The Spirit Cabinet

The Spirit Cabinet

PAUL QUARRINGTON

Atlantic Monthly Press
New York

Printed in the United States of America

FIRST AMERICAN EDITION

Library of Congress Cataloging-in-Publication Data

Quarrington, Paul.
    The spirit cabinet / Paul Quarrington.
      p. cm.
    ISBN 0-87113-805-0
    1. Magicians—Nevada—Las Vegas—Fiction. 2. Las Vegas (Nev.)—Fiction. I. Title.

  PR 9199.3.Q34 S65 2000
  813'.54—dc21   99-055840

Atlantic Monthly Press
841 Broadway
New York, NY 10003

00 01 02 03   10 9 8 7 6 5 4 3 2 1

"Never reveal the secrets in this book."

PRESTON THE MAGNIFICENT (SENIOR),
The Secrets of Magic Revealed

I'd like to thank Gabi Czech, who helped me with the German, and a host of magicians, from whom I learnt not secrets, but the nature of secrecy.

The author is also deeply indebted to the Canada Council for the Arts (I mean I owe them a debt of gratitude. I'm not giving back the money).

There are animals everywhere.

They sprawl across the broadloom and furniture, all pale bellies and matted fur. Barbary doves and aracaris rest on the bookcases, feathers falling from them like raindrops after a bad rain. The birdshit on the floor is oily and oddly colourful.

A rabbit thumps across the room, its legs stiff from disuse. The creature was once white, but shadows have turned it grey and taken the pinkness from its eyes.

A Van Hasselt's sunbird hides in the shadows. A mute swan hangs its head over a chairback and gives forth silent sighs.

The largest of the animals lies on the sofa. There is a sliver in his paw and he sucks at it in a desultory way, but it has been there for weeks and he is only slightly determined. Mostly he watches the television, a huge Japanese machine that occupies the entire far wall, surrounded by a small artificial pond filled with mottled carp. Most of the water has evaporated, though—the fish lie on their sides, flapping fins arrhythmically, making little bubbles that pop weakly in the stale air.

The largest of the animals—he is an albino leopard, snow-white but somehow still spotted, spackled by patches of light and dinginess—stretches, coughs up a furball, swats himself across the snout a couple of times.

On the television screen, young Kaz, having just dismembered and reassembled a woman, shoots his arms heavenward and thrusts his pelvis back and forth.

Rudolfo Thielmann enters the room at that moment, holding a scrap of meat in his hand. It is brown, almost spoilt. All of the animals *look at the meat for a long moment, but there are few healthy appetites in that room, in that house. One of the blond ringdoves squawks. Rudolfo mutters, "Fuck you, bay-bee," and flips the meat onto the sofa.*

The meat lands near the maw of the albino leopard, whose name is Samson. He lashes out with his tongue, colourless and dry, but the meat is too far away. He tries a couple of huge snorts, hoping to draw the meat closer. Unsuccessful, Samson produces a mournful sound and refixes his eyes on the large screen.

"Oh, look," says Rudolfo, "it is that asshole on my television set."

Words creep across the screen: THE WORLD-FAMOUS KAZ, THE WORLD-FAMOUS GALAXY HOTEL, THE WORLD-FAMOUS CONSTEL-LATION ROOM.

Everything in Las Vegas is world-famous.

Rudolfo himself was once world-famous, not even that long ago. It has only been a few months since he and Jurgen attended the auction.

Rudolfo lies down beside Samson, stretching his naked body along the length of the white leopard. Samson stirs slightly. Rudolfo picks up the morsel of tainted meat and gently pushes it into Samson's mouth. Many of the teeth are loose and Samson's breath is foul.

Rudolfo pulls weakly at the creature's throat, coaxing the food down into Samson's belly, which is bald in places and studded with colourless wens. The albino leopard sighs with what might be content-ment, but then spits the scrap back up. The meat falls to the floor with a small, ugly sound. A spotted genet, skinny and vicious-looking, appears out of nowhere and drags it away.

Rudolfo closes his eyes. Although he does not sleep, he dreams.

Chapter One

Preston the Magnificent, Jr., (or, as he preferred to call himself privately, Preston the Adequate) stood outside the George Theater dressed in an old morning suit that had belonged to his father. Being a much larger man than Preston the Magnificent, Sr., he had only managed to do up one button on the slate-grey jacket. The lapels wowed over his girlish breasts; the jacket fell away on either side of his belly and the tails splayed. Despite the fact that he complemented it with sandals, exhibiting his oddly shaped and quite hairy toes, Preston felt that the suit lent an air of mournful dignity to the proceedings. He undermined this formality by glowering at people as they approached the George, his face warped by fury. Preston conveyed the impression that he could turn people away should he choose to, and might choose to do so violently. So people darted by him, ignoring the grunt that he meant as a greeting.

Once inside, the people would approach the glass box containing the ashen and improbably beehived Mrs. Antoinette Kingsley. Mrs. Kingsley shoved a crude little booklet at them, sets of photocopied sheets stapled together. Then, still alarmed by Preston's bristling, sorrowful presence outside, the people would seek refuge in the old theatre hall, which smelled like time kept too long in an icebox. They would look at the little booklet, a catalogue of the McGehee Collection, as compiled by Preston. The script was produced by an old and infirm typewriter. The letters refused to sit upon the straight line, each jumping or dipping according to whim. Some letters were truncated, ghostly patches of grey left behind where serifs had broken off the keys.

Seeing as there were still quite a few minutes before the auction's commencement, the people would allow the booklet to fall open. It always did so to pages eight and nine, where the most prominent listing was for item number 112: "The Davenport Spirit Cabinet."

Preston didn't frighten everyone, of course. For example, he didn't frighten a very tall man wearing a white shirt with foppish collars and what appeared to be black tights. This man, the world-famous Kaz, had known Preston for many years. Of all the magicians in Las Vegas, Nevada (and there are many), Preston and Kaz were the longest resident. Kaz had moved to the desert when he was thirteen years old, there to perform illusions with towering topless showgirls. This accounted, Preston thought, for Kaz's acne-ravaged skin and the spectacles with the thick, yellowed lenses.

Kaz approached Preston and announced, "I'm buying it. Just try and stop me."

"Why would I want to stop you?" responded Preston. "Go ahead and buy it."

"I'm buying it because I *know*." Kaz exhaled heavily on the last word, and Preston noted the sourness of his breath. Kaz's breath was spectacularly awful. Preston had heard that Kaz had had two or three operations trying to fix it, though he couldn't imagine what sort of operations they might have been. He began reflecting on this question, but only as an evasive tactic, and could not escape the profound sickness that came to twist his belly. Kaz *would* buy it. Kaz had nothing but money; he made an obscene amount, half a million a week or something. Preston remembered hearing that Kaz was the highest paid act in Las Vegas—

No, wait. He took a breath and silently corrected himself. Kaz was the highest paid *individual performer.*

"Preston! Kaz! How are you hanging?"

The highest paid *act*, Preston realized, was coming down the sidewalk.

They were led by the albino leopard, Samson, who had lowered himself into stalking position but allowed the pads of his paws to slap the pavement heavily. The big cat knew this was a foolish way to get about; in a jungle he'd have cleared every living creature out of his path hours before he himself arrived. But he didn't live in a jungle any more and retained only the vaguest memories of those first few weeks of life so long ago. The jungles he'd seen on TV didn't look all that appealing, despite the presence of sleek young females. Not that Samson was interested in that so much, not since he'd awoken one day to discover that his testicles were missing. But, despite that grim morning, Samson was a contented and obedient animal, so he lowered his old bones and gamely continued the loud, menacing strut. When he felt a slight tugging on his jewel-encrusted collar, Samson licked his lips and produced a roar guaranteed to turn bowels watery.

"Oh, Samson," tsked Rudolfo, even though it was he who had pulled upon the leash, "put a lid on top of it."

Rudolfo's partner, Jurgen Schubert, came to an abrupt halt. "Preston and Kaz," he announced. "Two people."

"Two people," said Rudolfo, hurrying to help out, because

offstage his companion lacked confidence and tended to strip down his English to the barest of bones, "that are your favourite people."

"*Ja*," said Jurgen.

Kaz leaned down and whispered, his fetid breath stirring the hairs in Preston's ear, "What a couple of assholes."

Preston the Adequate merely grunted. He didn't approve of mean-mouthing fellow professionals, although it was hard to deny that Jurgen and Rudolfo were assholes. Leaving aside the fact that they'd brought a huge albino leopard to the auction, they themselves were done up in outlandish fashion. Jurgen, known as the more conservative of the pair, was clad in red leather, the jacket, pants and boots all the exact same bloody shade. Only his belt was otherwise, a foot wide, black and intricately tooled with a pattern of gnarled ivy.

Rudolfo was dressed in some sort of futuristic cowboy getup. His chaps were golden and the jeans beneath were made of a denim that was bleached until almost incandescent. His vest, which was all he wore on his upper body, was rendered out of metal and jewels and pieces of mirror, held together by thin silver wire. Beneath this peculiar garment, Rudolfo was all muscle, beautifully shaped and coloured. Due to an odd, utter hairlessness, his body looked as though it were made of porcelain.

"Hey, Kaz. Hey, Preston." Miranda appeared magically. Both Kaz and Preston, who between them knew the workings to every gimmick, rig and apparatus ever invented, thought of Miranda's appearance as "magical." She seemed to step out of a cloud of light, in a blink of Preston's eyes, in a sharp, sudden squinting of Kaz's. There she stood, towering above her employers, Jurgen and Rudolfo, dressed in some sort of plastic bodysuit that sucked itself to her flesh. "So," she asked bashfully, "how's everybody?"

Miranda seemed to be having a profound effect on Kaz, who

was panting audibly, although this might have had something to do with Samson, who was sniffing at Kaz's genitals, shoving bits and pieces around with his snout.

Jurgen grinned, the owner of a vast number of blindingly white teeth. As the corners of his mouth turned upwards, his eyelids began to flutter girlishly. "Don't worry, Kaz. Rudolfo has given Samson his lunchtime."

"*Ja*, but Jurgen," said Rudolfo, "maybe now is time for a little *schnawk*."

Everyone laughed, no one with much enthusiasm. Samson backed away and sneezed, fluffing the folds of skin that hung over his colourless lips. It was his attempt to laugh along, although only Rudolfo recognized it as such. After that, a silence descended as each man looked into the others' faces, trying to decipher purpose and plan.

The group paid no attention to the people who walked around them, through the open doorway into the George Theater. It was understood that these others were not players. They were lesser lights, mostly, magicians from the smaller hotels. There were a couple of illusionists of international stature, but they seemed to be down on their luck, sporting shiny tuxedos and cheap toupées. Preston recognized Theodore Collinger, a friend of his father, once famous for his work with the Chinese rings. Collinger was now badly wrinkled, and his hands, shrivelled and clawlike, trembled awkwardly at his side. Preston shook his head. If any of these people had thoughts of competing in the auction, they would soon be dissuaded. While there might be any number of people in the world who wanted to own the Collection, only three (two if you counted Jurgen and Rudolfo as a single unit) could afford to.

A photographer from *Personality* magazine rushed up with the desperate singlemindedness of an assassin, the camera already stuck to his eyeball. Rudolfo, Jurgen and Kaz smiled with practised naturalness, upper lips trembling as they each tried to display just the right amount of enamel. Miranda bent her knees so as not to loom over her bosses, and Samson shifted his weight onto his forelegs, assuming a heroic pose. Preston the Adequate scowled so profoundly that he would eventually be airbrushed out of the picture. The flashbulb exploded six or seven times, all within the same short moment, and then the photographer abruptly turned and darted away.

Preston stared at the other men, his dark eyes registering both wonder and judgement. He looked at Kaz, whose smallish eyes darted back and forth behind the lenses of his spectacles like small children trying to avoid the wrath of a bully. Then he looked at Jurgen and Rudolfo. The two men grinned still, somehow merrily frozen in time. Their faces were tanned, the whites of their eyes preternaturally white.

"Piss!" blasted Preston. He produced a cigarette and lit it clumsily. He looked at the others on the sidewalk and fashioned what he meant as a smile, although, judging from their reactions, his efforts again fell well short. He drew deeply on his butt and tried not to weep. It had been two months since Eddie McGehee had told him the Collection was to be auctioned off, but Preston's feelings upon hearing the news—disgust, panic and the deepest of sorrows—had not diminished in any way.

The McGehee Collection was originally assembled by Ehrich Weiss, the man we know better as Harry Houdini. Despite remaining itinerate throughout his life, never owning more than a series of *pieds-à-terre* in New York City, Houdini was obsessed with collecting. His chief obsession was with books, ancient and historical, the learned weight of which would lend his profession of Vaudevillian an austerity that even his father, the Rabbi, might respect. Houdini also liked to own the actual mechanical appurtenances of his forebears. He enjoyed demonstrating to people just exactly how these devices worked, pulling apart the boxes to expose trapdoors and helpfully pointing out the hiding places created by angled mirrors in dark interiors, the implication being (although even Houdini lacked the *chutzpah* to say it aloud) that his own stage boxes lacked similar subterfuges.

By the year 1920, Weiss laid claim to the largest collection in the world of material regarding magic, magicians, books, scripts, spiritualistic effects, documents, steel engravings and automata. Unfortunately, around that time Weiss also became involved with movies, creating the Houdini Picture Corporation, responsible for flickers like *The Man from Beyond* and *Haldane of the Secret Service*. These were not the successes he'd imagined. Houdini was one of the most famous men on earth, but what people wanted was to *see* him, actually view him in the flesh, as he did battle with chains and ropes, dangled from skyscrapers or was tossed into icy rivers. They liked to watch him go one-on-one with the Grim Reaper, but distrusted his smug, silvery screen image; they suspected that the stunts were done with photographic trickery (even when they were not). Weiss had invested much of his own money in the Houdini Picture Corporation, so with great reluctance he let it be known that he might be willing to part with a portion of his wonderful collection.

Edgar Biggs McGehee, the grandfather of the current owner, appeared almost immediately. He had made an incredible fortune in the oil fields, but the only thing that engaged his interest was conjuring and prestidigitation. He considered himself one of the great amateurs, although his grandson Eddie clearly recalled detecting, even at the age of five, every sleight of hand the old man attempted. Eddie quickly learned to exclaim with great glee, no matter which card was presented as the one he'd chosen. And it was a matter of McGehee family legend that Edgar Biggs only stopped trying to saw his wife in half when someone noticed blood dripping from the cabinet (made in 1878 by the great Harry Kellar and sold to Edgar Biggs by Houdini) onto the floor.

The actual nuts and bolts of the McGehee/Weiss agreement have never been known but they were hammered out during one of Houdini's performances. Prior to the meeting, Houdini had been handcuffed and manacled. Chains were draped over his shoulders; they somehow had the appearance of a ceremonial mantle. Houdini was placed in a large wooden box, which was hammered shut and it too wreathed in chains. Then the audience stared at the box for about an hour, an hour during which there was no apparent activity on stage. Finally, Houdini reappeared, dripping with sweat and dangling the chains from his hands like the severed heads of dragons. The chains about the wooden box remained unmolested, mysteriously mute.

During that hour Edgar Biggs had been ushered backstage, where he found Houdini sitting calmly in a rocking chair, sipping a cup of tea with lemon. Houdini dismissed his many assistants with a regal gesturing of his thick fingers and indicated a small stool where McGehee might sit. The men began to talk in whispers. They could hear the audience beyond, stirring nervously in their seats.

Houdini ended up selling perhaps a third of his collection. What remained was given to the Library of Congress after his death. The severance, the McGehee Collection, was taken to Nevada, where Edgar Biggs maintained a residence about fifty miles south of Las Vegas—which didn't exist in any substantial way back then—on the fringes of the Mojave Desert. It was a very modest residence for a multi-billionaire, a mud-covered hovel surrounded by three tilted outbuildings. For the first few years, Edgar Biggs would visit the Collection only occasionally, but the frequency and duration of his visits increased as he grew older. In his last days, Edgar Biggs dwelt in the desert continually. The few times he was seen, he was wearing only what appeared to be an enormous diaper. He had shaved all the hair from his head, except for a topknot, a spray of gossamer filament that stood bolt upright. He was so gaunt that his bones threatened to rip through his paper-thin skin with every movement.

After Edgar Bigg's death, his son, Edgar Biggs McGehee, Jr. ("Ed," he called himself, being a no-nonsense-type fellow), moved the Collection to Las Vegas proper, soon after the city had exploded upon the sands. He stored the books and pieces in a warehouse, where they were protected from the elements; other than that Ed proved to be an indifferent administrator, only mentioning the Collection around tax time, when it served to open a sizable loophole. (His indifference might have had something to do with the fact that it was Ed, a doting teenage son, who first noticed the blood dripping from Kellar's old cabinet and realized his mother's anguished screams were not as stagey as they sounded.) When Ed died, his son, Eddie, assumed control. He located—in the George, a run-down theatre where the ghosts of failed tragedians made the building groan and whimper—both a home and a curator. Preston the Magnificent, Jr., spent four years rummaging, cataloguing—the happiest years of his life—and when he was finished, Eddie had announced his intention of placing the McGehee Collection up for auction.

"I'm surprised you guys came," Preston said to the four people gathered around him outside the George, seeing how far he could push a bluff. "This is real boring stuff. Collectors' stuff. Some of the books are pretty damn dry. Very *academic*." He pronounced the last word with pompous precision. He still clung to the hope that a university would purchase the Collection, stick it in some cobwebbed storage room where it would be forgotten over time. Preston knew it was folly to imagine that universities had anywhere near the financial resources of these guys. Still, he'd fired off letters, listing the books and the pieces, making grand statements about the historical significance, though he doubted any university representative would show up. He had more faith in the arrival of an eccentric billionaire. Such creatures inhabited the deserts surrounding Las Vegas, after all. Some senile fart pumped full of monkey-gland juice could cart the Collection home—Preston wouldn't mind that so much. The only other satisfactory outcome to this whole thing—and in many ways the likeliest—would be for the earth to open up and swallow the auction hall and everyone in it.

"Oh, Preston," said Jurgen Schubert, "it is not a surprise that I am interest in this." Jurgen's skull was square and all of his features oddly rectangular, as though he'd been designed by an architect, planned out on blue drafting paper. His hair was made up of tight golden fiddleheads, a dense mat of curls that he brushed forward so that it draped evenly over his brow like a bedspread. He was deeply tanned, but, even so, his eyelids seemed much darker than the rest of his face, in a bruised, unhealthy way. "I am telling you a story."

"Hoo boy!" called out Rudolfo eagerly, clapping his hands together. "Tell us this story." This was how they behaved on television shows, Jurgen doing most of the talking, Rudolfo reduced to over-enthusiastic responses and exhortations, even though Rudolfo's English was much better than Jurgen's.

"I am hearing about a book in bookshop," said Jurgen. "It is cost twenty Deutschmark."

"Which," put in Rudolfo, "is a lot."

"*Ja, ja. Es war sehr teuer.*"

"So vot did you do, Jurgen?"

"I work at docks. I am eleven years old. But I am getting up every Saturday and Sunday at three in the morning and go to the docks in Bremerhaven, and I am lift with the men huge craters."

"Hold on," said Rudolfo loudly, laying a hand on his partner's shoulder. "You are making a mistake, my friend."

"*Was?*"

"Not craters. Crates."

Jurgen didn't bother to correct himself, but turned back to Preston and said, "Four hours on my old bicycle to Bremerhaven. Two hours to go, two hours to come home. Every weekend. So after many weeks, I have money. I buy the book. You know what book was?"

Preston shrugged.

"*The Secrets of Magic Revealed,*" said Jurgen. "By your father. Preston the Magnificent."

"Hoo boy!" shouted Rudolfo.

"So, it is not so a very big deal for Rudolfo and I to get into our very long limousine and tell Jimmy the driver to come here. So I don't know why you are surprise."

"Yeah," agreed Preston, "I don't know why I'm surprised either."

"That was my first book, too," said Kaz.

At first Preston thought this was just more evidence of Kaz's absurdly competitive nature, but he quickly decided otherwise. *The Secrets of Magic Revealed* was everybody's first book. Judging from the magicians who worked many of the smaller rooms, it was some guys' *only* book. A couple of times Preston had heard patter, taken word for word, from those pages, silly stuff that had been laughable when his father had said it. At least, Preston always found it laughable. His father, ornately moustached, his hair greased and moulded into an unlikely peaked coiffure, seemed to get away with it. "For just as our telluric orb is a moonlet of mighty Sol," Preston the Magnificent would say, aiming a finger at the little rubber globe that circled his head, "so we espy here testament to consonance and concinnity!" Magicians still performed the illusion and they still said essentially the same crap, the only difference being the statuesque near-naked women standing behind them, guilelessly gesturing at the revolving sphere.

"I would have been five, six," Kaz continued. He pulled off his thick spectacles and chewed on one arm, both to affect a more thoughtful air and to keep Miranda at a fuzzy distance, to break her spell. "I was performing the big illusions by the time I was seven. The close-up stuff took longer. I didn't master coins until I was nine." This, too, thought Preston, was talk-show behaviour, Kaz reciting his personal history, at least the one-pager used by his army of publicists. It was all Kaz was ever asked about and it was the only information he ever gave, the meagre outline of a strange life. Kaz was the youngest person ever admitted to the Inner Circle of the International Brotherhood of Magicians and given the status of Grand Wizard. It was true, Preston would admit, that the kid was sensational. His show-stopper was "The Mannequin," a classy little bit of animation involving a dress-maker's form that comes to life and follows the young Kaz around the stage. The kid would appear unmindful of his admirer, going about his business, turning away by chance whenever the ardent dummy tried to present herself.

"That was good," said Preston suddenly, alarming even himself. "*The Mannequin*. You still do that?"

"Are you crazy?" Kaz said loudly, driving everyone backwards with a gust of rancid breath, including the huge albino leopard. "I haven't done that shit since I was sixteen."

Preston the Adequate sighed, and a single teardrop rolled out, getting lost in the grey folds piled up beneath his left eye. Preston was a somewhat leaky man, often burdened by a runny nose, watery eyes and even oozing beads of white stuff from the pores of his face. "Okay, okay," he muttered. "Let's get this show on the road."

Chapter Two

Miranda led Rudolfo and Jurgen to their seats. At the end of the row, she gesticulated in a showy manner, aiming long index fingers in graceful unison. Jurgen went in first, followed by Miranda, with Rudolfo claiming the end so Samson could lie down in the aisle. The old beast immediately did so, collapsing and allowing his snout to hit the ground, even though the red carpet was redolent of the thousands of feet that had smoothed its nap. Kaz chose to sit closer to the front, seeking out some young boys and elderly women who had attended the auction only because of the prospect of spotting Kaz. He responded to their subdued applause in grand fashion, raising his long crooked arms into the air, throwing his pelvis back and forth a couple of times. Rudolfo leant over, digging an elbow into Miranda's side. "What a asshole," he whispered.

She nodded, although she wasn't sure exactly what was wrong. Kaz was only doing what his fans expected of him. She had a notion to point this out to Rudolfo, but the atmosphere inside the hall was uncomfortably churchlike. The people sat staring rigidly forward, their hands folded into pious little wedges. Instead of speaking, Miranda concentrated on crossing one long leg over the other without kicking the seat of the woman in front of her.

Preston the Adequate stood near the back of the theatre, clinging to the jambs of the main doors as if preparing to make a hasty exit.

The auctioneer, whose face was elongated and peanut-shaped, stepped out from behind the black velvet curtain that skirted the stage. He approached the wooden lectern, brought his gavel down softly and announced, "The McGehee family has requested that the Collection be auctioned not by lot but in its entirety."

The auctioneer allowed for a short silence in which this statement could sink in, a silence that was ruined by a nightmarish sound, something half fart and half death rattle. Just as the terrifying wake settled, the sound came again, and people turned and stared, realizing it was the snoring of the slumbering Samson. Rudolfo beamed at them brilliantly and spoke in a voice far too loud. "Oh, *ja*, this is time for his *nawp*."

"Well," said the auctioneer, pinching his face into the smallest of smiles, "let's try to hurry things up so as not to disturb him too much."

The people laughed. Rudolfo's hairless skin was suffused momentarily with red, which Rudolfo willed away by concentrating not on his anger, but rather on what he could learn from this. Why hadn't they laughed at what *he* had said? Why was it funny, what the man had said? More to the point, could he and Jurgen use it in the Show?

"This then..." the auctioneer waved his hand at the black velvet curtain behind him as the halves pulled apart in a herky-jerky way, "...is the Collection."

Apparently Preston the Adequate's duties as curator had not extended to cleaning or dusting. The books were stacked in piles three and four feet high, and cobwebs spanned the distances between. Flies hovered over top and little worms, chubby with pulp, tumbled from between the book covers. Vermin scurried for cover as the curtains waltzed apart, several mice and one large rat. Only Samson, lifting an eyebrow wearily and pulling his left eye open, noticed the rat, which was filthy and vicious-looking.

The books themselves were for the most part enormously thick, a four-foot-high stack containing perhaps only twelve or thirteen volumes. The pages were ragged, the edges blackened and devoured by old air. Smaller books littered the ground between the stacks—medieval chapbooks, squares of parchment laced together by lengths of crude hemp. There were even one or two brown and flaky cylindrical objects that were surely papyrus scrolls.

Rudolfo was paying absolutely no attention. He was petting Samson absent-mindedly because the albino leopard's head had jerked up suddenly, as though the beast had been startled or frightened, and even now Rudolfo could sense a small trembling somewhere deep in the animal's being. Rudolfo crossed his legs. He kicked the off-puttingly large bottom in the seat ahead, and a man spun around. Seeing that it was Rudolfo, this man (who came from Wisconsin and was quite active in amateur magicians' circles, calling himself The Mystifying Henry) smiled politely and mouthed the word *sorry.*

The stacks of books reached almost to the back wall, so some of the Collection was draped in gloom and shadow. This was the paraphernalia, the physical accessories of conjurers long dead. There were Chinese rings, green with tarnish, and small chipped china cups emblazoned with ornate suns, smiling faces etched inside the horns of flame. There were rusty chains and popped handcuffs, the locking mechanisms now filled with dust and spider eggs. There was the infamous Kellar woman-in-half rig, and what looked like a cheaply made steamer trunk, a crate of dried wood contained by straps of faded, disintegrated leather. There was also an automaton, a fat mechanical man who sat awkwardly cross-legged, his hands in the air, a fatuous smile painted on his lacquered face.

(These last two pieces had caused quite a bit of haggling and bickering between McGehee and Harry Houdini at the famous backstage negotiations. It is not that McGehee wanted them and Houdini demurred; rather, Houdini insisted they be part of the deal. McGehee restated his affection for the books. Houdini said that the books themselves were worthless and threw in the Substitution Box, which he and Bess had used in their famous act "Metamorphosis," as well as the automaton, constructed in 1767 and named "Moon.")

Of all the pieces, the most obtrusive (and the one that provoked the most intense discussion between McGehee and Houdini, a discussion involving specific dates many years in the future) was what appeared to be an oversized wardrobe, easily ten feet high and seven feet across. All of its angles seemed too great, obtuse; if you studied the individual corners it seemed unlikely that the box could fit together as a whole. The piece had double doors, and one had fallen open. Inside there seemed to be only a single shelf, fitted at an oddly low level.

The box was made from light, unfinished wood, whorly with grain. Small pieces had been taken out of it; bits of the door had been removed as if with a cookie cutter, leaving holes shaped like crescent moons.

Jurgen glanced at the small booklet he held in his hands— he couldn't quite remember where he'd gotten it—and allowed it to fall open. It spread at the pages numbered eight and nine. His eyes were drawn toward a large block of writing: "Number 112," Jurgen read, "The Davenport Spirit Cabinet."

The Davenports—Ira and William—were two young men from Buffalo, New York, who claimed to be in touch with the spiritual realm. This was late in the nineteenth century, when people were inclined to believe such things. At any rate, the Davenports seemed to be able to prove their claim, for the brothers would be bound, hand and foot, and placed inside this cabinet. The Spirit Cabinet was always most certainly empty; sometimes the Davenport Brothers were naked as well, so that there could be no question of trickery. The doors of the Spirit Cabinet would be shut. Moments later, noises would commence, strange rappings, hollow knockings. Next would come musical sounds, as from trumpets and plucked strings, and then melodies, pieces of songs sung by the boys who had died in the War between the States. Then, from the crescent-shaped holes in the doors came animals, a serpent slithering from one, a dove, wet and glistening, from another.

The doors to the Spirit Cabinet could be (and were) thrown open at any time during this, and Ira and William would be seen sitting on the bench, unmoving, still bound hand and foot.

At number 113 in Preston's catalogue there was listed a book: *Magie et physique amusante*, written by the great French conjuror Jean Eugène Robert-Houdin. It gave a very detailed account of how the Davenports perpetrated their fraud. When being bound, for example, the brothers would insist that each length of rope be doubled. People always complied, thinking this made it twice as strong, little realizing that, in fact, the doubling made knots and wrappings essentially useless, the rope acting against, undoing, itself. Once inside the Spirit Cabinet, Ira and William merely threw off the ropes, produced objects through various, and not very ingenious, ways. (Those interested might consult another seminal French work, *La Magie blanche dévoilée*, written by Henri DeCremps and listed in the programme at number 312.)

Despite these revelations, Houdini had pursued the Spirit Cabinet with great ardour and prized it above all other possessions. He'd first heard of it as a young magician on Coney Island, where he and his wife, "Harry and Bessie Houdini," had performed a simple routine consisting of two parts: mentalism (a tired carnival act) and a Transformation. It's popular lore that Ehrich Weiss began his career as an escape artist by scouring flea markets and second-hand shops for old locks and handcuffs (he learned the secret of each, one at a time, working at them with picks and needles), but it's not so well known that at each stop Harry hiked one of his dark eyebrows and stared into the shadowiest corners.

The auctioneer opened the floor for bidding, folding his hands together and leaning forward ever so slightly.

Jurgen crossed his arms with resolution. Kaz did likewise, pushing his feet out in front of him, sinking down into the chair as if none of this was of any concern. There was a long moment of weighted silence. Finally a gentleman from Ottawa, Canada, an eccentric millionaire merely, lifted his arm and spoke the sum of five hundred thousand dollars.

"Von million dollars," muttered Jurgen.

Rudolfo's impulse was to correct what was assuredly a language error. Perhaps Jurgen had meant to say, *I don't care about these silly books.* But Jurgen was grinning, and the arms folded across his chest were afire with the nervous flexing of small, knotted muscles.

To their left Kaz snickered, jerking his head with arrogance. The sudden force tilted his huge glasses and flipped the right temple away from the ear. Kaz adjusted his spectacles with long bony hands and spoke through them as he did so. "One and a half million dollars."

"Two millions," said Jurgen.

"Hoo boy!" sang out Rudolfo.

Preston the Adequate still stood at the back of the theatre, his bottom lip folded beneath his yellowed upper teeth, the pressure draining the colour from his face. He was not a man given to prayer, but that was, in fact, what he was doing.

Suddenly there was a stranger beside him, drifting through the doorway soundlessly despite being swaddled in acres of tulle and muslin. The man had a third eye tattooed between the two given by nature. He wore a topknot, a long spray of bone-white hair that stood bolt upright; the rest of his scalp was a prickly silver nap. This man wore an expression of bemused serenity. However, when Kaz called out "Two and a half million," the stranger—already very pale—blanched. "Shit," he whimpered, and disappeared.

Preston stared sadly after the man. "Things is tough all over," he mumbled.

"Tree—"

"Hoo boy!"

"—millions," said Jurgen.

Kaz gave the first hint of weakness: instead of adding a half million dollars to Jurgen's bid, he hesitated briefly, then spat out, "Three million four."

Jurgen stirred in his seat as though trying to surreptitiously release gas. He turned and looked at Rudolfo. His eyelids had become riotous, rising and lowering independently of each other. Jurgen lifted a thick eyebrow questioningly. Rudolfo shook his head, with considerable urgency. Jurgen's eyes darkened and he turned them toward Miranda.

Miranda lifted her hands from her lap, hands of an unnatural size and smoothness. She fanned fingers quickly and briefly. Three six.

"Three millions and sixes," said Jurgen.

"Three eight," snapped Kaz. He'd realized he'd made a

tactical error and was trying to make up for it with a kind of churlish aplomb. But this allowed Jurgen to say "Four" with finality. Even Rudolfo, alarmed as he was by the proceedings, was impressed with the muscular timbre of Jurgen's voice.

So now the onus was on Kaz to venture into the fours. He'd already exceeded what his accountant had told him he might spend, but he was driven on by a couple of thoughts. One was that he *must* own the books, the other was that he *should.* There was a rightness to it. Kaz was, after all, the greatest magician in the world, much better than those two Aryan faggots. The trouble was, Kaz knew perfectly well that Rudolfo and Jurgen made more money than he did. Not much more per week, but they worked almost every goddamn week. Kaz then tried to calculate their overhead and expenses. They owned their absurd mansion. Given that the place was laced with man-made streams and waterfalls, Kaz suspected their utility bills alone negated the disparity in weekly salary. And all those fucking animals! Kaz shot out an arm confidently and said, "Four million one hundred thousand."

"Four millions," replied Jurgen, "and two hundred thousands of dollars."

Kaz then remembered that it was not as though he rented a one-bedroom apartment or anything. He owned a mansion, too, not an absurd one, maybe, but one that likely cost about the same. Kaz also went through money pretty quickly. He had a huge staff, for one thing. He had office people, personal secretaries, no less than eight female assistants (showgirls with an average height of six feet, although he found not a one as tantalizing as he found Miranda), not to mention the Doubles and Confederates, sworn to secrecy and paid well to maintain it. "Four three," Kaz mumbled quietly.

"*Ja*, four millions dollars and four hundreds of thousands of dollars."

Kaz pinched the end of his nose with force, fanning pain into his forehead and eyeballs. Jurgen gave every indication of being willing to augment whatever bid Kaz made. But he could be bluffing. After all, there were several illusions, really elementary stuff, that Jurgen made work by sheer dint of mien and manner, his brow furrowed and his pupils dilated, staring into the eyes of the first row as though daring them to spot the mirrors and false fronts. "Four five," shouted Kaz, buoyed by this thought.

"Four eight," came a voice, a new voice, and Kaz spun around in his seat to see who the intruder might be. Judging from the circle of twisted necks, the voice belonged to Rudolfo. Rudolfo's thin lips were compressed into a shallow smile. Rudolfo took a deep breath through his nostrils, puffing out his chest until the tiny nipples poked through the pieces of metal and mirror.

Kaz was devastated. He couldn't play with these guys, not the two guys together. He couldn't keep up, the simple arithmetic wasn't there. He also couldn't say "five million." The accountant had told him that calamity would absolutely befall him should he say those words. Kaz rose out of his seat suddenly, making for the aisle with a haste that gave no one time to move crossed feet or knees. He stumbled most of the way, grabbing hold of tops of heads for support. He thought he might faint—he'd fainted fairly regularly as a young boy—so when he achieved the aisle, he doubled over and sucked in air. "Congratulations, boys," he groaned.

There was applause, awkward and halting, because no one was sure how to applaud at an auction.

As Kaz passed through the doorway at the back, he leaned in toward Preston the Adequate, close enough to bathe him in streams of putrid breath. "It's like a couple of chimps bought some books about brain surgery," he said bitterly.

Preston shrugged.

"We could have worked out a deal, you, me and McGehee. Private sale. Four million would have been no problem. Because I deserve the books. You couldn't handle them, could you? Only I can handle them. Only me in the whole fucking world."

"You don't know what's in the books," said Preston the Adequate.

"Oh, yeah, I do," said Kaz as he disappeared. "I *know*."

Chapter Three

"Well, that was brilliant," said Rudolfo, fuming in the back of the limousine. He pulled open the bar beside him and poked around until he found a bottle of Orangina. He wrenched off the cap and poured some down his throat. Outside the darkened window lay the wasted plains of Nevada.

"What's your problem?" wondered Jurgen, leafing through the catalogue with pursed lips. Jurgen's lids had slid down to cover his eyes almost entirely; they didn't rise up now, but there was some slight muscular activity, a weak electrical charge that caused them to quiver. "You made the final bid, after all."

"Right," nodded Rudolfo. "Because I had to go feed the animals, and I didn't have time for *four millions and seven hundreds and fifty hundreds of thousands of dollars.*"

Miranda laughed, mostly because she was surprised at the sudden spurt of thick and clumsy English. Both men stared at her, sitting on the seat opposite. "Sorry," she said.

"I've never bought anything before," said Jurgen quietly, even though he was reasonably certain that Miranda couldn't understand German.

"Oh, no? You bought the Lamborghini four-wheel drive."

"I didn't buy that," returned Jurgen. "You gave that to me for my birthday."

"Only because you asked for it."

"That's a different thing." Jurgen flipped a page and began to read studiously. "Look," he said, without removing his eyes from the print, "you buy all sorts of things. You spend millions of dollars every year on your animals—"

"*My* animals?" interrupted Rudolfo. "The animals are for the Show."

Jurgen sighed wearily.

Miranda could understand some of the things she heard— *die Tiere*, for example, *the animals*. It was a phrase the two often exchanged, Jurgen employing a tone of annoyance, Rudolfo one of gentleness. "*Die Tiere sind für die Schau, da,*" said Rudolfo. When he said *die Tiere* he moved his arms, throwing them away from his body and then allowing them to resettle gently, a vague kind of gathering motion.

Rudolfo leaned forward and touched Miranda's knee. It was an odd thing to do, as if her attention needed redirection from the window or something, whereas in fact she'd had her eyes aimed steadily at him. Miranda tilted her head slightly by way of asking what he wanted.

"Miranda," asked Rudolfo, "where can you drop off?"

"Oh," she shrugged, going through her not very extensive list of alternatives. "The hotel."

"*Ja*, Jimmy!" shouted Rudolfo. The driver raised his shoulders, wrinkling the folds of skin on the back of his neck. "Miranda is to the hotel going."

Jimmy grunted. Jimmy seemed to have only a specific number of words that he could utter on any one day—twelve, perhaps—so he usually grunted or made a chicking sound as though everyone else in the world were a horse.

Samson sat up front beside Jimmy, because it made him very nervous not to be able to see where he was going. The ancient albino leopard craned his neck back toward the other passengers and appeared to nod. His tongue hung from his mouth, a long slab of meat with just the slightest tinge of pinkishness.

"Christ is hot," said Rudolfo, throwing himself backwards into the leather seats. He turned his head sharply to Jurgen. "You could have told me."

"Told you what?"

"That the books were so fucking expensive, what else?"

"It was an *auction*," replied Jurgen. "How was I to know how much the books would cost?"

"You could have told me *the park of the ball*."

Jurgen shrugged and continued to flip pages. He couldn't have said what books he'd expected to find on the list, but the names he was reading didn't seem right: *Geeston en Demonen, Satanova Cirkev, Ho Leukas Magos, Tachydaktyklourgon Kai Thaumatopoion, Mejik Triksa*. So many in so many strange languages.

"Did you know," asked Rudolfo, "that Kaz the asshole was going to try to buy the Collection?"

"Sure," Jurgen nodded.

"You could have told me that," said Rudolfo.

"Why, what would you have done? Have him murdered?"

"We might have been able to negotiate a private deal with the auctioneer." A scowl blew across Rudolfo's face as he remembered the man with the peanut-shaped head and the laugh he'd gotten from the crowd. "By the way," he mentioned, "I'm thinking about a small change to the Show—"

Jurgen sighed.

"What?" snapped Rudolfo.

"Nothing."

"What?" demanded Rudolfo again.

Miranda, who this time *had* been looking through the window at the endless desert, spun her head toward Rudolfo and his harsh, "*Was? Was?*" She immediately saw that it had nothing to do with her, but she didn't look away.

"This silly guy," explained Rudolfo, jerking a thumb at his partner, "all I'm having to do is say *die Schau* and he is hurling his chests. Every time he is doing this." Rudolfo did a sarcastic imitation of Jurgen's breast-heaving.

"A small change," said Jurgen, leaning forward suddenly, adjusting his bottom on the leathery seat, sticky despite the air conditioning. "I'm tired of small changes."

Whatever Jurgen said, Miranda saw, had made Rudolfo angry. His skin, so smooth that he sometimes seemed waxed, coloured many shades of red, the deepest ruddiness filling in the hollows of his cheeks. Rudolfo's blue eyes widened and his nostrils trembled as though he were stifling a sneeze. Then he began to speak, softly, the German sounding to Miranda like nothing more than wet sounds and growls.

"Sure," he said to Jurgen, "what we really need to do is completely change the Show. After all, it has only won Act of the Year four years in a row. That means that it's not particularly good. Maybe we should reconsider the whole concept. Maybe we should do a fucking song-and-dance act, maybe we should try plate-spinning like that greasy Italian boy you thought was so adorable."

The limousine pulled into the driveway of the Abraxas Hotel. The driveway was four kilometres long, a huge circle that curved around tennis courts, an outdoor pool, a soccer field and a fountain. The grounds were crowded, largely with doughy blond people, German, Dutch and Scandinavian, the Abraxas being the hotel of European choice because of its association with Jurgen and Rudolfo. These people played tennis dolefully or hung about the bright blue water (the air sharp with the scent of chemicals) in tiny little bathing suits. Their children galloped around the soccer field in hordes. Jurgen sometimes stopped the limousine and got out to watch. Once or twice he had even joined in, rushing at the ball with unseemly determination, pushing children out of his path. But he was in no mood for that today, and didn't even bother to look.

Miranda was glad she would soon be getting out. There was a fight coming; the two men, especially over the past few months, had been relentlessly bickering and squabbling. Jurgen sat brooding and stock-still. Rudolfo's body quivered with small convulsions, as though things inside weren't working quite right, his lungs having difficulty drawing air, his heart pumping blood erratically.

Miranda watched as the fountain came into view. A huge spiral of water, lighted from within by all the colours in creation, shot two hundred feet into the air and then exploded with a muted thunderclap. The water fell and drenched all the honeymooners having their photographs taken below.

The road was lined with hotel staff. The doormen and porters tended to be pituitary giants, huge men with imbalanced faces, swollen noses and brows, tiny eyes obscured by shadow. They dressed in turbans and pink chiffon pantaloons. The limousine rolled to a stop and one of their ranks stepped forward, tearing open the rear door. Miranda alighted and gazed upwards into the craggy, lumpy face.

"Maurice," she said. "How's it hanging?"

"Welcome to the Abraxas Hotel," said Maurice automatically, his voice in the lowest register. "How are you, Miranda?"

"Aces," she answered. She turned back toward the couple in the car. "See you tomorrow night."

The men nodded simultaneously. Miranda swung the limo door shut and walked toward the awful tower that was the hotel.

Theirs was the most spectacular house in the desert. Any number of magazines had pronounced it such. *Der Spiegel* had called it *das eindrucksvollste Haus im Universum.* It may have been; at least it possessed an otherworldly quality that would seem to put it in the running. It was a curiously shapeless construction when seen from the outside, as though a colossal gelatinous mass had been dropped upon the sands from a great height. Alien vegetation, nurtured through frantic and relentless irrigation, had grown up around it—spruce, larch and oak trees that would have been more at home cradling the Alps. A stream ran around and through the house, twice, describing a large figure-eight that contained it within carp-filled moats.

The limousine came to rest by the front door, the tires crushing the sea-throws and shells that carpeted the driveway. Rudolfo and Jurgen climbed out, each placing sunglasses over their eyes. Jurgen marched toward the entrance and keyed in numbers on the futuristic pad that protruded from the wall. Rudolfo waited while Jimmy crossed in front of the car and released the albino leopard. Samson lumbered to the ground and shook the stiffness out of his bones. Rudolfo suddenly rushed forward, dropped to his knees and gathered the beast's huge white head to his chest. He kissed the leopard's brow, which tasted oddly of perfume. Jurgen had already walked through the front door and into the huge house; Rudolfo turned and stared at the emptiness where he'd been.

The first thing Rudolfo did when he got inside was change clothes, swapping the otherwordly cowpoke garb for a pair of olive-coloured overalls. He slipped his pedicured feet into a pair of crud-encrusted workboots, then went outside and attended to the animals, flinging seed, feed and raw meat into the appropriate cages. He leashed the larger, more dangerous animals and cleared out the shit from their living quarters. He orchestrated an exercise period, releasing all of the creatures, shrieking, and skipping alongside the ensuing stampede as it made a few circuits of the grounds.

When he finished, Rudolfo descended into the Gymnasium. He peeled away the overalls and stood among the equipment wearing only a tiny pair of sequined exercise briefs. He stretched as he approached the bench, locking his hands over his head and twisting his body sharply from side to side. Rudolfo wasn't actually certain that today was Upper Body; in fact, if pressed, he would have had to admit that he'd worked chest and arms only the day before. But he felt like doing the bench press, so he feigned confusion and started loading weight onto the bar. He put two big plates on either side and picked up some smaller ones. Rudolfo then paused and reflected, listening to a clamour from deep within. He dropped the twenty-pounders and went instead for more of the forties, carefully sliding them onto the bar and locking the load with a couple of clamps. This was more weight than he usually lifted, but his anger was going to do a great deal of the work. He removed his wig and draped it over one of the forks of the weight stand. He lay down on the bench and curled his fingers around the bar. There were two sections where the metal was roughed up and bumpy, the better to grip, but Rudolfo avoided these, preferring the feel just to the outside, where the steel was smooth and very cold. It made for a harder lift with his arms spread so, but he wasn't worried. He even muttered "*Kein Problem*," before shoving the bar up rudely, lifting it off the rack; he cocked his arms forward and lowered it. As soon as he felt the coolness kiss his chest he pushed upwards, screaming as loudly as his lungs would allow. The weight sailed through the sticking point; as it neared the acme he allowed it to come back down again, avoiding the lock-out zone where only lazy fat people went. Rudolfo screamed again, a stream of pained Indo-European vowels. He'd now lifted the weight twice and hadn't really exerted himself. As the bar came back down he elected to do eight presses. This seemed, at first blush, impossible, especially considering that eight really meant ten, because the only important lifts were the two anguished and trembling ones that were made after the supposed completion of the set.

The anger that made all this possible wasn't entirely due to Jurgen's squandering of five million dollars. In fact, the money played almost no part in it—their wealth was close to inexhaustible. And Jurgen was correct, if a bit surly, in pointing out that Rudolfo spent vast sums collecting animals. The animals were not *all* for the Show. Some he acquired simply to be near them. Many of the exotic birds were too obstinate to learn any tricks; the most beautiful, the blond ringdove for example, seemed to lose all dignity when placed upon a stage, squawking in an unseemly manner, throwing off plumage and streams of sick-looking shit.

Rudolfo's fondest memories involved his poorest days, when he'd lived as a beggar on the streets of Münich, a bizarre-looking fugitive from the law. That was when he'd met Jurgen, and they had been happy. Or so it seemed to Rudolfo. He had recollections of happiness, now lost, dried up in the vast desert that was their new home. So perhaps they had too much money—not that there was any way of getting rid of it. Not even spending five million on a bunch of old books and refuse from a lawn sale.

No, it was not the money that made Rudolfo angry.

The truth of the matter, which neared the surface as he completed six lifts and let the weight down for a painful seventh, was that he was infuriated by Jurgen's dissatisfaction with the Show. It was what Rudolfo worked hardest at, and it was Rudolfo's creation. When they met, all those years ago, Jurgen had known only tired and corny tricks, which he had performed in a silly manner, his eyes popped open with melodramatic intensity. His audiences were bored, always, and sometimes violent, there mostly to grope each other or watch a parade of near-naked people mount the stage, that being the main attraction at Miss Joe's. Jurgen's card tricks, coin manipulations, silk transformations and dove productions did not engage their imaginations. However, this had all changed the first night he, with Rudolfo standing by his side, had opened the lid of a makeshift Production Box to reveal the young Samson. The albino leopard bared his teeth and howled menacingly. The audience, after a long, stunned moment, applauded, at first meekly and then with enthusiasm.

That had been Rudolfo's doing, the first of many inspirations. While he understood little about the mechanics of the illusions—he knew his own part in several of them, but there were some he found as baffling as any child might—he understood Show Business. That thought came with the eighth lift, and it was inspiring enough that Rudolfo immediately brought the weight down and screamed again, forcing the iron up even as he lost feeling in his arms. The only sensation now was a prickly tingle around the elbows. The muscles themselves were consumed by a dull numbness which, when Rudolfo finally racked the bar, would be replaced by agony. His muscles were now "distressed," a word in English that Rudolfo liked and used whenever he could.

He allowed the weight to come back down, resisting it all the way with his trembling arms. If you weaken and simply let the weight fall, Rudolfo knew, it becomes impossible to regain momentum, to push again. So he resisted and then resisted hesitation, driving upwards with his numb and swollen arms. He screamed, but all that came out was a small sound. This tenth lift, Rudolfo realized, was a mistake. It was not so much that he'd abandoned belief in his ability to hoist it, despite the negative aspects of that last thought. He was adept at all manner of positive thinking techniques, had for years been listening to Tony

Anthony's "YOU!" series of motivational tape cassettes. But his arms were simply not responding to orders. He watched the bar begin to sway back and forth and was reminded of something he'd once seen on television. A suspension bridge was being buffeted by a hurricane, twisting and heaving in the storm. The bridge ultimately blew apart, just as the weight would soon fall, likely crushing Rudolfo's windpipe. He had one chance, he thought, and that was to throw the weight clear. Unfortunately, that would require at least a little control over his arm muscles. The bar was now pitching back and forth, and Rudolfo thought that he might be able to use some of this momentum to propel the weight away—but it was a vague and hopeless thought and occupied only a split second.

Just before his arms collapsed, though, a thick forefinger came and curled itself beneath the bar. "Up," said Jurgen, and that was all the assistance Rudolfo required—the finger or the word, he couldn't have said which. Rudolfo's voice came with force, almost a yodel, and his arms exploded with a firing of nerve and muscle so intense that he would not have been surprised to see flames shooting out of his elbows. "Up," repeated Jurgen, and Rudolfo pushed and somehow the weight rose, and then Jurgen pulled it backwards, guiding it still with just the one finger, and gently placed it on the rack.

Rudolfo bolted forward, and noted that oddly enough it was not his arms that hurt, but his stomach. He leaned to the side and retched, his belly wracked by spasms. Nothing was forthcoming (Rudolfo ate very little as a rule, mostly raw eggs and vegetables, and certainly never before exercise), and when the moment passed, Rudolfo realized that his arms did indeed hurt, hurt so much that it had made him nauseous. So he crossed his arms and took each bicep in hand and pinched and kneaded until close to tears. "Hoo boy," he said softly, "are my arms distressed."

Jurgen had crossed quietly over to the squat rack and was positioning himself under the bar. He was not dressed for the Gymnasium—he hadn't changed out of his red leather outfit—but he stepped backwards with the weight on his shoulders and descended gracefully onto his haunches. He made no response to Rudolfo, perhaps because Rudolfo had spoken in English, perhaps because there was no response to make.

"Where are you going to put all that crap?" wondered Rudolfo suddenly.

"I've been thinking about that," answered Jurgen. "Maybe that funny little room at the end of the hall, beside the wine cellar."

"Do you mean the Grotto?"

Jurgen stepped forward, slipping the weight from his shoulders back onto the support pins. He turned toward Rudolfo and nodded. His skin was mottled slightly from the brief exertion, his large square brow misted with sweat. His quivering eyelids had assumed a position of military readiness, dividing his orbs at sombre halfmast.

"The Grotto," said Rudolfo testily, "is supposed to be for the animals that don't like sunlight."

"We don't have any animals that don't like sunlight. All of the animals are always lying around the pool."

"There are the bushbabies," Rudolfo argued. He plucked his wig from the fork of the weight stand and fitted it carefully on his head.

"Sure, but you don't keep a special room for a few stupid little animals!" Jurgen raised his voice, although not angrily, really. It was more as if he were forced to speak above other sounds and voices, a din that he alone could hear.

Rudolfo sighed heavily as he tried to figure where best to attack that sentence. His mind was suddenly cluttered with thought. The bushbabies were stupid, that's true, but how intelligent could they be with brains the size of peppercorns? And there weren't a *few* of them, there were scores, and the number was ever-increasing, because if you flipped on any light in the middle of the night you would catch at least five tiny furry couples in the act of squeaky fornication. So there. Now, why not have a special room for them? For instance, wasn't there a separate room for Jurgen's old swimming trophies, which totalled exactly three? And leaving all this aside, why should Jurgen start screaming all of a sudden? "Why," spoke Rudolfo, "are you screaming all of a sudden?"

Jurgen waved his thick hand in Rudolfo's direction. It was dismissive and scornful, more so than he'd intended, Rudolfo knew. None of Jurgen's human interaction was subtle—unlike Rudolfo, who often intended a world of hurt and insult to be expressed through the flaring of single nostril. Or laced into the words of an innocuous sentence, for instance, "When would you like to eat dinner?" which is what Rudolfo asked now.

"I don't care," answered Jurgen, turning away.

"Yeah," said Rudolfo, flaring both nostrils. "I can see that."

Out on the desert, the sun doesn't set so much as surrender, plummeting melodramatically behind the horizon.

Rudolfo Thielmann doesn't notice, though, because for a year he has survived in a vast timelessness. Clocks are generally superfluous in Las Vegas, anyway—where all is ruled by the tides of chance—but Rudolfo has somehow pushed things beyond that. He has managed to warp time, to mangle and melt it until it's useless, until time has nothing to do with the dreary business of living. Suns, moons, the journey of the stars—this is time in its simplest form, time as nurtured by the first magi, grim men with grey eyes who spent many hours staring into the heavens.

So Rudolfo doesn't notice the sun going down; but there are creatures outside his door that do.

They pop up with the newly birthed darkness, tiny beings with hideous faces, their features frozen into grimaces and grins. They are, for the most part, black-clad, shrouded by velveteen cloaks. Some are more benevolent; they wear leotards of pinkish hues and stroke the air with sparkling wands. With the nightfall, they begin to move toward das Haus *with ginger menace.*

They clutch empty bags.

Chapter Four

Jurgen had not been entirely honest when he told Preston that his first book had been *The Secrets of Magic Revealed*, written by Preston's father, the Magnificent. True, his journey toward professionalism had started when he'd pulled open that cover and read: *Never reveal the secrets in this book.* The reading itself had been slow and laborious, because the book had been translated into High German, and Jurgen had his difficulties with languages. (He also had his difficulties with mathematics, sciences and anything to do with geography or history. It was Jurgen Schubert's well-kept secret that he was a dim-witted boy. He was handsome and could work hard, and he'd learned that a sober, silent industry was often confused with intelligence.) Fortunately, *The Secrets of Magic Revealed* was full of photographs, black-and-white images of a huge set of hands. These hands were pale and delicate, the nails filed into beautiful crescent moons. They were photographed from every angle, and Jurgen found it thrilling to see the secret photographs, the ones that showed the coin nestled between the second and third knuckles, the playing card bent and cupped in the hollow of the palm.

Jurgen had learned almost everything from that book. He learned the sleights and passes, shifts and manipulations. And whatever information Preston the Magnificent left out, he gave directions to its location, the wonderful Erdnase card book, for example, or the classic *Modern Coin Magic* by J.B. Bobo.

But, technically, it had not been Jurgen's first book. His first book had been *Houdini on Magic*.

Jurgen had found the book while hiking. Though there were no true forests anywhere in the vicinity of Bremen, only spare outcroppings of diseased trees and moonlike shelves of slate and granite, Jurgen often tramped away into the country-side. He had a vague sense that there was a romantic rightness to this, which he got not from poetry, but from some paper place-mats he'd once seen in a restaurant. The placemats showed a strapping blond German youth all decked out in hiking gear, his upper body criss-crossed with leather straps. The lad's legs were thick with muscle and dressed lightly with golden hair. Jurgen hoped, actually expected, to encounter this creature sometime on the trails. An even more compelling reason for his hiking had to do with the overcrowding back at his own house. The house was tiny to begin with (Jurgen would realize one day that he could fit his entire childhood home into the trophy room of *das eindrucksvollste Haus im Universum*) and the Schubert family grew as if by cell division. His mother was usually both pregnant and nursing, his father was frequently announcing a visiting relative, the elder daughters were constantly getting married and their feckless husbands were never working and the elder sons would disappear briefly and then return with their own burgeoning broods. Jurgen was a middle child, but what he was in the mid-dle of was a vast sea of humanity. This is why he loved to lace up his hiking boots.

The boots were actually street shoes into which he'd forced long, thick laces, twisted and ribboned into complicated outdoorsy knots. Lacking not only *lederhosen*, but shorts of any kind, Jurgen hacked off the legs of some faded flannel pants and then rolled up the bottoms to reveal the entire length of his pale blue thigh, blue because the rolled-up pant leg cut off the circulation below his groin. He crossed two small belts over his chest, cinching them so that they, too, were biting and painful. He found a hat which he managed to persuade himself was Tyrolean. The one good thing about his home was that strange articles of clothing were easy to find, especially accessories, materializing suddenly in odd places and remaining unclaimed. Ties stayed hooked over newels for months, sweaters languished on the floor and hats grew like buds on the furniture. This particular hat had been purchased by Jurgen's brother Oscar, who originally thought that it made him look like an American gangster, before realizing that it was far too large and made him look like the thing he least wanted to be, a country bumpkin. Jurgen, even at a very young age, had a head so large and blocklike that he had to take hold of the brim of this hat and tug it down over his brow. The hat made Jurgen look like an American gangster, and he could never understand the looks of mistrust he received when he'd tramp into restaurants for a cup of coffee.

Jurgen would sometimes hike from dawn until well past dusk, consulting his compass dutifully and recording his route in a small notebook. He would record landmarks and town names; sometimes he'd jot down his impressions of the same: *nett*, he would write, *sehr nett*. When he returned home, Jurgen was often surprised—not *really* surprised, not after the first few times—to find that no one had noticed his absence.

It was a day of no particular distinction, neither sunny nor cloudy, hot nor cold, when Jurgen came across *Houdini on Magic*. It was lying in a pile of dead and dried leaves the same colour as the cheap parchment used to bind the book. He would never have noticed it except for the light hitting the tarnished gilt of the cover's lettering, sending up a reflection that crackled with something like electricity. Jurgen hurried over, imagining that he'd stumbled upon a cache of gold or gemstones. Instead, he found the little book, the paper burned by time. As soon as he lifted it, the sunlight ceased to play upon the leaf, and the lettering, although ornate and curlicued, looked very plain indeed. *Houdini on Magic.* He almost tossed the book away. His arm actually moved, his wrist cocked and then snapped. Jurgen was never sure why his fingers never let go. The fingers themselves decided they wanted to hold on to the book, so Jurgen pulled it back in and opened it, mildly curious.

He'd heard of Houdini before, of course, but realized at that moment that he had no idea what Houdini actually did. This struck him as wondrous, that this man could be so famous, almost without reason. He was simply *famous*. Jurgen's heart began to ache for fame, for elevation above all the people, a thousand times higher than the shitty little hills that surrounded Bremen. Here, apparently, was how Houdini had accomplished it: *by magic.*

He took the book home and hid it in his drawer. He waited until, one afternoon, there were no cousins or brothers, either natural or in-law, hanging about the bedroom. Then he opened the book and read:

> THE PAPER BAG ESCAPE
> *An escape from a paper bag, as from the pasteboard box, is convincing because the item used is too simple and easily examined to be faked in any way.*

This man escaped from paper bags?

Jurgen reread the words, confident that he'd misread, been misled, but Houdini was clear on the point: he climbed inside a paper bag seven and a half feet long and then freed himself. Where did they have such bags, wondered Jurgen, and why?

He flipped more pages.

CARD IN EGG

Jurgen read on, if for no other reason than he liked eggs.

Oh, this was more like it. Houdini described an effect whereby a chosen card is torn up and then found, miraculously restored, inside a fresh chicken egg.

This would make them take notice, thought Jurgen, this would surely silence the riotous breakfast table.

> *The card selected must be forced; that is, you compel the party selecting a card virtually to select the card that you almost push into his hand.*

Jurgen could compel the members of the Schubert household to do absolutely nothing. He turned more pages.

LIFTING A HUMAN BEING WITH POWER FROM EYES
(A Rare Trick of the Cingalese)

Jurgen read on.

One stormy evening, Jurgen Schubert assembled his family in the parlour. He hadn't selected the night because of the tempest; in fact, he was a little annoyed with it, as if God were trying to steal his thunder. The Schuberts crowded in, the parents and Oma claiming the spring-poked sofa, others squatting on the floor, the smaller children perching on the credenza and woodbox.

Jurgen appeared suddenly and startingly, more out of

nervousness than showmanship, and announced the advent of the Cingalese.

His family loudly demanded to know what *um Himmels willen* he was talking about.

"The Cingalese," repeated Jurgen, realizing that he'd been wondering about this himself, just what exactly a Cingalese might be. He knew why it was necessary for there to be one, because of the eyes—

Reminded of the wonder he was about to achieve, Jurgen waved his hands at his clan and hushed them sternly. Remarkably, they hushed. For years to come, Jurgen would wonder why he was only able to control audiences when he was rude. When he tried to be cultured—in accordance with Preston the Magnificent's "Magician's Pledge"—people were disdainful, even disorderly. But when he stared at them with cruel eyes, his black lids quivering with rage, they pushed back into their seats and silently begged him to continue. (It was Rudolfo who understood all this, if not to explain it, then to capitalize upon it.)

"Ah!" exclaimed Jurgen, fanning his hand behind his left ear. "I hear the Cingalese approaching!"

Jurgen ran into the kitchen to get ready.

He had managed the donning of his costume in as little as one minute and forty seconds, but that night, full of nerves and jittery as he was, it took four times that long. We can use the interlude to meet Little Ha-Jo, who was to assist Jurgen with the illusion.

At that exact moment Hans-Joachim had no idea of this, because he was suckling at his mother's breast and, besides, Ha-Jo had no idea of anything. He was eighteen months old, still bald and vaguely bluish, the latest addition to the Schubert clan. Houdini had called for the levitation to involve a baby, so that's how Jurgen was determined to proceed, but if Houdini had been able to see Little Ha-Jo, he probably would have suggested using another child, perhaps even one of the smaller adults. Jurgen was not fully aware of the monstrousness of his baby brother, although many would have been alerted by the fact that Ha-Jo was transported not in the years-old perambulator, but rather in a souped-up wheelbarrow, cushions strapped to the metal sides.

In the kitchen, Jurgen pulled his head through the hole he had cut in an old blanket. The fact that the blanket was old hadn't qualified it for selection; all of the Schubert blankets were old. *This* one had a pattern of zigzags and circles and looked, if not Cingalese, at least foreign. Jurgen placed a hat upon his head, a cone he'd fashioned out of thick black paper and adorned with little paintings of the moon and stars. He was not artistically inclined, and the paint had bled, little rivers of dirty white flowing from star to star.

Jurgen poked around underneath the sink and removed the piece of apparatus he'd constructed, a mesh basket. He was very proud of this contrivance, meticulously rendered out of screening, wood and wire. Houdini had not been helpful here; there were neither instructions nor handy hints. Houdini tended to write about the "mesh basket" with such insouciance that it took Jurgen two or three days before he realized this wasn't something he could simply purchase in a shop. So he'd made one as best he could, and was very pleased with the results (although looking upon it right then, he briefly wondered if the basket didn't seem a little small to contain Ha-Jo).

He cast that doubt aside, and reached further into the recesses of the cupboard beneath the sink, searching for the eyes.

According to Houdini, it was necessary to disguise oneself as a Cingalese because Cingalese people had odd eyes, silvered, almost mirror-like. This was the secret of the trick; one wore false eyes. Lengths of silk twine, thin to the point of invisibility, were attached to them, and tiny hooks at the ends of the silk twine latched onto the mesh of the baby-laden basket.

If Jurgen had found it hard to purchase a mesh basket, imagine his frustration when he tried to locate a pair of silvery false eyes. One of his brothers-in-law, fortunately, had a small interest in metal work, and at the bench in the back of the garden Jurgen was able to find a scrap of tin. He cut out two ovals with snips, took a small ballpeen hammer and pebbled the pieces until they were lens-like, then sanded and buffed the edges. He was able, although his ocular muscles rebelled and his fingers trembled, to slip these under his eyelids.

Attaching the silk twine had been more difficult, mostly because, as far as he could determine, there was no such thing. But he had a brother, Karl, who was an especially avid fisherman, always in pursuit of the huge zander that prowled the mud-blown rivers, and Jurgen found in his tackle box some line, fairly invisible and rated to withstand a weight of seventeen pounds. He calculated, quite wrongly, that Ha-Jo could weigh no more than seventeen pounds. He drilled two small holes, side by side, in the centre of each tin lens, poked the line through one and back out the other, tied it as best he could. Also in Karl's tackle box he found some small hooks.

So he lifted his blanket there in the kitchen and fed the eyes up through the neckhole, allowing the hooked lines to dangle down below his knees. Then, after forcing his eyes open with one hand and plugging in the tin lenses with the other, he returned to the parlour.

Jurgen was quite blind with the tin in his eyes. What he could see through the line-filled drillholes was doubled and indistinct, which means that the first appearance of the Cingalese involved his reeling into the room after colliding with the jamb of the doorway. He quickly regained his footing and turned to greet the audience.

Beunruhigt, alarmed, is the best word to describe his family's reaction to the sight of the Cingalese, although there were variants on the theme of alarm, ranging from nervous guffaws and giggles to his grandmother's blood-chilling shriek and subsequent sobbing pleas for heavenly mercy.

The Cingalese placed the mesh basket on the floor before him, gesticulating at it. In his bedroom, Jurgen had assumed a voice and developed an accent that he thought sounded Cingalese, but this deserted him now. He was somehow mute, so he pointed at the basket several times and waved toward his blind, silvery eyes. Finally he pointed at Ha-Jo, who giggled muzzily and spit up all over his tummy.

Mrs. Schubert meekly surrendered the infant. The Cingalese cradled Ha-Jo in his arms and stepped backwards. He lowered the child into the basket. Ha-Jo's diapered butt occupied most of the space, and the baby was able to draw in an arm so that he could suck a thumb comfortably. Everything else—the other arm, the ham-hock legs, the enormous lolling head—remained uncontained.

Jurgen bent over the basket, lowering his head near the child's, as though transmitting mental information or casting a silent spell. In reality, he was moving his knees slightly, following Houdini's instructions, trying to direct the small fishing hooks into the mesh on either side of the basket. Jurgen had practised this, but sequestered and alone, and the presence of the audience unnerved him. Not to mention his grandmother, whose whimpering had increased markedly when she saw the Cingalese steal little Ha-Jo. Not to mention little Ha-Jo himself, who apparently had no problem espying the invisible lines and was waving his hands in the air trying to grab hold. Jurgen was forced to move his knees with greater vigour than Houdini had intended. Indeed, it looked like the Cingalese was bending over the baby and dancing the Charleston. The little hook on the left dug in first, so Jurgen listed to his right and moved that knee in a broad circle, swinging the line, bashing the tiny hook into the mesh. After about a minute of this, the hook caught, and although Jurgen suspected the connection was tenuous, he decided to move forward with the illusion.

The secret, Houdini had stressed, was to stand up and bend backwards, so that the line fell across one's chest, bearing the weight. This Jurgen did. And then raising his hands into the air, he began the levitation. He felt the reassuring sensation of the lines biting into his breast. He straightened his legs.

The Cingalese's head began to vibrate, as if it were mounted on a spring and had been given a little flick. Jurgen marvelled at how strong his eyelid muscles seemed to be. The tin discs were being sucked away with tremendous force—Ha-Jo had gotten hold of one of the lines and was jerking on it—but Jurgen squinted, pulling his lids together, and successfully resisted.

He took a step backwards. This is what Houdini had advised, although Jurgen knew immediately it was misguided, because the basket started swinging. Just a bit at first, but Ha-Jo, giggling and pulling harder on the wire, accentuated the pendulous motion. Jurgen's lids now had to resist force from the sides as well.

The Cingalese desperately waved his hands in the air, indicating that a great miracle had taken place.

The Schubert family applauded, genuinely amazed and awestruck, not so much at the lifting of the baby—although they recognized the sheer athletic impressiveness of the deed—as at the colouring of Jurgen's face. Bright purple circles had blossomed around the silver eyes, and the hues diffused outwards.

Jurgen's head vibrations increased in frequency and modulation. Indeed, he pitched his head back and forth, like a dog who won't let go of a sock, with such force that his conical hat, black and bleeding stars, flew off and landed on the far side of the room. The purple eyelids, darkening more deeply with every instant, pulsated and quivered, throbbed and vibrated, and just when Jurgen was bringing his head forward to lower the basket, the right eyelid opened and vomited up the tin disc. The basket hit the ground with a resounding thud, the left tin disc popped out audibly and Jurgen fell backwards with both hands pushed into his wounded sockets.

Oma Schubert truly believed that the Cingalese had made Ha-Jo fly, using only the power of his wonderful eyes. When she saw those eyes pop out of his head, Oma succumbed to dementia, from which she never quite recovered.

Chapter Five

In the hills that surrounded *das Haus* (ersatz hills bulldozed from a distant place) were the cages. Some were more like cabins or cottages, a little subdivision of happily familied creatures. Other pens were crudely dug out of the earth, but only for the timid, blinking animals that liked such things. The big cats had more proper enclosures, constructed with thick unbending pipe. The biggest cage was for the biggest cat (not counting Samson, of course, who lived in the mansion proper).

Rudolfo threw open the door to this cage, shoving it backwards into the bars and sounding them like dull, broken bells. He took up his stance in the entranceway, planting his feet with precision, clasping his hands behind his back. Across from him, the panther unfolded from slumber, rising to its hind legs and roaring all in the same instant. The creature lifted a paw and swiped it through nothingness, making the air whistle.

"Oooh," said Rudolfo. "I'm in my boots shaking."

Actually, he truly was in his boots shaking. He held his hands behind his back so that the animal could not see them

tremble. This was the crucial and perilous day, the day of opening the door. Every afternoon for three weeks, Rudolfo had taken
the same stance in exactly the same place, but always with the
door shut and bolted. The panther had growled and howled to
begin with. It had tried with startling determination to force its
lethal claws through the iron bars. Over time, the beast had
calmed somewhat and contented itself with lofty yawns, aiming
arrogantly half-closed eyes at Rudolfo. Occasionally, it would
make a menacing dash across the sawdust or rear up to expose its
genitals. For three weeks Rudolfo had stood there and gently
taunted the beast. "*Ja, ja, ja*. Big deal."

Now the panther, full of disdain, turned its back and lumbered away from him. Rudolfo braced, reminding himself of
what he had learned from General Bosco. The panther turned
suddenly and charged across the circle, sleek and lethal. Rudolfo
concentrated on the humping of the shoulders, the attitude of the
head. He saw immediately that the animal was not intent on a
true engagement—this was all bluff. When the panther drew
near, Rudolfo lifted a leg and deftly kicked the beast, his heel
connecting with the animal's furiously creased brow. The animal
flew backwards but was on its feet immediately. It shook its head,
making a few wet *wubba-wubba* noises, and then began to march
the perimeter of the cage, as if making a survey of the circle had
always been its intention.

Behind Rudolfo, across an artificial gully, at one of the
mansion's many rear doors, Jurgen was directing a small army
of fat men. Always bashful speaking English in public, Jurgen
tried to make do with imprecatory grunts and sounded, thought
Rudolfo, like an ape. But he hadn't much time for that thought,
because the panther, nearing once more, was pressing itself
against the bars of the cage, searching in vain for a corner from
which to pounce. Rudolfo seized an opportunity, at least, he intuited suddenly that the time was right, and took a large step

forward into the cage. The panther glanced up, and stopped in its tracks. Rudolfo now stood in its path, which gave the creature two choices. It could either move around Rudolfo, or it could eat him.

"Unh!" grunted Jurgen from behind, a negative sound. Rudolfo could imagine him shaking his head, waving a thick forefinger at one of the fat men and pointing him off in another direction. Most of the Collection was being toted downstairs, into the Grotto, but some of the larger pieces were being housed elsewhere. The huge, hideous cabinet, for example, was too awkward and hulking for any room except their bedroom, which was domed to accommodate the fabulous skylight.

The panther, giving itself time to think, planted its hindquarters on the ground and twisted back to lick its genitals. Rudolfo took quick, quiet strides toward the beast. The panther left off its licking, looked up and saw the human towering above. It growled, but it was a strangled cry, more kittenlike than the panther might have wished. The beast lifted a front paw and threw it toward the man's leg, but this small action knocked the animal off balance, so it ended up rolling onto its back. Rudolfo leapt then, impetuously and rather foolishly, digging his fingers into the cat's belly. The panther twisted and writhed and emitted a low growl.

"*Gucci koo*," whispered Rudolfo.

The beast opened its maw and lashed its prickly tongue up the length of Rudolfo's face. Rudolfo grinned, then giggled, then laughed out loud, a couple of huge, hoary barks. He hugged the panther tightly to his chest and pressed kisses on its head.

Rudolfo presumably was delivered upon the planet in a everyday manner, his mother bathed in sweat and gripped by pain, doctors and midwives hovering. But this event must be imagined only. There is no evidence of it, no birth certificate that names even the general locale. His *arrival*, however, is better documented. The first anyone ever saw of Rudolfo Thielmann, he was slung under his mother's arm like a bagpipe bladder. His mother stepped off a train in Bern, Switzerland, with such grandeur that a newspaper reporter, sitting in a nearby café and getting quite drunk, lurched to his feet and requested an interview. Anna Thielmann blushed and chewed her bottom lip, finally said a few confusing words and consented to being photographed. She then pushed the reporter away with her fingertips.

It was this reporter who first made mention of the baby, although he wrote that the infant was "cradled in his mother's arms." The accompanying photograph—the item was placed on the back pages of the morning *Zeitung* and given an illustration— belies this. Little Rudolfo is caught in the crook of his mother's left arm, facing downwards, his arms and legs splayed awkwardly. The baby in the picture is trying hard to raise his huge head, to look at the strange world around him.

Anna Thielmann, according to the photograph, was huge and regal, with a linebacker's physique and a face that seemed to be made up of too many features. Closer examination of the newspaper photograph (Rudolfo still had a copy, folded into a wallet that he never carried because none of his clothes have pockets) reveals that Anna had the basic makeup: two eyes (dark as night), a nose (oddly triangular, like the protective flap hinged to industrial safety glasses), a mouth (Anna smiled by raising her upper lip and crimping it in the middle) and a spectacular obelisk of red hair.

Miss Anna Thielmann, the story began, *arrived in the city yesterday having abandoned her career upon the great operatic stages of the world.*

Local opera aficionados were not familiar with the name *Anna Thielmann*, but when they heard her voice they were united in their support of her decision to abandon the stage. She spoke little as a rule—she named cuts of meat at the butcher's, rhymed off a list of inexpensive intoxicants at the wine store—but when she did her voice was froglike, not just in timbre but in character, leaping suddenly away up high and then landing with an awkward splat.

She seemed to have come not only from a strange place, but also from a strange time, the *fin-de-siècle*. She dressed in long scarves and feathered boas that seemed vaguely old-fashioned. Possessing a rump of exaggerated meatiness, she gave the impression that she wore a bustle, although she did not. Anna seemed to have missed the last fifty grievous years. She came to Bern imbued with a vague innocence, and this stayed with her even after it became clear to everyone that Anna was involved with drugs, that her apartment sat squarely on the Opium Route.

No one had ever seen Anna Thielmann herself smoke opium. True, they had seen her spill wild-eyed onto the cobbled streets of the old city, her monolith of hair tilted almost to the horizontal, but on such occasions she trailed substantial alcoholic fumes and vapours. No denying, however, that opium was smoked in her apartment. Anna's clientele was for the most part eccentric. The Bernese prided themselves on a hard-earned normalcy, and they were shocked to see their city suddenly giving up a host of freaks. There were fat women and men with tiny heads, dissipated dwarves and melancholy giants. They filed in and out with a regularity that suggested that there was a doctor's or dentist's office at the top of the staircase at Kramgasse 49, an address Anna and Rudolfo shared, although not at the same time, with Albert Einstein.

Some of the people who came to Kramgasse 49 were young women, and they offset Anna's quaint singularity with a violent embracing of modernity. They wore nylons and complicated brassieres. They wore shoes with long, thin heels, usually red and always so antithetical to locomotion that the ascent up the wooden stairs took hours. Young boys would push open the door at street level to gawk upwards and the women, clutching the walls and wobbling, would hurl down vile curses. These women tended not to go in and out; they would arrive in the early evening and leave with the dawn, nylons twisted, complicated brassieres abandoned and shoes slung over their shoulders.

It is not entirely true that Anna's apartment was an opium den, not in any strictly commercial sense. There were no tiers of flea-infested bunk beds; the furnishing was second-hand but comfy, long settees and big fat easy chairs. People did smoke opium, true, but they smoked many other things besides, mari- juana and Turkish hashish and pipefuls of a rare Tahitian stu- porific. Neither were the young women prostitutes, *really*. They referred to themselves as artist's models, and when they achieved the summit of the staircase they stripped off their clothes and stood in the middle of the living room while the people in the room painted them, or photographed them, or composed poems dedicated to their physical beauty. Anna Thielmann was actually the custodian of a Salon, and the people who came to visit were *artistes*. They were unabashedly third-rate artistes, gleefully turn- ing out childish drawings, blurred prints and clumsy rhymes, but they were artistes all the same.

Things could get pretty wild. There was a huge hump- backed piano in the living room, and it tended to herald the debauch. At some point near midnight, someone (usually Hein- rich Gissing, near-blind and proudly consumptive) would leap upon the machine, savaging the keyboard, playing jazz, which signified a careless admixture of white and black keys. The naked artist's models would break pose and posit certain transactions. The artistes, uniformly penniless, would undertake the negotia- tions with vigour and conviction. It was often some time before things were hammered out, at which point the charge of nymphs and satyrs would commence. Around two a.m. the drugs would

kick in, and Kramgasse 49 would ring with howls and half-for-
gotten lullabies. There were fights, often a stabbing. On one
occasion someone flew through the front window and ended up
a small crumpled pile on the cobblestones below, but this was a
failed experiment in flight rather than foul play.

Rudolfo had his own room; rather, there was a large walk-
in closet which had been allotted to him, his crib pushed into the
corner and his stuffed animals spread out around him. Little
Rudy had an astounding number of stuffed animals, because,
let's face it, if you were an artiste intent on getting cross-eyed and
rutting in the middle of the living room, you would bring a
stuffed animal to the little boy who would no doubt be standing
in the corner, sucking his thumb, wide-eyed with horror. Rudolfo
soon had hundreds of them, bears, lions, tigers and rarer things
besides, parrots with multi-coloured plush beaks, a well-crafted
baboon, its rump a quilting of vibrant satin.

Rudy had trouble—understandably—sleeping through the
night. Sleeping at all, really. Sometimes he drifted away into a
fitful trance, but there was always some loud noise to pull him
back. He would sit up in bed, wailing, but his cries could never
be heard above the piano, the grunts, the shrieks of hilarity. He
sought comfort in the glass eyes of his menagerie, grabbing one
of the plush pussycats and pulling it into bed.

Some nights were more sedate. Some nights, Anna Thielmann
would invite a youngish, long-haired man, whose name Rudolfo
remembered as Flowers. Flowers was slender and incredibly vain,
always throwing his chin high into the air and twisting his head
so that he showed a full profile. Flowers affected black tails and,
although his suit was shiny and the elbows put out, he did raise
the tone of the Salon. The artistes were quieted by his presence;
they sat placidly in the corners and picked things off their
sweaters, or rubbed at the luminous nicotine stains that covered

their hands. The models drew long scarves out of tiny handbags and draped them over their naked shoulders like prayer shawls.

Flowers would sit down behind the keyboard and, after cracking each finger meticulously, begin to play. He favoured the music of the Great Romantics, and he played with a grand knuckle-rolling style that involved grunting. Flowers was, by most standards, awful, a hammer-handed dilettante who closed his eyes not out of ecstasy, but as an aid to memory. Even so, he'd bog down halfway through any piece, allowing his fingers to drop from the keyboard, slumping forward and sighing, as though to continue would be more than the soul could bear.

At which point Anna Thielmann would enter the room, dressed as one of the great heroines from grand opera. She would take all roles, soprana, mezzo, alto; it made little difference to her. She was not focused on such niceties as pitch and tone; her accent was more on the dramatic. Although she might begin by standing erect with her fingers locked in front of her bosom, it wasn't long before she started drifting through her little crowd, staring deeply into eyes, caressing cheeks, pulling on forelocks. Soon she would take advantage of any purely musical interlude to kiss a listener or two, undo shirt buttons, perhaps even thrum a crotch. Of course, this was just for the love songs, the arias that dealt with romance and the stirrings of the heart. If tragedy were invoked, Anna would reel throughout the room, bouncing off walls, tears spilling over the ridges of muscle that formed her face. Her Tosca, Rudolfo remembered, was especially effective; when she heard the shots that meant that Cavaradossi had been shot—damn that Scarpia—she would wail and keel over backwards, landing with a thud that shook plaster dust out of the ceiling.

Some years before, when young Albert Einstein, an employee of the Swiss patent office, had lived at Kramgasse 49, he had already largely worked out the Theory of Relativity, bickering about it with his wife, Mileva, over the breakfast table. A tall reading stand stood in the corner as testament to Einstein's having lived there, although Anna, not given to reading, used it mostly as a place to dry her dainties.

Little Rudolfo had more second-hand contact with the previous tenant. In the quiet, dust-filled afternoons, Rudolfo prowled about the apartment. He was constantly finding pencil scratchings on the walls, formulae and brief exclamatory sentences. As a child, Rudolfo crawled about the place trying to make sense of these cryptic runes.

As a man, Rudolfo could still see the letters and numbers clearly when he closed his eyes. They remained a mystery.

Samson strutted into the cage, affecting an air of careless inquisitiveness, much like a janitor who has discovered the stockroom door left open. Seeing his master with another animal, he came to an abrupt halt, his head jerking back as if slapped. He recovered well, disdainfully squirting a stream of urine onto the sawdust. The albino leopard spied a sparkling ball, perhaps three feet in diameter, across the circle. He loped toward it, reached out and pulled the ball backwards with a huge paw. Throwing a glance toward Rudolfo and the panther (Rudolfo was on his feet, wiping sawdust from his dark blue bodysuit), Samson leapt on top of the globe. Unfortunately, it had been some time since he'd performed atop the gleaming ball. He was paddle-pawed and his joints were sore. Managing only a few clumsy minces, he rolled off sideways. He sought to regain some dignity by affecting a regal stance shortly before he hit, then there was a dull sound and a huge cloud of sawdust.

Rudolfo walked over to Samson, now pretending to be asleep, snoring with such conviction that his pale tongue curled and unfurled like a party favour. Rudolfo gave the beast a gentle nudge, saying, "Come on, Sammy. Let's go see how big a mess Jurgen is making."

Samson struggled up. He licked the back of Rudolfo's hand and then made for the cage's doorway. The panther roared at him, standing up and shaking his genitals. Without changing his gait, Samson contemptuously let loose another stream of urine. It was one of the few benefits of aging, the ability to summon piss at any time.

Rudolfo felt as guilty as a lover who has been caught humped over the wrong backside. While it was no secret that animals were being trained to replace Samson, neither had there been any open discussion about it. Jurgen maintained that the animals were Rudolfo's concern, covering any sign of affection for Samson with this impersonal professionalism. Not that Jurgen was *that* attached to the beast. Especially lately, especially after that show a few weeks ago when they had pulled away the curtain from the gaffed cage to reveal the albino leopard in a state of profound slumber. The audience had laughed, which always seemed to horrify and madden Jurgen. Rudolfo had tried to cover, guffawing with the exaggerated lip-twitching of a moronic donkey, slapping his thighs with stagy mirth. Samson awoke and, confused as to what was happening, had backed behind the mirrored panel, disappearing from view except for a ghostly, quivering snout.

Rudolfo and Samson neared the back of the house. The last of the movers emerged through the door, two overalled men chuckling and shaking their heads with bemusement. Rudolfo knew immediately that they were laughing at his partner, so he whispered to Samson, "Go play with those two fat piggies." Samson bounded with childlike enthusiasm, indistinguishable from brute fury to the movers. Rudolfo allowed a few moments for bowel-loosening, with Samson cavorting before the two men, alternately hugging the ground and springing high into the air.

"Guys, hi," he said nonchalantly, leisurely walking toward them and clapping his hands together. Samson crumpled like an old newspaper, lying down and then licking out of habit, shovelling up a tongue-load of gravel from a flowerbed and tossing it down his throat. "What company are you babies from?" demanded Rudolfo.

The two movers looked at each other and one pointed to the crest sewn over his breast.

Rudolfo squinted, stared, nodded his head. "Because when is a big mess in the house I get angry and phone the company."

"No mess, chief," said the man.

Rudolfo grinned at that, always happy to learn new colloquialisms. "Okay, chieves," he said, executing a quasi-military salute. "Is my friend in there?"

The two men nodded as one and hastily began down the bright golden path that led around to the front of the house.

Rudolfo pushed the door open for Samson, who hoisted himself from the ground and lumbered through. The hallway lay before them, a long tunnel of polished marble and burnished oak. They walked past the entranceways to the Gymnasium, the archery range, the theatre, Samson making a half-turn at each one, straightening out hurriedly when he noticed Rudolfo still walking determinedly.

At the very end of the hallway was the Grotto. This had been Rudolfo's idea, to construct a cave beneath the house, although the architect had embraced the notion with quixotic enthusiasm. Most of the stone was imported from the tiny emirate of Alqa'ar, although some of it was Himalayan, large pieces from the very summits imprinted, incredibly, with the fossils of sea creatures. The Grotto was vaulted, the light sources hidden in nooks and crannies. It was a large hole of shadows. There was no door as such, rather, a large remote-controlled boulder that rolled into place. However, the batteries had long ago run out on the remote, so the boulder remained parked just inside.

The movers had dumped the boxes of books, the few pieces, with no care or design. True, the Grotto had no real corners, where things might be piled less obtrusively, but Rudolfo didn't think that was reason enough for the confusion he felt.

Rudolfo was briefly alarmed to see a fat man sitting over in the shadows, but as his eyes got used to the gloom, he realized that it was the big wooden doll-man. (He would not have been able to name it—*Moon*—even though the word was carved into the top of the automaton's pedestal.) In the middle of it all, at a small schoolboy's desk complete with empty inkwell and the initials of children long dead, sat Jurgen Schubert, a large leather-bound tome clutched in his hands, the covers sealed by cobwebbing.

Jurgen flipped the front cover open and blew away dust. As he read the title page, his eyelids fluttered up and down rapidly like antique television sets that need adjustment with the horizontal hold.

"Hi, chief," said Rudolfo, from the hole that was the doorway, leaning up against the cool rock. "Anything good?"

"*The Art of Juggling, or…*" said Jurgen, reading the English. There was another word on the title page, *Legerdemain*, which he did not attempt. He switched to German. "It's a very famous book. Four hundred years old. One of the first books about magic."

"We have to the hotel be going." Rudolfo would often use English when petulant, peeved or baffled.

Jurgen looked up at his friend, nodded, and closed the book.

"So," asked their driver, Jimmy, "what's the story on this Tee-hee-hee Collection?"

Jimmy was a large man with a head that consisted of over-sized features—long, froggy lips, a bulbous nose marbled with exploded veins—stuck onto a billiard ball. Very unpleasant. Fortunately, they rarely saw his face.

"Why do you me this ask?" said Jurgen.

Rudolfo scowled, annoyed as always with his partner's English syntax.

"No reason, boss," responded Jimmy. Jimmy had originally come to Vegas hoping to become the driver for a shadowy under-world figure. He'd had a vision, which he found deeply exciting, of steering a long black limousine, willing himself to stare straight ahead, occasionally, very occasionally, glancing into the rearview mirror where he saw such goings-on as were unheard of in Missouri. "It was on television."

"What was on television?" snapped Rudolfo.

"The thing," explained Jimmy. "The Collection thing. They said as how you guys bought it. On the news."

"Oh, so it was on the news, *ja?*"

"Yeah," nodded Jimmy. "Not on the *news*-news, where there's a picture in the background and the chick is reading from a piece of paper."

"Whatever in the world are you blistering about?" asked Rudolfo.

"It was on that part at the end, you know, when the chick newscaster and the sports guy and the weather guy are all sitting together. And she says how you guys bought this Collection, and then they said some more stuff. Had a few laughs."

They hit the Strip suddenly, light and noise exploding upon the planet.

"*Ja*, well," said Rudolfo, "sticks and stones can break my bones, but local coverage will never harm me." He felt very sad momentarily, for without thinking he had quoted Miss Joe, their first manager.

"So this Collection thing," persisted Jimmy—this now qualified officially as the longest conversation Jurgen and Rudolfo had ever had with their driver— "is a big deal, huh?"

"It is," responded Rudolfo, "just a bunch of books and a few hideous pieces of wood."

Jurgen put sunglasses on, even though it was still daylight and nowhere near as bright as it would be at night. "I will tell you about books," he said quietly. He took a deep breath and chewed at his lips briefly, as if to draw blood and energy into them, and Rudolfo realized that he intended to continue in English, that whatever he meant to say was as much for Jimmy's illumination as his own.

"Was a man named Jean. In France, many years ago. And he was young man, eighteen years maybe, he is wanting to be, like his fodder—"

"Father?" suggested Rudolfo meanly.

"Watchmaker. Maker of watches. So he is asking the bookseller for book, you know, about making watch."

"You understand this, Jimmy?" wondered Rudolfo.

Jimmy grunted, threw his shoulders upwards in a loose and uncoordinated manner. "Sure. Like on the back of the matchbooks. It's got watchmaker right there with refrigeration and air-conditioning technician."

"So book comes, you know. It looks funny. It is name *Amusing Mechanical Devices*. Not about watch at all. It is about how to make, oh, Transformation Boxes and Automata and all sort of thing. So Jean becomes magician. Sometimes you no choose books. Books choose you."

"What the hell kind of stupid shit story is that?" demanded Rudolfo in German, the hard sounds and diminutives making him sound petulant and childish.

"He make his name 'Jean Robert-Houdin.' He was the greatest magician of his day," Jurgen switched to German.

"That's what you must do; that's all that counts. Being the greatest magician of the day. And then another day comes, but that's all right."

"And you are the greatest magician of your day," said Rudolfo.

"No."

"You are," insisted Rudolfo. "Who else is there? Preston the Unsightly? He's nothing. He's no better than a gypsy playing three-card monte. Who else? The asshole? Kaz is shit and he knows it! He's got all those people helping him. Half the audience are sticks, you know that."

"It's not that Kaz is or isn't good," said Jurgen. "It's that I am bad."

"Act of the Year, four years in a row."

"I'm so scared every time I do an effect. Even one I've done a thousand times, I'm afraid that people will see that it's a trick and point at me and laugh and say, *Jurgen Schubert, you big fake.*"

"Everyone's a *fake*," argued Rudolfo. "Magic is a fake. That's why *showmanship* is so important."

But Jurgen had turned away, and no longer seemed to be listening.

Chapter Six

Having not seen them for a while—had he ever seen them, other than on television?—Preston decided to go to the Abraxas Hotel and catch the Jurgen and Rudolfo Show. He had to cancel his own evening's performance, which he did simply enough. He telephoned Mrs. Antoinette Kingsley and advised her to stay home. She grunted groggily on the other end, having been newly woken. Preston offered to pay her nightly salary anyway, at which point she hung up.

For a man who dressed as poorly as he did, Preston spent a lot of time thinking about wardrobe. He considered wearing the morning suit he had worn the day before, the one that had belonged to his father, Preston the Magnificent. But he had sweated the garment out—there were dark skunky stains emanating from the armpits. He next considered wearing his show clothes, a sweatshirt with the images of the moon and stars stitched on and a pair of jeans that kept a crease because he only wore them for two hours a night. But Preston decided that this garb was too ostentatious. He opened his closet door and surveyed his apparel. He selected an ornate and colourful Hawaiian shirt and put it with the trousers from the morning suit, which had not been damaged too badly by perspiration. Then he forced his fat and puffy feet into a pair of snakeskin cowboy boots.

Preston went through the door of his apartment and descended into the theatre.

The George had been built in 1917, during a brief boom. Badgered out of the sands by the obdurate Helen Stewart—widowed on account of a duel in which her husband Archibald had been forced to defend her honour—Las Vegas was a random stop on the tracks being laid along the Mormon Trail. The George Theater lay in the heart of Block 16, the haunt of faro players and horny railway workers. It had been erected by a theatrical Englishman, Ivor Thicknesse, who was surely suffering from heatstroke, the skin on his pate perpetually blistered by the merciless sun. Thicknesse opened the George with a production of *Hamlet*, taking the lead himself, spinning about the stage in a state of advanced delirium. He managed to put on quite a few shows, even persuading some of the prominent thespians of the day—George Arliss, Edmund Breece, Lumsden Hare—that the George in "Ragtown" represented a fruitful and gratifying stop on any transcontinental tour. Thicknesse himself always took a part, at least he did until an audience member, caught up in the duel taking place before him, shot Thicknesse's Tybalt in the back of the head.

The theatre was then clapboarded and tarpapered, and it lay unused until Preston the Magnificent, Jr., bought it, refurbished it and started presenting his little entertainments in its hall. It seemed a very odd thing to do; Preston was rumoured to have a problem with strong drink.

The stairs snaked and curled, connecting the loges and the small auditorium below. Preston was forced to take hold of the banister, to place his feet with precision on the uneven, wobbly risers. The lamplight was dampened by the dust on the glass. It wasn't that Preston was lazy about housekeeping duties, but he liked the idea of dust so much he was loathe to wipe and feather it away. Dust was mostly human skin, Preston had heard, and in this unhygienic manner Ivor Thicknesse was still prowling about the George, his brains boiled by the heat.

In the tiny foyer was the small glass booth that contained, ordinarily, the pinch-faced Mrs. Antoinette Kingsley, who would make change and issue tickets with sober, churlish industry. Preston removed from his pocket a piece of paper (it was actually a Kleenex). He reached through the cut-out and fished around on Mrs. Kingsley's desktop until he located the stub of a pencil. Then he wrote the words SHOW CANCELLED—TAKE A RAINCHECK on the Kleenex, licked a corner and stuck it up.

He carefully locked the big theatre doors behind him with a massive, old-fashioned key, a heart wrought at one end, the works merely three truncated fingers. In Las Vegas, a town full of crooks and magicians, this precaution was more than useless. There were guys, Preston knew, who could undo the lock without even touching it. But he enjoyed old locks and old keys, so he worked the loud, clunky mechanism, whistling all the while, and when he was done he paused to look at his poster.

PRESTON THE MAGNIFICENT, JR., large letters proclaimed, although the man in the poster looked not much like the Preston we know. The man in the poster was slim and clear-eyed. He held his hands in an awkward manner, the fingers spread wide. They were empty, but the poster made one imagine that they had been full of things just the moment before, or would be the moment after—all manner of things, coins and cards and radiant doves. In the poster, Preston was wearing one of his father's capes, long, black and embroidered with a design of lightning flashes. Preston no longer wore that cape. In fact, he had no idea where it was. That thought made him chuckle a bit, because the cape was certainly left loaded, a collapsible wand tucked into the hem, along with the thin metal rod that controlled the flying ball. If anyone found it, his father would be exposed for the cheap cozening thimblerigger he was.

As far as Preston was concerned, his father had only ever performed one worthwile stunt. It had taken place in Cleveland, where Preston the Magnificent was giving a Saturday afternoon matinee. Preston could imagine his father standing on stage, unreasonably rigid (so that his huge, sculpted hairdo would not be knocked askew), announcing each illusion in an English that no one else spoke or understood. "Yea," his father might say, sometimes even adding the *verily*, "Wither comes this luminiferous orb? It cometh out of a mystic vacuity!"

So there he was, Preston the Magnificent, prestidigitating for all his worth, when the manager appeared in the wings making frantic hisses and come-hither motions with his index finger. Preston the Magnificent ignored him for a good long while, upset by this lack of breeding and manners, but finally and reluctantly he asked the audience's indulgence and went to see what was up.

"Fire," whispered the manager. Only then did Preston the Magnificent notice the smoke, the flame that was licking the edges of the scrim.

The story, as reported by the newspapers and repeated at chintzy conjurors' conventions, had it that Preston the Magnificent didn't hesitate at all, merely wheeled about and walked to his mark, stuck a finger into the air and began to speak. His son didn't buy that, exactly. He imagined that his father opened and closed his mouth wordlessly a few times, that his face coloured with anger. The idea of anything interrupting a show would make him apoplectic. So Preston the Magnificent probably swore at the fire (he used several childish words in place of curses, things like *fizz* and *pigwart*) and then spent long moments realigning and adjusting his clothing, feeling sullied by this proximity to vulgarity. Preston the Magnificent then turned and marched to the centre of the stage, raised the tiny pale finger and began to speak. "Laddies and lassies," he said, "the next miracle is the globally celebrated and much ballyhooed Hindu Rope Trick. I, alone in the Occident, possess the arcanum of this wonder, having learnt it firsthand from a Cingalese swami. But, hear me, why should I perform this *chef-d'oeuvre* inside this theatre, opening the doors for accusations of subterfuge and chicanery, insinuations of thin wire attached to the lighting grids holding up the rope?" (Preston, when he heard the speech repeated verbatim, knew just how angry and upset his father had been, because he had blown the effect right there.) "Instead, I shall perform the deed upon the *boulevard without*! If you therefore stand and effect an egress in an orderly fashion—the youngsters in the last row should go first, then the penultimate, etcetera—you will see a miracle that shall go down into the vaults of historical annals!" And the children did leave calmly, and were all outside when the theatre popped into full conflagration. Preston the Magnificent lost everything, from big apparatus down to his little bag of coin effects, but such was the publicity that he was booked for about seven years afterwards—largely for children's matinees—and it took him no time to reassemble an act.

When Preston arrived at the Abraxas Hotel, his clothes were soaked through with sweat; he was puffy and hacking up sputum. Although the bus stopped right outside the huge gates (bare-breasted angels were sculpted above, blowing on long bugles and plucking at lyres), it was a long way to the front door. He'd paused by the fountain, twice as a matter of fact, to scoop out a palmful of water and splash it across his brow.

Preston grew up in Las Vegas—insomuch as Las Vegas is a geographical entity, insomuch as Preston ever grew up—and he had struck a truce with the city's oddities and peccadilloes. But the Abraxas Hotel had always disturbed him. It was themed by the notion of fairy tales; the hotel itself was castlelike, circumvallated by jagged, dark towers. Old women with warts and beaked noses were hired to scamper through the hallways, laughing hideously. There were knights in armour, complete with visors and codpieces. There were children trailed by goats, old men with thick spectacles and nightdresses. Preston knew none of the referents. His father had never told him a fairy story, and his mother had only told him one, the story of a young girl whose life was destroyed by a powerful and cruel wizard.

Preston waved off the oversized and disfigured doormen, throwing silver dollars into cavernous palms. (He produced the coins out of thin air, but the doormen were all too jaded to notice.)

Preston wandered through the endless Casino. Along the way, women offered him snacks, women with wide, empty eyes and voluptuous bodies. Preston paused long enough to toss three or four coins into a slot machine. He was rewarded with a handful of money, enough, he hoped, to get him a ticket into the Theatre.

A ticket cost ninety-three dollars. Preston wondered how they'd arrived at that figure. All he could think was that the hotel accountants were into numerology; "ninety-three" was both pleasing and potent. As luck would have it, when he unclenched his fist and allowed the coins to dribble forth, they totalled ninety-four seventy-five, leaving him busfare home. Preston grunted with vague satisfaction and went to claim a seat.

The place resembled a lecture hall, the tiers heavily raked, the chairs small and hard. There were even, between the seats, small trays that could be pulled up and folded down. These were to support the drinks that cost an average of twelve dollars each. Preston, who no longer drank liquor, certainly not at twelve dollars a pop, produced his own glass and placed it gently down.

Beside him, an elderly woman pulled out a cigarette and lit it with trembling hands. She was from Winnipeg, Manitoba, and was a huge Jurgen and Rudolfo fan. She thought Jurgen was the most attractive man she'd ever seen; every illusion he performed made her flutter internally.

Preston aimed his forefinger at the empty glass and it filled with a dark liquid. Ice fell out of the air, even a slice of lime, and when the semi-clad girl came to take his drink order, she was surprised to see Preston already sipping peacefully.

Darkness fell with a thud. This then was broken by lines of light, threading quickly through the room as though taking a head count.

The music began, enormous and assaultive, a legion of Roman soldiers sticking the air with lances and pikes. Most of the people in the audience removed their hearing aids. Preston, denied this option, plugged his ears with napkins and hoped this would stop the blood from trickling down and staining his shirt collar.

The music was familiar and unsettling, like an old friend troubled by mental problems. Or in this case, Preston thought, like an old friend who'd become a furry, slobbering geek.

"Ladies and gentlemen," came a huge and beautiful voice, a voice such as God would have if He'd gone to community college and studied Radio Arts, "the Abraxas Hotel is proud to present the greatest show on earth...*Jurgen and Rudolfo!*"

Preston sat forward in his seat and shoved his fat hands under his thighs. The *Siegfried Idyll*, he realized suddenly. Buried underneath the prehistoric frequencies of the music was the fragile piece that Richard Wagner had written for his wife on her birthday. When Cosima awoke that morning, Preston remembered reading, nineteen musicians were sitting on her front steps. Her husband conducted them tenderly, his eyes half-closed, his mouth half-open. Now here the thing was, pumped up and snarling as though in the throes of 'roid-age. Preston had to physically tug at the grey skin of his jowls in order to fashion a more profound scowl than the one he typically wore.

The stage filled with acrid grey smoke. Jurgen and Rudolfo appeared suddenly, each caught in his own spotlight. For a long moment they did nothing, merely stood upon the stage, their hands on their hips, staring into the audience. Their costumes were of the same design—skin-tight jumpsuits, high leather boots—but Jurgen's was black and Rudolfo's white. The audience burst into applause—the old woman beside Preston clapped so furiously that she was winded within seconds—but the two stood there without response. Then they brought their hands up, pounded their palms together—these actions exact and simultaneous—and extended forefingers at the crowd. They smiled now, briefly, and got down to business.

The stage—about the same dimensions as a football field—became even more illuminated. There were huge geometric shapes arranged upon it, all rendered out of gleaming, pebbled aluminum. There was a metallic cube, an eight-foot pyramid, a ring with a wall three feet high, a few monoliths and a huge globe, perhaps twelve feet in diameter. The globe rolled forward now, as if of its own volition. Jurgen and Rudolfo corralled it, shoving it playfully back and forth, until they and the sphere achieved the centre of the stage. They placed their hands upon the globe and caused it to spin; the pebbled aluminum exploded the light and sprayed it throughout the auditorium. Jurgen stopped the ball abruptly and pointed to a small latch on its smooth surface. Rudolfo, standing on the other side, pointed to another. Each worked one of these, then together they lifted the top half of the sphere, hinged at the back, to reveal the emptiness inside.

Miranda arrived onstage now, dressed in what appeared to be cellophane. Many of the men in the audience dribbled rum and coke onto their shirt fronts. Miranda smiled at the crowd and then climbed into the silver ball. Jurgen and Rudolfo relatched it, spun it around, rolled it toward the front of the stage. Then they both took a step away from the orb and stared at each other, deeply, as though forgetting what they should do next. They clapped their hands—again with improbable synchronicity—and ripped open the latches.

Samson leapt out of the silver ball, howling fiercely.

Jurgen and Rudolfo looked inside the ball and then turned to express their astonishment to the audience, because there was no sign of Miranda.

The crowd erupted in applause, and Preston joined in eagerly. What he found most impressive was the cost of the gimmick itself, the huge aluminum ball, maybe a hundred thou right there. There was a hidden compartment, of course, and what hid it was a third piece of aluminum, tooled painstakingly to reflect exactly the inside of the half-circle above it. When the globe was flipped, this piece would move, freeing whatever was hidden there (a huge albino leopard, in this case) and allowing something new (the miraculous Miranda) to take its place.

The old woman from Winnipeg shook her head, so awestruck by what she'd witnessed that her first inclination was to disbelieve that it had happened at all.

Samson bent his head low and forced his front legs to bend. He was taking a bow, although it had the look of undignified servility. Then the big white cat turned and trotted offstage.

Jurgen and Rudolfo each placed their hands on the silver ball and made it go around in a circle, trotting beside it so that they each disappeared from view, momentarily, over and over again. Finally the globe was revolving at a furious clip (light attacked from all directions and was repulsed with luminous savagery) and neither Jurgen nor Rudolfo was anywhere to be seen.

The huge silver ball abruptly rolled toward the back of the stage and was swallowed up by the shadow. Jurgen and Rudolfo appeared, their hands cocked on to their hips. In a few seconds, the boys had managed to change costumes, to actually *exchange* costumes. Jurgen was now wrapped in a white bodysuit, Rudolfo was black-clad.

The lights began to dim and a black velvet curtain descended from above, separating the apron of the stage. Preston grunted with satisfaction, causing alarm to the elderly woman from Winnipeg. *Pretty clever*, Preston thought, as Jurgen stepped forward, his arms raised, his lids pulled apart, his dark eyes glowing like hot coals. What Preston appreciated most about the costume reversal was the way its true purpose was masked by another. Which is to say, people would assume that the switch was made so that Jurgen would stand out, for this was clearly a kind of solo or aria. From his raised hands came animals, first the small doves and Bengalese finches, then larger birds, rose-breasted cockatoos, and then raptors and giant carrion-eaters. But—more importantly in terms of the act—Rudolfo's new outfit of black made him part of the darkness. Rudolfo had merely pulled on a hood, tugged gloves over his hands and was busily feeding his partner the animals. That old Black Magic.

Preston appreciated that sort of thing. Like Houdini's chains. The chains were always part of Houdini's submersion escapes; his hands would be tied, his ankles bound, and finally a mantle of locks and chains would be draped across his shoulders. They looked as though they would make the stunt more hazardous, the escape more complicated. What they really did, of course, was quickly pull Houdini down to the bottom of the river or pool, so that his rather pedestrian little tricks could not be observed.

Miranda ran onstage, this time dressed in tiny triangular pieces of material that covered all the important bits and her navel. Preston found himself consumed by a fantasy concerning Miranda's navel when all of a sudden there was a huge explosion. He looked back at Jurgen and saw that he had produced, as a grand finale, two young cheetahs. He held them high in the air, by their scruffs. Preston burst into applause, not because of the illusion, but rather for the classic bit of misdirection. The way Miranda was dressed, the cheetahs could have been led onstage by an usher wielding a flashlight.

The stage went black, there was a sudden needle of light and in its centre stood Rudolfo, newly costumed. Preston was becoming awfully impressed with these costume switches. It took him much longer to even get his fat fingers on the zipper tug-tag. Mind you, Rudolfo was not wearing that many clothes, just a pair of tights that clung to his legs. His upper body was naked and oiled, his muscles so large and defined that he looked like an animated anatomical chart. The light bounced off his body with as much spectrum-smashing violence as it had bounced off the aluminum globe.

Jurgen suddenly descended from above—a clumsy bit of stagecraft that nonetheless earned a storm of applause—and spread his arms wide. He, too, was shirtless. Jurgen's muscles, especially those in the upper arm, were, if anything, bigger than his partner's. And, unlike Rudolfo's purely decorative bulges, Jurgen's seemed actually servicable, the accoutrements of an athlete.

This time the silver cube moved forward. Even though it looked about five feet by five, Jurgen picked it up and showed it to be without bottom and empty. This action made his nipples pop and flutter (which sent the old woman from Winnipeg groping for her drink). Meanwhile, Rudolfo and Miranda were hauling the thick silver ring forward. Jurgen placed his cube inside the ring; Rudolfo stood the ring on its end and showed it to be empty. They then replaced it around the cube. Jurgen and

Rudolfo looked at each other, their faces frozen into practised half-smiles, and clapped their hands hard. Samson came out of the cube, lazily vaulting over the aluminum perimeter.

Cheap trick, Preston thought. When Jurgen was showing the cube to be empty, Samson was hidden within the ring. When the cube was put inside the ring, it covered up the big cat, allowing the ring to be acquited, *acquitment* being the technical conjuror's term for—in its most popular form—showing the sleeves to be empty. The illusion relied on quickness and practice and a large dollop of *chutzpah*. But the crowd went wild, driven to a frenzy by a strange combination of things—the music, the ghostly leopard, Miranda's near-nakedness, Rudolfo's perfect glass body and Jurgen's black-eyed solemnity.

The music stopped abruptly and Jurgen stepped forward. A microphone stand blossomed from the stage; Jurgen tore the instrument out of its clip and slapped it against his thick red lips. "Okay," he muttered. "Is time for Up Close and Personal."

"Hoo boy!" said Rudolfo, coming now to stand beside his partner. He, too, touched a microphone to his lips. "*Ja*, Jurgen," he continued, "what nice person are we talking to?"

Rudolfo took a few determined strides forward; he squinted and stared at the faces in the audience. His eyes brushed across Preston's face quickly; a moment later they returned. Rudolfo may have even nodded at that point, but so subtly that the action was impossible to decipher. Was it a greeting or a lofty dismissal?

Rudolfo's eyes finally settled upon a middle-aged woman three rows from the front who sat clutching her handbag. There was nothing remarkable about the woman; she had brown hair and eyes, was perhaps twenty-five pounds overweight and dressed in a steel-blue outfit. When Rudolfo pointed at her, she rose as though hypnotized. She made no motion toward the stage, however, until the man beside her placed his fingertips on her backside and pushed her forward.

The woman climbed the stairs slowly and with trepidation, almost as though she were on her way up the hangman's scaffolding. Rudolfo smiled and offered a hand, which the woman latched on to immediately, with all the force she could muster. Rudolfo brought her forward and deposited her in front of Jurgen. Jurgen's dark eyes flickered like a matinee idol's. "Darling," he asked, "what is name?"

"Lois Sweet," whispered Lois Sweet.

"And where you from?"

"Fort Dix, New Jersey."

Jurgen produced a deck of cards and executed a couple of flourishes. This was his speciality as far as cards went, turning the deck into a fan that encircled his hand evenly and perfectly, or stretching out the packet until the cards in the middle seemed suspended in nothingness. He stared into Lois Sweet's eyes as he did this. "Okay, tell you what we going to do, Lois."

"Hoo boy!" sang out Rudolfo, although he was supposed to wait until after Jurgen's next statement.

"You going to name one card, okay? You just say name out loud."

"Six of spades."

Jurgen abruptly tossed the cards into the air. As they fluttered and turned he stabbed his hand upwards. The swarm of cards disappeared, fifty-one of them tumbling to the stage. Jurgen held the fifty-second between his thick fingers. He showed the face first to the audience—who roared appreciatively at the sight of the six of spades—and then he showed it to Lois.

"My goodness," she said. She covered her heart with both hands.

"Stick," muttered Preston.

"Okay, Lois," said Jurgen, producing a thick-tipped felt pen, "we going to sign this for you." Jurgen scrawled a hasty version of his name on the face of the card and then flipped the ducat and the pen to his partner. Rudolfo somewhat laboriously produced his signature. Then both men leaned forward and kissed Lois on her cheeks. "Thanks for coming up…" began Jurgen, and then he and Rudolfo finished with their eerie simultaneity, "…for Up Close and Personal!"

They clapped their hands and darkness and smoke claimed the stage. Preston recognized the new music, an ululation that filled the auditorium; it was Mendelssohn's *Italian Symphony*, formerly spritely, now manic. Rudolfo and Jurgen both executed balletic leaps, but their leaps had no apex; both continued upwards until they were gone from sight.

Miranda rushed onto the stage, dressed in some handkerchiefs. She twirled and gyrated, dislodging these tiny draperies, flashing patches of naked skin. Preston squirmed in his seat and tugged the material away from his crotch to give himself a bit more room. Jurgen and Rudolfo now reappeared—their costumes seriously abbreviated, tiny bathing suits and silver boots with curled toes—pushing a huge cage. As Jurgen unlocked the door, Rudolfo pounded on the iron bars with his hands, demonstrating their solidity. Miranda climbed into the cage (shifting her hips suddenly to the left, she relocated a couple of handkerchiefs and gave Preston a breathtaking view of flawless buttock) and then Jurgen and Rudolfo encircled the cage with velvet drapery. The cage was no sooner enclosed than the drapery was tugged away, and there, in Miranda's stead, stood Samson.

"There's an old chestnut for you," said Preston.

"Excuse me," snarled the old woman from Winnipeg. "I am trying to enjoy the show."

"Sorry."

"You might be insane," noted the woman. "Some of the things you say make no sense. *Stick*, for instance. Why did you say *stick*?"

"You know what?" said Preston. "I *am* insane."

"Thought so!"

The audience gasped as one, and Preston saw that the corn-ball transformation he had just witnessed was but preamble to a more ambitious illusion. Miranda floated in the air. The hand-kerchiefs clung to her like seaweed to a lovesick suicide. Miranda hovered above Jurgen and Rudolfo, who both reached up and laid hands upon her—Jurgen taking hold of her head, Rudolfo her feet—and spun her like a helicopter blade. Miranda rotated, airborne, toward the back of the stage, gaining altitude as she went, and came to rest atop the gleaming silver pyramid. Jurgen and Rudolfo pranced over and spun Miranda once more. The point of the pyramid lay just at the small of Miranda's back and as she turned she settled upon it. The audience—including Preston—sucked in their collective breath, because Miranda con-tinued spinning, unaffected by the laws of physics, and the point of the pyramid drove itself into her back. She was soon turning so quickly that she was just a blur of white linen (spackled by luminous fleshtones) and then the pyramid's point appeared above her middle, driven cleanly through her perfect body.

As Jurgen stepped forward to receive applause, Rudolfo began to corral and run animals. They appeared from anywhere and everywhere. There were clouds of butterflies, swallowtails and luna moths. There were gangs of African greys and forpus parrotlets. Then came the small mammals—sugar gliders, ten-recs, chinchillas—and finally the big cats, of which the biggest was Samson. Samson went to the front of the stage and allowed his wobbly front legs to buckle, crashing his forequarters onto the stage with a thud. This was his version of a deep bow, and as soon as he'd taken it, Rudolfo and Jurgen came to stand on either side.

Miranda was nowhere to be seen.

The applause was deafening, and Preston joined in with gusto. He even stuck fingers in his mouth and managed a whistle that wet the backs of many heads.

But Kaz (thought Preston) had made a valid point at the auction with his chimps/brain surgery comment. Most of what Jurgen and Rudolfo did was ancient stuff, variations on things created by venerables like Anderson (the Wonderful Wizard of the North), the American Philadelphia, Professor Pinetti and *L'Escamoteur Philippe*. Or else it was little stuff blown up to ridiculous proportions, like the silver ball. Most guys could afford a *tiny* silver ball with a false flap inside, where they could produce or unproduce a ring or something, but only Jurgen and Rudolfo could afford one twelve feet in diameter.

Preston rose from his seat, knocking the little tray that held the drink he'd barely touched. The drink tumbled; Preston rather absentmindedly aimed a finger. The drink slowed, stopped, then reversed, disappearing as it neared Preston's puffy hand.

"Stop that," snapped the elderly woman from Winnipeg, clearly annoyed.

"Sorry."

Still, reflected Preston, it was an impressive show. It had a choreographed austerity that people obviously responded to. In terms of sheer stagecraft—the needles of light, the bastardized music, the costume changes, the exotic animals—it was a pretty good show. But (Preston moved slowly toward the exit, engulfed in a sea of doughy, elderly people) sheer stagecraft is sheer shit. Jurgen and Rudolfo didn't have a shred of talent between them. Miranda was the magus on that stage. She was the one who slipped unseen into small shadowy places, who appeared suddenly bathed in light, who was impaled upon a pyramid, sacrificed to the small gods of showbiz. And Samson was impressive. The big cat must have crunched himself up pretty good to get into some of the secret places. That silver ball, for example, could only have a hidden compartment of a couple of cubic feet. And come to think of it—Preston snapped his fingers and, as he was now wandering through the wasteland of the Casino, a half-dressed woman materialized with a tray full of drinks—Samson must have been responsible for the animation of some of the geometric shapes. The bleak shining monoliths and pyramids had moved toward the front of the stage without obvious propulsion. They were then moved around by the boys, and usually yielded up the albino leopard. Preston chuckled. That was clever stuff, a good way to move props *and* sneak the load on stage. Get the load itself to do it.

Preston had only worked with animals once, long ago, as the fifteen-year-old "Presto." He did a few things with birds, although they often disappointed him. They rarely, once produced from nothingness, flew upwards with exaltation. They more usually crashed to the ground (made as awkward as dodos by domestication) and pecked around, searching for breadcrumbs. Presto had also worked with a rabbit, until that sad day when—entertaining at Courtney Bell's sixth birthday party—he pulled out a beast that had been claimed by disease. Blood trickled out of the floppy ears. The pink eyes were glazed. Courtney was never the same.

One of the giant doormen pulled open a huge glass door and Preston obediently wandered outside. He peered upwards, trying to see the night sky, wanting to see the stars coalescing into constellations. But, of course, the heavens were obscured by the neon radiance of Las Vegas.

His father, Preston the Magnificent, had worked with animals. Also briefly. He'd had a few exotic birds, an iguana (he claimed it was a miniature dragon and made the thing seem to exhale huge licks of flame) and a tiny dwarf pony. The last was an attempt to inject humour into his act, which was otherwise characterized by dour propriety. Toward the end of his set, Preston the Magnificent would clear his throat and massage his Adam's apple gingerly. "I'm getting a little hoarse," he'd declare. Then quickly he'd step aside and the dwarf pony would be standing there. "Aha!" Preston the Magnificent would shout. "A little horse!" Preston had once counselled his father that there was no need to hit the gag twice, but his father never listened to him.

For the most part, his father had found the animals intractable and insalubrious. Preston remembered very well coming home from school one day and finding the backyard littered with the corpses of exotic birds. The lizard hanging from a tree branch. The little pony had been shot through the head. Preston the Magnificent lay by the pool, stark naked, lost in drunken oblivion.

The doorbell rings.

Rudolfo starts up suddenly, which alarms Samson, because Samson is a skittish beast, perhaps the most skittish in creation. Samson emits a kittenish yawp and races off toward safety. Mind you, he begins his racing off before assuming a proper stance. He begins whilst still prone on the sofa, lashing out with his limbs. Instinct, the tiny residue of instinct that still courses through his veins, pops out his claws. So it is that he gashes his master and true love. As Samson tumbles from the sofa, his forepaw slides down Rudolfo's smooth chest, carving out four parallel lines that stud instantly with crimson beads. Rudolfo rises and touches the blood. He stares at his fingertips for a long moment, as though surprised to find the stuff.

The doorbell rings again and Rudolfo goes to answer.

No one has rung the doorbell in some time. For a few weeks after Jurgen's disappearance their manager, Curtis Sweetchurch, would drop in, waving his huge Daytimer like Moses wielding the holy tablets. Sweetchurch would keen forlornly, stumbling throughout das Haus. What he was doing was making certain that Jurgen wasn't merely hiding somewhere, because such pranks, such childish trickeries, were certainly not above Jurgen Schubert, not at the end when he was glowing and weightless and silver-eyed. It eventually became plain to Sweetchurch that Jurgen was gone, absolutely and forever, so he stopped coming over. For a few days he made phone calls, then he abandoned that, and Rudolfo had now all but forgotten that the man had ever existed.

The doorbell rings again, with insistence. The chimes are rhythmic and tonal, and it occurs to Rudolfo—which is to say, this realization sounds dully, a howl from far, far away—that they play a tune. He *cocks his head in order to better hear. (Samson, following fearfully in his master's wake, cocks his head also, wondering what they are wondering at.)* I know this, *thinks Rudolfo, and he clenches his fist to facilitate thought. He clenches his fist until the knuckles blanch. His nails, which are long and thick and curved, leave behind a series of halfmoons across the palm of his hand.* I know this. *Rudolfo has forgotten that he himself demanded that the doorbell be programmed to play this tune. The images that the music summons forth are confusing. He sees a golden key; he sees hands groping toward and around it. Fingers find the key and then, for some reason, surreptitiously slip it into a pocket. This is what Rudolfo sees, fleetingly, and then he sees a pale face, so very pale as to be ageless and sexless.*

Rudolfo remembers that he is headed toward the door and spins around to make certain that he is going in the right direction. Turns out he wasn't; he was retreating back into the bowels of the mansion, back to the shadows. He corrects himself and marches off with false determination, because really he has no intention of answering the door. He may achieve the door. With a little bit of luck, he may even screw one eye closed and apply the other gingerly to the peephole drilled through the thick oak. But he can't imagine whom he might see that would cause him to open—

He remembers suddenly what tune the doorbell sounds.

Rudolfo stumbles, weak-kneed. He holds his hands out to protect himself, but as the tiles fly toward him he calmly slips his hands behind his back so that his head can meet the floor. Although this place he goes to is not truly slumber, it is dark and silent.

Chapter Seven

Rudolfo never dreamt, as far as he knew, but he often awoke distressed, a sick feeling in the pit of his stomach. As a wet sidewalk might indicate that it had rained the night before, so his mind glistened with emotion and hinted at nightmares.

So when Rudolfo woke up, he popped his eyes open with such force that they almost produced sound. He did not, however, peel back the covers and bolt from the huge circular bed. Instead he lay perfectly still, this being some defence mechanism put into use by his limbic brain, that part of his consciousness that was prehistoric and inchoate.

Beside him, Rudolfo could see, resting atop an unreasonably firm pillow, the back of Jurgen's head. It was remarkable that a night of slumber had done nothing to muss or ruffle Jurgen's coiffure. Then again, Jurgen didn't move while he slept, lying perfectly still on his side, his breath even and not quite loud enough to be called a snore. Rudolfo, on the other hand, stirred, budged and thrashed. This he knew because he often woke himself up. More precisely, he woke the animals on the bed, and they in turn screamed him into wakefulness.

Sharing the bed, at that particular time, were Samson, three Japanese bobtails, a muntjac, a mute swan, and two Flemish giant rabbits. The smaller creatures were moulded into the folds of Rudolfo's naked body. Samson lay sprawled across the lower half of the round mattress, his mouth hanging open, his tongue dangling over the side and halfway to the plush mauve carpeting.

Rudolfo thought about what he must do that day (give the animals their breakfast, work with the panther, animal lunch and recreation, personal training—today was legs—animal dinner and baths, *die Schau* at ten o'clock that evening, fifteen hours away) and decided he must get going. He tensed then, preparatory to pushing off into the day, when his attention was caught by something most strange.

A hair.

The hair sat in the geometric centre of the back of Jurgen's head—and such was the nature of Jurgen's head that the geometric centre was unequivocal—and glowed. Because this hair was not merely grey (actually, Rudolfo knew there was no such thing; all grey hairs are actually bone-white), it was luminous and dazzling. Little of the dawn was able to enter the bedroom, but what little there was seemed to be trapped and reflected by this single hair, the kinky little strand that grew out of Jurgen's head.

Rudolfo reached forward and plucked the hair from Jurgen's scalp. He did this without thinking, but even if he *had* thought about it, he certainly couldn't have predicted the anguished howl that came from Jurgen. The animals on the bed became a maelstrom of feathers and fur, the swan beating its wing upon Samson's head, the rabbits finding no purchase on the satin sheets for their panicky hind legs. Jurgen flung himself out of bed, one thick hand grasping the site of the plucked hair with knuckle-whitening force, as though fearful that his brains would squirt out the tiny fissure.

Jurgen spun around to confront Rudolfo. "Vot in the hell you are doing?" he demanded in English, his voice a thick, dripping porridge of diphthongs and grunts.

Rudolfo slowly raised his hand, the hair between his fingers glowing in the shadows. "Look, Jurgen," he said softly, "look what it is."

Jurgen focused his eyes, his lids tensing and setting like football players on the line of scrimmage. "What?"

"A grey hair," whispered Rudolfo.

"So what?" raged Jurgen. "I'm old enough to have a few grey hairs."

"If I had a grey hair, I hope you would pull it out for me."

Jurgen grimaced, and then allowed his eyelids to relax. They fell and then lumbered back up, and the anger seemed to be gone from his eyes. He said nothing, an act of kindness. He glanced down and seemed to realize then that he was naked. He pulled a bathrobe across his shoulders and disappeared.

Rudolfo remained in the bed, biting at the tip of the tongue that had said such a foolish thing. Rudolfo Thielmann could never have a grey hair, having no hair whatsoever.

He'd had hair up until his tenth year, and then it had vanished. Rudolfo remembered it disappearing overnight, although many doctors and specialists had since advised him that this was unlikely; *alopecia universalis*, they said, usually takes three or four weeks to render the body utterly without hair.

But Rudolfo recalled it this way:

He came home from school. By this point he had proven himself to be a spectacularly poor student. This was largely due to his constant exhaustion, for he managed to sleep only an hour or so per night, kept awake by the desperate merriment of his mother's friends. He had been held back in class many times, and now his classmates were six and seven years of age. Rudolfo

towered above them, but, even so, he was the object of much bullying. Many of his tormentors adopted a morally superior stance,
causing him pain on the grounds that his mother was a drug
addict and a whore. Rudolfo had long ago given up trying to
argue with them. For one thing, the children had no idea what
any of it meant. Rudolfo, who did, conceded that it was to some
degree true—his mother at least had some *connection* to these
things—and so suffered his beatings in silence.

It was his daily habit to pass by the bear pits. The name
Bern, of course, comes from *Bären, bears*. Bear was the first animal successfully hunted by the town founder, Berchtold V of
Zähringen. Since the twelfth century, the creatures have been
posted at the gates of the town, and the tradition of keeping
this ursine sentry has continued. Today they abide in the heart of
the grown city, in a square excavation at the end of a bridge span-
ning the River Aare. When Rudolfo was a boy the bears numbered four, two adults, two cubs. Each time he stopped by the
bear pit, he would clutch the bars, pressing his face between
them, and stare down at the rock ledges. He would purse his lips
and make little sucking noises, which drew the attention of all the
bears, the mother in particular. She would cant her head upwards
and search him out, squinting. The mother always looked as
if she half-remembered him, found something familiar about
him but could not put her claw on it. Once or twice, she whined
pitiably.

"*Hallo, Mama*," Rudolfo would call. "*Wie geht's?*"

On that day, the mother seemed distracted. She reacted to
the noises, but only to execute what could well have been a
yawn, opening her mouth and exhibiting her huge greyish maw
for nearly thirty seconds. Then she rolled into the waterhole,
because it was a hot day in August.

Rudolfo continued on his way, underneath the tower that
marked the limit of the old city. It was nearly four o'clock, so he

paused to watch the exhibition of the clockworks, automatons scurrying along the miniature parapets. Then he set off toward Kramgasse 49.

The silence surrounded him when he was still well away from the apartment, before he had set foot on the sidewalk or passed under the stone archway that canopied the front door. While it was quite true that he could, ordinarily, hear nothing from the street, Rudolfo was disturbed by this profound quiet. He pushed open the door at street level and his cheek was brushed by a tiny, cold wind. He considered running to get someone at that point, an adult who would take him by the hand and lead him away with kind and consoling words, but he knew no adults. None who cared for him, anyway. So he climbed the stairs slowly. It occurred to him that the silence was no such thing; it was sound that had always been masked by the furiously merry laughter of his mother and her friends. Like wind stirring in the belly of the piano or causing the curtain chains to knock against the wall. Rudolfo took the stairs two at a time, not out of haste, but because it was what suited his too-long legs. Sometimes he would step up and his legs would wobble, as unsound as those of a newborn colt.

The apartment door was slightly ajar, which spoke volumes to Rudolfo. He pictured his mother's friends leaving in a panic, the whole opiated gang of them stampeding through the doorway at once. He looked through the centre pane of the door, trying to see past the edges of the small curtain. He saw a foot, his mother's huge foot, pressed into a fuzzy slipper. This seemed unreasonable to him, that he should only spy a foot, not enough to turn around and run. He pressed his fingertips against the glass and pushed. The door sighed open. Then he saw enough. Even so, he descended the staircase with admirable calm.

Which is more than can be said for the local police, who with undisguised panic received the report that a boy was trapped

in the bear pit. They flew about the station gathering up anything that might be used in the rescue: rifles, ropes, poles and
billy clubs.

There was a crowd gathered around the iron railings, a curiously sedate gathering. They murmured, but in a very, very,
sober-sided way, as though commenting on a scientific lecture.
The reason for the orderliness of the mob, the police soon determined, was the domestic scene being enacted in the bear pit
below. The cubs, almost fully grown at this point but still play-
ful, were pushing each other into the waterhole. The father had
situated himself in a corner, squeezing his furry fanny into a
crevice so that he might sit upright. He held his forelegs in
a curious manner; they seemed suspended in front of him as
though by guywires, and this made their emptiness all the more
apparent. These were paws waiting for a newspaper and pipe.
And over on a small ledge, the mother was curled up and applying all of her maternal affection to a human child.

The police fired tranquilizer darts into the beasts. The
crowd bristled; one or two even booed softly. After perhaps a
minute the bears went down, the youngsters half-in, half-out of
the stagnant water, the father with his jaw hanging open. The
mother rolled onto her back, revealing that the human boy was
naked and chewing contentedly on a piece of raw meat.

At the police station they placed Rudolfo inside a cell
because they thought he might feel more comfortable, but also
because everyone was a little afraid. The boy was, apparently,
incapable of speech. He grunted and occasionally sent up howls
of muddled outrage.

It was during that sleepless night—this is how he remembered it, with certainty and conviction, unswayed by the theories
of professionals—that Rudolfo lost his hair. The dawn found him
curled up in the centre of the cell, one eye closed, one eye war-
ily opened, and all around him lay golden brown tufts. Every

hair on his body had come out, his eyelashes riding to the ground borne upon his tears.

In the newspapers the next day, competing with the story of *der wilde Junge*, were reports concerning Anna Thielmann. Not about her death or the manner of it (which was in truth a little suspect) but the revelation that Anna Thielmann was a man. This was not in any way ambiguous. She, rather *he*, was anatomically intact, nothing added or subtracted, except for a little hair. Above the knee and below the neck Anna's body was covered with tiny dark curls. Authorities then remembered that he/she had had a child, but when they went to look, found no one. In the meantime, *der wilde Junge* had been sent to live in a huge grey building. It called itself a vocational school, *eine Berufsschule*, but truly it was an institution that dealt with society's young oddities by hiding them from view and pretending they didn't exist.

Rudolfo climbed out of bed, grabbed the hairpiece from its stand and fixed it carefully on his slippery head. The wig made him look like he needed a haircut, an effect that cost many thousands of dollars to achieve.

He found himself standing in the shadow of the hideous monstrosity, number 112 in Preston's catalogue. Rudolfo did not know it was called the Davenport Spirit Cabinet, nor would he have cared.

The lefthand door was open. Rudolfo peered inside. The interior was rough unfinished wood, stained only by time. The single bench was cockeyed, tilted lamely toward the middle.

The albino leopard joined him, laying his pale snout upon the bench. He pulled back sharply, having gotten a whiff of something foul and decayed. The skin on the beast's neck wrinkled up like an old dirty sweatsock.

Rudolfo left the bedroom and began to prowl around the mansion, Samson at his side.

He was reaching a few decisions. One, he and Jurgen needed some time apart. This display of petulance and irritability was only the latest in a series of similar outbursts. Actually, the series was one of disdainful glances and hard, dark silences, but it made Rudolfo marvel to think that all it took was a tiny little thing like a plucked hair to escalate one of these into a maniacal rage.

A lemur scurried underfoot, and squealed pitiably as Samson mashed it into the tiles. Rudolfo, lost in a thought, didn't notice.

His thought was this: Jurgen was not without justification. Rudolfo was willing to shoulder a certain small amount of the responsibility. For example, he *was* reluctant to change the Show. Mind you, that was because it was damn near perfect, as any idiot could see, but perhaps there was some tiny tinkering that could be done—

And then Rudolfo had an idea. He wasn't sure if he got the idea and then started whistling, or if some nether region of his psyche, the font of creativity, had caused his lips to purse and emit a tuneful flutter, which in turn gave him this wonderful idea.

The music. He could, he would, change the music. And he knew exactly what to do.

He rushed off to find Jurgen, and such was his excitement that he checked several of the other rooms—the Music Room (essentially, a large speaker with a sofa in it), the Trophy Room (where the three silver cups sat, laden with dust, the stands o'er-mounted with tiny, naked swimming boys)—before reluctantly admitting that Jurgen was likely in the Grotto, his nose stuck inside the old and dusty books. So he descended the staircase—Samson heeling like a bulldog, although Rudolfo's abrupt about-turns caused the leopard to go skidding into the occasional wall—and ran down the hallway.

The stone, the remote-controlled boulder, was rolled into place, blocking the entranceway to the Grotto. Jurgen had replaced the batteries, Rudolfo realized, which irritated him. It seemed like a great deal of trouble to go to, locating batteries in their huge house. Jurgen must have sent Jimmy out to purchase them, or demanded the same of Tiu, the housekeeper. But Jurgen had obviously found it important enough to block off the doorway that he was willing to undergo this battery-changing hell. Rudolfo snorted, and because his nostrils lacked cilia and filament, they produced a loud whistle that brought half a dozen animals running. Rudolfo knelt down to receive them.

The two didn't actually speak until after that evening's Show.

When they returned to *das Haus*, Rudolfo said, "We need to talk."

Jurgen merely grunted. He did not turn to face Rudolfo, or even slow down, continuing steadfastly down the hallway toward the Grotto. The boulder was still in place—*again* in place, Rudolfo corrected himself—and Jurgen removed the sleek black remote control from somewhere on his person and blasted it. The stone creaked and rumbled and began to move.

"You see," explained Rudolfo, "I'm having an idea."

Now Jurgen spun around, and his eyebrows raised and bumped into each other. "Yeah?" Before Rudolfo could respond, Jurgen turned and nearly bolted through the newly made opening, which seemed barely wide enough to accept him.

Rudolfo took a step or two after him. He caught the wall on either side of the doorway and leant forward, so that his head stuck into the Grotto.

The books were still in teetery stacks, but the stacks had been shoved about until they formed a large, lopsided circle, in the centre of which Jurgen had positioned the wooden automaton. Jurgen approached the automaton now and—although Rudolfo didn't see him press a button or throw a switch—activated the mechanical man. The doll began to hum and vibrate, turning slightly from side to side and raising, abruptly, its arm. A deck of cards was clutched between the shiny carved fingers. Jurgen plucked one of the cards, studied it briefly and then approached a stack of books. He counted down three, pulled out the volume quickly and returned with it to the little schoolboy's desk, settling into the seat. Placing his elbows on the tabletop, Jurgen knuckled his hands and rammed them on either side of his head, pulling his crippled purpled eyelids up so that he might better read without interference.

"Yeah," said Rudolfo, "I'm having a great idea."

"Speak German," snapped Jurgen, turning a page, eagerly following the words with a thick forefinger.

"Maybe you're right. Maybe the Show has been getting a little, um..."

"...dull," Jurgen completed the sentence.

It was a damning word, *eintönig*. The one inheritance Rudolfo had from his mother was a delivery from dullness. What no one understood—not even Jurgen, Rudolfo reflected bitterly—was that Rudolfo was an artist, that he had been brought into this world to create. His Art was the Show. It could have been painting, or music...

Rudolfo suddenly remembered his inspiration. He smiled brightly and lifted a forefinger. "Bruckner's Fourth."

Rudolfo began to sing, by way of illustration, waving his hands before him to suggest motion and pageantry unfolding on an unseen stage. Jurgen glanced up briefly. "The Romantic," he nodded, and then returned to the ancient tome.

Rudolfo's hands stilled themselves in the air. How would Jurgen know that Bruckner's Fourth was nicknamed "The Romantic?" His taste was decidedly more everyday, what Rudolfo characterized as "goatherding music." Jurgen usually enjoyed listening to squat men strum guitars and squeeze accordians, plaintively bellowing about lost loves.

Rudolfo decided that he must have told Jurgen about it at some point; perhaps he had played the symphony one night as an overture to lovemaking. This would have been some time ago. "Yes, the Romantic, *but*," said Rudolfo, loudly enough to make Jurgen's square head pop up, "the Sturm and Drang version."

Sturm and Drang was a duo, two dour, middle-aged heroin addicts. When they performed (which they did with merciful infrequency), they stood upon the stage dwarfed by a towering monolith of speakers. They themselves hunched over racks of emulators and samplers, pressing down upon the tiered keyboards with the dispassionate propriety of pathologists. They had few fans, but were fortunate in that one of them was Rudolfo Thielmann.

"So here's my idea. What we should do is—"

"—cancel the Show for a few days," supplied Jurgen. "You go to Los Angeles and make the music. I'll stay here and work."

"Work?"

"I have a few ideas myself." Jurgen glanced up and winked. Or, at least, that's how it seemed, but it was impossible to say for certain. Jurgen was always appearing to wink, a spasm sending one or the other of his eyelids bouncing down and up.

"The only problem with that is, you don't like to be alone."

"I don't?"

"No."

"How do you know that?"

"You told me," said Rudolfo, treading very carefully because he didn't know exactly where he was. "You've told me that many times."

"I don't see how I could have told *you* that," said Jurgen, "because I don't know that. I've never *been* alone."

There was some truth in that. When they met in München, Jurgen was living in a tiny apartment with several brothers and cousins. They slept three in a bed, two on a fold-out couch; there were always at least four of them up to various off-putting things in the single washroom, and for all these Schubert men, it was luxury. "Because," they'd say, "it's so *crowded* at home." And since then, Rudolfo reflected, he and Jurgen had been together. "Well," he spoke aloud, "it's not that great. Being alone. It sounds like it might be wonderful, but in the end, it's just lonely."

Jurgen didn't appear to have heard. "You go to Los Angeles," he said softly. "I'll stay here."

Rudolfo didn't see Jurgen reach out and press a pad on the remote control, but he must have done, because the boulder shook and began to move. Rudolfo moved his head out of the way and the rock rumbled into place.

Chapter Eight

After performing the Cingalese Eye Levitation, Jurgen had immediately given up Magic, throwing away the cheaply bound *Houdini on Magic* and reapplying himself to other, more wholesome, interests. Soccer, for example. Jurgen was a talented footballer, and he took to the fields with a vengeance, playing with a grace and savageness not seen in many twelve-year-olds. His only weakness was that, occasionally, as he neared the enemy goal, his eyelids (still brilliantly purple) would flutter and fail, causing him to stumble and kick the ball well away from the net. Jurgen also took up swimming, joining a local aquatics club. The Sharks, *die Haie*—that was the name given to the division of young boys— met at five o'clock on alternate mornings. They stripped naked and dove into the warm, milky water. Jurgen swam laps with industry, vaguely aware that some portion of his mind was far away in another place.

Despite her having entered a higher level of feeblemindedness, it was Jurgen Schubert's grandmother who rekindled Jurgen's interest in Magic. He noticed that whenever he came home from school, Oma's face would change. She was perpetually sitting on the sofa, her hands nested in her lap. She usually stared straight ahead, her mouth set in a light half-smile, as though expecting an old friend to arrive at any moment. An endless parade of Schuberts had no affect upon this expression. There could be a youngster with his head cracked open from a fall, there could be a near-naked young girl tiptoeing in to grab her nylons from above the kitchen sink, there could be a shiftless uncle drunkenly falling face-first onto the carpet, and Oma Schubert would remain placid and pleasant. But whenever she saw Jurgen, her eyebrows would fly up to mix with the wrinkles, her eyes would bug open and her mouth would shrivel into a tiny creased ring of wonder. "*Der Zauberer!*" she'd exclaim. "The Conjuror!"

Jurgen would walk by, nodding politely. "Hello, Oma." But his grandmother would get agitated by this, raising her trembling fingers, long after he'd gone, in a desperate attempt to clutch at his shirt sleeve. Jurgen was too polite a boy to keep ignoring her, particularly when he began to suspect that she was weeping in an odd manner, would have actually *been* weeping except that she seemed to be dried up inside and could summon no tears.

He felt very bad about all this. In a sense, it was his fault, or rather, the fault of the Cingalese. But it was Jurgen who had unleashed the Cingalese into the Schubert living room. Oma had never been very far from gaga, not even as a young woman, but she had undeniably been pushed over the edge by the Baby Levitation. Now she sat, her brittle body all a'thrimble, calling out desperately to the haughty *Zauberer*.

But Jurgen knew no magic secrets. The things in Houdini's book, he realized bitterly, were traps, set-ups for little boys to humiliate and destroy themselves. It was Houdini's way of protecting his vaunted status as Master Magician, to dissuade if not to actually maim, disfigure, possibly *kill* any pretenders to that throne.

Jurgen found help in an unlikely place—at home. His brother Dieter, nine years older, a pudgy and pale young man with clownish circles of flushing on his cheeks, one day pointed a deck of cards at him. Dieter belched, and Jurgen was made faint by the previous night's effluvia, spiced by cigarette smoke and marinated in slumber. Dieter was a great frequenter of beer cellars and taverns, and it was there that he learned the trick he was about to show his little brother. "Pick a card," he muttered, making a very clumsy fan with the deck. "Any fucking card. I don't give a shit."

Jurgen pulled out a card, the king of clubs.

"Right. Okay. Now, put that card back on top. Yeah. Now. We're going to cut the deck, right, so the card is in the middle. Here. Take some of the deck. Okay. Now I put my half down and you put your half on top. Now, your card is in the middle, right? So watch this." Dieter lifted the cards into the air. "This is great," he muttered. "Hocus-fucking-pocus." Dieter allowed the cards to drop, carpeting the floor. One card—the king of clubs— lay overturned.

Jurgen wrapped his hands around his brother's throat. He was almost as big, and certainly more powerful. He spoke calmly, although Dieter was clearly alarmed. "Show me how to do that."

"Yeah, sure, Jurgen," said Dieter, which gained his release. "It's easy. Look. When you cut the deck, I take my half and go over top of yours to put it down. And then I say, *put your half on top*, okay. You see?"

"I put the cards back where they came from in the first place?"

"Yeah!"

"But I'm not *that* stupid," he insisted.

"Nobody ever notices. It's because I move my cards over yours. It seems like it was always the top part."

"Nobody notices that?"

"You know what? People just aren't as bright as you think they are."

"Huh."

"*Then*," continued Dieter, shoving the cards together, "you just shove the top card over a little, like this, so when you drop the deck it flips over." Dieter demonstrated.

The next afternoon, Jurgen sat down beside Oma on the sofa.

The old woman allowed herself to keel over so that she butted up, shoulder to shoulder, with her grandson. She smelt as though she'd been kept in an old wooden chest for many years. "Show me magic!" she whispered.

Jurgen took the deck of cards from his shirt pocket and spread them into an awkward fan.

"Pick a card, any card."

Oma nodded and reached forward with a trembling hand. "Tell me," she asked, "will it be very painful?"

"No, Oma," answered Jurgen truthfully.

Oma excitedly ripped a card out of the deck and studied its face. "Oooh," she grinned. "A good one."

"Remember what it is, Oma."

"Yes."

"Really remember what it is very well, Oma."

"Yes."

"Put it back on top."

Oma lingered with the card, not impressing it upon her memory, merely studying the face as though she found it pleasing.

"Okay, Oma, cut the cards, okay?" He offered the cards, cradled upon his palm. Oma lifted off three cards, about as much weight as she could bear.

"Yeah, that's right," said Jurgen encouragingly. "Now..." He was still unsure about this next part. It angered him, somehow, that the art was based on people's stupidity. Suppose people weren't stupid? Suppose only Jurgen Schubert was stupid, and every time he assayed this trick he was discovered and ridiculed?

He passed his portion over those trembling in his grandmother's hand and placed them on the coffee table in front of them.

"Oma," he said very quietly, "put your cards on top of those."

She did so without hesitation, and as gleefully as she could manage.

Having gotten away with it (though his grandmother wasn't much of a test), Jurgen sighed and reached for the deck.

"No, no, no!" shouted Oma.

"Hmmm?"

"*Magic*," said Oma, with trenchant precision.

"Yeah, watch." Jurgen reached for the deck again.

"No, no! *Magic*." Suddenly her face was in curious motion, the wrinkles flowing, bumping up against each other. Her eyes widened, her mouth all but disappeared. Jurgen was about to call for his mother when his grandmother's face suddenly blanched and recomposed itself. "Like that," she explained.

"Oh!"

Even as a twelve-year-old, Jurgen Schubert could fashion a pretty intimidating face. He ran the two halves of his huge, squared brow into each other, producing creases as sharp as lightning bolts. He pursed his mouth, flared his nostrils and then, to deal with the dark, flickering lids, he forced his eyes open until the irises were like little blue stones in a pond of milk.

"Good," nodded Oma appreciatively.

Jurgen suddenly and urgently threw the cards to the ground. He threw his eyes heavenward, cupped his hands and raised them as though to say, "You want me? Come and get me!"

He'd expected one of his grandmother's skittish shrieks.

Instead there was silence, or what counted as silence given her rheumy lungs. Jurgen looked down. Oma was smiling at the overturned seven of diamonds, smiling like a young girl walking in the forest who notices a rare bird perched on a low branch.

Every day she asked to see magic. Jurgen had a great problem, however, in that he only knew the one trick. Even his grandmother eventually grew bored, sometimes not even bothering to look down to see her card, merely muttering, "*Nicht schlecht*," and going straight to sleep.

Jurgen brooded about this at night. He enjoyed performing for his grandmother, he enjoyed the way she said *Der Zauberer* without irony and he was determined not to lose her. It occurred to him one night that as long as she remained none the wiser about the "cut," he could produce the chosen card in many different ways. One day, for example, instead of hurling the deck to the ground, he held it up in his left hand, showing Oma the faces. "Look," he whispered, raising his right hand, holding it over the cards, waggling his fingers in an odd manner, overly strenuous and jerky. He pushed with his forefinger, which was bent against the top card. The four of clubs appeared to rise from the deck, summoned by Jurgen's strange magical finger waggling.

"Good," said his grandmother, touching the tips of her fingers to his cheek. They felt as cold as plumbing on a winter's morning.

Jurgen canvassed his siblings and their mates for new tricks. One cousin, Volker, a pale young man who, like Dieter, spent far too many hours in beer cellars, nodded and placed a cigarette between his thick lips. "Okay, watch." He fumbled with the deck of cards, not shuffling them so much as forcing them to commingle, bending the edges. Volker made a fan. Instead of saying "Pick a card," Volker merely nodded toward the deck in a cursory manner. Jurgen selected one, looked at it and then, at Volker's urging, shoved it back into the middle of the closed deck. "Watch this," muttered Volker. He again fanned the cards, showing Jurgen their backs. One—the king of spades, Jurgen's selection—faced upwards.

The secret, Volker divulged willingly, was to reverse the card on the bottom. When the person isn't looking, flip over the deck and offer that for the reinsertion of the card.

"Ah!" said Jurgen, racing off to show it to Oma.

Some of the boys at school knew little tricks too. One friend showed him a neat effect with safety pins—and God knows, the Schubert house could yield up any number of safety pins—interlocking two in such a way that they could be pulled free of each other and yet both remain closed.

In this manner Jurgen managed to assemble a tiny repertoire. He did a trick with a box of matches: you half-open the box, demonstrate that all is normal, then turn the box over and pull the inner compartment out all the way. None of the matches drop until you say the magic words, "Hocus-fucking-pocus." Then they shower like spring rain. The secret is a broken matchstick inserted crosswise. It holds the matches in place until you squeeze, and then it falls to the ground with all the other matchsticks.

But Jurgen's true education in magic came about in a magical way. One Saturday morning he came downstairs for breakfast and found the dining room table deserted. The oddness of this cannot be overstated. The table should have been thronged. There was evidence that the clan had been there only recently. Pablum decorated the high chairs. The table was covered with half-cups of coffee and empty cereal bowls. And the newspaper was spread across the length of old oak.

Later that afternoon, Jurgen learned what had happened. Oddly—*magically*—it was not a single exigency that had ripped the family from the breakfast table, it was a series. Papa Schubert cracked a tooth and began to roar with pain. He lashed out and knocked over one of the high chairs, toppling Ha-Jo to the ground. Ha-Jo himself was unharmed, but he bounced and rolled and acted as a kind of bowling ball, taking out the legs of all the other high chairs. Infants tumbled to the ground. Brows cracked and limbs were twisted. Mothers screamed and picked up children, husbands began to race around searching for car keys. Dieter and Klaus collided head-on. Dieter, never far from unconsciousness, blacked out immediately. His wife, Maria, screamed, not because she cared particularly, but because her water had just broken. There was nothing for it but a mass exodus to the local hospital. No one gave a thought to Jurgen, who was just waking up.

He'd been having a dream in which he was a great Conjuror. In the dream he wore a long cape, emblazoned with silver and gold stars. He was otherwise naked. Lately, Jurgen was naked in many of his dreams. This was vaguely erotic, true (he usually woke up with a tingling sensation at the tip of his penis), but had more to do with the fact that he could never decide what to wear.

Anyway, in this dream he was performing miracles. He motioned at his baby brother, for example, and the bloated Ha-Jo floated into the air, making a loud sound, half grunt, half giggle. Suddenly Jurgen was levitating all the babies in the family, and the air was filled with their startled gurgles. The mothers started to scream. Jurgen merely smiled sardonically and left the infants suspended in nothingness. The fathers rushed toward him, his graceless brothers and brothers-in-law, but Jurgen threw up his hands and they collided with eldritch invisibility. Dieter fell to the ground; Maria screamed. Jurgen waved a hand and they all disappeared.

By the time he arrived at the dining room table, the dream was forgotten and Jurgen was startled to find his family gone. Alarmed, even, but not so much that he couldn't pour himself a

small cup of coffee and sit down. He realized that he could, however briefly, conduct his life as a man of leisure. He leaned back
in his chair, scratched where there was only the vaguest of itches,
and then, as his father had done many times, he reached out and
gathered in a section of the newspaper.

His eye was immediately drawn to a small box in the corner
of the page. It was an advertisement for a bookstore. It was a
very unremarkable advert, too, merely a listing of books that had
recently arrived, trails of dots leading to numbers designating
prices.

So the magic is there to see, if you linger over it, and unwrap
each moment as though it were a cough drop: that Jurgen should
be alone in his house, that he should have access to the newspaper at all, let alone decide to read it, that this book title should
immediately catch his eye:

THE SECRETS OF MAGIC REVEALED
(PRESTON THE MAGNIFICENT)..........*DM 20*

At the same time as young Jurgen Schubert was earning those
twenty Deutschmarks, labouring at the docks in Bremerhaven,
loading the supercargos that could not navigate down the silted
Weser, Rudolfo Thielmann was having a hard go of it at the
Berufsschule. Rudy was not regarded there as an interesting case
study. He was regarded as a moron. Considering that his fellow
students had misshapen heads and wore glasses with lenses as
thick as the bottom of coke bottles, that was going some. Rudy
learned welding, lathework, and during lunch hours he was taken
into the shower stalls. The other boys would tear off his clothes
and then bugger him, biting their tongues with concentration,
their heavy glasses knocked askew.

When Rudolfo was thirteen, his body began to fill out and
harden, at which point he began swatting away these boys like

vermin. Girls appeared, equally googly-eyed and thick-lipped, equally eager to abuse him in shower stalls.

At no point did he perceive any of this as unfair or unjust. He was a little surprised at how odd life turned out to be, that's all. But he was prepared for all manner of twists and turns. So when the circus appeared, three tilted tents hastily erected in a soccer field, he merely shrugged and began to pack his few belongings into a knapsack.

Jurgen Schubert diligently worked his way through *The Secrets of Magic Revealed*. He began with the card tricks, because Oma seemed to like them, progressing from effects that were based on pure mathematics to the sleights-of-hand. As per the instructions given by Preston the Magnificent, Jurgen practised the Two-Handed Shift for one hour a day, until the transposition was silent and instantaneous. He laboured over Chenier cuts and buckle displays, little finger breaks and false counts. Then he started working with coins, which required an additional hour of practice each day, perfecting things like the Improved French Vanish. He couldn't work with silks, *per se*, not the elegant silks that Preston the Magnificent wrote about and which were pictured in his book, but Jurgen purloined some underthings from the mountain of dirty laundry, cut them up into squares and added tricks like the Sympathetic Cut and Restoration to his repertoire. His daily practice session now totalled three and a half hours.

Mind you, Jurgen continued an adolescence that was essentially normal. (Unlike Rudy, over there at the circus. The first chore Rudy was given was the feeding of Boris, an ulcerous and peppery lion. Rudy impressed everyone, especially the lion, by merely wandering into the cage, the meat hanging limply in his hand, and placing the food into the maw of a rather stupefied Boris. "Eat that," he commanded.) Jurgen continued to swim with *die Haie*, competing several times a year, often finishing in the top rank. He was widely sought after for soccer teams, wooed by coaches, changing affiliation easily with no qualms or guilt. Indeed, it never truly occurred to Jurgen that people might be angry with him. He never noticed the increased viciousness of former teammates, the boos and hisses from their parents.

His first public performance, not counting the Cingalese swami incident, was given at Ha-Jo's fourth birthday party. Ha-Jo had by this time achieved an even more remarkable size, and at his birthday party he sat squeezed into a chair, cake in one hand, flagon of punch in the other. His friends looked like royal minions, clustered at his feet.

Jurgen entered wearing a dark suit that had been discarded by one of his older brothers or brothers-in-law. Appearance had been stressed over and over by Preston the Magnificent. One should look "prepossessing and as well-heeled as one's present economic modality would mitigate." Jurgen bowed deeply ("courtly manners impress more indelibly than any number of illusions") and spoke ("never betray an abbreviated education nor paucity of breeding").

"Ladies and gentlemen," Jurgen began.

"Hey, idiot penis," croaked Ha-Jo, spraying cake crumbs. "There's no ladies here."

Fortunately, Preston the Magnificent had supplied a retort to this very heckle. "Nor gentlemen neither," said Jurgen, smiling suavely.

"Shut up, crazy testicles."

The little crowd began to stir, excited by Ha-Jo's brashness.

Jurgen began to perform the Miser's Dream, pulling coins from thin air. As he did this, Jurgen maintained an idiotic expression, which he'd adopted from the photographs in *The Secrets of Magic Revealed*. His eyebrows were raised, as though by astonishment. His mouth was bent into a small grin ("one must look confident and unfearing, though never smug"). The little crowd was not impressed. They shifted their bottoms in happy expectation of further invective from Ha-Jo.

"Hey, fart hair," the little despot ventured, "give me that money."

Though Preston the Magnificent warned against it ("never exhibit a negativity of demeanour"), Jurgen scowled. He could feel his eyes tightening into black stones, and when his eyelids began to flutter, he wrenched them apart by sheer dint of will, until they framed his eyes with blackness.

The little crowd hushed, and when Jurgen produced a tiny speckled dove they gave forth a whisper of obedient awe.

The *chimes fill* das Haus *again, simple round notes that bump and collide like footballers trying to dance ballet. The music rouses Rudolfo; it prods and shakes him like a landlady. He climbs to his feet, then freezes, his body cocked as though ready for action but his face washed with an expression of bafflement. He stands there for a very long moment, motionless except for a small flickering of his eyes. The doorbell rings again, and this forces his decision. He smacks his hands together, which is what he always did in the Show to indicate that he was about to do something worth watching. The resulting sound is barely audible. In the old days, Rudolfo remembers vaguely, he could make little thunderclaps with his long, naked hands. He and Jurgen would punctuate the Show with meaty cannonades and rim shots.*

Rudolfo is marching down the hall once more, toward the front door. Samson falls in beside him. Samson walks with an aged, twisted gait, his hindquarters swinging in a wide, sloppy arc. The albino leopard's tongue is caught between white lips and fangs. There are animals hidden in the shadows that line the hallway. Little grey eyes dot the way like markers on a runway, but Samson pays no attention. He has too much dignity to turn and recognize these critters, these stupid squawkers and mewlers.

The front door yaws up suddenly, blocking Rudolfo's path. He certainly hadn't expected it to appear so soon; he thought the door was miles and miles away. But here it is and he's so startled that he doesn't think to turn and flee. Besides, maybe it is someone Rudolfo wants to see. It might be Miranda, for example, who appears periodically with groceries and little presents for the animals. Or it might be Jurgen; after all, he disappeared, so he could reappear. Rudolfo remembers

Einstein's symbols, the pencil scratches the physicist made on the walls at Kramgasse 49, and thinks that Jurgen's unvanishing is within the realm of possibility. So he takes hold of the solid gold knob (a huge thing as big as a cantaloupe; Rudolfo has to use both hands to twist with all of his might) and makes a crack into the night. The October wind does the rest, blowing across the desert and nudging the door open with great force.

A little figure stands in front of Rudolfo, a horrifying spectre. The face, small and pale, is slashed and half-hidden by a huge moustache, the ends curled and waxed into sharp swordpoints. The figure's torso is wrapped in a crimson jacket, festooned with brass buttons. Cutting diagonally across the chest is a Sam Browne, and holstered at the connection to the belt is an oversized gun. In one hand the tiny figure holds a whip. It raises the handle and jerks it, making the length of leather snap in the air.

Rudolfo screams.

Samson faints.

Rudolfo slams the door shut and joins the big cat on the floor.

Chapter Nine

When Rudolfo returned from Los Angeles, Jimmy was not there
to meet him. The airline people, always eager to participate in
surreptitious activities, had hustled Rudolfo through some back
corridors. He wore a nylon shell, the hood pulled up around his
head, and walked with a slight hunch, pinching his shoulders
together as though he could be identified at a distance merely by
his phenomenal physique. The airline people—joined by a couple of policemen who strutted alongside with their hands resting
on their pistol butts—banged through a doorway far away from
the usual pedestrian traffic. They pushed Rudolfo outside and
then turned away abruptly, dispersing into the airport; that was
part of the game plan, to act suddenly as though nothing were
unusual. No one except Rudolfo noticed that the long white limousine was not sitting where it should have been.

Rudolfo set his travelling bag on the ground. He cursed
silently and determined to fire Jimmy.

Actually, firing Jimmy was not necessary. Jimmy had already quit. Jimmy was far away at that moment, down in Mexico

drinking too much tequila and consorting listlessly with dark young beauties. Jimmy was wracked with guilt. Jimmy, you see, had accepted a monstrous amount of money to dismantle the security system at the mansion, this act of disloyalty being accomplished by the simple pressing of a button. Then he fled and would spend the rest of his days in alcoholic misery, never knowing that no one suspected him of playing a part in the break-in, because no one, *almost* no one, was ever aware that a break-in had even taken place.

Though Rudolfo was standing beside one of the roadways that girded the airport, there was no traffic on it. He suspected that there was a cabstand somewhere and, had he been braver, might have launched himself back into the river of humanity inside the airport, in hopes of emerging ultimately through the appropriate doorway. But that seemed drastic, dangerous. That asshole Kaz, he knew, was forever getting molested in airports. True, Kaz brought it upon himself, never attempting to disguise his outgrown features, not even removing those eyeglasses that made him look retarded.

Rudolfo also had a terrible hangover, the result of a single glass of champagne, forced upon him by one of the suicidal musicians comprising Sturm and Drang. When one is in such great shape as Rudolfo Thielmann, one's system becomes very finely tuned, and anything out of the ordinary sends it for a loop.

The champagne had been in celebration of the completion of the Sturm and Drang version of Bruckner's Fourth Symphony. Sturm and Drang were very pleased with their work, elated for at least twenty minutes, during which they forced champagne upon Rudolfo. Then Sturm and Drang plunged back into despair, because perfection had come tantalizingly close.

Rudolfo was also very pleased. The music was perfect for the Show, so much so that he wondered why it had never occurred to him before. The Fourth started quietly—as quiet

as Sturm and Drang ever got—and then grew in volume until
a simple melodic line floated earthward like a heavy snowfall.
Rudolfo got very excited, goosepimpled, imagining the entrance
he and Jurgen would make with this regal fanfare pounding
down upon their shoulders. That's why he'd accepted the glass
of champagne, had even, like Sturm and Drang, dashed the flute
to the floor of the recording studio.

And now, with his head buzzing and his tiny stomach full of
acid, Rudolfo wondered what to do.

Almost no one knew about the break-in the night before.

Samson knew.

The albino leopard had been prowling nocturnally, which
made him feel a little bit wild and untamed. He was a different
cat late at night, not quite so dandified. Running across other
night creatures—the bushbabies were typically scampering
around—he was likely to roar, quietly, and to bat the wide-eyed
varmints out of the way with a huge paw. He would climb defi-
antly on the furniture (countenanced by Rudolfo, forbidden by
Jurgen) and lick furiously at his ghost balls.

That's what he was doing when he was startled by the sight
of a black-clad figure tiptoeing past him. It was an animated
shadow, blended in with the night, but Samson had night vision
enough to recognize it as human. The elbows were raised high,
the toes tapping with the ginger thoroughness of a white cane.
Samson realized that just as the dark human mixed with the
blackness, so he was invisible upon the cream-coloured sofa.
What he should have done was unleash a huge and mighty
roar, then perhaps pounce and maul. He even licked his lips
preparatory to the howling; the shadowy human spun around,
alarmed by this sound like wet sandpaper. But there was no roar
forthcoming because Samson had immediately pulled in his
tongue and shut his eyes, hoping that he was therefore totally

invisible. Samson was terrified. When he opened his eyes, the figure was gone.

When they had met, Rudolfo and Samson, many years ago, Samson was a miniature version of himself, a puffy little white ball with fangs and claws. He was placed in Rudolfo's hands and immediately started savaging, getting a nice piece of flesh between his teeth and tearing away with all his might. Then there came a pleasant sensation, Samson being cooled by a gentle breeze, and then there came an unpleasant one, Samson being crumpled up against a wall.

He slid to the ground, then turned around to look at the human being who had done this to him. He had seen relatively few. There was the fat one who had taken him away from his mother, a dastardly act that actually worked out well, since Samson's mother much preferred his brightly spotted brothers and sisters. And there was the young man who had attended to him on the ship, although this attendance only amounted to shoving thin strips of desiccated meat through the bars of his cage.

In those days, Rudolfo Thielmann wore a wig of alarming blondness, long near-white strands that he had to keep pulling out of his face. Perhaps this was to cover the acne, or perhaps the acne was caused by it. Whichever, the nineteen-year-old suffered a horrible case, his face bubbled and pocked.

Rudolfo was generally surly back then. He'd been with the circus for five years, years spent travelling from grimy town to grimy town. His purview was the care, maintenance and training of wild animals. He took the job very seriously, removing himself, as far as possible, from the society of people. The only person he had anything to do with was General Bosco, the Lion Tamer.

General Bosco stood about five-foot-four and looked even

shorter because of an odd disproportion of his limbs. His arms seemed truncated, for example, and culminated in tiny fingers that lacked knuckles. And not only were his legs short, they were bowed in a dwarfish manner. So General Bosco gave the impression of severe tininess, an impression he did his best to correct through the discipline of bodybuilding.

Bodybuilding was not a popular sport in those days. It was considered odd and was tainted by an aura of slightly squalid homosexuality. General Bosco likely had a lot to do with this general perception. In the gymnasium (these would have to be located, town to town, and were usually designed for boxing or gymnastic training, with a few free weights tossed over in a corner), General Bosco would traipse out of the change room in a skin-tight, old-fashioned one-piece bathing suit, with a lifting belt cinched so tightly that his torso seemed ready to pop toward the ceiling like a champagne cork. General Bosco would stop in the middle of the room and assume a pose, usually one that accentuated his strong points, his calves and biceps. He'd lick his fingers and stroke his moustache, exciting both sides into sharp, uplifted spears. Then he'd slap his hands together, announce his plan to the world at large and set about with furious industry. General Bosco did squats an awful lot, loading so many plates on either end of the iron bar that it formed a huge frown across the hump of his shoulders. And as he lifted he would not only scream and grunt, he would shout at invisible beings: "*Ja*, dat's good!" he'd howl. "*Ja*, baby!"

Rudolfo accompanied him, more often than not. At first he'd been reluctant to, but General Bosco needed a lifting partner, and he was able to intimate that accompaniment on weight-lifting outings was part of Rudolfo's job description. General Bosco was not Rudolfo's actual employer, but he acted as though he were. It was General Bosco who had, that first day years ago, sent Rudolfo into the cage with meat for the irritable lion, Boris.

General Bosco had been very impressed with the boy's ability to not be savagely attacked and/or eaten alive, so he'd determined to make Rudolfo a protegé. He'd accomplished this through a combination of veiled threat and petulant remonstration. Slowly, Rudolfo's attitude changed from a grudging tolerance to an odd admiration.

It was not long before Rudolfo entered the cages because he was the only one qualified to do so. Soon, all of the animal trainers came to him for counsel, even Zofia Himmler with her lugubrious elephants. Rudolfo likewise benefited from his exposure to the discipline of body sculpting. Soon he too was hunkered beneath the iron bar, dropping down and then pushing heavenward with all his might, blasting his thighs into striated hams.

Given the smooth sculpted bulk and the platinum-blond wig, Rudolfo presented an odd-looking figure. This was a vision that imprinted itself instantly on the young albino leopard's retina. Samson, his mind still clouded from having been thrown against the wall, fell in love.

A taxicab screamed up and came to a wailing halt in front of Rudolfo, the brakes applied so suddenly that the cab continued to shiver and shake for moments afterwards. It was an oversized contraption with puffed-up fenders, painted a bright silver that sang with light. On top a small unlit plaque announced "MERCURY."

Rudolfo bent over to look through the window and saw that the driver was concentrating on his own activities. Rudolfo realized that he'd been standing so still that he'd managed to blend in with the surroundings. This was, of course, habit from his animal training. He'd often remain motionless for hours and hours, until his presence meant no more to the beasts than the individual bars that made up their cage. Still, he was a little hurt to realize how easy he was to overlook. He was stung by the feeling that the entire planet was, at that moment, ignoring him.

The cab driver's own activities consisted of reading a paper-back book and smoking a joint. He was a middle-aged man, black, dressed in what seemed to be ceremonial robes and adorned with a number of necklaces and bracelets, uniformly gold. He wore some kind of military or service headgear, per-haps what had once been an airline pilot's hat. All that remained now, however, was the shiny black visor, held in place by a tattered ring of material. The driver's scalp was decorated by thin, tiny rows of coarse hair, angled and curved intricately. The resulting design seemed to contain meaning, although Rudolfo could make nothing of it.

The book-reading and joint-smoking were being conducted with furious industry. The driver's fingers didn't so much hold the joint as prevent it from being hoovered through his lips. The fingers on his other hand hovered above the book, trembling with raptorial excitement, so that page-turning could be executed in an instant. He was, Rudolfo saw, nearing the end of the book, but Rudolfo had little sympathy for readers. He took a step for-ward and rapped on the window.

The bracelets and necklaces sent forth a musical clangour; the book shot up and collided with the roof just before the dri-ver's head did. When he fell back to earth he disappeared, lost beneath the ceremonial robes.

Rudolfo pulled open the passenger door and tried to put the man at ease. "Baby!" he said, employing the tone of moronic heartiness he used in the Show. "Don't get so jumpy with me!"

Rudolfo threw his bag into the back seat and climbed in the front. The driver's eyes were bugged open with apparent horror. "*Was?*" Rudolfo snapped, catching sight of this look. His first thought was that his wig had fallen off; it was his belief that with-out his wig he presented a truly hideous spectacle. He reached up and touched the curls and locks and then, reassured, became haughty and imperious. "You must take me to where I am living," he said. "I am Rudolfo."

The driver thought about that for almost a minute. He then turned and formally addressed the dashboard, placing his left hand on the steering wheel and working the gear selector slowly through "R" and "N" before putting it to rest in "D." Changing hands on the steering wheel, he depressed the signal indicator so that a loud ticking and flashing light announced his intention of pulling out to the left. He checked his blind spot many times, craning his head backwards, righting it, then snapping it back once more, ever wary that some madman could come screaming around the corner. Despite all this driving activity, the car did not go anywhere for many long moments. It was as though the man were awaiting clearance from an unseen tower, an impression he furthered by touching his ears occasionally.

Finally, the silent word was heard, and the car screamed into the heat of Las Vegas.

The driver began singing. Or making musical noises with his mouth, at any rate, because along with plaintive falsetto melodies and guttural lowings came odd percussive sounds, tongue-clicks and such. He began to drum along with his fingers, smacking them down upon the steering wheel with sufficient force to produce tympanic pops. Soon his whole body was involved, his neck jerking back and forth like a turkey with a full crop. His left foot began a steady tapping, his right foot a more erratic one. Seeing as how the man's right foot rested on the accelerator, Rudolfo was tossed back and forth. He shouted, "Cool off!" but the driver seemed to interpret this as encouragement and exaggerated the jerky spurts.

The airport disappeared abruptly and the vehicle sambaed into the desert.

Samson grew at an alarming rate, his limbs sprouting visibly. He was a miserable beast, for the most part, shunned and reviled by the other animals. Total whiteness is freakish beyond conception. A God so absent-minded as to forget to put colour into a creature was capable of anything. So Samson was hissed and swatted at by the other big cats. General Bosco seemed to share this unkindly view. He would snap his whip with what was either very good or very poor aim—instead of cracking the air just above Samson's head, the stinging tip would tear at his ear, or at the end of his snout, and for an instant the albino leopard would experience excruciating pain. The only moments of happiness came when Samson was close to Rudolfo, the boy with hair of similar colourlessness. It was to please Rudolfo that Samson learned the basic stuff, to rear up on to his hind legs and paw in a mincing way at the emptiness before him. Samson learned to jump through a hoop, although he found it very boring to do so, no less so when the hoop was set aflame. He'd found that very *surprising*, the first time, but boring nonetheless.

Samson found himself thinking of other, untried stunts. Somersaulting, for example. He'd seen the men with the painted faces do that, and it seemed to delight the human beings, especially the smaller ones. So Samson worked on somersaulting, although his head was too large to simply turn to the side, and his back end, comparatively puny, often waggled in the air in an unbecoming manner. Samson worked on this when perhaps he should have been applying himself to other things, and he worked on it with such single-mindedness that he was often unaware that other things were going on. Such as the time General Bosco, ramming his hands on his hips and staring daggers in Samson's direction, shouted, "*He, Schneewittchen! Mach dass du den Arsch hoch kriegst.*"

Samson continued his somersaulting. He'd developed a kind of sideways roll, pivoting on one of his shoulders and snapping his little pelvis mid-air to gather momentum. He was in the midst of one of these turns when the tip of General Bosco's whip flicked his rear-end.

For the first, and only, time in his life, Samson knew what it was to be wild. His mind was licked clean by a tongue of fire. The pain filled his being so completely that his claws seemed to give off sparks, his moist snout steam.

He completed the somersault and landed upright on his paws. His mouth was wide open, the skin pulled back so far that it gathered in tight folds just under his eyeballs and revealed much glistening pink gum and many white teeth. Samson made a sound that he'd never made before—and has never made since—a musical howling that seemed to make the bars of the cage vibrate, to make the air sound with eerie polyphony. Then he rushed forward. That is, he *rushed* in the sense that he covered the twelve feet that separated him from General Bosco in a thrice, although his motion was very methodical, gross muscular actions that rippled the sinew.

General Bosco attempted to crack the whip again, but he was clearly flustered, and the snap came well above Samson's head. Or perhaps the General was desperately trying to demonstrate that he still possessed the lion tamer's knack, using the whip to startle rather than hurt, but Samson was beyond caring. He sank his teeth into General Bosco's leg and clamped his jaws together with all the force he could muster. Indeed, the bite itself was not the most serious aspect of that first injury, even though the teeth ripped apart the beautifully defined calf, making it pop and deflate like a balloon. More serious from a medical point of view was the fact that Samson had cracked the tibia, webbing it with fractures. General Bosco screamed, not just from the excruciating pain, but also from the realization that he would now be cursed with a gimpy and embittering gait.

"*Das genügt*," said Rudolfo gently, and he watched the

tension disappear from Samson's body. Samson removed his mouth from around General Bosco's leg, walked away and then sagged to the ground, laying his pale head upon the sawdust disconsolately. General Bosco, in the second he had left before fainting, turned and speared him with a hateful look. As Bosco collapsed, Rudolfo understood that he'd spoken too calmly; at least, too calmly for Bosco's liking, although if you want to quiet a panicking animal, it is much better to whisper than to shriek. His choice of words could have been better, too, Rudolfo supposed calmly. *Das genügt*, as though some measure of the torture were acceptable, even called for.

The other big cats roiled and writhed upon their stands. They were reared up onto their hind legs, their upper bodies twisting in serpentine undulations. Their master was down, dead apparently, and they were an inch away from rioting, from destroying the cage and running wild in the howling streets. One—it was Frederick, the last lion Rudolfo would have expected to behave this way—slinked down from its stand and batted General Bosco across the head, leaving behind three neat rows of gash. The sawdust darkened with blood. General Bosco woke up momentarily, sat bolt upright. Some part of his system must have deemed the situation hopeless, because he immediately lay back down again and closed his eyes, seeking refuge in a black coma.

Rudolfo kicked Frederick in the snout and called, "Back!" Frederick, startled, obeyed. Rudolfo surprised even himself with the evenness of his tone; then again, he didn't fear death in any profound manner, having never found life that precious a gift. So when Helmut bounced down from his stand almost playfully, Rudolfo swung around to confront the cat and momentarily stilled the beast with a look of almost holy quiescence.

Now, Helmut, he was the *first* lion you'd expect to take part in an insurrection. He had always been recalcitrant, ever since he was a cub; indeed, Helmut hadn't been trained to any real degree. He could leap on and off his half-barrel, but he would do this almost at his own discretion. Whenever another cat performed a stunt, Helmut would hog a portion of the applause, jumping down, roaring briefly, leaping back aboard with more lethal grace than his companion. The rest of the time Helmut spent in restless motion, picking up and replacing his huge paws on the smallish circle that was his roost. The only time he quieted was when General Bosco performed the old head-between-the-jaws routine, when Helmut would stare at Bosco and Gregor— old Gregor, hoary and grizzled and virtually toothless—with a look of calm menace. *Hey*, Helmut's eyes said, *try some of that shit with me.*

So that explains the eagerness with which he descended to the ground. When Rudolfo snapped his whip and stung the tip of his ear, Helmut pulled back his lips and grinned. Rudolfo continued to snap the whip as Helmut crossed over and gingerly mouthed Bosco's foot, testing it for tenderness. He spit it out disdainfully, roared at Rudolfo, crossed over to the other side of Bosco's body and tenderly licked at the hip.

Only then, and with some reluctance, did Rudolfo draw his weapon, the war-vintage Luger that hung at his side. He had never used the gun, was afraid of back- and misfirings, and he was fond of Helmut, for all his faults. But he raised the gun and aimed it as best he could, concentrating on Helmut's head. The head, after all, was the largest target. Rudolfo might have preferred to shoot at the hindquarters, to cripple young Helmut rather than destroy him, but that might only anger the cat, leaving him with enough rage-filled life to kill not only General Bosco but Rudolfo and all the other cats as well.

Rudolfo turned toward the rest of the lions, who were now sending up a unified howl, an eerie chorus. He hushed them sternly; they lowered the volume but did not stop.

Then he pulled the trigger.

Rudolfo's memory of the event is made up of a series of stark images, Rudolfo's logic forcing them into order. First, there's a picture of Helmut chewing into the General's chest, apparently having elected it as the choicest cut. The image of Helmut lifting his head with nothing but a shiny gold button caught between his teeth comes next and must coincide with Rudolfo's pulling of the trigger.

Which means, of course, that the lion's head was no longer Rudolfo's target.

What he hit instead was General Bosco, exploding the brocaded jacket that covered his heart and sending up a geyser of blood. He then aimed once more at Helmut, knowing that the cat was about to explode, just as all the cats would, driven senseless by the proximity of death.

But Helmut instead turned away indolently and remounted his stand. He collapsed his bones with feline laziness and dropped the gold button daintily between his forepaws.

Rudolfo glanced down and saw that the albino leopard was beside him, quivering with fear, pressed up against his leather boot. "Yeah," said Rudolfo, one outcast to another, "let's get out of here."

The cab rolled to a stop, the tires crunching heavily on the drive. Rudolfo had a small tote bag cinched around his waist; he unzipped it and fished out one of the hundred-dollar bills that were always there. He handed it to the driver and waved his hand brusquely, indicating that the man should stop looking for change. The man, actually, had been doing no such thing. He had lifted the bill up until it was but inches away from his face, flipping it over and over. He was, likely, examining the bill for signs of counterfeiting, but it seemed somehow conceivable that he'd never seen one before.

Rudolfo pushed open the front door of the mansion, startled at how easily it moved. He and Jurgen had paid something on the order of a hundred thousand dollars for their security system, but far from being an impenetrable fortress, the mansion seemed as accessible as a derelict barn. The hinges howled; there was a creaking sound like the cracking of old bones. And then silence. He was reminded briefly of the discovery of his dead mother—the dead thing that had pretended to be his mother—how the silence had hunched over her, as though the silence itself were the culprit and had been caught red-handed.

And where, it occurred to him, were the underlings? Where was, for example, Tiu, a young women curiously obsessed by dust and dirt? She should certainly be hovering about, a feather duster trembling in her hand, her lips set with grim zeal.

His stomach, already made tender by the single glass of champagne, suddenly soured and crumpled. He made a low sound, a musical hum of misery, because he was not far away from hopelessness, and never had been. The sound lasted many seconds, and just before it died away, Jurgen appeared.

He emerged from the gloom just in front of Rudolfo, walking out from behind a curtain of shadow. Rudolfo was both relieved and startled, an odd combination that left behind a residue of annoyance. When Jurgen said, "Hi," Rudolfo sidestepped the greeting with the grace of a matador.

"Jimmy the headfuck never at the airport showed up," he snarled. "That headfuck is fired."

"Jimmy is confused," said Jurgen. That gave Rudolfo pause, and he tilted his head and stared at his partner. There was something not right. For a moment he thought it was simply that Jurgen was smiling, when ordinarily he maintained a visage of stern propriety. Or perhaps it was the eyes, which were contained in little nests of wrinkles. This was due in part to the smile, Rudolfo thought, but there were clear signs of fatigue, even ill-

health. Jurgen had lost all control of his eyelids, which were raising and lowering at random intervals and frequencies.

But as odd as all that was (very odd), it was Jurgen's hair
that caught and held Rudolfo's attention. It was messy. The curly
fringe that ordinarily lay across his square brow with such precision was bolt upright and fashioned into a series of little tufts
and horns. And the whole disaster area was pointed with more
little white hairs.

"Guess what?" asked Jurgen, still smiling.

"What?" snapped Rudolfo, craning his neck this way and
that, disturbed at the stillness that existed inside *das Haus*.

"I got new card trick."

"How nice is that for you."

"Say the name of a card. Any card."

"Nine of diamonds."

"Ta da!" intoned Jurgen tunelessly. He snapped his thick
fingers in the air and the nine of diamonds appeared there.

"Good," muttered Rudolfo, but he didn't really give a fuck.
Why would all the animals be sleeping at this time of day?

"I could do it in *die Schau*," suggested Jurgen shyly.

"You do it *die Schau* already."

"In Up Close and Personal, you mean? *Nein, nein*. Is not
same trick."

Das eindrucksvollste Haus im Universum should have been
echoing the soft, rhythmic sounds of little padded paws. "Holy
Jesus," Rudolfo said suddenly. "You didn't feed the animals."

"Uh-oh." Jurgen looked instantly remorseful, although the
grin remained carved into his face. "I lost track of time."

Rudolfo stormed away. As he went he let out a series of
whistles and grunts, and animals rose out of their torpors and
began to gather behind him. They followed with dangling, dry
tongues and wet eyes. Those that had tails wagged them weakly.

Samson climbed down from the sofa in front of the huge

television. Actually, he didn't climb down so much as fall off, his old bones sending up a clatter. Then he stretched, achingly, because he hadn't moved from the sofa since Rudolfo had left. He'd watched old movies and black-and-white sitcoms. Toward the middle of the third day, just before Rudolfo's reappearance, Samson had begun to think just how appealing Mary Tyler Moore looked, appealing as in *succulent and juicy*. But here was Rudolfo, his love and his life, so Samson fell in behind. They walked through the house and out onto the grounds beyond.

The big cats were howling.

Chapter Ten

It was unusual, this rehearsal, but Miranda didn't mind. Anything to break up the day, that was her thinking. It was almost her motto. From the time she awoke—sometime around nine a.m., absurdly early by Las Vegas standards, shamefully late by her parents'—until the Show at ten p.m., the day stretched out, empty as the Saskatchewan prairie she'd grown up on.

Lately she'd been going to churches, churches of all sizes and denominations, but there were few services held in the late mornings and early afternoons of weekdays. And those that she had found were decidedly weird. They featured either gamblers inveighing against their ill fortune, demanding angrily that God get with the program, or else gaunt men and women who spoke of the meads of asphodel and held their brass crucifixes upside down.

The traditional time-waster of her ilk—her ilk being known in the trade as a box-jumper, although she wrote thaumaturgical assistant on credit card applications and such—was, of course, keeping in shape. But such was the nature of Miranda's body that flabbiness could be erased with just a couple of snappy stretches. She still belonged to Shecky's Olympus—the shadowy Hades where she'd first encountered Rudolfo—but only needed to go a couple of times a week. Actually, she didn't really *need* to go at all, but she sometimes craved the human company, even if it was silent and surly. (The bodybuilders worked with grim industry, exhaling heavily with exertion so Miranda was buffeted by many small winds. She'd first noticed Rudolfo, Miranda remembered, because he alone acted otherwise, driving upwards from his squat with a long howl of ecstatic pain, ending with a rapid series of grunted *ja*s.)

Miranda also never seemed to gain weight and sometimes resented the fact, because that would at least give her a foe and a fight. She did sometimes go for runs in the desert, but the Bod usually located whatever little pockets of fat existed, tossing them out in desperate appeasement.

Miranda was perforce a hobbyist, one with an artistic bent. Watercolours, wood carving, photography. Her hotel room—she couldn't bring herself to consider it an apartment, what with the furniture being bolted to the floor and all—was crowded with an easel and drawing table, the walls adorned with prints and parchment. None of it, Miranda knew, was much good. Some of the photographs were all right, the bloodless landscapes of the desert, and she'd once done a fine painting in the Chinese style, sitting cross-legged for thirteen hours and then lowering the brush to the rice paper, scraping it across and leaving behind a line that came from deep inside. Basically, though, she was a hacker. Her work was all just one step removed from jigsaw puzzles and paint-by-numbers.

All of which left her in a vast desolation of neon-lit timelessness, which is why she welcomed this rehearsal.

The two men were standing together on the stage, but each was so thoroughly up to his own business that they looked, even from four hundred feet away, to be in totally different worlds. Rudolfo was directing the lighting guy, gesticulating at the ceiling as though he were God creating the universe. "Okay, blue," he commanded, and the air became suffused with azure. Rudolfo stared through the shafts of illumination. "*Nein, nein, nein!*"

Jurgen's business was much harder to define. He seemed to be investigating the air itself, wiping a hand through the emptiness and then examining his fingertips as though there might be residue. Miranda was not so quick to notice his white hairs, nor the fact that his once-orderly locks were rebelling atop the blocky head, or that his tan, so deep a few days before, had faded away. But she did notice the odd expression he'd adopted, at once both somber and addled, as though Jurgen were at the same time pondering the universe and having his belly tickled.

Miranda leapt up on the stage. "Hey," she said. "What's up, guys? You got something new for me?"

"I don't know," said Rudolfo churlishly. "Is Jurgen's idea for rehearsal."

Jurgen nodded. "*Ja*, I got something new." He turned, placed thick fingers in his mouth and whistled like the beer-swilling football fan he had been all those years ago.

"More, what the fuck is it called, *lavender!*" sang out Rudolfo, and he trusted that his disdain was manifest. He became aware of some disgruntled trudging across the stage, a few workmanlike grunts, a creak and some clumps. Rudolfo turned to see six unionized stagehands unloading what looked to be a huge old steamer trunk.

Jurgen rushed over, locking his fingers together, twisting his arms like a small girl who has just received a puppy. "Beautiful!" he enthused.

"Jurgen," said Rudolfo patiently—he was determined to maintain his calm here— "what the fuck-shit is that?"

Rudolfo knew what it was, more or less—it was part of the Collection, a piece of junk that his partner had paid hundreds of thousands of dollars for, but he didn't know what it was doing on the bright shining stage at the Abraxas Hotel.

"Is new Substitution Box!"

"It's not new," noted Rudolfo. The wood was pale and green with age. The leather straps had been fed through the buckles so many times that the edges had been tanned to near-suede.

"*This* Substitution Box," explained Jurgen, pointing help-fully, as if the stage were littered with Substitution Boxes, "is same one Houdini used." Jurgen turned and gazed at Miranda. "You know routine?"

Miranda nodded. "Sure thing, boss. I used to do this chest-nut with the Amazing Leonidas." Miranda threw open the trunk and pulled out a huge canvas sack. (Rudolfo reeled, because the sack smelled as if it had been kept in Hell's musty rec room.) "I cuff you. You get into the sack, I tie it, I close you and the sack inside the box and do up the padlock. I climb up on top, pull up a curtain. Meanwhile, you lose the cuffs. You cut through the bag at the bottom." Miranda walked behind the trunk, reached out with her left big toe and pulled the lower part of the back wall away. "You roll out here, reach out and take the screen, I drop and crawl into the box. You drop the curtain, *bang*. Inside the box, I climb into the sack, I hold the bottom of the bag closed with my toes. You unlock the padlock, open up the box, untie the bag and *pow*, there I am. Metamorphosis."

"Okey-dokey," said Jurgen. "That sounds easy enough."

"It's kind of," said Miranda hesitantly, "a corny bit."

"*Ja!*" said Rudolfo, even though he was trying not to pay attention. "Is corny like piss." Rudolfo turned away and contin-ued screaming at the lighting guy. "Put another gel on the spot-light right away now!"

"There's a lot of acts with a sub box in it," Miranda went on. "The Pendragons are the best. They do the switch so fast, it's amazing. Our routine won't be anything special."

"Miranda," said Jurgen seriously, "it gonna be special; you better believe it."

"Well, okay, sure, let's try." Miranda bent down and dug through the stuff in the trunk, finally coming up with a pair of old handcuffs and snapping them around Jurgen's thick wrists. The handcuffs were gaffed; all Jurgen had to do was knock the sides together and they would open and fall away. Jurgen stepped inside the canvas sack; Miranda raised the material over Jurgen's head, pulled it tight and cinched the ropes. Jurgen folded himself into the Substitution Box and Miranda closed the lid, snapping the oversized padlock that fastened the latch.

Then she pulled off her sweater, socks and sweatpants, stripping down to a white leotard, because the main reason thaumaturgical assistants are usually almost naked is that clothes interfere with what they must do: crawl through tiny holes, make themselves as small as possible, etc., etc. Miranda picked up a large square of velvet and stepped up onto the Substitution Box. She planted her feet firmly and raised the curtain until both she and the trunk were hidden from view.

The moment just hung there, like washing on a line. It lingered for so long that Rudolfo turned away and placed his hand above his eyes, peering through the light into the darkness. "Okay, chief," he said to the lighting guy. All of a sudden there came the strangest sound, a pop like a fat boy makes with finger and cheek. And there stood Jurgen atop the Substitution Box, grinning like the idiot he seemed intent on becoming. He jumped to the ground, produced a huge key, worked the padlock and pulled open the lid. The canvas sack rose up from inside the Box, its contents visibly shaking. Jurgen pulled at the ropes and the sack fell away from Miranda.

"Wow!" Her cheeks were flushed; indeed, her whole body was flushed, great circles of red bleeding through the whiteness of the leotard. Her hair was messy and her eyes were bleared with tears. "Holy fucking cow!" Miranda virtually leapt out of the Substitution Box; she sprang up and landed some feet away in a defensive crouch, as though terrified beyond reason. She wiped at her nose and eyes as though she were crying, but when she fell over backwards clutching her stomach, her long legs raised heavenward, it became more than clear that she was laughing.

Jurgen was laughing too, a chuckle that might be employed in a church should the pastor attempt a witticism.

Rudolfo stopped short. On talk shows Jurgen could be counted on to heave out a couple of overburdened breaths should the host say something meant to be funny, but beyond that Rudolfo had always believed that Jurgen had no laugh.

Only then did it hit him, the realization that should have come many hours earlier. He had never told the strange dope-sucking cabbie where to take him. He had not said where he lived. He didn't know why this was connected to Houdini's ugly old Substitution Box, but it was, the first idea stopping short and the next bumping into it like a hackneyed vaudevillian act.

He looked at his partner and he was afraid.

The only time Rudolfo had been more afraid was when he thought he would be arrested for General Bosco's murder.

He and Samson had fled into the night.

The one thing Rudolfo had learned in the grim *Berufsschule* was how to function even when scared senseless. He thought through his predicament logically. How much did *die Bullen* know about him; how much would they have been told? His fellow circus performers thought his name was Rudy, because that's what General Bosco had called him and General Bosco was the only one who ever talked to him. No one knew Thielmann and, anyway, Thielmann was not a name entered in any birth certificates or records. So at best the police would be looking for a youth with platinum-blond hair (he quickly stuffed his wig into a trash container) known only as Rudy. He would simply cease to be that person.

Samson remained a larger problem. A fugitive does not benefit from the companionship of an albino leopard. Rudolfo headed for a department store to remedy the situation.

Curiously enough, Jurgen was in that same department store, although this was not the occasion of their first meeting. This was a near-miss, if you will. You could, conceivably, even perceive it as a miscalculation on Someone's part. You could dismiss it as coincidence. But the fact remains that Jurgen Schubert was standing before a set of mirrors in the men's department, trying on a suit of improbable colour. Preston the Magnificent, Sr., had been very clear in his instructions that the performer dress "not as a member of the drab and drear citizenry—for from these pedestrian ranks his Art has elevated him—rather as a latter-day Priest of the Sun, a Flamen of Fire, a wondrous robed Magi." For some reason Jurgen seemed to think that magi had very bad taste, that they favoured the vomity tones of the spectrum. He had located a suit of such a profoundly ill hue, a bile green with little flecks of rust, that its manufacturer likely went out of business immediately following its creation. Jurgen stood before the mirrors and appraised himself, noting that the colour suited his deep plum eyelids. He struck a pose, placing a hand in front of his chest and twisting the fingers upwards. If he'd had a deck of cards, he would have produced a perfect fan; as it was, it merely looked like his hand was suddenly twisted by infirmity, retribution for even trying on the suit.

At that moment Rudolfo was skulking behind the racks of jackets and trousers, sneaking toward the hosiery. He glanced over, saw Jurgen and laughed. Jurgen spun around with darkened eyes.

He saw a strange white hairless creature looking at him from behind some clothes. This monster shook its head and then disappeared from sight.

Jurgen turned around and inspected himself once more. He decided not to buy that particular suit.

Meanwhile, Rudolfo had picked up and paid for a pair of black socks, shoe polish, a dark blue watch cap, three belts and a pair of sunglasses. He and Samson then took to an alley and awaited nightfall.

Some hours later they emerged, the watch cap covering the greater part of Rudolfo's baldness, the sunglasses balanced on his nose. He walked in a stiff, awkward manner, his shoulders pulled back and his chin tucked into his neck. In his right hand he clutched the loop of a buckled belt; this belt was attached to and through the others, so as to form an odd kind of harness; this jerry-rigging girded young Samson's chest and belly. It was Rudolfo's inspiration that he should disguise himself as a blind man, and Samson as his Seeing Eye dog. Toward that end, he had blackened the albino leopard's body with the shoe polish. It was impossible to do more than impart a kind of sootiness to Samson, but it was enough to cut the glare. The other problem, the animal's pointed ears, Rudolfo solved in a clever manner, pulling the black socks over them to dangle with canine goofiness.

They hadn't gone more than fifty feet before a passerby pressed a banknote into Rudolfo's palm. He had found a new career.

Chapter Eleven

Jurgen Schubert was buying a new suit because he had just gotten his first engagement at a nightclub. He was a veteran of birthday parties, corporate luncheons and county fairs, but this was his first proper job, a full month contracted with more promised. So he was using his savings to buy himself a suit, a fine and expensive suit, even though he was going to tear out the lining and bulk up the sleeves with hidden pockets. A small pouch would be sewn into the back vent, a place to keep the doves, which wouldn't do much for his broadbeamed silhouette. The trousers would be eviscerated too, so that he could put his hands into his pockets and gain immediate access to a modified machinist's apron full of little rigs, gags and decks of cards. The legs would be too long, and he'd turn the cuffs up once only; he needed very deep cuffs because many things came from, or ended up, there. People might think Jurgen had found his suit in a trash heap, though at least he'd selected a nice colour, a gunmetal grey that rippled light with every movement.

A few days later, he went down to the club with his gear—

two huge suitcases, a birdcage, a small rabbit pen and a collapsible presentation table—to prepare for his debut. The door was locked—not that he'd expected the club to be open so early—so he knocked. There was no response. He began to wonder if perhaps he wasn't *too* early. It was, after all, only eight-thirty in the morning. Still, he was buoyed by the fact that pedestrians were scurrying around behind him.

He raised his knuckles and then paused, making certain that he was at the right address. There was nothing to distinguish it from the other houses on the street except for a small sign, very crudely painted, that read "MISS JOE'S."

He pounded on the door. "Hello?" he called. There was nothing but a deep and still silence from within. He considered going back to the crowded apartment, returning later in the afternoon. But the sun was up and Münich was singing. "Hello!" he shouted once more.

At last there came a muffled response. "Who is it?"

"It is I," Jurgen answered uncertainly. "The Great Schuberto."

"The magician?"

"The magician."

"Do me a big favour, okay, Mr. Magic?"

"Yes?"

"*Go fuck yourself.*"

Jurgen smiled stupidly at the door and saw that there was a small peephole drilled into the middle of it. Not knowing what else to do, he took a step to his right so that his face would be framed within the circle. "It is I," he repeated quietly, "the Great Schuberto." His eyelids were flickering.

"Why don't you come back in a few hours?" demanded the voice. It occurred to Jurgen that he couldn't determine whether the voice belonged to a man or a woman. "The nurse hasn't even made her morning rounds," the voice continued. "She hasn't given us our medication or emptied the pisspots. It's too fucking depressing in here. This is no place for a strapping young, um, *youth*, such as yourself. So please go away and come back in a little while. Okay?"

The Great Schuberto pulled back his eyelids and stared into the peephole. He could understand that he'd come too early, been too anxious, but he could not stem the anger. He disliked being turned away. He hated being counted as third-rate, even if he himself suspected that's what he was. "I have to prepare," he said firmly. "Let me in."

Tumblers fell and latches loosened. The door creaked open with a horrible sound. Jurgen peered into the shadows and could see nothing. "Okay, Mr. Magic. Come in." Using the voice as a guide, Jurgen finally found, some six feet in the air, a face. That is, he recognized it after a moment as a face, although originally he'd thought it was just a nose. A huge nose, crooked and hooked. Then he noticed two small eyes attached on either side, dark irises floating in stagnant yellow pools, and he was able to infer the existence of a mouth, because there was a smoking cigarette suspended up there.

The creature withdrew and Jurgen stepped over the threshold, dragging the presentation table and the heavier of the two suitcases with him. "It is necessary for me to prepare the stage," he said once again. "That is why I have come."

"What the fuck is *this*?" The creature was staring at the ground a few feet away. There were no clues as to gender. It was impossible to say whether the hair was long or short, because it was contained in a stocking, a black nylon that clung to a bullet-shaped skull. Emaciated and draped in a housecoat, a drab checked thing with a feathery fringe, the body gave no clues. The hand and forearm that poked out one of the sleeves were nothing but skin and bone, and precious little skin at that, thought Jurgen. The hand and forearm pointed toward the ground and trembled with disease or fury. "What is *that?* I'll tell you what that is, my young Magic Man. Someone has puked up an internal organ. You tell these people to go easy on the sauce, but will they listen?"

Jurgen nodded and went back outside for the the rest of his stuff.

"Oh, little fuzzies!" The creature—Jurgen guessed this was Miss Joe—bent over to peer into the birdcage, and Jurgen noticed the residue of makeup, patches of powder, lipstick packed into the crevices of chapped lips. "What do you do?" the creature wondered. "Bite their heads off?"

"Oh, no," responded Jurgen earnestly. "I make them appear and disappear."

"Hmmm! Well, aren't we all looking forward to that!" Miss Joe spun around and marched off into the shadows, this time with a very exaggerated sashay. "Let there be light," Miss Joe intoned, reaching out a bony finger and stabbing at a control box mounted on the wall. Light bulbs flickered, for some reason accompanied by the sound of groaning pipes. There were flashes of great illumination, as though lightning forked from the ceiling, but when the lights finally burst into being they barely sliced through the gloom. Jurgen could make out a small stage, several round tables, a few disparate chairs and countless articles of discarded clothing.

By Jurgen's foot there did indeed appear to be an internal organ. Miss Joe returned with a dustpan and broom, hunkering down to sweep the thing away. The housecoat fell away from the bony knees; Jurgen stared but could see nothing. "That's cheating," said Miss Joe, without looking up from her labour. (The broom was not equal to the task; Miss Joe now scraped at the thing with the blade of the dustpan.) "You're going to have to find out the hard way."

Jurgen spun around, took a few steps away. "The stage," he called over his shoulder, "is inadequate."

"Hmmm?" Miss Joe finally picked the thing up with her hands, throwing it onto the galvanized scoop, then came to stand beside him. Like the rest of the nightclub, the stage was littered with discarded clothing, but these were smaller pieces, items that Jurgen was able to classify as "underwear" in a very broad sense.

"The stage is too small."

"Hey, Mr. Magic, I've had forty-one people on that stage doing the African Cluster Fuck. There's plenty enough room for you."

"We could take away these tables; I could use all this space here at the front."

"Look, Schuberto. I don't like to burst your little bubble, but you are the *Chaser.*"

"*Chaser?*" The word sounded like English. Jurgen had only a smattering of the language, perhaps nine or ten words. This wasn't one of them.

"Yeah, right." Miss Joe lit a cigarette, then spit out a puff of smoke that drifted over top of the little stage and loomed there like a rain cloud.

"What does this mean?"

Miss Joe spun around and stared at Jurgen for what seemed like a full minute. "Oh, well," she said quietly. "The Chaser is the big star."

"So I must have more room."

"Yeah, yeah." Miss Joe glanced around the nightclub. "I guess I don't need all these fucking tables."

Rudolfo meanwhile had staked his claim on Bayerstrasse. His career as a blind beggar was going exceptionally well, although he couldn't have said exactly why. Every day he made refinements that added Deutschmarks to the battered tin cup he clutched between his fingers (tilting his head at an angle, pointing his toes inward, hunching over even more). But as to why he was successful and not Peter Bloch, the sightless man three store-fronts away, Rudolfo couldn't say. He didn't realize that in large part it was his hairlessness, which lent him an unearthly sheen. And he didn't know, because his head was always snapped forward, that Samson, hanging back and adopting the posture of an old hound dog, would often glance up at the pedestrians and pull the corners of his mouth back sharply, exhibiting, for a brief moment, a furious snarl. The passersby would quickly dig into their pockets and hurl coins into the tin cup.

"*Danke, mein Herr*," Rudolfo would intone.

As successful as the disguise seemed to be, Rudolfo still expected to be arrested at any moment, taken away and charged with the murder of General Bosco. Sometimes the fear was so intense that his skin spotted with sickly sweat. He'd rented a tiny squalid room—he could afford better, but few innkeepers wanted his bizarre dog—but his nights were as sleepless as his days. So certain was he of arrest (and then what, probably execution) that he didn't even bother making idle plans. He stood on the corner and, despite the wheel of weather, wind to warmth to wind once more, existed in a state of timelessness.

Until the day he recognized some people.

That statement warrants some clarification. Rudolfo didn't *know* these people; he was certain that he had never seen or met them. But he knew, instantly, *what* they were.

There were two, a man and a woman. Or so it seemed. The man was fat, with a tiny pointed head, so that his silhouette was that of a huge teardrop. He sported a goatee. A fringe of wispy hair encircled the point of his skull, shaven like a monk's tonsure. He wore sunglasses and a scarf; the rest of his habit was less easy to classify—maybe drapery and carpets hacked apart with a dull knife and placed willy-nilly on the fat body. Great grey billows of smoke exploded from him, more than could be accounted for by the thin black cheroot in the ebony holder.

The woman, too ridiculously feminine to really *be* a woman, pranced down the street as though she were the front half of a clown-horse and didn't realize that she lacked both the costume and her partner. Her mission in life seemed to be relocating her outlandishly large breasts from one place to another. Everything else—the flaming red hair, the glistening purple lips—seemed as inconsequential as the mudflaps on a transport truck.

These were the people, Rudolfo realized, who had come to his mother's Salon. The freakish and the misfit. The people who lived in the shadows. And these particular people moved, if not with determination, at least with purpose. Rudolfo understood suddenly that they had a harbour and a haven.

He whistled sharply. Young Samson uncoiled himself from his sitting position and caught himself short halfway through a tight, feline circling. The beast wet its lips—the tongue showing up dazzling white against the sooted fur—and let loose a passable *arf.* "*Ja*, Rover," said Rudolfo. "Come, boy." The two fell in behind the strange couple.

At night, Miss Joe's was more conspicuous. Signs had appeared throughout the day, hastily written, the characters childlike and awkward. These were stuck to the edifice with masking tape, most at eye level, some higher, some so low they seemed designed to attract only the attention of people lounging in the gutters. JOACHIM'S GOING TO DO HIS THING, IF YOU THOUGHT LAST NIGHT WAS BAD, JUST WAIT, COME ON IN, BOYS AND GIRLS. One of the signs—better lettered than most, as if the creator had laboured at it with a touch more care—read THE GREAT SCHUBERTO, THE MAGIC MAN, PERFORMS NIGHTLY.

By ten o'clock in the evening these signs surrounded the thick oaken door, covered it, obscured it. By ten o'clock in the evening it took keen skills of observation, or foreknowledge, to even realize the door was there. Luckily, Rudolfo, crouched around a corner with Samson, saw his two freakish people walk through it. He waited a few minutes and then turned to the albino leopard.

"Okay, I'm going to go in there."

Samson trotted out onto the sidewalk, only to be hauled back into the shadowy alley, Rudolfo yanking hard upon the makeshift tether. "You better wait here." Samson looked instantly saddened, betrayed. Rudolfo felt his heart melting, but, really, Samson had no idea of how absurd he appeared, like the offspring of animals that should have been destroyed as monsters. It wasn't just the disguise, which truthfully worked pretty well as long as the socks didn't fall off his ears. It was Samson himself who queered the game, largely through his efforts to act like a dog. He would come upon a fire hydrant and eagerly raise a leg, sending out a steaming stream of pee. Usually, though, he threw himself off balance, the support leg buckling, sending the cat to the sidewalk with a thud. So it would be best for him to remain outside, rather than have him attempt to beg food with a ludicrously dangling tongue, or whatever else he might have in mind.

"No, Sammy," he whispered. "Wait out here." And Rudolfo hurried away before he could be swayed by doleful pink eyes.

He pushed at the door and his ears were stung by the piercing howl of the hinges. He slipped through and stepped to the side, pressing his back against the wall. This is how he'd been taught to enter the cages of dangerous animals. He looked around the shadows—there were figures there, probably human, roiling in the darkness—but his attention was caught by the man trapped in the shaft of light.

In those days, it should be mentioned, Jurgen modelled his hairstyle after his hero, Preston the Magnificent. The curls were rolled and worried into geometric shapes and balanced upon one another. The creation was then virtually shellacked. Jurgen's face was sternly set too, the dark unruly eyelids tamed by the trick of pulling them up into his vast brow. He looked like a frightened man, or a man about to sneeze, or a man who might somehow shoot his eyes from his head as though they were peas. And yet Rudolfo thought him extremely handsome, that Jurgen's face was one that God might make for a hero doomed to a tragic end.

The man up on the stage raised empty hands into the air, rubbed them together briefly and, suddenly, silk handkerchiefs began to materialize, many of them, variously coloured and knotted. When he had produced perhaps ten linear feet, the man suddenly bunched them all together into one hand and made an exaggerated throwing motion toward the tables in front. Nothing there. Rudolfo brought his hands together, but his was the only applause—so unaccompanied that it startled several people, including the magician. Jurgen turned his head sharply toward the source of the sound, knocking his hairdo askew. The entire assemblage started sliding and he was forced to abruptly jerk his head the other way. The balls and wedges shifted, and then settled into a brand-new hairstyle, no less ornate. Jurgen found Rudolfo with his eyes—although Rudolfo wondered if he could see anything, given the bright spotlight—and smiled. The magician lifted his own hands and brought them together. The sound was loud and cut easily through the other noise, a soup of mulches and moans. When he pulled his hands apart, two doves flew away. Although the white doves were not quite white, and obviously suffered from great dietary deficiencies, Rudolfo found this overwhelmingly beautiful.

After Jurgen fled the stage, three rather dissolute gentlemen mounted it. One carried a guitar, one a bass fiddle, the last a soprano saxophone. They looked at each other and mumbled song titles, each running through a long list, and they did this until by chance they all said the same song title at the same time. This was the song—"No Greater Love"—that they began to play. Rudolfo remembers this, but when he replays his first conversation with Jurgen in his mind, he chooses other background music. Ravel's "Pavane for a Dead Princess," often, even though it is achingly sad; or sometimes the slow movement from Brahms' First Piano Concerto, which sounds no less melancholy, but rings with Johannes' love for the lovely Clara Schumann. Both of these pieces Rudolfo imagines as performed by Sturm and Drang.

And the first words that passed between them? They were Rudolfo's, of course. Rudolfo had spoken first words before, to men in small towns, to boys in acrid locker rooms. He knew to choose first words with care. It was important not to alarm the other; it was also important to announce, even in a very muted fashion, one's desires. So Rudolfo moved through the tables—noting that there were pale backsides moving in the gloom like moonlit waves—and said to the magician, "Know any more tricks?"

Jurgen was occupied with trying to retrieve his doves. They had roosted on some rusty water pipes, their tiny heads buried beneath wings, and Jurgen was bouncing into the air, increasing the force so that each leap brought him closer, swiping his hand, opening and closing his fingers. But with these words he settled onto the earth and stared at Rudolfo.

Rudolfo instantly reddened, sickened, because he'd given no thought to how he himself looked. The watch cap covered most of his head, but what of those ghastly barren inches between his ears and the wool? His eyes were burdened with huge blue pouches of sleeplessness; worse, he had no eyebrows. In better times he would have drawn some on with a makeup stick, but he'd abandoned this since becoming a beggar. His clothes had been filched out of refuse bins, bought from the cheapest of second-hand stores. He could not blame the magician for widening his eyes with what seemed to be terror.

It was out of the purest, most burning embarrassment, then, that Rudolfo raised his eyes toward the water pipes. He lifted a hand into the air and extended his index finger. A simple whistle, a chubby musical note that bounced into the air, and suddenly the doves were fluttering down. They lit upon the finger, covered their heads, went back to sleep. Rudolfo held them out toward the magician, who nodded curtly. He took them—hardly gently, Rudolfo noted, each bird encircled by thick fingers—and placed them somewhere behind his back.

When the magician's hand reappeared, he was holding a deck of cards. "Perfectly ordinary playing cards," he noted.

Rudolfo reached for them. "May I see?"

"I shall demonstrate," said the magician and held out the deck and riffled the edges with his slightly calloused thumb. Rudolfo watched the faces fly by, a random ordering. "I will do this once again," said the magician. "You must stop the procedure via the sudden intrusion of a digit."

"Stick my finger in?"

"Indeed."

Rudolfo didn't watch the cards this time. He stared into the magician's eyes. The magician stared back, and their eyes remained locked until the magician's left eyelid came crashing down like the curtain on a dying act. As it struggled back upwards, the other eyelid, dark as blood sausage, descended, but only halfway, bouncing there ever so slightly.

Rudolfo placed his finger into the deck, silencing the small whirring sound.

"*Ja,*" said Jurgen. "Deplace the ducat upon which your finger presently resides."

"Why do you talk like that?" wondered Rudolfo, although he was surprised that he had spoken aloud.

"Deplace the ducat upon which your finger presently resides. I shall determine its value and suit via psychic empathy."

Rudolfo slid the card out, shielded it carefully with both of his hands and peeked at the face.

"Concentrate!" sang out the magician sonorously. "For just as Science has just declaimed the Wave Theory of Light, so now do we conjecture a similiarity of Thought processes. So concentrate, my friend, emit great pulses of ratiocination."

Rudolfo smiled at this man. He had decided that the magician was crazy, so his basic plan was to keep smiling and move away quietly. The magician raised a hand and pinched his square brow between thick fingers. "Emanate," the magician whispered. "Emanate pure cognition."

Rudolfo took a step backwards. The magician's head jerked up sharply, pinning Rudolfo with dark eyes. "The two of hearts," he growled.

Rudolfo looked at his card again, not that he couldn't remember it, more to add to the effect. He handed the card back to Jurgen and winked. He whispered, "Good trick."

The chimes sound, and Rudolfo finds himself singing along. "Bella come un'aurora," he chants. The words are flattened because his cheek is mashed up against the Panamanian tiling. He raises his head enough to perceive that he is lying on the ground. His bones are chilled because he no longer has much substance covering them. His penis and testicles are shrivelled, almost gone from sight.

He staggers to his feet, still singing, "Se lo rammento…" and he sees the front door looming before him. He stumbles forward and wraps his hands around the doorknob, pulls the door open — and sees fiends, devilkins and familiars, gnomes, trolls and wraiths. Rudolfo raises his arms and clacks his ulnae together, thereby fashioning a crude cross. It is protection against the horde on the doorstep, kelpies and bogies and loups-garous. The pack sends up a hideous yowling, "Trick or—" and then silence falls suddenly.

"Mister," says a naiad, streamers of green tinsel threaded through her golden hair, "you got no clothes on."

Chapter Twelve

The explanation for Jurgen's odd behaviour was of such a charming simplicity that Rudolfo immediately heaved a great sigh and felt good for the first time in days. *Sleep deprivation.* Rather than getting the eight-and-one-half hours that he himself claimed were necessary, Jurgen had been slipping into bed late and rising early. In fact, some mornings Rudolfo was fairly certain that he'd spent the entire night all alone in the huge circular bed. So of course Jurgen was acting very oddly, grousing about the Show and behaving like an idiot. Of course his hair was turning white, because sleep is what holds age at bay.

It was actually humorous, in a way, because usually it was Rudolfo who cheated Slumber. He felt comfortable in the mansion late at night, when all the animals were asleep (except of course for the bushbabies, the round moons of their eyes cutting through the darkness), and he would often stay up until three or four in the morning. He would load up the CD tray with discs of various operas, hitting the random button so that the stories became intermingled and confused—Cio-Cio-San pursued by a strapping, hormone-addled Tristan. The Music Room had speakers mounted everywhere and Rudolfo would sit in the middle of it and exalt in the melody, splendour and infinite sadness.

Jurgen would caution him that no good could come of this. Jurgen dispensed advice and wisdom like a balloon-breasted dowager, speaking in cretinous aphorisms and tapping his listener on the chest. "For every hour we don't sleep," he might say, "comes closer the appointment we all must keep." Now here he was, with his black puffy eyes, and it was really very funny, in a way.

So it was Rudolfo's idea that in order to encourage Jurgen to bed earlier, he would try to rush through the customary Post-Show Photo Op.

The Post-Show Photo Op was one of Miss Joe's innovations, put into place years and years ago when Jurgen and Rudolfo were just starting out as a duo, doing five minutes of magic between naked people. They would finish, Rudolfo remembered, holding hands and bathed in sweat. The applause would be deafening, even though there were but seventy or eighty people on the most crowded night at Miss Joe's. Jurgen and Rudolfo would bow—the young Samson gingerly folding his forelegs, inclining his upper half elegantly to receive the ovation—and then the stage would be plunged into total darkness. Moments later a single spot would light the stage and Miss Joe would be standing there, usually caught in the act of balancing her towering hairdo, because it was she who cut the lights from the back of the room and then bolted forward at full tilt.

"Okay, kiddies," Miss Joe would say, devouring the mesh head of an ancient microphone. "We all know our memories aren't what they should be. I mean, I sweep up more brain cells than dust, right? So, why not have your picture taken with the boys?"

It seemed a very peculiar idea and, indeed, very few people took advantage of the offer. But Miss Joe's showbiz adage was:

"Act like stars and then become stars." Over time, people began to gather backstage, and soon there were great big jostling crowds. Now, at the Abraxas Hotel there was a long lineup in front of a single door where two giants dressed in genii garb screened the potential subjects and allowed only the rich and famous into the inner lair.

These people would shake the duo's hands, make an effusive statement concerning their wonderment, place one arm across Jurgen's shoulder, the other across Rudolfo's, and pose for a Polaroid.

These photographs, of which there must be tens of thousands, have a sameness about them. Rudolfo's smile is wide but not enthusiastic, as though his teeth acted as some kind of force field to deflect the camera's evil. And Jurgen adopted the mien of Preston the Magnificent, fashioning his features until they asked darkly imponderable questions.

So, on this night, Rudolfo tried to rush things. Following the Show (which had not gone particularly well), he went to the dressing room door, opened it slightly and stuck the tip of his nose through. Maurice, one of the giants, grunted interrogatively.

"Okay, chief," said Rudolfo. "Only be letting in maybe ten peoples."

"But," returned the giant, "there are perhaps two hundred and fifty people waiting on line."

"*Ja.* So what?"

The giant shrugged. When Rudolfo shut the door, Maurice began walking the length of the lineup, ruthlessly shoving people toward the exit signs.

Their first visitor was a famous athlete, a huge man with a tree trunk for a neck. His head was shaved so close there was only a light nap, no heavier than a day's growth, and he was dressed in a ridiculous short-sleeved suit, his arms blasted into obscenity by steroids. He had a tiny woman by his side. Jurgen greeted this man as though he were a relative, grinning and pumping the puffy hand. Mind you, Jurgen did know many athletes, maintaining his enthusiasm about sports, especially soccer and hockey. So Rudolfo was willing to dismiss this display of friendliness. He himself posed beside the tiny woman, slipped a hand around her minuscule waist and was surprised to feel her trembling ever so slightly. Miranda worked the button on the Polaroid; a flashbulb popped.

Next up, a television actor. Rudolfo knew he was a television actor because Samson greeted the approach of television stars with excitement, pulling forward and straining his bejewelled lead. The television actors often found this disquieting, as this one did, stopping dead in his tracks and flinching spastically, his hands flying like little birds in a hurricane, trying to protect all vital organs, body parts and hair. "No worries," Rudolfo said. "Samson won't bite." Which, indeed, he wouldn't. Samson had only bitten a human being once. Since that day he had been gentle and civilized, or so he fancied, although Samson knew at the bottom of his pale heart that he was simply cowardly and pitiful.

The television actor—who had no one with him, which was a little odd; most of these boys usually came equipped with a woman so as to throw particularly stupid *Personality* magazine reporters off the trail—came forward and shook first Rudolfo's hand, then Jurgen's. "I'm still shaking," the television actor whispered. "I've never seen anything like it." Jurgen kissed the boy on the cheek. This kiss was alarming, of course, but still not as unsettling as the grin Jurgen was dealing out. Surely this would have been a good moment for his Sorceror's look, where he set his jaw firmly, affecting the whole of his head, squaring up the corners. The flashbulb popped and the television actor withdrew.

It was at this point, as a Supreme Court judge and his wife

drew near, that Rudolfo noticed the odd man lurking in the corner. Security surely wouldn't have let such a bizarre creature into the dressing room. Jurgen and Rudolfo often received death threats or menacing statements, invariably cryptic because they'd been written by idiots. DIE, SPONG OF STAN was one that had puzzled them for weeks. Miranda had solved that one, suggesting that the message meant "spawn" ("spong" because that's what the moron thought the word was) "of Satan" (the dimwit forgetting that important "a" in the passion of the moment).

When the aged Supreme Court judge took his hand and made it tremble in consort with his own, Rudolfo merely muttered, "*Danke, ja,*" keeping his eye on the odd creature who was suddenly drawing nearer. He was wrapped in tulle and muslin; his arms popped free of the diaphanous material naked and pale, tinged with newborn blueness. His head was bald, almost blindingly so, except for a topknot, a plume of pure white in the centre of his pate.

The politician's wife kissed Rudolfo on the cheek, pleading for the return of his attention. She clutched his hand between hers and moved it absentmindedly across her body. "Tell me a secret, Rudolfo," she whispered. The woman was far younger than her husband, but then again, everybody was far younger than her husband, who was wattled and melting, his only distinguishing feature being a pair of horn-rimmed spectacles. Rudolfo remembered that he had a stock response to this demand, *tell me a secret*, one he'd paid some young television writer four hundred dollars for, but it would not come to mind. The judge's wife pressed the back of his hand to her breast. Rudolfo smiled and then gasped, because the odd man suddenly loomed not two feet away. The creature had three eyes.

An explosion of light blinded Rudolfo. He heard the soft whirring sound of the Polaroid camera spitting out the image. Miranda handed it to the judge. "Here you go," she said.

Rudolfo blinked frantically until he could see again, and was alarmed to find Jurgen in conversation with the creature. Rudolfo saw now that the centre eye was unmoving, the colours not quite right. This third eye was a tattoo, although to Rudolfo this seemed odder than actually owning one. One of the creature's thin arms suddenly disappeared within his folds and wraps. Rudolfo was suddenly filled with dread, at least, the dread that filled him always suddenly came to a boil. But the creature's arm reappeared, not with a weapon but with a piece of paper. *Parchment* might be a better word; it was yellowed, the edges browned; it seemed as though one could see the individual wood chips that comprised it.

Jurgen took up his pen, a large felt-tip, aimed it at the piece of parchment and signed his name. The creature was some sort of bizarre autograph hound. Rudolfo reached out both hands, one going for Jurgen's pen, one for the piece of paper. Both were suddenly gone, and he was groping through emptiness. There was a flash of light, but of a different magnitude than the previous ones, much brighter and somehow pulsating, as though the light came from a star that was going supernova.

And in that instant, the creature's face appeared in front of Rudolfo, and he saw that the two eyes, the real eyes on either side of the tattoo, were silver and empty of iris and pupil.

When his own eyes cleared (although tiny mites of light swam across his field of vision for days afterward) the creature had vanished and Jurgen was pulling on his arm, saying, "Let's go home."

As they entered *das Haus*, Rudolfo yawned and reached his hands heavenward. He clasped them together over his head and twisted his body languidly. "Okay, chief. Maybe is time for bed."

Jurgen smiled, nodded his head. "Okay, chief."

Rudolfo happily headed off toward the bedroom and had

gone quite some distance, all the way to the Tiki-Tiki Room, when he noticed that Jurgen was not following. He whirled around and bolted back down the hallway. He turned left and descended a flight of stairs, turned right as he landed at the bottom and then raced along the darkened passage. He first heard the boulder rumbling, then could see a patch of light growing small, evaporating. When he reached the Grotto, there was just a sliver of space remaining between the wall and the rock. Through it, Rudolfo saw Jurgen standing in the centre of the circle of ancient books, his arms held high—not in triumph, more in mute announcement, the same way Rudolfo often spread his arms to tell *die Tiere*, "Here I am. Here I am, home."

Rudolfo spun around and kicked at the wall, although what he actually ended up kicking was the snout of an alarmed and deeply wounded Samson. Rudolfo immediately sank to his knees and pulled the cat's head to his breast. "Sorry, Sammy," he whispered, "it's just that…" He couldn't say what. But ever since he'd met Jurgen, all those many years ago, being alone left him bitter and confused.

Jurgen said, "The two of hearts," all those years ago. Rudolfo winked and whispered, "Good trick."

"Come back to my dressing room," said the magician, his face relaxing into a smile. "That's where I keep my smokes."

"Yeah, okay," shrugged Rudolfo, and he followed the magician through the writhing shadows. As they neared a long bar at the far end, a rail-thin figure suddenly flew off a bar stool, shrieking like a giant bird. "Hey, Magic Man!" screamed this being. "What have you got there?"

Again, Rudolfo felt the warming sensation of recognition. Here was a collection of bones held together by the thinnest skin, a translucent wrapping that glowed with the blue of disease. On top of the figure's head was a magnificent headdress, blond curls so ornate that it seemed likely that animals with quite an evolved social order made their home in it. Its dress—adorned with clownish polka dots—was very short, and every movement raised it above the limits of modesty, although only shadow was revealed.

The magician planted his feet and said, "Miss Joe, this is—"

"Rudolfo." Rudolfo reached up and moved the woolen watch cap around on his smooth skull, which he hoped passed for good manners.

"Jurgen and Rudolfo," mused Miss Joe, leaning forward suddenly and kissing both men on the cheek.

They continued on to the dressing room, which was actually a broom closet. It was not a broom closet that had been pressed into service as a dressing room, it was a fully functional broom closet, filled with brooms and mops and a huge metal pail. The magician's gear was shoved in there, including some empty cages.

The magician reached out and picked up a pack of cigarettes from a little shelf piled with sponges and rags. He shook them so that three or four poked their filters out of the opening, pointing them at Rudolfo. "Smoke?"

Rudolfo merely shook his head. He was tempted to caution the magician about the habit, but that would have reminded him of General Bosco, who was violently opposed to any bad habit he himself did not actually have.

The magician shrugged and lit a cigarette, sticking it between his lips so that the smoke greatly increased the fluttering of his eyelids. He put his hands behind his back and produced the two doves, placing them into a cage. They stepped onto the perch and immediately sank their heads out of sight.

"Your birds are sick," Rudolfo noted.

"Hmm." The magician took off his jacket now, loosened his tie, undid the button at his thick neck. "Doves are pretty sickly," he noted. "I have to buy new birds every two weeks."

"The birds die every two weeks?"

The magician shrugged again and continued unbuttoning his shirt. Rudolfo suspected he'd misjudged the situation. Here, apparently, was a take-charge kind of guy, eagerly wrestling out of his clothes. But then he saw that the magician's upper body was heavily bandaged—no, not bandaged. There were thick pieces of duct tape stuck to his body, from which dangled thin wires, springs and strings. The magician began to remove these, grimacing stoically. When done that, he gestured vaguely with a downward motion. "I've got something in my pants."

"Hmmm?"

"If you don't mind."

Jurgen's manners were impeccable, which meant that for Rudolfo they were incomprehensible. He tilted his head. "You have something in your pants?"

"Something big."

"Oh, yeah."

"So if you wouldn't mind turning around."

"Oh!" Rudolfo spun about. A square of sheet metal was hanging on the wall serving as a sort of mirror, although the image it reflected was warped and indistinct. Rudolfo watched the magician work at the zipper and buttons of his trousers, letting them tumble to his knees. He was wearing boxer shorts, which he shimmied down onto his hips. The magician pulled out something white and furry, set it down upon the ground and then pulled up his pants. "Okay."

Rudolfo turned around and saw a small rabbit sitting on the floor, its hind legs quivering. Rudolfo bent over and scooped up the animal, pressing it to his breast. The creature had rancid bunny breath and was emitting irregular little puffs of putrid air. "Let me guess," said Rudolfo. "You leave the rabbit in this little room, where it's cold and dry, except for when you perform, when you stick it down your pants, where it's warm and, um, moist. Right?"

The magician butted his cigarette, pulled out a comb and started rearranging his locks. "Right."

"Why don't you just step on it?"

The comb paused mid-flight, little strands of golden hair clinging to it. "What?"

"It would be much easier to simply step on its head and crush out all its brains. Easier on you, easier on the rabbit."

The magician processed this sentence, and it seemed to take him quite a while. He set his jaw with furious concentration and trained his eyes on Rudolfo. The dark eyelids moved up and down like pistons; the comb remained frozen in the air. After many moments, he asked, quietly, "That's bad for the bunny?"

Rudolfo pulled off his watch cap and nestled the rabbit into its woolen warmth. It was only when he looked up and saw the magician staring at him, startled, that Rudolfo realized what he'd done. "It's a sickness," he said calmly. "I have no hair anywhere on my body."

The magician—who was either very kind or thick as pudding—said, "My uncle Fritz, he's got hair in his *ears*."

Rudolfo smiled, placing his thumb upon the rabbit's head and rubbing gently. "I had hair until I was ten," he began, and he didn't stop speaking for a long time.

Chapter Thirteen

Preston worked Monday evenings, when other Shows were dark. On a good night, he might get as many as fifty people inside the George Theater. Midway through his act he would descend into the seats, a deck of cards clenched in his fat hand. He would ask that the house lights be put on. They would be, after a long moment's delay, Mrs. Antoinette Kingsley complying only grudgingly, as she didn't feel the flipping of electric switches was part of her job description.

On this night—like all nights—Preston raised the cards into the air and said, "This is just an ordinary deck of cards. They aren't rigged or gaffed. They're not strippers. They're not marked. It's not a Svengali deck. Just an ordinary pack of blue-backed Bees. But you don't have to take my word for it. Probably half the people in here are magicians. So let's just have these cards checked by—"

Preston glanced around at the small crowd, his brow only slightly lifted, his eyes struggling upwards. His attention was caught, his head stopping so abruptly that upper vertebrae gave forth audible cracks. "Oh, hey," he muttered. "I guess we could have this deck checked out by the world-famous Kaz."

Kaz sat in an aisle seat, sunk low, his long legs stretched out in front. His bony hands were laced over his chest, his chin nestled on his clavicle. When his name was mentioned, the audience erupted into applause. Kaz—very atypically—did not respond, other than making a tiny grimace, as if the sound hurt his ears. He merely extended a hand, turning up the palm to receive the cards.

As Preston passed him the deck, Kaz said quietly, "Hey, Preston. I'm suing your fat ass," and sprang suddenly to his feet. Preston supposed that he'd meant the action to be dramatic, but Kaz's forte did not lie in the physical realm. He bolted too far forward, smashing his hips into the chairback in front. He folded up, bent backwards to correct and landed once more in his seat. Then he rose again, this time with greater care. "Ladies and gentlemen," he said, turning around so that he could be seen by more of the little crowd, "I believe this deck is none of those things he says it isn't."

"Hey, Kaz," put in Preston, "nice sentence." The crack got a little chuckle.

"But you have to be careful around guys like Preston. Maybe he left something out. For example, he might have a locator card in here. That would be a card shaved just a little bit shorter than the rest, so Preston could find it any time he wanted just by running his fingertips over the end of the deck like this…" Kaz demonstrated, once, twice, again. Then he shrugged and handed back the deck. "Ordinary deck of cards," he pronounced.

"All that palaver," mumbled Preston, "and he couldn't even find it." He shuffled the deck a few times, trying to think of what to do. Not about Kaz and his silly threat to sue—*fuck Kaz and the elephant he rides offstage on*—but this portion of the show was unplanned. He simply did five or six card tricks with various members of the audience. He knew thousands of card tricks—he likely knew more than any other human being on the planet—so they changed from night to night, according to his mood or whim. "Here's a good one," he said aloud, selecting an audience member—in this case a small man who sat across the aisle from Kaz—and fanning the cards under his nose.

"Did you hear me?" whispered Kaz as Preston turned his back.

"Pick a card." As the man made his selection, Preston executed a small half-turn and demanded, "Sue me for what, Kaz?"

"Collusion."

"Yes, well done, sir." Preston, relieved to see that the man had taken the force card, said, "I'll turn my back, you show the face to the people around you."

Now Preston could direct the full bloodshot scorn of his eyeballs at the world-famous Kaz. "What the hell are you talking about, Kaz?"

"You and those two German faggots are buddy-buddy-buddy."

"Rudolfo," countered Preston, "is Swiss." He spun back to the small man. "Now, look. I'm going to give you the rest of the deck. Put your card back in and shuffle them."

"See?" hissed Kaz behind his back. "You *know* that. Rudolfo is Swiss; only someone very close to them would know that. And when that someone was involved in what was supposed to be a fair auction—"

"Have you shuffled the cards well, sir? Very good. Now go through the deck and find me your selected card."

"We've been watching you," said Kaz. He was breathing very heavily, creating a huge cloud of rancid effluvium. "You went and saw their show. You never came to see my show."

Preston suddenly felt very sorry for Kaz, who could be wounded by such a small thing. If he hadn't been in front of such an audience, Preston would have told Kaz the truth, as much of the truth as he knew. Kaz might have gone away happy and contented.

"I can't find the card," giggled the small man.

"Can't find it? What the hell did you do with it?"

"I don't know," the small man said with effort, now almost consumed by giggles. "It's just not there."

"You lost the card?"

"I guess so," agreed the small man.

"Then you owe me two-and-a-half bucks. Because a fifty-one card deck is useless. What card was it, anyway?"

"The eight of spades."

"Damn," said Preston. "That's one of my favourite cards."

"Sure," whispered Kaz, "'cause it's the one you palmed off."

"Ladies and gentlemen," said Preston loudly. "I know what you're thinking. You're thinking, hey, aren't magicians bound by a code of brotherhood? Well, I want you to know that Kaz and I are actually in—what was that word?—*collusion*. Accusing me of palming off that card was classic misdirection. Because, you know where that eight of spades is right now? It's in his underwear."

"Bullshit," sniped Kaz.

"Seriously."

"*I* couldn't even have put that card in my underwear."

Preston shrugged modestly. "What can I tell you? That's where it is."

Kaz rose from his seat, a skeptical look drawing his face even longer, and ran his thin hand down the back of his tight jeans. He rummaged around for the briefest of moments, and then withdrew his hand. The eight of spades was caught between the tips of his first and second fingers.

"Kaz, ladies and gentlemen!" shouted Preston, gesticulating in the general direction of the gaunt conjuror with halitosis. The people applauded, so Kaz had no choice but to bow deeply, which he did with all the grace of a puppet with snapped strings.

He then fled the theatre, leaving behind only lingering fumes.

"There goes," said Preston to the audience, "one very talented—and strange—guy."

Rudolfo had to revise his sleep deprivation theory. Jurgen didn't suffer from sleeplessness. Jurgen got *no* sleep, but suffered no ill effects. He seemed somehow to have lost his need for sleep. For the past few nights Rudolfo had woken up at all hours—once as early as three-fifteen—to find the other half of the circular bed deserted. He had floated dreamily down to the kitchen, feigning an interest in a midnight snack, filching a carrot out of the crisper, perhaps an apple or banana. Chewing peacefully (the ghostly white spectre Samson walking silently at his heels) Rudolfo had drifted through the mansion. He'd made no special effort to pass by the Grotto, but he knew that if he continued drifting, he would do so soon enough. And always the remote-controlled boulder was rolled into place, and a little light from inside bled slightly around its hulking shape.

One night Rudolfo stood stock still some ten feet away from the Grotto's boulder and was overcome with shivering. His breath came out in short gasps and his skin, every square inch of it, prickled and beaded with sweat. Jurgen must be sick.

Preston's Show was going very well, indeed. He was somehow buoyed, made cocky, by the encounter with Kaz. Preston didn't consider himself a competitive man. He disdained the Magic Olympics, for example. He thought the event was adolescent at best, likely harmful to the craft, so he never went even though it was held in his hometown. But if he did, he knew he would surely kick some international butt. The truth of the matter is that Preston wasn't competitive because he knew he was the best, in his own small way.

So Preston did some tricks he didn't always do, stuff that

even he found a little difficult. Stuff that required a gambler's confident recklessness, counting off three cards when he was really clutching twenty, making blind forces, disregarding sight-lines so that—were he not the best and his fingers the quickest—all of the sleights could be detected.

"Okay," said Preston, truing the cards on his little production table. "I need another volunteer from the audience."

He watched arms flower upwards. He eliminated the hairy ones first of all. He disregarded the ones with fat drooping beneath the muscle. He generally tried to pick a fairly good-looking arm, hoping that someone fairly good-looking was attached to it.

On this night, no particular arm seemed quite the ticket. Preston took much longer with the selection than he should have. Good thing he had nothing but scorn for his father's corn-ball and antiquated theories of Entertainment. *Alacrity*, that's what Preston the Magnificent had always counselled. His son appraised each arm with some care, looking for, well, he didn't know what. But there was no denying the sensation of unique-ness that infused the night, an ember of excitement in his tummy where there had been nothing previously.

Then the arm appeared, unfolding with mechanical preci-sion, as if controlled by levers and pulleys. When it was fully extended, its fingers blossomed into a little bouquet, long thin petals tipped with golden nails. Preston lifted the deck of cards and motioned vaguely in the direction of the arm.

The arm rocketed upwards then, and in its wake there came a shoulder, a breast, a hip. "You," Preston grunted, and such was the brilliance of the smile that Miranda returned that the heads in the audience snapped back, startled.

"Oh, say, look who has come! Long see, no time." Rudolfo stepped back into the foyer and allowed Dr. Merdam to enter. He had to move back quite a bit because Merdam weighed over four hundred pounds.

Despite the fact that the audience at the Abraxas had an average weight of well over two hundred pounds, Rudolfo disliked fat people, generally. But Dr. Merdam was different, because in some peculiar way, he didn't *seem* fat. He gave the illusion of daintiness, in this instance executing a little half-turn so he could fit through the doorway and then shuffling through with tiny balletic minces. He wore a dark suit, as ever, a plain white shirt and a florid bow tie. All remarkably clean; Dr. Merdam appeared always to be dressed in new clothes. He was a very handsome man, despite the roundness of his face, an olive-skinned beauty with large dark eyes and full lips.

"Hello, Rudolfo," he said. "You seem surprised to see me. I thought we had an appointment."

Rudolfo's eyes widened briefly; he closed his mouth so tightly his thin lips blanched.

"You know," Dr. Merdam said, "you don't look at all well." Another remarkable thing about the doctor was that despite carting around all that extra weight under the heartless Nevadan sun, he didn't sweat. He often—as he did now—removed a handkerchief from his breast pocket to pat daintily at his upper lip, but this seemed to be more emotionally palliative than anything else, as though the handkerchief were laced with his mother's own perfume.

"Doc," said Rudolfo with soft urgency, "keep a button on the yapper."

The doctor, a little alarmed, turned and waltzed daintily toward the sunken living room, tiny animals nipping at his polished heels.

"Jurgen!" Rudolfo bellowed. "Guess what? Today is an appointment to be medically examined which we have made many weeks ago and completely all forgotten about!"

Merdam executed a nimble glissade down the short flight of stairs. The animals, far less graceful in comparison, tumbled off the top riser.

Rudolfo actually had quite a bit to do with Dr. Merdam's gracefulness, although he'd forgotten this. When they'd first met, years ago, Merdam had been merely chunky, a perspiring man who couldn't keep his shirt tucked in properly. Rudolfo had gone to visit his office complaining about a strange pain in his left shoulder, a snarling bite that chewed at the muscle and sinew whenever he executed the military press.

These were the days before the Abraxas Hotel. These were the days when Jurgen and Rudolfo did only ten minutes between bare-breasted bubble-bottomed showgirls at the hotels and motels on the fringes of Vegas, for which they received exactly one hundred dollars per night. These circumstances embittered the duo, because just a few months previously they had been a huge sensation in Paris, so much so that when something truly weird occurred, your average Parisian was likely to comment, *"Mais, c'est trés Jurgen et Rudolfo!"* In Las Vegas they rented a single room in a motel that had the very strange name of Tophet—it was actually "Top of the Town," but several of the neon bulbs were blown—where they lived with Samson, three vermilion flycatchers, a snowy egret, a crimson stilt and an overweight rabbit.

Jurgen spent his days sitting on the edge of the bed, his hands folded in a genteel manner, staring forlornly at the ghostly images produced by the antique television set in their room. He watched American football and American baseball, even though he found it all very baffling. Occasionally he would pick up a deck of cards or a stack of coins and practise, but his enthusiasm was gone. He would lay the stuff aside and refocus his fuzzy attention on the television screen. When the crowds cheered, Jurgen would produce a small, hollow grunt.

Rudolfo rather desperately cooked up a surfeit of ambition and enthusiasm, simply to battle the ennui that threatened to devour them. He first found an affordable gymnasium. It was called Shecky's Olympus and was buried at the intersection of Paradise Road and Sahara Avenue. You pushed through a door at street level and then descended an almost endless staircase. With each step the temperature went up a degree, the miasma of sweat becoming more acrid and stinging. At the bottom was a huge room full of medieval torture devices. The people working them were stripped down to the barest of ribbons, worn more to bind potential hernias than to cover body parts. These people were extremely serious. General Bosco had been single-minded and industrious, but compared to these people he was a dabbler. Bosco would hunker under the bar and do squats, and he would howl and scream and when he finished his face would be slick with tears and his thighs and hams would be quivering. These people didn't howl, as a rule, which meant that one could hear the muscle tissue ripping apart. Sets were stopped, most often, not because they were done, but because the lifter had passed out, vomited or ruptured an internal organ.

Rudolfo noticed that all of these people had strange black boxes strapped to their sides; a thin cord led from there to plugs, little foam-covered stones that they popped into their ears. They were tape players, not nearly so common back then. Everyone would listen with intense concentration and were very hard to distract, which meant that Rudolfo found it difficult to find anyone to spot him.

There was one non-maniacal member, a very tall and beautiful woman who would descend into the sweat-bowels for the purposes of toning only. This woman would straddle a preacher's bench, curl her fingers around the steel bar and begin to lift. One could actually watch the biceps enlarge, inflated as though by a foot pump. The skin would begin to glisten, light and dark would play in the newly formed hollows. This woman would work a few major groups and then, having barely raised a sweat, would nod vaguely in the direction of the lifters and disappear.

This woman did not wear a headset; she seemed to prefer to accompany her exercise with her own humming, sometimes quietly but mournfully lowing out words. Rudolfo had a hunch this was country-and-western music, because the few words he recognized were all the names of animals. Anyway, one afternoon their activities brought them into proximity, Rudolfo standing patiently near the incline bench as this woman puffed up her pectorals. By this time the two had smiled at each other on a handful of occasions. When she straightened out, Rudolfo touched the brim of his hat—he wore a California Angels baseball cap to keep his hairpiece in place—and said, "Hi, baby."

The woman jumped off the bench. "How are you doing?"

"Abdominals."

"No," said this woman, pulling at her leotard, "that's *what are you doing? How are you doing* is like *fine* and that."

"Oh, *ja*. Dunky-hoary."

"Me, too." The woman gesticulated at the incline bench. She had a lovely manner of gesticulation. "Need a spot?" she asked.

Rudolfo nodded and eagerly added plates to the bar. He lay down, hooking his feet under the rollers so as not to slide away. He did his set and, before the final two repetitions, jerked his head ever so slightly. The woman wrapped her hand around the bar, whispering, "Upsadaisy." When he was done, Rudolfo sat up, wiped away a little bead of sweat and asked, "You know all these people with little machines on their heads?"

"Sure."

"Vot are they listen to?"

"Oh, right. What's his name, Tony Anthony or something. You know, *The Power of One*." The woman pointed at her own head. "How to overcome adversity and—"

Rudolfo interrupted here. "Ad-ver-sity?" he pronounced carefully.

"Shit, basically," the woman said, motioning for Rudolfo to clear the incline bench and lying down herself. "How to shovel shit without getting your hands dirty." She curled her fingers around the bar and pushed.

"Whoa, baby," said Rudolfo, although not by way of encouragement. "You didn't take off plates." The woman was pressing sixty more pounds than she'd done previously.

"Oh, don't worry," she answered, her voice just slightly strained. "The Bod can handle it."

Rudolfo actually cut his routine short, passing over much-needed work on his calf and thigh muscles, in order to go and buy a little tape player and Tony Anthony's tape. Actually, there were about forty Tony Anthony tapes, but after purchasing the cassette player, Rudolfo could only afford one. He selected the first, and apparently the best-selling, which was called only *YOU!* On the cover of the little box, Tony Anthony pointed his finger with alarming directness. His mouth was curled into the little circle that would come with saying "You!"

Anyway, it was three weeks later that the pain came to Rudolfo's shoulder. He got Dr. Merdam's name from the woman at the gymnasium. The woman had no professional relationship with this doctor—the Bod, she maintained, simply never broke down—but she lived in the building where he kept offices. So that was how Rudolfo met both Miranda and Dr. Merdam— Merdam, by the way, has for the last half hour been in the Grotto, poking at a naked Jurgen Schubert—and at his first appointment Rudolfo had unplugged his ears and offered the little foam stones to the chubby man. "Dig this, Doc," he muttered.

It was a part of Tony Anthony's weight-loss regimen that one ideate oneself as a slim person. *Create the person within*, was part of the litany, *then without*. This aspect appealed immensely to Melwood Merdam, much more so than the actual restrictions of caloric intake. He abandoned those after a few days, although he continued to ideate himself as a slim person. More than slim, he pictured himself as tiny, elfin, a creature so insubstantial he could be knocked over by a strong wind. Over the next few years he put on weight at an alarming rate, but he never lost this internal picture of himself, and that is why he now came reeling out of the Grotto with the nimble peppiness of a song-and-dance man.

"Yes, well," said Dr. Merdam. "He is, er, healthy."

"Ur-healthy. What does this mean?"

"He is healthy. He is fine."

Rudolfo was both relieved and disquieted, because the mystery was back, sitting in the corner like a mooncalf. "Okay. A bunch of thanks, Doc."

"There *is* one thing that is a little odd," mentioned Dr. Merdam. He picked up an animal from the carpet—it was a civet but the doctor evidently thought it was a cat, chucking the creature under the chin, rubbing the pointed skull between the ears. "He is somewhat underweight."

"Jurgen?" Rudolfo's eyebrows—etched carefully with make-up pencil—crawled up his forehead. "But I keep telling him he's getting poodgy."

"How much would you say he weighs?"

"One seventy, one seventy-five?"

Dr. Merdam nodded. "That would have been my guess, too." He set the civet back on the ground and spoke as he straightened up. "One forty-seven."

"*Was?*"

"I checked the scales. Twice. He weighs one hundred and forty-seven pounds. Very odd. But aside from that, he seems right as rain."

Rudolfo had heard that expression before, and always found

it baffling. It seemed to make sense, now, *right as rain*, right as water falling from heaven and making everything earthbound wet and shivering cold.

Preston had never worked with an assistant. Well, once he had, as a very young man of seventeen. He'd gotten work at a convention, and the contractor had implied that it might be nice if he had an assistant. "These people," the man explained, "like *diversion*."

Preston telephoned his father—they lived in the same house, but Preston the Magnificent maintained a separate apartment in the basement, handy to the wine cellar.

"Hello, sir. I need an assistant," said Preston, who back then still billed himself as The Amazing Presto.

"Why?" demanded his father. "Whatever are you doing up there?"

"I'm doing a convention next week," he explained, sullenly. Preston was sullen because he knew his father was befuddled and confused, more befuddled than could be explained by his constant imbibition of Chablis.

"An assemblage," said Preston the Magnificent. "A congregation."

"Yeah."

"Say no more," commanded Preston's father, hanging up abruptly.

It was a Convention of Rendering House Operators. These people, having no real business to discuss, having attended a few brief seminars relating to new methods of disposing of animal carcasses, all got blind drunk. They had a huge banquet dinner where they handed out awards to each other, prizes for cleanliness and efficiency. Then the Master of Ceremonies introduced The Amazing Presto and he walked onstage to a chorus of jeers and catcalls.

The Amazing Presto did a few tricks, pulling playing cards out of thin air, making perfect-circle fans, and then beating these lightly until a brilliant white dove materialized. The Rendering House Operators booed, as if they'd seen this all done better. Which they hadn't, of course, because Preston was already the best. He was an awkward, hulking teenager, splay-footed and pear-shaped, and his face was rippled with acne, but he was already the finest mechanic in the business. Even the old guard acknowledged this, everyone except his father, who had never come to see him perform.

The Amazing Presto turned to the wings and extended his hand, silently beckoning the assistant his father had sent. Viv, for that was her name, rushed onstage with admirable alacrity. Suddenly the crowd was applauding as eagerly as they'd booed. Their enthusiasm was caused by an apparent plethora of body parts and a comparative absence of costume. As she walked toward Preston she turned her upper body and extended her arms, which pulled her breasts out of the little sequined cups. The Amazing Presto blushed deeply on her behalf, but Viv herself didn't mind, even grinned at the ensuing roar of approval. She spun around then and waggled her bottom, which was costumed with a piece of ribbon. Viv even stopped in order to give her keester a licentious rotation. The Rendering House Operators cheered until they choked, several of them fainting, a couple of the older ones actually succumbing to heart attacks. Viv continued on her way then, and when she reached The Amazing Presto she beamed widely and stuffed her breasts back into the cups. Preston stared at her, which Viv assumed had to do with the breast-stuffing, so she winked and stuck out her tongue playfully. Truly, though, Preston was wondering how she could have failed to do the simple task assigned to her. For walking onstage was not the point, no matter with what ecdysiastic grace it had been accomplished; no, Viv was supposed to fetch the production table. Without it, the act would grind to a halt, which it did. The boos and jeers flew up like a flock of pigeons alarmed by a car-honk. The Amazing Presto stormed offstage then, to get the damned apparatus himself, but Viv interpreted this as handing over the entertainment baton and quickly peeled off what little costume she wore. Preston returned with the production table but Viv was already lying on her back with her feet stuck up in the air. The Rendering House Operators were stupified and reverential.

The Amazing Presto resolved never to have an assistant again, although as Miranda stood beside him on the stage he wondered idly if he shouldn't rethink that. Preston was shuffling cards, explaining what was about to happen, but part of his mind was observing that Miranda was contributing a lot of, what would be the word, *intangibles.* For example, just a slight incline of her head evidenced a keen but polite interest that the audience could share in, perhaps even emulate. "So, I'm going to show you these cards," said Preston. "Look at them and pick one. Just think of it, don't say it out loud."

Preston pointed the faces toward Miranda and pushed the cards from one hand to another. He gazed into her eyes, which made his fingers tremble slightly, and he watched the tiny flickering of her irises, which were as blue as the sky above a frozen prairie. Miranda said, "Okay," and Preston the Adequate feared that for the first time in his professional life, he'd fucked up big time, because he didn't know if Miranda's eyes had lingered on the right card or not. He had no choice but to continue. He stuffed the cards back into their case and then said, "Okay. Name your card."

"Queen of hearts."

"Yeah." Preston the Adequate bit his bottom lip and tried to think of what to do next. Because the cardcase in his hand was rigged to eject—with considerable force and dramatic impact—

the four of diamonds.

"Hey!" said Miranda, her eyes widening with surprise. "You sneak!" she chided, pulling the elasticized waistband of her sweatpants away from her body. Preston the Adequate snuck a quick peek. He spied athletic-looking undergarments. Miranda slipped her hand into them. "What gives?" wondered Miranda aloud, pulling her hand back out with the queen of hearts held gingerly between two long and flawless fingers. She handed the card to Preston and touched his elbow gently but significantly, making him turn so that he might acknowledge the audience's applause.

They both made deep bows.

Clothes.

Rudolfo floats into his bedroom, pulling open the huge closet door with the elaborate "R" carved into the oak.

Across the room is another door, this one bearing a rococo "J."

Between the two sits the huge and hideous cabinet. Rudolfo chooses not to look at it, ignoring it as though it were an old, crazy woman.

He rushes into his walk-in closet and picks an outfit, in this case a jumpsuit the colour of bruised fruit. He slips it on.

The jumpsuit seems to have been made for someone else, and, of course, it was. It was made for a man with an inflated upper body, and a lower half mortified into insect-like tininess. Now the suit flaps over his chest and shoulders; Rudolfo's arms are lost in the sleeves. The rest is like ground meat in sausage casing.

There are animals hiding in the closet. Rudolfo sees them—a couple of bushbabies, an Egyptian mongoose—and begins to whistle, to put them at their ease. But his lips are dry and the lullaby amounts to nothing more than a couple of dusty puffs.

And then he drifts down hallways, staring straight ahead.

When the doorbell chimes once more—"Aiutavo il destino…"—Rudolfo launches himself toward the kitchen. He has figured out that it is Hallowe'en and, even though the realization sickens him, actually studs his skin with foul-smelling beads of sweat, he is willing to play along. He locates what he can in the kitchen and then heads for the front door. "E cerca, cerca," sound the chimes insistently.

Rudolfo wrestles the door open. The child is disguised as a woman, a tall woman with glorious breasts. "Nice outfit," says Rudolfo, and *before the child can blurt out, "Trick or treat," Rudolfo flings the treat at her.*

The meat, red and rancid, bounces from her face, leaving behind a stain of blood.

Miranda whispers, "Hiya."

Chapter Fourteen

At first Rudolfo found Jurgen very complicated and mysterious, because he was looking at him through a veil of infatuation. Before he realized that Jurgen was, well, simple, he puzzled over his personality and penchants. For example, Jurgen liked to discuss football. Between sets they would sit at the long bar—Miss Joe hovering behind—and Jurgen would keep up a one-sided conversation concerning the sport. "I think *Bayern München* is pretty well unbeatable this season, especially with Sepp Maier in the net." For a long while Rudolfo was certain that this was all some code he could not work out, that meaning laced and impregnated statements like: "Franz Beckenbauer, Bertie Vogts, who could stop them?"

When it dawned on him that Jurgen meant no more than he'd stated, Rudolfo looked for meaning in the accompanying gestures. Jurgen typically sat staring straight ahead. He'd drink beer, virtually inhaling it, three or four sips to drain a Pilsner glass. (This, of course, only after he was finished for the evening.)

He smoked in those days, Revals, and Rudolfo wondered if the lighting of the smoke was significant. Jurgen would often stop mid-sentence in order to do this, leaving a strange half sentence sitting there awkwardly. He would exhale heavily, moving his mouth so that the thin stream of smoke circled and roved like a searchlight.

During this time, the enchanted first month, Rudolfo's career as a beggar suffered. For one thing, he simply wasn't putting in the hours. He would spend most of the night at Miss Joe's—which remained open until five or six in the morning—and then he would crawl off to his seedy hotel room. This room was in the basement and was, Rudolfo suspected, usually leased to vampires. Rudolfo felt very like a vampire in those days. Sometimes dawn would catch him as he stumbled through the streets of Münich, and he'd gasp and whimper, screwing his hands into his eye sockets. Mostly he felt like a vampire because of the way he'd cup his chin and stare at the young man babbling on about football. He feigned interest, he smiled and nodded and made soft noises, but basically he was just waiting for that moment when he could bite down and taste blood.

At any rate, by the time Rudolfo did get to bed he'd collapse into a dark sleep. When his eyes fluttered open, it would be late afternoon and Samson would be sitting in the corner staring daggers. Rudolfo would leap out of the grimy bed and drag the beast out to the street corner, and the two would put in three or four hours, and then Rudolfo would take Samson back to the hotel room and leave for Miss Joe's.

Samson was miserable, feeling abandoned and betrayed. The hotel room had a television set. Actually, it had five, because the room was used for storage, junky old antiques that had been ripped out of the much more livable rooms upstairs. The albino leopard learnt how to turn them on, although it was tricky, because the knobs were little and could only be caught and worked with the flatter teeth well to the side of his mouth. He would get all five going at once, even though three of them usually showed nothing but snow, and he would lie in the middle of the room and turn his head languidly from set to set, as though keeping track of his harem and offspring.

Rudolfo, over at Miss Joe's, showed signs of financial strain. When it came time to pay for Jurgen's beer—Jurgen, preoccupied as he was with football, never offered to pay for one himself—Rudolfo would dump handfuls of coin onto the bar and pick out pfennigs carefully. Miss Joe, noting this, one night asked, "Would you like to make a little money?"

Rudolfo merely grunted. Truth to be told, Rudolfo didn't care for Miss Joe, not in those first days. It wasn't that he was frightened or confused by Miss Joe, not after all those years with the addled Anna Thielmann—well, that's exactly the point, isn't it? On more than one occasion Rudolfo found himself on the verge of ordering, "*Nach ein bier, Mutti.*" So on this occasion he merely grunted, allowing it to be interpreted however Miss Joe wished.

"Here's the thing, Rudolfo." Miss Joe folded long brittle arms across the bar and collapsed upon them. The wig, a towering burial cairn, pitched forward and smote Rudolfo upon the head.

Over on the stage, Jurgen was going through his routine. This was the word that Rudolfo used, not *show* or *act* but *routine*, because the lack of variation was astounding. Even the doves, despite being healthier due to Rudolfo's intervention, behaved always in the exactly the same manner, fluttering out from behind the fans, flapping four times, tumbling to the ground. And given that the clientele was mostly the same night after night, Jurgen's act became routine very quickly. Several people left the club as soon as he mounted the little stage. That was, in effect, Jurgen's function, although Miss Joe kept up the fiction that the

Chaser was the big star. Miss Joe even gave Jurgen a raise, not that he'd asked for it or deserved it in any way.

"Here's the thing, Rudolfo." One good thing about Miss Joe, she never took liberties with his name, never called him *Rudy*, the name of the long-haired boy who had shot General Bosco in the heart. "Karl—you know Karl, the dark one with the big mole on his forehead?—well, he has larked off to America, to fucking Cincinnati for Christ's sake, where his uncle operates a rendering house, so bye-bye Karl, which leaves me a little in *el lurcho*, because he at least had a sense of fucking rhythm even if his only dance move was the Buttock Clench-and-Release. Though, I must say, it is a crowd pleaser. So, I'm shy to the tune of one Go-Go Boy. What do you say?"

Rudolfo accepted without hesitation, or contemplation, and became an immediate success. Although it had been months since he'd been inside a gymnasium, his body was still exaggerated by muscle and his beggar's hunger had devoured much of the subcutaneous fat. His stomach was especially impressive, because Rudolfo did sit-ups constantly, that being an exercise he could, and would, do anywhere. Rudolfo would do them on the street corner, when the pedestrian traffic was distant and infrequent. He would command Samson to sleep, and the boot-blackened beast would collapse with appalling servitude. Rudolfo would then lie down on the pavement, hook his toes under Samson's belly and begin an agonizing series of crunches. The result of all this was a little rippled oval in the centre of Rudolfo's being. Miss Joe framed it nicely with his costume, a pouchy G-string and a truncated fishnet singlet. Of course, Rudolfo lost these early in the set, peeling them off so that the patrons could admire, without obstruction, his physique.

Mind you, his popularity was not based on looks alone. There was something in his manner that made him a favourite at Miss Joe's, something to do with his circus training. All of his

gestures were outsized and ridiculously self-aggrandizing, because, as General Bosco had told him constantly, you play to
the benches at the back of the tent. So Rudolfo would spread his
arms wide, stretching the fingers until the tendons connecting
them almost sounded with pain. He would smile so hard that his
neck became laced with suspension-bridge cabling. And when he
was in motion, he became, once more, a lion tamer, in a cage of
invisible cats; every movement was imbued with menace and
authority.

And there was his hairlessness, too, which polished his
body and made even the weak light at Miss Joe's explode in all
directions.

So Rudolfo would finish every dance to an ebullition of
applause rarely heard at the seedy shadowed nightclub. He would
leap off the stage and race to the back of the bar, barely able to
breathe, his heart all twitchy and spasmodic. There Jurgen would
be, pulling a bottle of beer out from between thick lips. "You
know," he would say, drawing deeply on his cigarette, "I don't
think Stuttgart will make it even into the semi-finals."

As Rudolfo's status ascended, Jurgen's stalled on a remote
road where no one even noticed or cared. The audience passed
from indifference into, well, a more profound kind of indifference, one with physical manifestations. Some patrons would
immediately fall asleep. Others would rise and attend to business
long neglected. The lineup at the washroom during Jurgen's set
snaked through the little round tables and almost out the door.
Jurgen didn't seem to notice. He stood unreasonably erect, his
complicated hair balanced perfectly atop his head.

One day Jurgen said, "I've got us a couple of girls for after."
Rudolfo was in the process of stuffing things into the little
G-string, of climbing strenuously into the fishnet singlet.
"What?" he demanded.

"Girls," said Jurgen. He, too, was preparing for performance. He ran a filament, thin as spiderwebbing, through a pocket, up through the waist, into the sleeve of his shirt. "Good-looking girls," he stated flatly. "Big tits."

They met the girls in a tavern, very late at night. Their names were Monica and Monique. Actually, they explained, speaking together and performing an elaborate ritual if they should happen to speak the same word at the same time, both of the girls were named Monica, but they were roommates, so they had tossed a coin and one took the more Gaulish version. As if to live up to this, Monique wore a dark, pointy brassiere that lingered menacingly beneath her white sweater. She wore hot pants and long boots. Her hair swept like a blade across her face, covering features that were small and budlike. Monica was more Germanic, a large girl, heavily muscled from the two miles she swam daily. (Jurgen had encountered her at the pool. He swam only occasionally, but when he did, it was with relentless determination.) Monica's hair was black and short. She wore straightforward clothes, but didn't seem to wear enough of them. Those that she did wear weren't up to the task of coverage or protection from the elements. Her short skirt rode up her thighs, and when she sat down her panties were plainly visible. Her sweater gaped around the armholes and folded back above her stomach. Her breasts, smoothed and tightened by the swimming, didn't need a bra.

She was clearly Jurgen's favourite. Rudolfo knew this because Jurgen chose to sit down beside her. That was the only clue. Jurgen didn't speak to either girl, really. He ordered some food for them, meats and pastries that they clearly didn't want, and every ten minutes or so he would flip open his pack of Revals and stab at them with cigarettes. Neither girl smoked, although Monique finally gave in and had one. Otherwise, Jurgen remained silent, staring at the other patrons cautiously, as though he suspected that an assassin lurked amongst them.

So Rudolfo engaged them in conversation as best he could, although the oddness of his life didn't allow for much of a connection to other people. Monique, for example, frequently announced how much she loved movies. Rudolfo had never seen one. General Bosco, he recalled, had once taken him into a small dark room where images flickered upon an uncovered wall; images of men and women, greyly naked, people intent on devouring each other. Rudolfo intuited that Monique was speaking of a whole other experience. He pressed her about it, asking that she tell the stories. Monique complied, and showed an aptitude for condensing complicated narratives into five or six short sentences, but finally she decided that Rudolfo was strange and fell silent. Monica's life was informed by athleticism, so Rudolfo asked how much weight she could bench press, how big a load she carried during squats. Each of Rudolfo's questions served to make Monica feel monstrous and outgrown. She shrivelled up, drawing in her broad shoulders and sinking her chin toward her chest. That's how the date proceeded, in silence, broken occasionally by Jurgen's irritating, "Anybody want a smoke?"

Despite this, Jurgen and Rudolfo were invited back to the girls' apartment. Monica took Jurgen by the hand and dragged him off to her bedroom. Monique, for whatever reason, didn't take Rudolfo to hers, even though she did point toward the door. Instead she sat Rudolfo down on the sofa in the living room, and began an amateurish striptease, peeling off the long white boots and hot pants. Her panties were blood-red. She worked off her brassiere, her hands hidden behind her back, her elbows thrust so far forward that Rudolfo involuntarily grimaced with empathetic pain. Naked, Monique flitted over to the sofa and sat down rather daintily. Rudolfo felt her left breast, but was slightly alarmed when the nipple flared up. He pulled his hand away. Monique chuckled at this, which deepened Rudolfo's sense of plummeting down a deep well of mystery. Monique undid Rudolfo's zipper and lowered her head; Rudolfo, resigned, leaned back, closed his eyes and lost himself in the sensation.

There was noise coming from Monica's bedroom, grunts and padded thuds. Rudolfo imagined that the two were playing soccer, Monica guarding a makeshift net, Jurgen prowling nakedly before her, suddenly launching the ball with the thick calloused side of his foot. "Score," Rudolfo muttered, just as Monique grunted with some dismay, and the door of Monica's bedroom opened. Jurgen walked out with a fresh cigarette caught between his lips. He was obviously on his way home; Rudolfo stuffed himself back together and ran out after his friend.

They walked in silence, both absorbed with the moon's reflection. It covered the river with light and made the garbage look like sea serpents. Rudolfo wondered where they were going, but soon realized that they were wandering aimlessly. "You know what?" he said suddenly. "I live near here. Do you want a cup of coffee?"

It was a bit unfair, really, to bait the trap that way. It was one thing to play on a serious vice or addiction, it was another to ensnare a fellow because of his affection for caffeine. It was likewise a bit underhanded for Rudolfo to claim that he lived nearby, which was true only in an astronomical sense. Indeed, his squalid apartment was no less than four miles distant. He considered raising an arm and flagging a taxicab, but he felt that that would make Jurgen suspicious and put him on the defensive. At the same time, he half-suspected, half-hoped, that Jurgen knew what was going on. He was sorely tempted to simply state out loud, "The thing of it is, we're both queers. Right?" But he couldn't quite predict Jurgen's response. He would either a) make a tiny grunt of agreement or b) punch Rudolfo until his eyeballs popped out of his skull.

The dawn came, leaking through the bricks, bleeding into

the skies. But the dawn only seemed to come so far; the light ascended and then was stopped dead by a curtain of black. Thunderheads approached the city, the bottom of the formation smooth, as if cut by a heated knife, the upper portions in constant motion, as restless as pitted vipers. Jurgen, much more of an outdoorsman than Rudolfo, nodded toward the clouds and muttered something about bad weather. After his forecast, he smiled slightly, perhaps the first true smile that Rudolfo had ever witnessed. Rudolfo was now even more smitten. "What?" he asked quietly.

"I like storms," answered Jurgen.

"Oh, you do, do you?"

"Sure."

It wasn't much of a conversation, Rudolfo thought, but it was something. They walked in silence and felt the first few raindrops fall.

Then, astoundingly, Jurgen began to speak. "One time, I was hiking, and I got caught out in a storm. A big storm, a terrible storm. I was near the top of a mountain, well I guess it was just a big hill, but it was like a mountain. I was near the top, and lightning was shooting all over. The rain was falling very hard, just pounding down. And in a few seconds my clothes were soaking wet, and very heavy, so I took them off. Then I was naked, on top of the mountain, and the trees were shaking and the ground was rumbling, and all around me was lightning."

"Wasn't that dangerous?"

"Yes, I suppose."

"You might have been hit by lightning."

"Exactly." Jurgen smiled again, and Rudolfo, even though he felt more at sea than ever, made his move. He slipped his hand into Jurgen's, then moved quickly to press his body against the other, knowing that his only chance lay in Jurgen's sensing the urgency and magnitude of his need. He then knew that he'd

184 THE SPIRIT CABINET

made a large miscalculation; Jurgen wrested his hand away and stepped back, bracing for a fight. Rudolfo knew of no other way to react other than as with a big cat, so he continued to press physically, advancing with all the confidence he could muster. He tried soothing words, "Just calm down," but they didn't work; suddenly his nose was popped and bleeding. Rudolfo hadn't even seen Jurgen's fist move.

Neither had Jurgen, mind you, because he hadn't hit him. As far as he could tell, a rock had fallen from the sky and bounced off Rudolfo's face. Jurgen craned his neck to look skyward and was alarmed to see a turbid black cloud filling the sky, as rough and boiling as an ocean hungry for ships, spitting stones. The one that had smacked Rudolfo was merely the vanguard; in its wake came thousands, millions, more, many of them not much smaller. They landed upon the two men with the power and enthusiasm of crazed football hooligans, pummelling them to the ground. Jurgen was the first to right himself, drawing up onto his hands and knees so that his broad back received most of the damage and pain, although it was impossible to tuck his head completely out of the way. Rudolfo was folded over onto his side, desperately trying to protect vulnerable parts of his anatomy. Jurgen placed a hand on Rudolfo's shoulder and pushed with all his might, righting him. The two began to crawl into the darkness, searching for shelter, searching blindly because they could not raise their heads. Stones continued to fall from the heavens.

Jurgen received a blow to the crown that made him nauseous with pain and was in fact on the verge of passing out when he saw that they were not ten feet from a doorway, a deep bricked alcove. He shouted to Rudolfo. The other man was close by, their shoulders butted, but Jurgen suspected that his words were never heard. The roar of hail filled the air, sharp *twoks* as the stones smote the earth, snakelike hissings as they immediately began to melt, dying like so many tiny kamikaze pilots. Rudolfo, fortunately, had spotted the same doorway. He sped up, although this made him less stable. He was put down by a sudden concentration of hailstones, so quickly that his chin cracked on the ground. He bit the end of his tongue off in that moment; his mouth filled with blood. And then he had a very difficult time regaining purchase. Ice-cold balls were everywhere, and the palms of his hand would slip away, his knees would skid and buckle and lay him out once more. But Jurgen managed to turn himself around, aiming his backside at the doorway, and he took hold of Rudolfo, wrapping his fingers around the soaking wet denim of his jacket, pulling the other man in his wake. The two slowly covered the distance, and when they were in the doorway they sprang upwards, trying to push each other into the corner. Both men looked frightful. Jurgen's hairdo had been destroyed utterly. Rudolfo was neater, in that his hat had been knocked off to display his perfect baldness, but blood poured from his mouth and he'd received a black eye, when and how he couldn't remember.

The men hugged each other, and in doing so it became clear that both had erections. There was a kind of laudable defiance in this, an act of affirmation, a final indulgence of the senses, because it seemed almost certain that the world was ending. Rudolfo was the first to move his hand downwards, forcing it through the clamped wet bodies. He began to work Jurgen's penis through the material of his trousers, not at all gently, not at all for Jurgen's benefit. Jurgen's hand then made its descent. He managed to find Rudolfo's zipper; Rudolfo's penis found its own way out. Jurgen took hold like a helicopter pilot takes hold of a joystick, tilting the lever of flesh backwards as though he could get lift and thereby escape the storm.

Hailstones continued to bounce and whiz inside the refuge; many rolled to rest there and soon the two men were knee-deep in ice.

Rudolfo slid his hand down the waist of Jurgen's pants; at the same time his mouth searched out Jurgen's lips. Jurgen resisted this—he pulled his own mouth away and cranked upon Rudolfo's penis brutally, as though exacting punishment. Rudolfo remembered that his mouth was leaking blood, so rested his head on Jurgen's shoulder and spat repeatedly. The blood stained the brick wall. Rudolfo tried to kiss Jurgen again, but Jurgen was having none of it. Rudolfo didn't really care at that moment; it was something he could work on over time, provided he had any time left.

The screaming roar and hiss stopped abruptly—then came snaps and crackles from deep in the ground, as though all the corpses in all the coffins in Münich had decided to pop their old knuckles. The silence that followed seemed almost absolute; the only sound in the world was that of two men breathing heavily, grunting with inarticulate pleasure.

Chapter Fifteen

Rudolfo awoke, sometime deep in the heart of the desert night, and saw to his surprise that Jurgen was for once in the circular bed with him. Jurgen had his back to him and had thrown the bedclothes aside, perhaps in troubled slumber. He was naked.

This was good news, Rudolfo thought, because *das Glied* was as hard as concrete. Not only that, it was in a mood, twitching like a dowsing rod. This coincidence, Jurgen's naked presence and Rudolfo's snarling tumescence, was almost too good to be true. Rudolfo suddenly cautioned himself, perhaps this was a dream, although Rudolfo didn't dream, as far as he knew.

Rudolfo bounced himself across two feet of empty mattress. His penis nudged and burrowed its way between Jurgen's muscled cheeks.

Jurgen stirred slightly; Rudolfo curled his fingers around Jurgen's shoulders, both to steady and to reassure him. It was as he did this, just as he squeezed ever so slightly upon the cool flesh, that Jurgen lit up like an electric bulb. There was a brief but undeniable diffusion of light, spreading throughout the whole of Jurgen's naked body. For a moment, he seemed to be made of glass, and from within came a glowing, a luminescence.

Rudolfo was instantly many inches away. His fingertips were numb. He rolled over onto his back, sighing deeply—because weariness was much easier to cope with than terror—and found himself staring up through the skylight. The heavens above were laced with lightning; a storm raged up in the welkin, gods sporting with each other without affect or influence on the puny mortals lying below. It must have been the lightning that flashed and lit up Jurgen's body, Rudolfo thought. He closed his eyes and tried to return to slumber, vaguely dissatisfied with the explanation.

It would be hard to say at what point Miss Joe and Rudolfo became friends; maybe it would be inaccurate to claim that they ever did. They never exchanged pleasantries, certainly not histories, never feelings, but after a time they assumed great importance in each other's life. Rudolfo became Miss Joe's righthand man; he would orchestrate the evening's talent, coralling the performers toward the stage, he would take the squawking microphone in his hand and make glib, unctuous introductions, and he would make the frantic slashing motions across his throat when the act started to go stale. Rudolfo the Go-Go Boy continued to be very popular, taming invisible cats in his zircon-encrusted G-string. He alone knew that he was snapping an unseen whip at the corners of the room, grimacing to display dominance and courage. The patrons at Miss Joe's were mystified but mesmerized; as he puffed out his chest and paraded around the perimeter of the room, the audience would stir restively; they would hang their heads and turn doleful eyes upwards, silently asking how they could please their new master.

One night, Rudolfo dismounted the stage and found Miss Joe standing behind the bar with her bony arms criss-crossed lazily, her painted lips pursed with consternation. "It's not quite there, is it, Rudolfo?" Miss Joe muttered.

Jurgen sat at the bar with his hands wrapped around a beer glass. Rudolfo sat down beside him, touched his knee gently. Sometimes he did that just to watch Jurgen bristle, which he did almost audibly, his body vibrating with irritation and embarrassment.

"What do you mean?" Rudolfo demanded of Miss Joe.

"Don't get testy with me, young man," she said. "Look, your act is good, god knows it's got no competition around this joint. All I'm saying is, you got a goulash but you've left out an ingredient."

"It's like Stuttgart," posited Jurgen, raising his beer and drawing off three or four inches. "They've got a good team, but they need a top-notch striker if they want to really go places."

"Thanks, Magic Man," said Miss Joe. "That's the very analogy I was grappling for."

"I don't know what else I can do," Rudolfo protested. "I can only get *so* naked."

"True," nodded Miss Joe. "But it's not that. It's..." Miss Joe raised a hand and snapped her fingers, making them clack woodenly. "It's that music. That dreary disco shit. You dance well, but that beat, I don't know, it makes your cock flap in a kind of unseemly way."

Rudolfo shrugged. The music was B4 on the huge Wurlitzer jukebox that hulked in the corner, that's as much as he knew. He didn't know it was entitled "Goulash" and he certainly didn't know that it had been composed and performed by two young men who, after this small success, would dabble in soft drugs, become addicted to heroin and arrive in America years later calling themselves "Sturm and Drang."

"You like music, don't you?" asked Miss Joe.

"I like music, sure."

"Give me a for instance."

"Of something I like?"

"Yeah."

Rudolfo exhaled heavily and allowed himself to drift briefly in memory. He remembered his mother, whatever his mother had been, careering through the Salon, her hands locked and twisted across her heart. He remembers her best, most vividly, as Lucy Ashton, Lucia di Lammermoor, mad and murderous. "Grand opera," he whispered.

Jurgen said nothing. He raised a thumb and chewed at the nail.

Miss Joe whistled lightly. "La-di-fucking-da," she said. "Still, if it works for you."

She produced an old turntable from one of the back rooms—her place had a seemingly endless number of back-rooms, all of them filled with refuse and junk—and Rudolfo bought some records from a second-hand shop: Gounod's *Faust*; Wagner's *Götterdämmerung*; lots by Puccini, his favourite composer, *La Bohème, Turandot, Madama Butterfly*. He also bought some pure music, the first piano concerto by Brahms, all the Beethoven he could find, and the *Gymnopédies* of Satie, which were, after all, written specifically for naked athletes.

Miss Joe liked the effect. She eventually had all of the old records removed from the Wurlitzer and Rudolfo's classical albums put in their stead. Now if one pressed the button "B4," the shadowy room echoed with Rodolfo's lament for the consumptive Mimi.

Miss Joe's establishment began to acquire a reputation; no wait, that's ill-put—the place always had a reputation, but it began to acquire a *favourable* one. Miss Joe's became known as a place of genuine (if slightly peculiar) entertainment. The only downside, Rudolfo often reflected bitterly, was his friend and lover, The Great Schuberto. Jurgen simply never changed his act, never refined or augmented. He didn't seem to notice, for example, that the Scarf Production was capable of inducing slumber, even paralysis. Rudolfo tried to suggest a few times that Jurgen replace that portion of the act, but Jurgen would usually turn defensively haughty. "Hey," he'd say, "I'm the *Chaser.*"

This was vexing, as vexing as Jurgen's refusal to be kissed on the lips. Jurgen seemed to think that as long as he never *kissed* Rudolfo he wasn't really homosexual, despite all sorts of evidence to the contrary. They would release each other from the most intimate of embraces, and Rudolfo would fold his lips together and search for Jurgen's, but the man would be out of the bed, stalking about the room, scratching his ass and searching for his smokes.

Which was vexing, maddening, finally infuriating. One night, sitting in the small room they shared in the back of Miss Joe's, Rudolfo snapped at him, "You're too small."

Jurgen finished lighting his cigarette. The smoke curled into his lashes and made his bruised eyelids blink rapidly. Jurgen shook out the match, tossed it into an ashtray, pulled a shred of tobacco from his lower lip and then grunted interrogatively.

"Your act," explained Rudolfo. "Your act is too small."

"Hey," announced Jurgen, "I'm the *Chaser.*"

"Do you know what a *Chaser* is?" retorted Rudolfo angrily. He leapt out of the bed—it wasn't a bed, actually, it was an old spring-poked sofa, the back flattened to accommodate the two men. "A *Chaser* is…" Rudolfo used some approximate synonyms: *rausschmeiber, lückenfüller.* "It's someone with a shitty little act," he explained. "He comes on between marquee attractions so that he *chases* people out of the theatre. Then they can get more paying customers in and after they get their money, it's on with the fucking *Chaser.*"

"That's what a *Chaser* is?" asked a dumbfounded Jurgen. He butted out his smoke and sat down on the bed. Rudolfo touched him on the shoulder. Jurgen raised a fist. "Leave me alone."

"I can't help what words mean."

"I'm thinking. I'm thinking bigger."

"Okay."

"Well," said Jurgen uncertainly. "I could escape from a big paper bag."

"Uh-huh. Yeah. Yeah, that might work."

Jurgen said no more about it, but the next day he put on his raincoat, even though the day was fine, and headed off to make a tour of second-hand bookshops. He didn't find what he was looking for in the first, or the second, but in the third store he located—by purest chance—a copy of the cursed book, *Houdini on Magic.*

Jurgen took it back to Miss Joe's and showed it to his lover, saying nothing, merely exhibiting the parchment cover with the gaudy gold lettering. Rudolfo nodded. "I see," he said.

"Think big," said Jurgen. "Think like Houdini."

"Right."

Jurgen thumbed through the book until he came to a crude line drawing showing a Production Box, a broken line showing how one of the sides pushed in from the bottom. "You see," he said, showing the page to Rudolfo. "I push the box onstage. You come in behind it, hiding. I can open the top, tilt it forward, show how it's empty. Then you push here and crawl in. Now when I open it, you jump out."

Rudolfo nodded, but already had other ideas.

"We need lumber," said Jurgen. "And some paint and velvet cloth."

"Okay." Rudolfo removed his wig and fixed the old blue watch cap over his gleaming skull.

"Where are you going?"

"I'm going to beg. Then I'll come back with the supplies."

"You'd go begging for me?"

"I'd go begging for *us.*"

Some nights later, Miss Joe made this introduction: "Ladies and gentlemen—and if someone doesn't stop what he's doing *right now*, I'm taking that 'gentlemen' back—we the management are proud to present the hottest act in Europe..." (Miss Joe giggled in an unseemly manner here, flapping the back of her hand against her crimson lips; she was silenced from the darkened wings, where four eyes glared like headlights, where two mouths clenched in grim rebuke) "...all right, all right, here they are are, ladies and gentlemen, the hottest act in Europe, *Jurgen and Rudolfo!*" The names were shrieked at such a high pitch that several of the patrons clapped without thinking. They stopped when they saw the figure step up onto the stage, his back toward them. They recognized the satin cape; they recognized the top hat—it was that magician fellow, the dull guy. The magician stood motionless for a long moment, apparently intent on sending the notion of *dullness* right up to the top floors. He slowly raised his arms above his head—there was an accompanying cymbal crash, which was kind of alarming and caused people to inch forward on their cheap wooden seats—and then slowly brought his hands down to his shoulders, lifting away his cape and allowing it to fall to the floor. The magician was revealed to be naked. Actually (the magician spun around quickly), he wasn't quite naked, he was wearing a G-string, a little sequined pouch for his privates. The audience, those that liked that kind of thing, applauded in a desultory fashion.

The magician thrust his hands up again and suddenly there were two doves fluttering from them. The magician tossed them into the air (he doffed his top hat then and smiled grimly at the audience, his eyes bugged open) and the birds flew into the shadows, where they landed on the shoulders of yet another nearly naked young man. This man took a large step forward so that he now stood within the stage lights. Those in the audience that liked this kind of thing applauded with much more enthusiasm, because this was the Go-Go Boy, the young man with the un-likely body, sculpted and oiled so that he seemed somehow like a mannequin come to life.

With Rudolfo's appearance most of the members of the audience noticed the music for the first time. Some merely found it unsettling, some found it beautiful, one or two were able to name it, the "Adagietto" from Gustav Mahler's Symphony Num-ber Five.

The magician again lifted his hands, and scarves began to materialize, long and brilliantly coloured. He tossed them into the air, where they described long, graceful arcs. His associate received them, with abounding grace, in preternaturally slow motion, all of his muscles rippling sequentially. The audience applauded heartily, somehow thinking, believing, that the act of catching tossed scarves constituted a feat of great difficulty.

After all the scarves had been produced, tossed and caught, the two men stepped forward and took grand bows, like concert musicians who had just pulled off a notoriously tricky piece. The audience seemed to realize as one that this bit of stage business looked ridiculous unless they themselves were applauding with something that neared frenzy, so that is what they began to do.

Suddenly the void between the two men was filled by a large wooden box. It had been painted a sky-blue, and someone had rendered puffy clouds upon it. The nearly naked men exchanged knowing glances and then both took hold of the box. They tilted it forward and the magician lifted the top, showing the velvet-lined interior to be empty. They rested the box back down. There was a long moment where nothing happened—but the perform-ers managed to fill it with such profound nothingness (staring into the audience, their lips pulled away as though their sole intention was to display some recent dental work) that the effect was one of suspense. Many of the patrons couldn't resist a little nibble at their fingernails. Then both men clapped their hands together with improbable synchronicity, and the magician lifted the top of the box once more.

A huge white creature leapt out and bolted toward the audience with its fangs bared. It reared up on its hind legs, roaring operatically, and clawed the air with vicious whistling swipes, tearing it to shreds.

Three people fainted. (Three became the minimum. Samson on subsequent nights managed as many as seven, although one teetered on her feet over by the bar, and Samson was forced to stalk over and growl at her from only a few feet away in order to force the topple.) Those who remained sentient threw up a cheer of enormous approval. Jurgen and Rudolfo joined hands, waved rather demurely, and then they themselves disappeared.

That was their act. It lasted about three minutes. There was no aspect to it that was mysterious to anyone with even a slight knowledge of illusion or stagecraft. The doves had been nestled under the shoulders of Jurgen's dark cape; as he worked the clasp at the neck preparatory to throwing the cape away, he merely hooked the birds and scooped them into his palms. The scarves came from within false thumbs where they waited, folded and pounded to the size of peas. The most impressive bit of business was not the production of the roaring beast but the production of the Production Box itself, which seemed to move forward of its own volition. The secret there is that Samson himself pushed the box, hunkering low and placing his forehead against the wood. It fooled people because no one ever suspected a lion (there was much confusion as to Samson's species) of being capable of it.

Rudolfo leads Miranda through the house, das eindrucksvollste Haus im Universum. *He is aware that Miranda is upset. There exists a state of decay inside the house that is filling her with misgiving. Animals are draped everywhere like furry opium addicts, as glassy-eyed as if they'd just come from the taxidermist.*

Miranda is carrying two bags of groceries, and Rudolfo understands now why food sometimes materializes in the kitchen.

"So, Miranda," says Rudolfo, leading her through dark hallways, "what are you doing?"

"Same as I was last month. I'm over at the Lodeo." Miranda notices a ghostly form trembling in the shadows. "Hey, Sammy," she says softly. When Samson sees that the intruder is Miranda—I've got to do something about these old eyes, he thinks—he ventures out and lies down on his back to have his tummy rubbed.

"Hey, Big Boy," Miranda chuckles, setting aside her groceries.

"The nudie show?" demands Rudolfo suddenly.

Miranda's fingers play on Samson's belly, each stroke pulling out the few tufts of white fur that remain. "What?"

"The Lodeo is a nudie show."

"Topless," Miranda concedes. "No big deal. But let's not worry about me. You—"

"Me?"

"Yeah. You. You look like a piece of shit—no offence—"

"Ja, because I am not doing my exercises!" Rudolfo is filled with resolution and, as fortune would have it, they are near the Gymnasium. He peels off the bruised-purple jumpsuit, strips down to his tiny exercise briefs—quickly realizing that he is not wearing any, but his

resolution is such that this doesn't stop him—and marches into the Gymnasium.

The bench is covered with a patina of dust. The bar and the plates are connected to the rack by intricate cobwebs.

The plates are quite large. Rudolfo has lost what little aptitude with figures he ever had, so he has little hope of calculating the aggregate weight. The months since Jurgen went away have not been processed mentally. The days are like newspapers that get thrown into the recycling bin unread. The last time Rudolfo lifted weights, this is how much he lifted, so he lies down on the bench and takes the bar into his hands.

"Don't," says Miranda.

Rudolfo silences her through concentration. The key to everything, it occurs to him, is concentration, and the act of concentrating feels wonderful to him. This is what his life has been lacking—focus—a brutal trashing of sensory input. He wraps his hands around the bar. The metal has been roughed up in two short sections, the better to grip, but Rudolfo slides his hands to either side where it is cold and smooth.

He pushes. It is as though he is lying under the foundation of an office building and attempting to hike it skyward. He does not manage to budge a single molecule.

"Spot," he cries out faintly.

Miranda's voice almost cuts through his mindset. She is saying a single word over and over again. But the word is deformed by weeping and he can't make it out.

Rudolfo takes a deep breath—didn't his chest use to rise and fall splendidly whenever he took a deep breath, didn't there used to be more than this wheezy clattering?—and pushes once more against the bar. He screams, remembering suddenly that this helps, and howls and shrieks and wails and when all the air has fled his body he passes out and goes, unwillingly, into the past.

Chapter Sixteen

"In America," Miss Joe proclaimed, "they are going to line up around the block to lick the shit from between our toes." These words were spoken on the deck of the *Corinthian*, a liner bound for New York City. "Royalty," said Miss Joe, "that's what we're going to be. Royal-fucking-tee." There was nothing around them, only a sea infinite in all directions. It was white-capped and roiling; most of Miss Joe's proclamations were punctuated with gagging sounds, and she'd often have to pause in order to spew a strange greenish substance over the railing.

Because she spent so much time bent over the railings—and this is to say nothing of the nor'easterlies and sou'westerlies, the cruel salty winds that buffeted the trio every waking moment— Miss Joe had developed very advanced methods of hairpiece stabilization. She had found some enormous clips and bobby pins, made of a silver so bright that one imagined the metal to be a product of the Space Race, that either the Russians or the Americans had developed the clasps to withstand the unimaginable heat of orbital re-entry. Miss Joe linked the hairpiece not to the blackened snood that lay beneath, but rather to her own costume. The back was anchored to her collar, and the sides were fixed to the straps of her undergarments, of which she wore many, despite the fact that she lacked virtually all human substance, to say nothing of the bits and pieces that contribute to gender differentiation. So the hairpiece was able to resist both gravity over the railings and the bullying winds, although it was a bit of chicken-and-egg deal, because without the hairpiece, which acted as lugsail or spanker, Miss Joe would have been able to stand in one place, not be thrown up and down the gangways and metal staircases.

They had been outward bound for six days now, and Miss Joe had done nothing but predict adulation and world domination. Even Rudolfo—who sometimes went so far as to fantasize actual regal apparel, mantles of sable and fiery crowns—was tiring of it. And Jurgen, immune somehow to seasickness, but unable to sleep more than an hour or two a night, was irritable, even hostile. "It's just a few cheap tricks," he growled. "I could teach you to do them in a few minutes."

Miss Joe shrugged. "Cheap tricks are good."

"Just once," said Jurgen, "I'd like to do something that isn't a cheap trick. Even if it's small. Even if it's just to make a grain of sand disappear."

"There's entertainment," said Rudolfo, as a joke. Jurgen spun around and glared at him, his purpled eyelids crashing and pounding.

"There's no such thing as magic," insisted Miss Joe.

"Listen," said Jurgen, and for a moment he tried to reposition everyone, moving and nudging his companions until their triangle was more arithmetically precise. Then he bent forward, inclining his head secretively. "I've never told anyone this."

"Which isn't hard to believe," commented Rudolfo, "considering you've never told anyone anything."

"When I was sixteen," Jurgen continued, "I heard a noise in the middle of the night. That wasn't very unusual; I mean, I heard noises all the time in that house, but this was a strange noise. Very musical, like a flute, but at the same time very, what would be a good word, um, wild." Jurgen used the word *barbarisch*. "It was coming from Oma's room. So I got up and went to see what was the matter. And I pushed open the door, you know, and I'll tell you what I saw."

At which point he fell stone-silent and turned his attention to the endless face of the sea, which crested as though huge humpbacks romped just below the surface.

"Yes?" prompted Miss Joe.

"You'll think I'm crazy," Jurgen demurred.

"Tell us," whispered Rudolfo.

"Okay. I saw Oma. She was naked. And she was glowing like a coal in the fire. She was floating three feet above her bed. And she, you know, was making this little whistling sound, like she was a bird, but when I came into the room she turned her head. And her eyes were like mirrors, I remember, silver and shiny. Oma looked at me and said the word *Zauberei*. Then she floated down, like a leaf, floated down onto the mattress, and her eyes went black and her body turned the colour of stone, and she was dead."

"Haven't you ever heard of *dreams*?" demanded Miss Joe.

"It wasn't a dream," stated Jurgen evenly.

Rudolfo had no opinion on the matter, not being entirely sure what a dream was, or should be. He was glad he was not afflicted by them if they launched naked old women into the air and made them glow.

"So ever since then," said Jurgen, "I've known that magic is possible."

Miss Joe blew a thick and watery raspberry, but Jurgen didn't seem to notice.

"I do the cheap tricks," he continued, "but maybe one day…"

"Maybe one day nothing," snarled Miss Joe. "One day the bitch Mother Nature will turn your lights out. That's it. Magic." She spat disdainfully. "There's no such thing as fucking *magic.*"

Although Rudolfo was not then the amateur naturalist that he would become, he knew, judging from the size, that a royal albatross was descending from the foggy heavens. These birds have the largest wingspan of any bird, sometimes more than thirteen feet. They are three years out to sea, these giants; the first years of their lives they spend flying above the ocean, often in the middle of nowhere, looking for food and/or a resting place. It is hard to say whether this particular albatross saw Miss Joe's hairpiece as the former or the latter. It's true that the bird came at it headfirst, burying its long hooked beak deep into the multicoloured complex of artificial hair. But then it brought up its feet in order to assay a landing. Royal albatrosses have a hard time landing. They hit the ground running; their legs buckle and they tumble butt over beak. Mid-sea landings are even harder, so albatrosses try to nail them emphatically, which is what this bird did, applying the brakes, lifting up its flippers, slamming into the monolithic coiffure. Miss Joe, that is, her substance and being, was not enough to stop the bird. She was simply and summarily picked up over the *Corinthian*'s railings and carried away. The albatross tried desperately to extricate its beak, but it was caught surely, Miss Joe's hairpiece acting like a huge Chinese Finger Trap. The albatross squawked and shook its head, hopeful that the wig would perhaps separate from its odd human owner, but that didn't happen. This might have been because of the futuristic bobby pins, or it might have been due to Miss Joe's near-weightlessness, but either way, the giant creature soon settled down—finding Miss Joe not so great a burden—and ruffled the air with huge and decisive flappings. Guided by a certain system of celestial navigation that makes sense only to royal albatrosses, the bird turned to its left and disappeared.

They now had an agent named Curtis Sweetchurch. Jurgen and Rudolfo never referred to Curtis as their *manager*, mostly because of a hopeless fidelity to Miss Joe. It was as though they still expected Miss Joe to return, soaking wet, seaweed threaded through her hairpiece. Curtis Sweetchurch had attached himself to them only when success was nigh, after the gloomy dark days spent in the desert. He'd had a stable of showgirls and lounge singers, but he shed them all when he found Jurgen and Rudolfo performing at the "The Oasis." The duo made Curtis filthy rich, although he actually did very little for them. There simply wasn't a lot of Jurgen and Rudolfo-related business to attend to. Their contract with the Abraxas Hotel reached far into the next century; raises, bonuses and increased patronage percentages had all been negotiated and laid out. (That was done by Rudolfo. He'd been flanked by lawyers, of course, but they were mere minions, tiny pawns with briefcases and bad toupées. He'd conducted negotiations like a dauphin, sitting at the huge oaken table and heaving sighs of prodigious ennui. When offers were made, Rudolfo would leap to his feet and march over to the boardroom's window. He'd gaze out upon the desert, which stretched away until it turned into distance's vapour. Rudolfo would communicate without turning around, his language as haughty and crude as he could manage: "Fuck yourself and also a horse.") As if to atone for the lack of business, Sweetchurch undertook what little he had with zeal, chartering an airplane and dropping out of the sky to announce things that could have as easily been communicated over the phone lines that linked Los Angeles, California, and Las Vegas, Nevada.

Rudolfo was in the cage with the panther. He was teaching the beast to flatten itself to the ground, to spread legs both fore and aft, to exhale air until the lungs were as deflated as blown tires. This was essential, of course, to many of the illusions—the Silver Ball, for example. There wasn't much room inside the secret compartment, and the false bottom moved with power, carried by centrifugal force; any body part above a certain line would likely get guillotined cleanly. So Rudolfo pressed the panther's head to the ground, drove and twisted it until sawdust came up to the creature's bottom lip. Animals, Rudolfo knew, only related to their heads; in a sense they conceived of themselves as nothing but heads. *Teach the head*, one of General Bosco's axioms went, *and the body will follow.* The panther's body was trying to follow, squirming and worming as though squashed under a giant jackboot.

Suddenly Curtis Sweetchurch was there.

"Hi!" he said, startling both Rudolfo and the animal. Rudolfo loosened his hold momentarily and the panther became a confusion of limbs. The black creature brought its teeth together and Rudolfo muttered, "Fuckshit." He grabbed hold of the loose skin at the back of the panther's neck and twisted until the huge cat produced a whine of pitiable meekness.

Rudolfo climbed to his feet, raising a bleeding finger and directing the panther back to its stand. The beast, evidencing great shame, prostrated itself. "No," said Rudolfo. "Too late. You have been naughty."

The panther slunk away and Rudolfo turned to confront Curtis.

"Whoops!" said Sweetchurch, brushing a hand across his lips, hiding a giggle that never came. "Sorry."

"That happens," answered Rudolfo, referring to the gash on his index finger, although this wasn't true. It didn't happen, had never happened before. Rudolfo didn't know how many days he'd lost, how far behind schedule this placed him. He was even concerned that he'd lost the panther forever. Even though the creature now cringed atop its stand, trying hard to summon up tears, *anything to please the human*, Rudolfo knew that it wouldn't forget. Mayhem was now an option. He stuck his finger in his mouth and sucked. "Vot you vant?"

Curtis Sweetchurch carried a huge Daytimer, clutching it to his chest like a schoolgirl. He now tore it open, savaged the pages with his fingers and eyes and said, "The Reno Show wants you. In two days."

"Who else is on?" demanded Rudolfo. He was still stinging over an appearance on one of these late-night talk shows. The other guest had been a gaunt comic who talked in a rapid, staccato fashion. He'd insulted Jurgen and Rudolfo, belittled and ridiculed them. Rudolfo comprehended almost none of the words, but he understood the cruel roar of the audience.

Curtis Sweetchurch referred to his Daytimer again. He slid his fingers along the edges, locating little plastic tags and flaps. He flipped pages and consulted subheaders. "Umm," said he, running his eyes over the pertinent page, "some up-and-coming starlet and a man who whistles the classics through his nose."

"I don't know," said Rudolfo. "Jurgen has not been feeling that well."

Jurgen picked that moment to come dashing out of the house. Rudolfo's first thought was that some enormous snake had chosen Jurgen as its next meal, but Jurgen was not wrapped up in a snake; he was wrapped up in a thick piece of rope.

He also seemed to be wearing a diaper, but as he drew nearer, Rudolfo saw that it was the unassuming loincloth of a fakir or swami. It barely clung to his meaty love handles; the front swooped low and exhibited a few downy, curly hairs. The loincloth was dingy and greyish, and Jurgen's skin seemed all the more pale in comparison.

"Am working on new trick!" he shouted, even though he was now within ten feet of the cage. Rudolfo stepped out and quietly shut the door behind him.

"Jurgen," said Curtis Sweetchurch, "is it true you're not feeling well?"

Jurgen ignored the question, which possessed an obvious and profound foolishness. Though he was pale, Jurgen exuded good health and vitality. "So look," he said, dumping his burden, the rope, upon the ground. "So Rudolfo, first of all you say, um, for intro…"

Rudolfo interrupted here. "Hold on to the horses," he said. It was not Jurgen's role to suggest introductions, after all. Not Jurgen Schubert, who, some years ago, had actually marched toward the audience and barked, "Here is trick!" with such crude brutality that several people choked on their martini olives.

Jurgen suddenly adopted a very odd pose, laying one hand over his heart, sticking an index finger into the air. "Laddies and lassies," he intoned, "the next miracle is the globally celebrated and much ballyhooed Hindu Rope Trick."

"Uh-oh," moaned Curtis Sweetchurch, "will we have to pay royalties?"

"Is *miracle*," snarled Rudolfo. "You don't pay royalties on miracles."

Jurgen now picked up the rope and raised it over his head. "Here is music and dancing," he said, setting the imaginary scene. "Miranda can show everyone her tits."

"Aha!" said Curtis Sweetchurch. "Misdirection."

"No, no," said Jurgen. "Is not that. Everyone wants to see Miranda's tits. Even me." Then he threw the rope back onto the ground, where it lay, limp and lifeless. Except for the last five feet, which remained upright, undulating like a blade of grass in a strong wind. "Not bad, eh?" bellowed Jurgen, and he leapt upon it eagerly. For a few seconds he rode it back and forth, and then it collapsed and Jurgen crashed to the ground. He lay there with his face buried, emitting a strange sound that Rudolfo thought was sobbing, although when Jurgen lumbered to his feet it became clear that he'd been giggling. Still was giggling, as a matter of fact. He looked at Rudolfo and spoke German. "I'll keep working on it."

Rudolfo only nodded, once, up and down.

Chapter Seventeen

Rudolfo argued against any appearance onstage of the hideous old steamer trunk, the Houdini Substitution Box. He did so with admirable restraint, pacing back and forth in the cavernous dressing room contained in the deepest bowels of the Abraxas Hotel. Jurgen sat on one of the couches, very placidly, his fingers interlocked. Interlocking his fingers seemed to be his current favourite pastime. Jurgen would make his digits mesh with care and precision, almost as though he were three years old and the exercise just a little beyond him.

"It's not just that the box is ugly," explained Rudolfo (that was top of the list, certainly), "it's more that it doesn't fit in. Everything else is very modern, high-tech."

Jurgen made the steeple, opened his hands and saw all the people, although his nails, which had grown so long they curled like ram's horns, interfered with the process.

"Stop that," demanded Rudolfo.

"I agree it's different," said Jurgen. "That's what's good about it."

Rudolfo slyly abandoned the discussion then, and allowed the Substitution Box to be wheeled out on the stage for the show one night. Jurgen's mien changed abruptly. Instead of lumbering around the stage with the grace of Frankenstein's monster, his bruised eyes pried apart, Jurgen became like a child on Christmas morn, racing around the old crate and clapping his hands together. Miranda trotted on in his wake, trying to take control of the situation, but when she reached for the lid, Jurgen had beaten her to it, throwing it open and bending over to pull out the canvas bag, the draping, the padlock, the ropes. In his giddy impatience, he presented his back to the audience, so for a few moments much of Miranda's attention was devoted to the surreptitious application of her fingertips at strategic pressure points, hoping to turn the man about. But Jurgen only turned after he'd fished out the handcuffs, handing them to Miranda. He placed his wrists together and held them out. Miranda fastened the cuffs and then helped him into the canvas sack, binding the top with old frayed ropes that had been handled by Bess Houdini herself, all those many years ago. Jurgen disappeared into the crate.

Rudolfo watched all this on a black-and-white monitor in the dressing room, the pale ghostly Samson trembling by his side. Rudolfo didn't wonder, then, why Samson was trembling, but he would later on that night, lying (all alone) in the huge circular bed.

Miranda closed the lid and fed the hasp of the padlock through the clasp. She clicked it shut, the sound alarmingly loud even in that grand hall, then she crossed behind the Substitution Box with the drapery in her hands and stepped up on top of the crate. She lifted the curtain and for a brief moment, except for the fingertips curled over the edge of the material, was hidden from view.

On the monitor hanging above Rudolfo's eyes there was

static and distortion, the picture suddenly fractured, but it as quickly recomposed itself, accompanied by a whooshing sound that issued from the tiny speaker beside the monitor and from the stage some fifty feet away, and from the emptiness surrounding Rudolfo.

The curtain dropped and there stood Jurgen. He spread his arms with admirable aplomb, but there was no applause forthcoming. "You see?" Rudolfo spit toward the monitor screen. "Is *shit*."

This didn't seem to worry or concern Jurgen, who clambered down off the crate and removed the padlock. He threw open the lid (the canvas sack rose full of lumps and agitation), undid the ropes and then stepped back to reveal Miranda.

Miranda looked very odd. Her cheeks were flushed, her hair was tousled and her leotard no longer seemed to fit perfectly, the seams askew by a millimetre or two. The armpits were darkly dampened and the front was pricked by erect nipples. Now the applause started—at the back of the room, heading toward the front like a slow-roller at Coney Island—but Miranda didn't wait around to acknowledge it. Instead she turned and trotted off the stage. The material at the back of her costume was wedged between the globes of her buttocks, and as she ran Miranda tried to pluck it out, and for some reason the audience was delighted at this. The applause was redoubled and decorated with cheers and bravos.

Rudolfo grudgingly allowed the bit to stay in the Show. He even took part, standing off to the side of the stage and delivering a kind of lecture. "It is Substitution Box owned by Houdini himself," he told the audience. "The greatest magician that ever lived. Except for Jurgen."

Rudolfo told Miranda she should keep picking material out of her ass, even though he himself found it indecorous and offputting. When he told her this, Miranda's eyes widened and her nostrils flared. "What do you like about it?" she demanded. "The fact that everyone can see my bare butt or the fact that I look like a buffoon?"

Rudolfo shrugged. "Is combination."

"You know, I'm the best box-jumper in this city. Hey, I'm one of the best *magicians*. All you want me for is my tits and ass."

Rudolfo didn't really contest the point. "Why you bring this up?"

Miranda stiffened so that she towered over Rudolfo. "Let's just say," she said, "that my eyes have been opened to some possibilities." She turned on her heel and disappeared.

When she pushed open the door that led to the service hallways of the Abraxas Hotel, Miranda didn't go to the bank of elevators that ascended to her gloomy suite. Instead she marched through the casino proper, a voyage that lasted many minutes, and emerged finally at the seemingly endless circular driveway. Standing amidst the giant half-naked doormen, smoking a cigarette with industry, was Preston.

"Hi," said Miranda.

Preston flicked the cigarette away, even though it was freshly lit, and turned awkwardly. Miranda saw that he'd made some attempt to tame his hair, adding oil and forcing all of the strands to straggle off in the same direction. He had even shaved. "Hi," he said. "How was the Show?"

Miranda nodded, which one would have thought an unsatisfactory response, although Preston accepted it easily enough. "So what do you want to do?" he wondered. "A movie or something?"

"I want to go to the desert."

So they took a cab twenty miles to the north, and when the emptiness seemed vast enough, they got out. Preston tipped the driver half a buck. The moon was full, which pleased Miranda.

She hadn't known it would be, had no way of reading the moon in the city of Las Vegas, Nevada, which was neon-bright enough to obscure the heavens. In her hometown, Maple Creek, Saskatchewan, the moon was practically a neighbour, lighting the night in a conscientious manner. But here was a full moon bathing the desert, and for a long time neither one of them said anything. They stood still and waited for the desert to come to life. That was how it felt, even though Miranda knew the desert was always alive, that the quickening process was really one of allowing oneself to perceive it.

So, for instance, it wasn't that the lizards suddenly started darting to and fro, racing up and down the saguaros. They'd been doing that all along, that was essentially all they did, but, Miranda realized suddenly, Las Vegas can blind you to such subtleties. Or non-garishnesses, if one could coin such a word, because it was only in a vain and very human way that a lizard's existence was subtle.

"So…" She flapped her arms up and down, as though half-heartedly testing her ability to fly. "It's nice to be here with you."

"Yeah?"

"Sure. Nice to be here. Nice to be with you. Nice."

Preston shrugged, or so it appeared, although he was in truth shivering from the sunless chill and at the same time twitching somewhere deep in his being, tickled by the fingers of desire. But it looked enough like a shrug that Miranda turned away and folded her arms across her chest.

"So," she demanded quietly, "have you been thinking about what we talked about the other night?"

"Thinking about it, sure," Preston answered. "Deciding anything about it, no way."

"I don't know what's to decide," said Miranda, spinning around. "Anyone in town would jump at the chance. I'm the best."

"I'm not disputing that. I'm just not sure."

"You're just not sure that having a thaumaturgical assistant with years of experience and a flawless body would enhance your act any."

"You see, Miranda, that's just it, I don't have an *act*, I'm not like the boys, I do different things every night—"

"That's cool. I'm adaptable."

"I'm just not sure I need an assistant with a perfect body."

"Hold on. I never said *perfect*. I said *flawless*."

"There's a difference?"

"Sure. Check a dictionary. First definition under the word *perfect* is *complete*."

"Your body isn't complete?"

"You said a mouthful."

"But it is flawless."

"No shit."

"What are you missing?"

Miranda jerked her shoulders, looking up at the stars as if trying to fix her location, and looking then to the ground to see if she was rooted and stable. When she opened her mouth, it was to speak very quietly, almost too quietly for Preston and his furry ears to pick up. She said, "You don't have to take my word for it."

"Take your word for what?"

"That the Bod is flawless."

"I have no problem accepting that."

"You could check."

"Oh, no, no, that won't be necessary."

Miranda laughed, a short euphonic howl that pierced the desolate night. "Hey, Preston," she said, "I'll make you a bet. If you find a flaw, I'll drop the subject and never bring it up again."

"Suppose I don't find a flaw?"

Miranda crossed her arms and took hold of the bottom of her sweatshirt. The shirt not only announced the existence of *The*

University of Saskatchewan Huskies, it pictured a huskie, half-dog, half-wolf, although the beast looked slightly addled. Miranda pulled upwards, raising the curtain slowly on her belly and her breasts. Preston bit down hard on his bottom lip. Miranda hooked her thumbs in the waistband of her sweatpants, peeling them and her underwear—they looked like black jockey shorts, which for some reason made Preston gasp in a subdued, strangled, manner—and then she hopped around briefly, removing these garments over her sneakers. She placed her arms at her side and came to military attention. "Okay, Presto," she said. "Do your best."

"You're right, I can't see anyth—"

"Of course you can't see anything from there, doofus. It's not like I'm missing an arm. Come on, get over here. Check it out."

Preston took a few steps closer and then hesitated, but Miranda reached out quickly and took hold of his arm. "Come here," she said, and Preston stumbled forward. His mother had been a thaumaturgical assistant—Gwendolyn, her name was but called Guinevere on stage—"the fair maiden Guinevere." Preston saw what he thought was a blemish, but it turned out to simply be a little pool of shadow nestled in the nape of Miranda's neck. He stooped slightly then, and looked at her breasts. "Flawless, right?" muttered Miranda. "Yup," agreed Preston. His mother had performed with his father for many years, until Preston was six or seven years old. Then she began to cry on-stage, sometimes fleeing into the wings, more often remaining there, the tears running down her face and staining her satin costume. Preston fell to his knees and inspected Miranda's navel, a likely site for imperfection, but whoever had attended at her birth had been meticulous, even artistic, leaving her with a fine and tiny crescent. Then Preston the Magnificent had performed with a series of younger women, several of whom actually stayed at their home, one of whom, Preston recalled, was perpetually getting lost on her way to the washroom. This woman would stumble through the hallways late at night, tipsy and naked. Preston leaned forward to look at Miranda's ankles and tarsi; he was bent as though the desert were an endless prayer shawl.

"Did you come?" asked Miranda quietly.

"Oh, yeah," said Preston, clambering to his feet. "A while back."

Miranda made a chicky sound with the side of her mouth. "There you go," she said. She bent over and picked up her clothes from the ground. "So what do you say?"

Preston nodded very slowly. "Okay."

A huge truck came and collected the silver ball, and later a helicopter landed on the grounds of *das eindrucksvollste Haus im Universum*. Curtis Sweetchurch leapt out of the plastic bubble and bolted for the house. He was running behind schedule, which was *absurd*, he had a personal time-management counsellor, for goodness sake, but on any occasion when he had to be somewhere—at the network television studio at 4:30 that afternoon, in this instance—the hours conspired to waylay him. He had gotten up at three o'clock that morning, and the pertinent page in his Daytimer was only partly festooned with yellow Post-its, but despite all that, it was now 2:45 and the minutes were dripping away. "Yoo-hoo!" he bellowed, still at some distance from the mansion, which Curtis thought was positively hideous, a half-digested piece of meat that had been spit up by some vast interplanetary being. "Rudy!" Sweetchurch shouted. "Jurgie!"

Curtis found a door and rapped upon it, not at all sure that this was an effective strategy, because he had no way of telling, based on the otherworldly architecture, if this was a front or side door or some out-of-the-way service entrance, but as he rapped and fretted the door opened and there stood Jurgen Schubert. "Hello," he smiled, "Curtis Sweetchurch."

"Yes, okay, let's scurry, hi, go grab your outfit."

But Jurgen wandered out the door without valise or garment bag. He seemed startled by the sunlight; his head twitched and jerked like that of a small animal catching the scent of something much larger.

"Jurgen," chimed Curtis. "Aren't we forgetting something?"

Jurgen spun around, sending his long white robe into a swirl near the bottom; it rose up and for a moment his naked, pale legs were visible. "Forgetting something?" he asked.

Rudolfo flew into sight, attempting to do up fly-buttons on a ridiculously tight pair of leather pants without stopping or even slowing down. On his upper half Rudolfo wore a white satin shirt; those buttons he'd neglected, so the shirt gaped open and displayed his smooth musculature. Curtis Sweetchurch chuckled under his breath, realizing that Rudolfo had dressed in a Kaz-like manner, and in so doing showed up Kaz for the scrawny ill-begotten pinhead he was. Curtis hated Kaz, although if Kaz ever considered changing agencies…

"Rudy!" shouted Sweetchurch. "What the *what* is your partner wearing?"

"Is robe," pointed out Rudolfo calmly, giving no evidence of the extremely vicious argument he'd just had over that very topic. He hadn't objected to the white robe itself—he half-admired Jurgen for making such a bold statement—but to the crudeness of the thing. It was rendered out of sackcloth and poorly tailored, the arms too long, the neck hole uneven and gaping. And someone—Jurgen himself, presumably—had attempted to embellish it with representations of the sun and moon, executed with all the talent of a four-year-old about to be advised by his kindergarten teacher to abandon art and find other pastimes.

"Well, yes, I can see that, but, you know, *hmmm?*"

Jurgen was proceeding toward the helicopter; Sweetchurch realized that time was running out, so he shrugged and scampered along. Rudolfo turned back toward the doorway and gave forth a whistle; Samson appeared almost immediately, even though moments before he'd been very deep in slumber.

Rudolfo stared at the back of the helicopter pilot's shoulders and head. It was very odd. The man's cap was ruined; all that remained was a visor and a thin elastic strap. Vestigial bits of serge clung to this strap, but there was nothing to cover the man's skull. The pilot was a *Schwarze*, and his hair, tight tiny curls, had been mowed and rutted so that patterns emerged. Rudolfo stared at these and tried to make some sense of them. He gazed into the designs and was reminded of the strange jottings and scribblings back at Kramgasse 49, the faint pencilled notions of Albert Einstein.

Samson sat near Rudolfo's feet, curled into a painful little ball between his master's and the pilot's seat, as if the people who'd designed the helicopter had never considered the possibility of a noble albino leopard travelling aboard. He was breathing heavily, hyperventilating, because he was scared. True, he was scared much of the time, vaguely possessed of an unlicked and amorphous fear. But helicopters made no sense to Samson. Airplanes had a birdlike logic; besides which, they were roomy and contained flight attendants. Helicopters blasted straight up toward the clouds, unexampled in the jungle or, more to the point, on any nature show on any of the four hundred and ten channels that the huge Japanese television received.

The helicopter landed atop the television studio. The entire production team clustered there, even the makeup people, so Jurgen and Rudolfo were set upon as soon as their feet touched the tarred and pebbly rooftop.

"Your big ball came," announced the producer, whose name

was Clair. Another woman flitted about, asking what they'd like in the way of beverages and pre-taping snacks. Rudolfo tried to think of things that would be hard to locate, because he was always very impressed by the cunning and resourcefulness of television people. "Toasted zweiback," he said, "and sweet-potato juice."

Someone screamed, silencing the little crowd for a brief moment. A woman rushed forward and fell to her knees before Jurgen. "Oh, sweet mercy," she whimpered, taking Jurgen's left hand gingerly into her own, raising it upwards as though she might lay her lips to it tenderly. This woman looked around at her co-staff and shrieked, "Can you fucking believe it?"

On a list of unsettling oddities, Jurgen's fingernails were well near the bottom. They were just long, that's all, and uncared for. Rudolfo sighed, shrugged, and waved an exasperated hand in the direction of his friend's hands. Still, Jurgen was rushed away by four or five flushed young people, as though there were an emergency makeup room and time was of the essence. Rudolfo didn't see his partner again until the sounding of the brassy fanfare heralding the commencement of the Barry Reno Show.

The green room was packed—a young actress wearing what looked like rubber underwear, an elderly man who had trained his nasal flutings so that he could produce melody, Curtis Sweetchurch talking on a variety of tiny telephones, producing them from every pocket, not to mention scores of Reno Show production assistants—and in the middle of it all sat Jurgen. He had not, apparently, resisted the ministrations of the makeup people. They had shampooed his hair, and sculpted it. Curls and ringlets coiled on top of Jurgen's head, as oddly complicated as the coifs he had given himself as a young man headlining at Miss Joe's. But the makeup people had failed in their attempts to deal with the nails. The one on the left index finger was chipped, but

Rudolfo imagined that the rasp had suffered more damage. He imagined it shattering like a champagne glass upon contact with the thick yellowing chitin. The makeup people had also applied fleshy goo to Jurgen's bruised eyes, the thick cosmetic forcing his lids down so that he looked dreamy, ready to fall asleep.

And though Jurgen still wore his robe, it had been brushed and de-linted and some resourceful person had managed to throw in a hem. So all in all, Rudolfo decided, Jurgen didn't look too bad.

At that moment, a strange half-sob almost strangled Rudolfo and a tear popped from his eye. He decided that he'd go wait in the wings.

When Barry Reno shouted "Jurgen and Rudolfo!" Rudolfo's head snapped and he was momentarily confused. Surely he could not have drifted away while standing in the shadows thrown by the velvet curtains. Still, his brain was full of that cloudy residue, the ash of dreams. Then Jurgen was beside him, peculiarly animated. He opened his mouth and hollered "*Ja!*"—the war cry they had made so long ago for moments like this. Rudolfo tried to shout "*Ja!*" but his throat produced only a small sound. He placed his hands on the huge silver ball and took a deep breath, preparatory to the physical labour required to roll the damn thing. Out of the corner of his eye he noticed Jurgen waving his hands, the long whorling fingernails trembling slightly. Suddenly the ball was in motion, and Rudolfo's hands slipped uselessly from it.

"Let's go," muttered Jurgen. "It's showtime."

They pranced onto the stage—the audience broke into hugely enthusiastic applause—and began the Silver Ball routine, at least, the version they used for television appearances. Rudolfo's own part required very little in the way of talent or concentration; he had merely to flip latches and make certain that the ball was rolled into the right position to move the false panel. But the ball was not behaving exactly as it should; it quivered and bucked and if Rudolfo leaned on it even slightly it would move away as though coy. Together they opened up the huge silver ball and Jurgen climbed inside, although he didn't jump in like the squat ex-footballer he was, but slipped in like a priestess easing into a milkbath. And as Rudolfo closed the latches the silver ball suddenly rose sharply off the ground and Rudolfo had to pull it back down. But again, he hardly noticed, because, of course, if he *did* notice then he would undoubtedly be reduced to tears, he would collapse upon the stage and sob and demand to know what was wrong with everything, *was zum Teufel ist hier los?*

"Hoo boy!" he sang out desperately, tunelessly.

Rudolfo undid the latches and Samson leapt out as though springing from behind a veil of jungle greenery. He even let out a roar of formidable volume, a deep hollow death cry that stirred all the bowels in the house. Then he sank his head and vomited all over the stage.

"Oh ho!" said Barry Reno. He was a florid man with white hair that shot straight upwards from a rumpled scalp, making him seem perpetually startled. He wore spectacles with heavy, raven-black frames. Audiences liked him because, unaccountably, it had not occurred to them that he was a hateful, twisted man. "Come on, guys!" he shouted. "Come on over here and take a load off."

Rudolfo bristled, suspicious of this phrase. It seemed vaguely sexual; perhaps Reno was making some allusion to their relationship. Their gayness was hardly a secret, but a vast percentage of the public was blithely unaware of it, preferring to conceive of them as *flamboyant*. Reno was actually forbidden to mention or hint at their sexuality—it said so in the contract. So when Rudolfo heard *take a load off* he pushed himself into an exaggerated, manly strut, pitching his pelvis forward so that his *Schwanz* pressed against the leather of his pants.

Jurgen, Rudolfo noted out of the corner of his eye, didn't seem to be walking toward the couch so much as floating, the burlap robes billowing out behind him as though he stood in the centre of a great storm. "Barry Reno!" shouted Jurgen. "Greetings!"

It was now Barry Reno's turn to look confused, because guests never hailed him with such directness.

"I am very pleased to be seeing you!" continued Jurgen.

"Sit down, fellas," said Barry Reno, ignoring this appalling politeness. "Hey, your pussy is a little under the weather, huh?" The audience roared at this. Rudolfo found himself saying, as he set his tiny bottom upon the sofa, "Is not pussy. Is leopard."

"Ha!" brayed Barry Reno. "I thought it was a great big pussy!"

"Then," pronounced Jurgen with some gravity, "you are an idiot." He gathered his robes prissily and sat down on the sofa.

"Hoo boy!"

The audience, after a momentary silence, sputtered with applause.

Barry Reno's eyes, behind his spectacles, had been re-designed into thin slits. He placed his elbows on the table in front of him and leant forward. Rudolfo became very uneasy, sensing that Reno was now out for blood. "So," Reno hissed, very slowly, "how long have you guys been together, anyway?"

Hoping to defuse the situation, Rudolfo grinned so hugely that his cheeks ached and the tendons in his neck tightened like banjo strings. "Long time!" he shouted, praying that the loathsome Reno would move on and ask them, as he always did, to relate stories about their animals defecating on stage. He trusted that Jurgen was grinning, too, but when he turned he saw that this was not the case. Jurgen was decidedly not smiling. He had spent the last few weeks grinning like an idiot and now, when grinning like an idiot was the thing to do, he was affecting a thoughtful, even philosophic, air. "We've known each other for a long time," he said, and then he reached over with his hand and gathered in Rudolfo's fingers. Rudolfo didn't panic, because panicking would be deadly. Such behaviour, he thought quickly, could be excused on account of their being European. Americans thought that all European people were very free physically, Americans thought that all Europeans went to nude beaches and shared saunas and kissed each other repeatedly whenever they got within striking distance, so he thought they might let this pass, but Jurgen showed no indication of letting go. Indeed, he repositioned himself until they were more properly *holding hands*, and that was how he seemed intent on carrying out the interview, he and Rudolfo connected like an ancient couple sharing lemonade on an old porch swing.

Even Barry Reno was a bit stupefied by this. He flapped his gums a few times, adjusted his heavy ebony eyeglasses and asked, "So…is animal puke and caca a big problem for you guys?"

Jurgen ignored this question, intent on answering the previous. "I was young *Zauberer*," he recalled. "*Aber* not really. I just knew some little tricks. And Rudolfo, he was famous lion tamer with circus."

Rudolfo blanched emphatically. "N-no I wasn't," he stammered. Rudolfo was still fearful of being arrested for the murder of General Bosco. That's what he told himself, at any rate, to explain the icy ball of guilt and shame that came to sit in his belly whenever he thought of that day, perhaps the worst of his life. "I was never lion tamer with circus."

"Hey, guys," chortled Barry Reno. "Get your story straight."

"Hey, Barry Reno," said Jurgen suddenly. "Give me your eyeglasses."

"Oh! A little trickeroony, huh?" Reno pulled the heavy spectacles from his face and held them out toward Jurgen. Jurgen gently pulled his hand away from Rudolfo's so that he could clutch the glasses between two thick paws. He twisted the ends in opposite directions; the plastic warped and bulged and spit out the lenses. Jurgen trod on them with his ancient leather sandals. There was a sound of small crunching. When Jurgen removed his feet there was nothing left but circles of cloudy dust. He then continued to mangle the frame, rendering the plastic almost formless. He tossed this away and then began a small game of *here's the church, here's the steeple.*

Barry Reno grinned appreciatively. "Okay, man," he said. "Do it."

Jurgen suddenly flipped his fists and opened the doors. He waggled all his finger-people under Reno's nose. "Do what?" he asked quietly.

"You know. Make my glasses come back."

"But Barry Reno," said Jurgen. "You don't need glasses."

"What?"

"Take a look around everywhere." Jurgen gesticulated at the vast television studio. "You can see hunky-fine."

Barry Reno's head jerked up. He lowered his eyelids against the glare of the lights and peered into the recesses of the room. "Hmmm." He turned to his left and then his right, then sought out his producer and raised his eyebrows in nervous bewilderment. "Huh," said Barry Reno, repeating the sequence in reverse, this time ending up gazing at the far wall, some three hundred feet away. "Well, this is the damnedest thing." He cleared his throat and spoke to the studio audience. "I can see, I mean, everything is very clear and…how the hell did you do that?"

"Oh," said Jurgen, "is just little trick."

Chapter Eighteen

Curtis Sweetchurch, sitting in the green room, wasn't paying much attention to the little monitor, concentrating instead on one of the young production assistants, an overly healthy boy whose skin almost exuded a miasma of vitamins and vegetable juices. But the actress in the rubber underwear said, "Wow, did he really fix his eyes?" and Curtis shrieked, "Oh, yes, he did, baby! He's the miracle man!"

"I wish he would do that for me," said the actress, pulling out the front of her gear to give her breasts a little breathing space. "I'm just about blind."

The old man with the whistling nose (who annoyed Curtis quite a bit, because the wrinkled old bogue actually couldn't *stop* his damn nose from whistling) announced, "I don't buy any of it. Reno was just pretending. It's all a fake."

"Oh yeah," agreed the actress sadly.

That's what most people would think, thought Curtis. Pausing to reflect, Curtis realized that's what *he* thought. He then had a good idea, one of a handful that had visited him during his lifetime. He pulled a telephone out of his pocket and stabbed at buttons, connecting with Information.

So it was that, as the television show waned following a nasally fluted performance of Rachmaninoff's "Vocalise," Barry Reno glanced at his producer, looked briefly confused and then announced, "Oh, hey. I guess there's an optometrist or something here gonna check my eyes and see if old Jurgen and Rudolfo really did pull off a little bit of magic."

Dr. Kenneth Beaver came onto the stage awkwardly, a lettered chart held in front of him like a shield. Dr. Beaver was an unsightly looking man and a poor dresser. The suit he'd thrown on—having received the frantic phone call from Curtis Sweetchurch—was threadbare and flecked with old, dried soup. As the credits rolled, Dr. Beaver pointed to lines of type, the letters ranging variously from huge to minuscule. Barry Reno rhymed off their names without hesitation and only toward the end, when the figures ran together in a grey smear, did he squint and grimace. In the show's last moments, Dr. Beaver said, "Excellent. Better than excellent. In fact, Mr. Reno's vision seems to be about thirty/twenty, which puts him in a range of sightedness shared by approximately only three per cent of the adult population." Mind you, much of that statement went unheard by the television audience because the producers, having heard the word "excellent," went to commercial.

And at the George Theater, in an old dressing room with velvet curtains and an ornate daybed, Miranda said "Huh!" and wiggled her long toes. Her toes were framing the portable black-and-white television set, at least they were from Miranda's point of view, because she had her feet propped up on a huge puffy ottoman. She herself was pushed back in an easy chair, surrounded by luxuriant, if ancient, cushions.

Preston was pacing around the dressing room, agitated by

the lust he'd been accumulating since his teenaged years. He lit a cigarette with trembling hands, although another burned in an ashtray in the corner.

Both Miranda and Preston were stark naked, having just coupled with sweat-popping fervour. Which is to say, Preston's large and amorphous form was studded with milky droplets that rose out of his grey skin and beaded at the end of his body hair. Miranda was not so damp, merely suffused by a vaguely skunky radiance. "Now how in hell did the boys do that?" she wondered aloud.

Preston threw a slope-shouldered shrug. "First off," he said, "Rudolfo did nothing. Second of all, you've got to examine your assumptions."

"Right," said Miranda. "Because all magic, all illusion, is predicated on the fact that human beings make assumptions."

"Hey! Who's the pedantic asshole around here?"

"You. Sorry."

"So in this particular case, the assumption is made long before Jurgen ever shows up onstage."

"Which is?"

"Well, we assume that because Barry Reno is wearing glasses that he *needs* them."

"Hey. That's right."

"Reno just thinks he looks more intelligent with glasses on."

"Do you know that for sure?"

"Yeah, yeah. Everybody knows that."

"Really?"

"Okay, maybe I don't *know*, but it seems highly probable."

"*Highly probable* don't get to cut the cake, Presto."

"Look. Jurgen is in the right position to look through Reno's glasses. He sees that the lenses are just plain glass, so he decides to pull the stunt. Remember what he said? *But Barry Reno*, he said, *you don't need glasses*. Right on. So then the doctor comes, he does the little eye test, Reno has great vision, and no one ever thinks to ask Barry if he ever needed the spectacles in the first damn place."

"I dunno," mused Miranda. "That seems awfully intelligent for the boys."

"I guess you have to give them notice, huh?" demanded Preston.

"Say what?"

"You have to give the boys notice. Right? You can't just quit, you know, you can't leave them in the lurch."

Miranda seemed not to have thought about this. "I guess so," she shrugged. The ensuing ripple effect made Preston weak-kneed. "Yeah," continued Miranda. "I'll give them plenty of notice so that they have time to replace me. Mind you I'm the best there is."

Miranda actually experienced a little pang of guilt, because she felt she owed the boys something. After all, at a time when things looked very bleak, they'd offered her employment. Of course, they'd had their own selfish motives—they knew she'd learnt a few things from Emile Zsosz, Master of the Black Art.

They, the boys and Miranda, had become acquaintances, in a strange manner, following the conversation at Shecky's Olympus in which Miranda informed Rudolfo about the existence of Tony Anthony. Rudolfo took the audio cassette entitled "YOU!" back to the Tophet and played it for Jurgen, who had not reacted to begin with. There was a soccer game on the antique television set, the screen blizzarding with electronic snow, but Jurgen stared at it with his stained eyes pried apart.

"Listen," said Rudolfo, plugging in the tape. He pressed the play button. After many, many empty moments, a spit-polished voice hollered, "*You!!*"

Jurgen didn't budge, didn't even blink, he merely continued

to watch the soccer players swimming in the static. Rudolfo, on the other hand, jumped two feet in the air. "*You* are nothing!" screamed the man on the machine. "*You* are insignificant! *You* are nothing!"

Jurgen rose suddenly, crossed over to the television and poked at it with a thick forefinger, silencing the storm. "*You* are but a germ infesting the body of society," continued Tony Anthony. Jurgen cocked his head in order to be more attentive, a strange half-smile playing upon his face. It was unlikely that he comprehended anything other than the frantically shouted *you*'s. Rudolfo understood more, but was unclear as to what precise point Tony Anthony was making. Surely he didn't think he was telling Jurgen and Rudolfo anything they didn't know. Here they were, lost in a desert, their haven a stable rendered out of clapboard and flypaper. "*You* are nothing," Tony Anthony repeated, and Rudolfo actually snorted. "Tell me about it," he thought sardonically, he who had been a blind bald beggar on the storm-buffeted streets of Münich.

Still, it wasn't long before Tony Anthony's voice began to raise their spirits. Jurgen and Rudolfo started to breathe heavily, drawing in great draughts of dry desert air. They began to rock back and forth on the balls of their feet to flex their muscles and by the end of Side A, they were both ballooned with hormones, the pasty smoothness of their skin marbled with ropey vein. At the end of Side B they shouted "*Ja!*" in frenzied unison, and then they raced out of the Tophet and began to put their lives in order.

Among their first stops was Shecky's Olympus, where Jurgen joined merrily in the mortification, trying to shed the sad dimpled fat hanging over his belt, American fat he'd acquired in an American way, motionless with his eyes glued to a television set. Jurgen had never worked out with much frequency, but he was a much more gifted athlete than Rudolfo. Having descended the long stairs into the sweaty gymnasium, he lay down on a crunch board and immediately cranked out a rapid series of sets, thirty crunches each, ten seconds rest. When he was through, sweat had collected on the ridges of his forehead. He next arched his body across a bench and began to launch a fifty-pound dumb-bell from the ground to the emptiness above him. When he was done that, the sweat spilled over and filled his eyes. "*Ja!!*" he screamed, exultant with pain.

"Jurgen, this is Miranda," said Rudolfo, pointing to the woman who lay on a mat in the middle of the room, her body fashioned into an enormous pretzel.

"*Guten Tag*," said Jurgen, but he didn't pay her any further attention. He leapt up, took hold of the chin-up bar and raised his legs, the resultant angle having a mathematical precision, ninety perfect degrees. His stomach was, for the time being, cowed into submission and merely ached dully. Once he stopped, the muscles would flame up and probably disintegrate, so he didn't allow himself any respite. Rudolfo felt Jurgen was being very rude. He was, it's true; then again, Jurgen was unintention-ally rude to most people. Manners were not highly prized in the Schubert household, where brute bullying was the only force that conferred any advantage. Rudolfo, tsking his tongue in his part-ner's direction, decided to make amends. He was forgetting, for some reason, that he was a rude person himself, his rudeness aris-ing out of a surly haughtiness. "So," he asked, "what you do?"

"Legs."

"No. Not what you do today, what you do every day?"

"Like for a job?"

Rudolfo grinned and nodded.

"I'm a thaumaturgical assistant," Miranda said, at which point Jurgen tore himself off the machine with an extended yodel of excruciation. He assumed a half-crouch in the middle of the floor and looked for some other machine with which to flay the few remaining muscles in his abdomen.

"Which is to say," said Miranda, responding to a new cloudiness in Rudolfo's eyes, "I'm a magician's assistant."

"Hey, *Jurg*," said Rudolfo, attempting to truncate his friend's name in an American, palsy-walsy way, "this woman is assistant to magician."

This news almost engaged Jurgen's attention. "*Sehr gut*," he said, and marched off to an incline bench in a corner of the room. He hooked his toes under the roller at the high end and began to struggle upwards.

"We are magicians!" exclaimed Rudolfo.

"No fooling around?"

Rudolfo thought about that for a few moments before repeating, "We are magicians."

"So, where are you working?"

He shrugged. His English was not up to hiding the truth in a tiny pile of half-truths. Moreover, he wasn't inclined to. "We no work," he said. "In Münich and Paris, we are big stars. But here we are nothing."

"Most people here are nothing," said Miranda, unfolding her body, rising to her full height.

Rudolfo stared at this monstrously beautiful woman. He sucked on his lips as though doing a mathematical calculation, trying to total tall columns of long numbers. Inwardly, he was resolving not to be nothing, to cease being nothing, to be nothing never again.

Jurgen came to stand beside him; his breath was uneven and halting, undercoated with moans.

"If you're not working," said Miranda, adding, "this week…"

That was such an act of kindness that Rudolfo briefly considered falling in love with this woman.

"…you should maybe come out and see Emile Zsosz's show."

Of course, Rudolfo misunderstood. He misunderstood to

such an extent that he failed to realize Miranda was actually enunciating words—it sounded as though this woman's teeth had suddenly fallen from her gums and were stuck down her throat. Miranda was used to this. "The show," she said evenly, "of Monsieur Emile Zsosz."

Jurgen's head had been aimed skyward, his throat distended and his Adam's apple bobbing. But at the mention of this name his head snapped downwards and steadied itself at Miranda. "Emile Zsosz?" he repeated. "But is not he dead?"

"Well," said Miranda, "not technically."

The Oasis was an aptly named establishment, being as it stood, virtually alone, in the middle of the desert. Two highways intersected nearby, and gas stations studded each corner. These way stations had taken the concept of "gas wars" to new extremes. They'd not only lowered prices until they were virtually giving the stuff away, the owner/managers had grown murderously antagonistic toward each other, and from time to time the wasteland rang with gunfire. The Oasis flowered from the sand, a column six stories high, each floor indicated by a different-coloured balcony.

The nightclub was encased in glass on the roof, so that the night sky surrounded the patrons. When that sky was cloudless, the stars seemed to bump up against the glass like confused little birds. Sometimes, though, the mere presence of The Oasis, substance in the middle of nothingness, caused puffy little thunderheads to form, and rain and lightning banged the glass rumbustiously and demanded entry. Quite often—and such was the case on the evening that Jurgen and Rudolfo chose to visit—both climes occurred together, the storms lasting about half an hour, followed by short periods of fineness.

Jurgen and Rudolfo doubled the size of the audience.

"*Ja*," said Rudolfo, "I am having green chartreuse."

Rudolfo addressed this comment to the strange person standing beside their table, who, despite nurse's shoes and a white frock with the name "Flora" stitched above the breast pocket, looked for all the world like Bertie Vogts, one of Jurgen's football heroes. Suddenly nostalgic, Jurgen ordered a beer, even though beer was on the "Forbidden Foods" list that Rudolfo maintained. The list was not written down anywhere, but no less tangible for that; it was so familiar to Jurgen that he fancied he knew which position beer occupied—three, just underneath *bratwurst* (one) and *zabaglione*.

"Ladies and gentlemen…" A husky voice sounded in the room, an accent shading all of the words, which, oddly, made them easier for Jurgen to comprehend. "It is our privilege to introduce the Master of the Black Art, Emile Zsosz." Jurgen and Rudolfo applauded politely. Music began abruptly, the phonograph needle bumping off the first note and clearing three full bars before settling again. It was Ravel's "Boléro," realized Rudolfo. It had been one of the favourites at his mother's Salon. The recording, he recalled, consisted of four thick plastic plates. In the middle of the long crescendo, the music would suddenly stop and everyone—all of the artistes and all of the models—would hurry to replace the disc. Even those most somnambulant with drugs would somehow launch themselves toward the antique machine.

In the middle of that memory, someone turned off the house lights, plunging everything into a faintly starlit darkness. The night sky pressed upon the glass all around. The moon was shaped like a scimitar, the stars scattered like seeds of light.

The stage before them was shrouded in shadow. A point of light appeared some six feet above the ground, then shot suddenly down, the point elongating until it met the ground and revealed itself as a long, gleaming zipper. Then the zipper came apart, starting at the top. A tiny metallic razoring sound filled

The Oasis. When the zipper was fully opened, hands appeared between the parted teeth and pushed the two sides apart. Through this rent in the air stepped Emile Zsosz.

He would have been a spectacularly handsome man, thought Rudolfo, when he was young. This would have been, oh, around the time of the French Revolution. No, no, that was just a joke; Zsosz wasn't that old, only a hundred and ten or so, but he seemed more ancient due to his bizarre efforts to appear otherwise. For example, his hair was dyed jet-black, and where there was no hair Zsosz's scalp itself was japanned. He had drawn black eyebrows over his dull grey eyes with a trembling hand so that his expression was all things all at once: terror, surprise, jollity. Zsosz's most prominent facial feature was his moustache, which blew from the sides of his mouth like the wings of an small airplane. It, too, had been painted black, and where it met the philtrum the connection had been filled with ink. His nose was still fine, although it was spiderwebbed with veins and leaked white stuff. The rest of Zsosz's face had been dulled by time, just as stones are smoothed by the sea.

Emile Zsosz wore a robe, an ornate silk affair that featured intricate stitching and brocade. He raised and spread his arms— the silk of the sleeves forming two perfect semicircles—and doves appeared on his palms; no, not doves, Rudolfo saw suddenly, but cloud pigeons from Madagascar, extremely rare, the name derived from the fluffy immature down which the birds retained into adulthood. The cloud pigeons flew away and in their stead were two crows—actually, Rudolfo saw, Icelandic ravens—birds as black as soot. They bounced up and down on Zsosz's pale palms like heavyweight contenders aching to get a poke at the other guy. Then these birds, too, were gone.

The old man remained with his arms outstretched, motionless except for a trembling of the fingertips, tiny in amplitude but of such frequency that it likely produced a pitch that dogs could hear. The silken robe began to move to the side, although the head remained where it was, and after a few seconds the two parts of Zsosz's body were separated by a good five feet. The head, floating in the air, didn't seem to care about this situation, particularly; it spun like a moon and wore an expression of stale melancholy. Across the stage, the hands rose up; between the fingers of one was a cigarette, and upon the palm of the other a tiny ball of blue flame. The hands brought these two together, so that the cigarette's end glowed and smouldered and mare's tails of grey smoke ribboned through the darkness. Then one of the hands threw the cigarette toward the head. Emile Zsosz opened his mouth slightly to receive it and the ancient man was soon puffing away happily.

Clouds had been bumping up against the tower in the desert, clinging to the dirty windows; The Oasis was now yoked by a dark cumulus ring. Suddenly a wheel of lightning spun about the glass and brickwork like the rotor on a child's toy. It lit the innards of the nightclub with the power of a battery of kliegs, and there was no mystery now. Emile Zsosz stood, humbled as though naked, which of course he was not; he was wrapped from the neck down in a black leotard, the bulge of his hernia disquietingly visible. And the "body" did indeed have a head, although it was sheathed in an eyeless hood.

The lightning completed its journey to heaven—lightning bolts drive upwards, not down—and the stage was once more darkened. Zsosz's head was again disembodied, but a change had come over it. His eyes were gone, leaving little nests of wrinkles in their stead. The tip of his tongue stuck out from between his lips. And what little colour there'd been in the head abruptly disappeared, leaving behind a paleness that cut the shadows like a beacon.

The head plummeted and met the stage with a dull thud.

The body in the silken robe was suddenly animated. An arm

lifted, the fingers groped about in the emptiness above and Miranda's face appeared. She fell to her knees and gathered in the old man's head; she bent over and covered the withered mouth with her own. She huffed and puffed into the head as though she could inflate the rest of Emile Zsosz. But it soon became clear that she could not, and she broke her lips away, lifted her head and said, very quietly, "Someone want to get the lights?"

The overheads flickered and filled the room with purple fluorescence.

Jurgen and Rudolfo rose from their seats and moved closer, seemingly to help, although neither knew the first thing about first aid, and both knew that Emile Zsosz was a long way past aid of any kind. All that they could think to do—and they thought of it at pretty much the same time—was to look at the beautiful weeping woman and ask, "Do you want new job?"

When Samson lashes his face with a long pale tongue, Rudolfo opens his eyes and crosses back into consciousness. We cannot really say that he awakens. He sits up on the bench and gathers his few thoughts. Miranda was here, he remembers. Miranda came back and now she is gone again.

Samson makes an odd kind of noise, stepping backwards and puckering his old white maw, emitting a startling woof. "Was?" demands Rudolfo, and Samson, by way of answer, turns suddenly and paces purposefully for the door of the Gymnasium. Then Samson heels about and makes another of the woofing sounds, and Rudolfo realizes that Samson is imitating Lassie. Rudolfo is willing to play along. "What is it, boy?" he asks, rising to his feet. His legs wobble, his tiny shrivelled stomach sends up a mouthful of bile, which he spits onto the floor. "Is one of the animals in trouble?" Rudolfo has been negligent in the care of his charges. He is aware (although he has not really acknowledged it until just now) that there are tiny feathered and furred corpses littering the house. So now he will be able to save something. Perhaps one of the moon-eyed bushbabies has gotten into some mischief and is dangling from a chandelier, or perhaps one of the birds of paradise, which are beautiful but as stupid as mud, has his head stuck down the toilet.

Samson disappears through the door and Rudolfo follows behind. They do not bear right, which is the way to the staircase that will guide one to upper levels and light. To bear left is to invite ectopia and shadow. There is no place to go there, there is no destination, other than the Grotto. So Rudolfo takes only a step or two in that direction and then he swings about—if an animal is dying down there, then the *animal must die. But after he has turned, Rudolfo registers what he has seen. There was a hole of light in the wall, gaping and irregular, the kind of hole that would be made if someone had rolled back the giant boulder that stopped the entrance to the Grotto. He sneaks a look over his shoulder. His stomach throws up a thimbleful of vomit. The boulder has indeed been rolled back. Rudolfo inhales deeply and wonders what to do next.*

He doesn't wonder for long, although he comes nowhere near decision or resolve. Someone brings an old-fashioned wooden cudgel down upon his perfectly naked head, propelling him brutally over the cliff and back into the void again.

Chapter Nineteen

The young woman Tiu had not been cleaning *das Haus* with the zeal and discipline for which she was renowned. Why, she had not been cleaning at all; in fact, she not been spotted by Rudolfo for many, many days.

(Tiu had gone to live in Yellowknife, where, she believed, the arctic air would kill airborne germs and mites. This move was financed by a strange and mysterious man who had given her a lot of money, more money than she could have made in seven years of featherdusting. Tiu did not intend to give up feather-dusting, of course; it was more passion than occupation. In exchange for all this money, Tiu had drawn a crude map of *das eindrucksvollste Haus im Universum*. She had scratched a circle around the lopsided representation of the Grotto, had drawn a thick *X* through the window that was most proximate. The strange man had rolled up the piece of paper between his thin, bony hands. He had laughed in an unseemly manner, and Tiu suddenly smelled death and decay.)

Rudolfo considered placing a phone call and hiring a new maid, but he couldn't see himself allowing a stranger into *das Haus*. So he elected to clean up the place himself. He had some notion of how this sort of thing was accomplished, although he'd never really done it. Since he'd become world-famous there were servants to do that sort of thing. Before he'd become world-famous, he'd had nothing, and nothing rarely needed straightening up. Before that he'd lived at the circus, and you don't clean up circuses. Before that, he'd lived in stainless-steel institutions. Before that, he'd lived in a walk-up at Kramgasse 49, and his mother didn't care about order, and besides, one of the previous residents had written all over the walls, so why bother?

But Rudolfo intuited that cleaning was a simple matter of methodical disposition. So look, here is a magazine on the floor, when it should be instead on the coffee table, or what would be a coffee table if anybody in the gloomy *Haus* ever drank coffee. Rudolfo bent over and plucked it up. It was a *Personality* magazine. He recognized the distinctive lettering before he recognized that he himself was pictured on the cover. Jurgen and Rudolfo. Curtis Sweetchurch must have brought, or sent, the issue over. Curtis had mentioned that the Reno show had raised their recognition factor significantly. Rudolfo considered the show a complete debacle, of course, a disaster from Samson's listless puking, through Jurgen's adolescent hand-holding, to the very undramatic mangling of Reno's thick spectacles.

Rudolfo flipped through the magazine, searching for the accompanying article. He found it, four pages crowded with photographs. Most prominent was a picture that occupied the whole of one page. It showed Jurgen standing atop the hideous old Houdini Substitution Box. The photograph caught the instant of Jurgen's sudden and startling arrival, his improbable replacement of Miranda. Rudolfo stood off to one side with a sleek silver microphone held up to his mouth. This photograph

interested Rudolfo very much. He stared at the image of his
own face and attempted to decode the expression frozen there.
His nostrils were pinched, flattened by a sudden inhalation of
air. Rudolfo did this often, and for a variety of reasons—to
convey superiority, *ennui* or disapproval of airborne pungency.
Or horror.

Samson, meanwhile, was watching a television show because
the two were in the Television Room, the huge machine surrounded by a mini-moat full of carp. The hungry fish kissed at
the water, puckering the surface. Samson ignored them. He sat
with his brow furrowed with feline concentration, his tongue
lolling over the pale gums. Samson was, in truth, not so en-
grossed in the broadcast fare as he made himself out to be; it was
a cooking show, and cooking shows made little sense to a creature whose custom was to inhale raw, blood-spurting victuals.
But through concentration Samson could ignore, or pretend to
ignore, the presence of the black-clad human beyond the oval
windows. Samson had spotted the prowler many minutes ago,
had been alarmed to see a shape materialize on the other side of
a nearby pane of glass. The creature peeked into the room, made
eye contact with Samson, and then disappeared in a twinkling. So
Samson yawned and stretched and watched the schoolmarmish
woman on the televison prepare a *ballottine*. He was struck, as he
often was while watching such shows, by the fact that the woman
herself, soft-skinned and nicely fatted, would probably taste
much better than the meal she laboured over.

Rudolfo flipped to a photograph taken on the day of the
auction. It pictured Jurgen, Rudolfo, Miranda and Samson standing in a corner with the world-famous asshole, Kaz. It was recent,
only a few weeks old. Jurgen still possessed his rather bottom-
heavy muscular substance. His hair was curled heroically. His
eyes twinkled; well, that is not entirely accurate, Jurgen's eyes
never twinkled, but they emitted a light of some low wattage.

They evidenced *life*. Staring at this photograph, Rudolfo was forced to admit to himself how much had changed in just weeks, days. Because Jurgen's eyes now possessed a kind of turbidity. They were very still, as though not functioning as eyes should.

Samson stuck out his tongue and lassoed the remote control, dragging it back and into his mouth. He jerked his head, tossing the box lightly between his teeth, until his left fang came to rest on the Δ button. He began to chomp lightly, travelling through the frequencies. He watched out of the corner of his eye until he saw something interesting. It was so interesting that Samson coughed out the remote like so much phlegm.

It was so interesting that Rudolfo, wandering around the Television Room staring at the photographs in *Personality*, dropped the magazine. It landed with a splash in the carp-filled water.

On channel 79 was Preston. It actually took Rudolfo a nanosecond to recognize him, because Preston had shaved or something; somehow his ruddy boiled face had been depilated. His hair was combed, *managed* anyway, drowned in cream and then forced backwards. His clothes were new and ironed and fit his peculiar body as well as any clothes might. All in all, Preston looked half-human. (Although, as Preston himself often pointed out, he *was* half-human.)

Preston sat behind a round felt-covered poker table and shuffled a deck of cards, his fat fingers working with improbable facility. Clustered around the table were tiny mewling children, and presiding over them, obviously older but not much larger, was Uncle Rupert. Uncle Rupert wore a cardigan, reading glasses and owned hair that wrapped around his head like seaweed bandages a drowned man. Rudolfo knew Uncle Rupert because— well, he couldn't really remember, he had encountered him at a club or party somewhere. Occasionally, Rudolfo would feel stifled, irritated by Jurgen's stiff-backed solemnity. (Although

Rudolfo was now rather nostalgic for that solemnity, the way
Jurgen would march slowly into the kitchen for a glass of juice,
not saying a word, unwittingly imbuing the simplest facets of his
life with pomp and circumstance.) So, feeling stifled, Rudolfo
would sneak out to some party or club. He wouldn't do much,
not in a sexual sense. Once or twice he kissed boys. He sat beside
them on tall stools and took hold of the backs of their necks and
drove their mouths forward to meet his own. He locked lips and
twisted his own head, tilting it frequently like a bewildered dog.
He would kiss the boys until their pale manicured fingers came
creeping along his thigh, then he would shove them away
brusquely and complain to the bartender about the freshness of
his carrot juice. So it was in such a place that he met Uncle
Rupert, who behaved abominably all night then rose at dawn to
host a show for small children. And on the show this early morning was Preston, shuffling a deck of cards.

"Okay, Uncle Rupert..." began Preston.

"Ah-hmmm?"

"Tell us all the name of the card you chose."

"It was the, what was it now, oh yes, it was the, what was it,
the king of clubs."

Preston abruptly threw the deck up into the air. He reached
into the cloud of playing cards and came away with the king of
clubs caught between his thumb and middle finger.

"Why," ejaculated Uncle Rupert, his eyeballs bulging with
hungover veins, "bind my BVDs!"

The children swarming around the table grinned with
appreciation, impressed not so much with the magical aspects as
by the fact that Uncle Rupert looked momentarily even more
foolish than usual.

Preston lifted the card over his right shoulder, holding it
there so that his assistant might replace it with a new deck.

Samson gasped. A moment later Rudolfo gasped, too, but

Samson had beat him to the gasping punch, opening his blanched mouth and emitting a gust of injured air. Because Preston's assistant—wearing an outfit that was hurtling all of the little boys toward puberty—was Miranda.

Samson's reaction was to inhale hugely, sucking in the remote control. He bit down hard, shattering the huge screen into a million dots of light which then slowly faded away.

"Time for bed," said Rudolfo. He was a bit surprised to discover it was near dawn. He knew that he'd been avoiding the huge, empty bed, but he was amazed to find out he'd avoided it so successfully, and for so long.

Samson knew that he should stay up. There was a prowler outside the house, after all, a terrifying human wrapped in black, and Samson, the grandest of all the animals, should assume the role of protector. But Samson launched himself toward the bedroom, his gait a slack, butt-wiggling trot. Samson was very upset, because, although it was clear that Rudolfo wasn't going to talk about it, Miranda had left them for Preston.

"I'm having a new idea for the Show," muttered Rudolfo.

Samson nodded, rounding a corner and spinning out on the Mexican tile. He fell hard, lumbered back up and continued on his way. Samson was now extremely miserable, knowing full well what Rudolfo's idea was—put the old white beast out to pasture, bring on one of those young cats, one of those saliva-dripping brutes with swollen testicles.

The pair arrived at the bedroom. The ceiling was high and vaulted, and on it was painted a parody of Michelangelo's "Creation," one with Rudolfo and Jurgen rendered in place of God and Adam. (This had been Rudolfo's idea, so he was the one pictured to the right. Rudolfo had never asked for much, after all, so it was only fair that he should be God.) Rudolfo bent over to remove his clothes and was a little startled to see that he wasn't wearing any. He then reached up to pull off his hairpiece, and was even more startled to feel the cool smoothness of his head.

He picked up the pace then, heading for the round mattress. As he passed the hideous Davenport Spirit Cabinet, he thought again that he really should try to find another place to house the thing. There must be some other room that could accommodate it. It could even be used for storage; it could be filled with old clothes and jewellery. He was pleased with this thought and resolved to move the cabinet as soon as possible. Rudolfo could pretend his determination to move the Spirit Cabinet had nothing to do with the animals that were currently flying and crawling out of the crescent-shaped holes in the front panelling. And through these openings came animals, which a portion of Rudolfo's mind catalogued without reflection: yellow-headed amazon, kittiwake, hamadryad.

Then the twin doors flew apart, and Jurgen emerged from inside.

"Hello, Rudolfo!" he said, a cheery and hale greeting such as acquaintances might exchange at a party. *"Wie geht's?"*

Jurgen floated to the ground, stark naked, his body glowing softly. His descent to the carpet was odd, as though it had been filmed and was being played back at a slower speed. His skin threw off light, light that chased away the gloom and shadow far more effectively than the dawn leaking through the cathedral-style windows.

Rudolfo smiled, nodded, and waved toward the round mattress; for some reason words were not forthcoming. Rudolfo yawned to illustrate the fact that he was very tired, exhausted even. He headed for bed.

The black-clad creature remained outside *das Haus*, working with a pry bar on a side window, although he obviously lacked expertise in this field. At one point the blade of the bar skipped out from under the window's metal rim and flew backwards. The creature, alarmed by the weapon it was now swinging, tried to duck out of the way. The metal bar bounced off his head with an audible *thwonk*, knocking a pair of thick spectacles into the shrubbery. He stumbled backwards, turning dizzy, woozy circles. During one of these spins the sun rose over the distant hills, bathing the creature in weak, golden light. He gave out a whimper worthy of Count Dracula, recoiling, covering the eyeholes in the raven-pitched hood.

The bells keep sounding, filling the air with clouds of mournful music. Outside the doors of das Haus, strange creatures continue to appear. When no one responds from within the mansion, the little monsters turn petulant and vengeful. Many have urinated on the stoop. Some have scooped up the shells and sea-throws from the drive and tossed them at the windows, often with enough force to crack the glass. Two of the uninvited visitors, brothers aged seven and five, have made a special point of disguising themselves as Jurgen and Rudolfo. The five-year-old is in a cowboy outfit. He wears chaps and boots and a ten-gallon hat, but leaves his chest bare. The older boy wears a crude white robe. When no one answers the doorbell, these two pound on the oaken door with their tiny fists. Still no one shows—so the little boys begin to circle the irregular perimeter, searching for weakness in the defenses, possible points of entry.

Inside das Haus, *Rudolfo* is lying on the huge circular bed. He was led to the bedroom, practically carried, by the fair Miranda. There are soft pillows propping him up into a semi-sitting position. Rudolfo's heart is pounding quickly, bouncing against his rib cage. Across from him sits the hideous Spirit Cabinet. Creatures crawl from the openings—tiny creatures, for the most part, cockroaches, spiders and beetles.

Miranda comes out of the washroom, a folded wet cloth stretched across her palms. "Someone gave you a hell of a bonk on the head." She gingerly lays the cool square onto his brow. It seems to Rudolfo that he hears sizzling, so strong is his fever. He notices that the Spirit Cabinet is now glowing slightly, light from inside leaking through the tiny cracks.

"What you do, Miranda?"

"*Remember when we first met, how simple everything was? Because you'd say* what you do *and I'd say like* legs, chest, back. *Those were the good old days.*"

"*Why are you at the nudie show?*"

"*Topless.*"

There are larger creatures coming out of the Spirit Cabinet now, skinks and iguanas, serpents from the desert. "So," asks Rudolfo, and he props himself up on his frail brittle elbow, "Why you not with Preston?"

Miranda shrugs. "It's a long story."

"So, what, Miranda, you have an appointment?"

Miranda laughs and wipes a tear from her cheek. "Hey, Rudolfo," she says quietly, "that was almost a joke."

"So tell me."

"What about the intruder?"

"Oh..." Rudolfo waves a hand dismissively. "Samson take care of him."

"Right."

"I always liked Preston," he lies, hoping to get her on track.

"Yeah, me too. So, things went pretty good for a while..."

Chapter Twenty

On the night of Miranda's final performance, something happened that provoked Rudolfo into action. He'd been avoiding true and significant investigation, but he realized, on this night, that he must understand what was happening to Jurgen if ever he was to stop it.

Miranda brought her boyfriend with her. She entered the green room with her perfect hand linked through Preston's bloated and hairy one. "Hey, everybody," Miranda said, "is it okay if Preston watches from the wings?"

The green room had, lately, become very crowded. Curtis Sweetchurch was always in attendance. He had acquired an assistant, a particularly unctuous young man named Bren. Bren was thick and muscular, which gave his unctuousness a threatening nature; Rudolfo often felt that a failure to accept an offer of carrot juice or Orangina would earn him a sound thrashing. The Abraxas management had also materialized, fat men who reeked of cigars. The offending cigars were never in evidence—it was forbidden by Rudolfo—but that didn't prevent the stench from coming in. The fat men brought their wives or girlfriends, doe-eyed young girls, a year or two out of the chorus lines. So this is why Miranda had addressed her question to "everybody."

They all turned to look at Jurgen, who sat cross-legged on a sofa. He held a deck of cards in his hands and shuffled with effortless grace, despite his fingernails. Jurgen had played *here's the church, here's the steeple* until his digits formed a solid, even architecturally sound, church; when he opened the doors he displayed a host of tiny, fleshy worshippers, more than could be accounted for by eight fingers. After he had gone as far as he could with that very limited art form, he had moved on to card shuffling.

Feeling the weight of eyes upon him, he made the entire deck disappear. The hangers-on clapped dutifully. Jurgen looked up and shrugged. The lights hit his eyes and robbed them of their blueness, leaving him with two pale stones. "Ask Rudolfo," Jurgen said.

Rudolfo, of course, resented this meaningless deference. He could feel power shifting; even as the Show gained popularity, Rudolfo's hold on it weakened. Still, he opened his mouth to say "no." Magicians do not stand in the wings during the performances of other magicians. It was a transgression against the rules that sorcerers, even weak and ersatz ones, should adhere to. Then it occurred to Rudolfo that he himself was no fucking magician and couldn't care less. "No problem," he muttered.

"Thanks," said Preston.

So they had done the Show with Preston standing backstage with his hands in his pockets as though he were waiting for a bus. Rudolfo had to admit that he didn't really seem to bother anybody. Jurgen even slapped him on the back before trotting onto the stage, like the two of them were teammates participating in one of the barbaric contests Jurgen found so riveting on television. (*Used to find so riveting.* Jurgen no longer watched televised sports, or televised anything.) Miranda, darting on and off, threw a number of warm smiles in Preston's direction. Several times she'd make her costume changes beside him, peeling off one outfit, exchanging it for another, all the time looking at him with impishly raised eyebrows. Preston would blush and look away, leaning forward as if to see more exactly what the shadows between the curtains held. The only one who seemed quite upset with the rival magician's presence was Samson, who refused to climb into the silver ball as long as Preston was watching.

The Show went along very nicely, Rudolfo thought, until it ground to a halt with the Houdini Substitution Box. But Rudolfo had resigned himself to this grinding. He went to the silver stand and wrenched the pistol-shaped microphone off the head. "Okay, ladies and gentlemen," he said. "Everybody is hearing of Harry Houdini."

Suddenly the microphone disappeared from his hand; it took Rudolfo a moment to realize that Jurgen had yanked it away and was now wandering about the stage, flipping the mike cable in his wake. "Everybody, tonight is special night, and also very sad. Because tonight we going to lose our Miranda."

Miranda, Rudolfo saw, was crying. There were slick patches under both of her eyes. Rudolfo was furious with Miranda. (Actually, he was simply furious, and Miranda was a handy target.) It was her decision to leave the Show after all these years, it was her choice to throw in her lot with Preston and the shoddy little George Theater. So, thought Rudolfo, *fuck you, bay-bee.*

"But instead of be sad," said Jurgen, spinning now so that the cable didn't become tangled with the hem of his long sackcloth, "we going to have a little bit of fun. How about that?"

Rudolfo clapped his hands together. "Hoo boy!" he called out listlessly.

"Okay, so this is Substitution Box. Same one used by Harry Houdini. Here is how it work."

Jurgen held the microphone out to the side. Rudolfo stared

at it for a few seconds before realizing that he was expected to
trot over and claim it like a menial stagehand. Still, he did so,
and he pressed the soft mesh to his lips and went, "Hoo boy,"
once again, in a darkly ominous way.

Miranda stood above the box, raised the curtain and then,
in the slimmest of moments, the curtain was lowered and there
stood Jurgen. The Substitution Box was opened and Miranda
was found bound and manacled in the sack that, moments before,
had held Jurgen. The audience applauded enthusiastically. "Is
same trick Harry Houdini did!" explained Rudolfo. "Exactly the
same. No change in seventy years."

Again the microphone disappeared. Rudolfo made a mental
note: *two* microphones. "Okay, ladies and gentlemen," said
Jurgen. "Rudolfo is right. No change. Never any change in metamorphosis routine. Except tonight, Miranda and I going to do
something little bit different."

Miranda cocked her head sideways, suddenly. This was
obviously news to her.

"We going to do it again *without* the curtain!" Jurgen
clapped his hands together, meaning to kick-start the stage into
animation. But Rudolfo and Miranda (and Samson, over in the
corner) merely stared at him blankly.

"Come on, let's do it!" said Jurgen, driving the palms of his
hands together once more.

"Um," questioned Rudolfo, raising a finger into the air, "can
you do it without curtain?"

"Why not?" demanded Jurgen.

Well, thought Rudolfo, this is hardly the place to have this
discussion. Still, if he gave his words a kind of goofy, comedic
spin, maybe everyone would assume it was part of the Show. Too
bad he wasn't any good at giving words a goofy, comedic spin.
"Well, if you don't use the curtain, Jurgie, everybody going to see
how you do it!"

"That's okay," said Jurgen. This time, when he clapped, the sound cue trumpeted, new lights speared the stage, and Miranda bolted forward.

What did people see in the moment of exchange, in that instant when Miranda disappeared and Jurgen took her place? Talking about it afterwards, audience members were divided in their opinions. Some claimed that there had been a kind of trans-mutation, that Miranda's limbs had shrivelled slightly, that her torso rippled with new masculine muscle, that her hair had receded and whitened and then there stood the conjuror in her stead. Others claimed that there had simply been an exchange, as though the Almighty had spliced one piece of time, containing Miranda, to another piece of time, containing Jurgen.

What did Rudolfo see? He saw nothing, because he had turned away. This was only partly out of fear. There was, in the split-second before the transformation took place, a realization, and Rudolfo turned abruptly to look at Preston. What Rudolfo saw was Preston fashioning his face into the most profound of scowls. Preston mouthed the word "Shit" with great venom and fumbled for a cigarette.

So it was that the following day—a dark Monday—Rudolfo determined to attend Preston's Show at the George.

Ever since Jimmy there had been a succession of chauffeurs. Men and women were sent from a firm whose job it was to con-nect menials with masters. Chauffeurs changed on an almost daily basis, because Rudolfo, finding some paltry ennoblement in the ruling of the roost, dismissed them with aristocratic hau-teur. This one talked too much, this one talked too little, this one smelt bad, this one used too much cologne. Rudolfo went out to the garages not knowing who or what to expect.

He threw open the door, hoping to catch the newest chauf-feur picking his nose or idly toying with his *Schniedelwutz*. It

252 THE SPIRIT CABINET

would have afforded Rudolfo a tiny amount of satisfaction to fire a driver just seconds after having laid eyes upon him. His initial thought was that the garage was empty, at least of humanity. The limousine sat there, washed and gleaming; the chauffeur's table and chair was nearby, a logbook unfolded upon the table top. But no chauffeur, or so Rudolfo thought, until he glanced down.

A dark little man, his skin the shade of eggplant, squatted there in a ridiculously squashed way, knees parallel with his rounded eyes, his bum just a fraction of an inch from the floor. His hands held stones, round and pale as Jurgen's eyes. He tossed these onto the ground, allowed them to roll to a stop, then scooped them up again. Rudolfo stared down at the man's scalp, where designs had been cut and razored into the short black curls. He cleared his throat.

The man leapt up, not from alarm so much as a kind of elasticity, his legs snapping and propelling him skyward. He displayed a set of blindingly white teeth and hooked a palm over his eyes, a hasty and sloppy salute. Then he produced his cap and spent many long moments putting it on, even though it was nothing more than a brim with a few tatters of material miraculously attached.

Rudolfo was momentarily too stunned to fire him. By the time he had his finger lifted and poised, by the time he'd prepared his throat for the appropriate volume and tone, the black man had turned around and was skipping for the limousine. He pulled open the rear door and gestured madly at the leather interior. There was something in his smile, an almost insane desire to please and be helpful, that weakened Rudolfo, so he shrugged and said, "You are taking me to the George Theater."

The man shrugged, compliantly, philosophically, arrogantly, Rudolfo couldn't tell. "The George Theater," he repeated and climbed into the huge stretch limo.

Rudolfo was wearing his nylon anorak, the hood pulled up and cinched tightly under his chin. He also had on large wraparound sunglasses that effectively hid half his face. And he assumed his hunch, the stooped posture that obscured his lovely physique. So he was very surprised to hear, as he hobbled toward the George Theater, a voice calling, "Oh! Hi, Rudolfo!"

He spun around and saw a man beside him, also headed for the George. He gazed upon the man with utter bafflement.

"Sam Rochester," the stranger explained. "The Amazing Romo. I work the Byzantine."

"*Ja*," said Rudolfo, picking through the man's words with some distaste.

"Come to see Preston's new show, huh?"

"Preston is very good friend of mine," Rudolfo announced grandly. This was the tack he had decided to take if cornered by bloodthirsty journalists—that he, Jurgen and Preston were good friends, that the transference of Miranda was more along the lines of a trade or a loan than a heartless defection.

"He's a great guy, isn't he?" said this Sam Rochester, this Amazing Romo of whom, of course, Rudolfo had never heard.

"He is," repeated Rudolfo, "good friend."

Suddenly it was his turn to purchase a ticket. Behind the glass sat a woman with huge hair and enormous glasses that rose and cut into the air like wings. She did not possess a nose, but rather a beak, and her mouth, crudely outlined in thick black lipstick, moved constantly, as if waiting for worms to be dropped inside. "How many?" she screamed at Rudolfo.

Rudolfo thought about that for a moment, certainly not a long moment, but long enough for the woman to raise her voice until it rattled the glass booth. "How *many?*"

"One!" shouted Rudolfo.

"Fifteen smackeroos," said the woman. Rudolfo began to dig around in his little waist-purse, silently praying that this odd phrase had something to do with money. He fished out a hundred-dollar bill and, not noticing the mouse hole through which business was customarily conducted, reached up and tossed the bill over top of the glass. It floated down like a leaf and settled on Mrs. Antoinette Kingsley's head. Rudolfo didn't wait for change.

He clung to the shadowed wall at the back, not even claiming one of the old, worn, velveteen seats, but people continued to spot and recognize him. What was infuriating was that there was no excitement attached to the recognition; his presence sent no bristling ripples throughout the dusty room. Instead he got a lot of nods and mumbled pleasantries: "Hey, Rudolfo, how's it going?" "*Ciao*, Rudolfo." Who were these people who knew who he was but didn't fully comprehend *who he was*?

Miranda walked onto the stage, dressed in a man's tuxedo jacket. Underneath, she wore a t-shirt heralding the Swift Current Broncos, faded blue jeans and cowboy boots. So piebald, faded and time-chewed were the boots that Rudolfo guessed that she'd pulled them from the feet of a dying cowboy. There was applause, enthusiastic even; Rudolfo began to suspect that strange things were going on, when Miranda could get applause without showing her breasts or perfect buttocks. He even spanked his own hands together listlessly.

Miranda raised a hand (the applause died away quickly, obediently) and snapped her fingers. A deck of blue-backed Bees appeared there. She fanned these, imperceptibly coaxing the cards into a perfect half-circle. She then tossed them into the air, where they hovered momentarily, and during that moment a fat hand appeared from nowhere, swiped the air greedily and grabbed one of the cards. The remainder of the deck fluttered to the ground. Then Preston stepped out of the shadows and approached the apron of the stage. "Hey, buddy," he said, stabbing his finger at a young man. "Name a card."

"Um…" said this fellow, "the seven of hearts."

Preston snapped the card out from where it sat upon his palm. It was the seven of hearts.

Rudolfo knew how that was done, of course. The kid was a stick, a plant, a student from UNLV who picked up a few bucks nightly by saying the words "seven of hearts." (The "um," Rudolfo calculated, was improvised; the kid was probably a drama major.)

More card tricks followed. Miranda pulled a seemingly end-less supply of blue-backed Bees from thin air. Preston would then perform illusions, all of which Rudolfo put down to the presence of sticks until about an hour into Preston's act, at which point it dawned on him that half the audience seemed to be sticks and that Preston couldn't afford so many, not with his measly fifteen-dollar ticket price. Even he and Jurgen could hardly afford so many. Indeed, they only had the one, the chubby woman pulled from the audience during the intimate, heart-to-heart Up Close and Personal section. Rudolfo tried to recall the woman's name. He thought it might be Anna, but that was wrong—that name belonged to his mother.

Rudolfo was startled by applause, caused by the execution of another minor miracle by the fat, ugly man standing on the stage. He shook his head, clearing it, and fled to the lobby.

Some time later, applause blossomed again inside the stale and dusty hall. It went on for quite a while. Rudolfo imagined Preston and Miranda taking their calls, the fat man stiff-backed and formal, Miranda fluid and touched by grace. Then the dou-ble doors blew apart and the audience emerged, their faces uni-formly flushed and grinning.

It didn't take long for the hall to clear, because the hall only held perhaps eighty people. Eighty people at fifteen dollars a pop. Rudolfo no doubt made more as a beggar back in Münich.

His insides were momentarily twisted by the memory of happiness. He realized that this was foolish; there was no logical reason why he should have been happier as a penniless fugitive from the law than as a world-famous, infinitely wealthy, Las Vegas show business legend. He swiped at his clothes, certain that the exiting crowd had raised a cloud of dust that was now settling down upon him. Then he turned and wheeled into the theatre.

"Tell me what is in books!" he shouted.

Preston looked up from where he was crawling on hands and knees, gathering up playing cards. Rudolfo momentarily felt very sorry for this unsightly ill-complexioned man who must gather up his own cards, painstakingly reorder them and stuff them back into their boxes.

"Hi, Rudolfo," he said. "I thought you'd come sometime."

"Jurgen is not himself. He is acting very strange. You see how he dresses. He doesn't weigh enough. He glows in the dark. What is in books?"

Preston scrambled to his feet, throwing a shrug through his lumpy, fluid body as he did so. "Just information," he mumbled quietly.

"Help me," said Rudolfo.

"I'd like to help you," said Preston the Adequate. "I really, really would. But I can't tell you what's in the books. You wouldn't understand."

Rudolfo was so far from understanding that this statement held no sting. "Help me," he repeated.

Preston clutched a stack of blue-backed Bees. He stared at them for a second, fanned them to make sure he held something resembling a deck. Then he pointed to the velvet-topped table centre stage. "Go sit down there."

Rudolfo sprang up onto the stage and threw himself into the chair—not the stiff-backed wooden chair reserved for the audience participant, but the big stuffed easy chair where Preston sat.

Preston approached with the cards spread so that Rudolfo could see the dissimilar faces. Then he flipped and stacked them, gave them a couple of riffle shuffles. "Right," he said, squaring up and aiming the deck at Rudolfo. "Here's what I want you to do. Take a card. Don't look at it. Put it face down on the table and cover it up with your hand."

"I don't have time for tricks."

"Do it."

Rudolfo reluctantly slipped out a single card, laying it on the table, covering it with his hand, which was as smooth and cold as china.

"If you want me to help you," said Preston, lowering his voice now so that it was barely more than a thick, wet whisper, "you're going to have to make a little effort. Take a leap, kind of. So this is the thing. Do you believe that when you lift up your hand, that card is going to be there?"

"Yes," said Rudolfo, because that was his firm belief.

"Okay, okay, sure," nodded the fat man emphatically, scattering hair grease and sweat-beads. "But *can* you believe that when you lift your hand, that card is going to be gone?"

The syntax was baffling; Rudolfo stared ahead without making a response.

"It's like this step you have to take or nothing I can say will make any sense," Preston said. "Okay? You have to believe that there's a chance, even the slimmest of chances, that when you take your hand away, that card is going to be gone."

"Gone where?"

"That's not the point."

"Gone where?" persisted Rudolfo, because that *did* seem to be the point. He needed to know the nature of the emptiness.

But Preston shook his head gently. "When you take your hand away," he asked, "is that card going to be there?"

Rudolfo nodded in a small but violent way. "Of course it is," he said cruelly, lifting his hand from the table. The card lay there crookedly. Rudolfo scowled and rose from the seat. "Thanks for the nothings," he said.

"Hey," said Preston. "Don't you want to know what card it is?"

Rudolfo stabbed his long fingers at the table, digging the manicured nails under the pasteboard and flipping it over: the two of hearts.

Chapter Twenty-one

Years ago in Münich, after sharing their first night in their first proper bed, Rudolfo rose and began to prowl. Samson lumbered to his feet and did likewise, driven by love and instinct, but it was obvious from his cloudy, half-lidded eyes that the albino leopard had no idea what they were supposed to be looking for. He watched muzzily as Rudolfo flipped open the lid of Jurgen's velvet production table and sifted through the silver wands and dove pans.

The bed Jurgen and Rudolfo shared—an old wooden bed pilfered from atop a mountain of Münich refuse—was situated in a back upper room at Miss Joe's establishment. Their love-making had been hitherto confined to dark alleys or the Englischer Garten. Rudolfo knew that this suited Jurgen, in a way. He preferred that their fucking have this athletic, outdoorsy nature; then it was not so much deviant, degenerate sex as a kind of wrestling, a physical manifestation of dominance and control. Jurgen had yet to kiss him, to allow a kiss, other than a kind of cousinly cheek-bussing. All this would change in a bed, Rudolfo knew. The mattress would put them on equal footing. The mattress, puffy with dustmite dung, would bring romance.

So they moved in, Rudolfo hauling a single duffle bag, Jurgen producing countless battered cardboard suitcases. Jurgen covered the walls with posters featuring footballers and professional swimmers. He also brought proper exercise equipment, albeit a small collection: a few dumbbells, a wobbly preacher's bench, a chest expander. Jurgen finally moved his magical props and impedimenta from the broom closet below, and it was this stuff that interested Rudolfo. He was most interested in the "two of hearts" routine, the first trick that Jurgen had performed for him and him alone. And a trick that Jurgen repeated now, often, as if it were as close as he could bring himself to an avowal of affection. He often thrust the deck at Rudolfo almost brutally, snarling out the magician's imperative, "Pick a card." Jurgen would riffle the edges gently. Rudolfo would poke in a finger, draw out a card, and then he'd overturn it slowly, his heart thumping, scared to death that the card would *not* be the two of hearts. But it always was the two of hearts. No matter how Rudolfo tempted fate and the gods—he might stick his finger in without hesitation, he might wait until the last possible instant, stopping the riffle with only a card or two left to fall—the card was always the two of hearts. Rudolfo thought this was so lovely that he might die of happiness.

But he could not stop himself from wondering how the thing was done.

So he rose while his lover snored and began to prowl about the room, looking for the special deck. He'd noticed that the backs were different from the cards Jurgen usually preferred, red cards with a diamond design, woven tiny and tight. These special cards featured concentric circles of various sizes, overlapping like rings on a puddle in a hailstorm.

Jurgen sputtered over on the bed. A foot jerked spasmodically, booting away the sheets and leaving him naked and pale. Rudolfo squinted so that he could see his lover through the gloom. Jurgen's arms were bent in front of him, both hands slapped together as though in prayer and slipped under his squared head. When his eyes were closed they were simply two patches of bruised dinginess. Rudolfo sighed and got back to work.

The doves cooed lightly upon his approach. One began jumping up and down slightly, bending and snapping its twiglike legs. Rudolfo fashioned his mouth into a tiny puckered thing and made a few light noises of affection. Samson, fully woken now by the sting of jealousy, opened his mouth, spreading his teeth wide, showing the little birds just how big and spacious death could be. They shut up immediately.

Rudolfo came upon a pile of ropes. He yanked a segment upwards, and the rope snapped in half cleanly. He stooped to pick up the discarded half and, as his two hands neared each other, the ends of the rope seemed to come together of their own volition. The rope was now miraculously restored. Rudolfo grunted quietly in the gloom and once more snapped the rope apart. Each broken end was studded with a tiny plate of metal. Magnets, he realized. He chuckled, pretending to be amused, but in reality rather ashamed and embarrassed on his lover's behalf. The Cut and Restored Rope—an effect Jurgen executed with dour sobriety—was suddenly a baldfaced bit of cozenage. It made both of Rudolfo's artistic pursuits (begging and nude dancing) seem exalted by comparison.

Rudolfo came upon Jurgen's show pants abandoned on the floor and realized that this was the most likely hiding place for the magic deck. Jurgen usually produced them from somewhere behind him, a hand pushing aside the ends of his jacket and snaking back. Rudolfo picked up the pants so that the backside— the rather too large backside, he thought, noting how the material shone where it was stretched across the seat—faced him. A little pouch was sewn into the waistband, and in the pouch were three decks of cards. One box was decorated with the concentric circles. Rudolfo pulled it out, snapped open the lid, slipped out the cards. Drawing a deep breath, Rudolfo turned the cards so that they faced him and managed an awkward fan.

Every other card was the two of hearts. Rudolfo bit his lip and pushed the deck back together. He was blushing slightly, as though he'd pushed open a door and discovered someone hunkered in *der Klos*. It occurred to him that he now knew the secret without understanding how the thing worked, so he reluctantly re-fanned the deck.

It took a few minutes to comprehend. Every other card was the two of hearts; that was the obvious and distressing truth. But each two of hearts was also, Rudolfo discovered, slightly smaller than the other cards. If one squared the deck and thumbed the edge, the tip would catch only the larger cards, showing their faces to the stooge. When the stooge inserted his finger, it would fall automatically atop a smaller card—always the two of hearts.

He walked back to the bed, sitting upon it heavily enough to bounce the mattress, spraying the gloom with silvery dust. Jurgen's eyes opened laboriously. "What's the matter?" he muttered, sensing, even in that first moment, that Rudolfo was angry and vengeful.

"Pick a card," snarled Rudolfo, "any fucking card." Rudolfo squeezed the cards between his fingers, spreading them unevenly, bending and warping them.

"It's called a Svengali deck," Jurgen confessed.

"Cheap trick," spat Rudolfo.

"That's what I've been trying to explain to you." Jurgen propped himself up on one elbow. "They're all cheap tricks. But one day..."

Rudolfo grabbed Jurgen's chin, which afforded him quite

a handhold. Then Rudolfo bent over and kissed his lover, un-
gently.

Following Miranda's departure, chaos began to infect the Show.
Chaos—*Wirrwarr*—there was no other word for it. They had to
find a replacement for Miranda; a tiny ad in the showbiz trades
drew countless beautiful girls and women out of the desert.
Rudolfo auditioned them with a surliness that he hoped masked
his distraction. He saw scores of applicants—he dispassionately
bade them smile, turn around, display their breasts—but Rudolfo
simply had nothing upon which to base a decision. Smiles meant
little to him, all of the women could manage the most graceful of
pirouettes, and tits were tits. So at one point during the process
Rudolfo stood up, aimed a forefinger and pronounced, "She is
good." He'd selected an eighteen-year-old from Flint, Michigan,
named Rhonda Byng. He fled the dance studio before his decision could be questioned by Curtis Sweetchurch or his menacing
assistant Bren.

But it was a mistake, Rudolfo knew that almost immediately.
Eighteen was simply too few years for Rhonda to have achieved
any effective onstage management skills, and the stage needed
rigorous and stern management. Jurgen seemed to have forgotten that there ever was a plan, a pacing and a rhythm for the
Show. He was as likely to open with Up Close and Personal as
the Silver Ball. One evening he walked to the foot of the stage
(his hem floating gently around his naked feet) and stared into
the blackness. "I want to get up close and personal!" he shouted.
Rudolfo rolled the silver ball toward his partner, hoping to bowl
him over into the laps of the fucking people. Rhonda Byng
appeared and threw her body in front of it as a kind of human
shield. Rhonda, Rudolfo realized, had a teenager's heart, howling and heavy, and she had already fallen in love with Jurgen.

But the worst insult, the most evil transgression, was

Jurgen's sudden introduction of half-learned, poorly planned effects. A case in point was the Hindu goddamn Rope Trick. Jurgen would come onstage dragging his length of rope behind him as though it were a slaughtered snake. Rhonda Byng would circle around him, executing muted balletic leaps. Rudolfo would stand off in the wings and scowl. The trick differed each time out. But even Rudolfo would have to admit that the effect progressed and transformed and was now nearing a point where they could consider *rehearsing* the fucking thing.

One show—ten o'clock Saturday, the busiest night, one or two extra people crammed into the already packed house— Jurgen dragged the rope to centre stage and allowed it to drop unceremoniously. "*Ja*, ladies and gentlemen," he said, "is much ballyhooed Hindu Rope Trick. I alone in accident um capable of unrivelling the arcanada."

Rudolfo, standing in the shadows, snapped his fingers and made a mental note to hire a writer to punch up that introduction.

Jurgen bent over, picked up the end of his rope and threw it upwards. With very little apparent effort, it rose in the air and stayed there. The end of the rope slowly bent back and forth, responding to an ethereal breeze.

"*Ja*, dat's good!" said Jurgen, and the audience broke into applause. Rhonda Byng stood beside the rope and clapped with the enthusiasm of a three-year-old. Rudolfo made a mental note to fire her ass—which, he noticed, wasn't big enough to excite the old farts from Pasadena.

Jurgen held both hands in front of his face, palms turned inwards, and summoned spit from deep pockets inside his mouth. He then horked twice, depositing bullets of saliva and sputum into the centre of each hand. He rubbed them together rapidly and his hands began to glow, as though the rubbing excited some phosphor that powdered the skin. Then he slapped his hands across his butt; his hands seemed to cool and turn greyish.

Taking hold of the rope, he pushed and pulled, like he was checking the trueness of a knot. Grunting with satisfaction, he leapt aboard the trembling, standing strand. He wrapped his legs around it and shinnied up with surprising speed. The flimsy erection teetered and wobbled. At one point, the thick twist went wowing way out toward the audience, threatening to toss Jurgen onto the laps of a young honeymooning couple in the front row. "Whoa!" Jurgen shouted musically, and as he neared the couple he flicked his eyebrows quickly, almost lecherously, as though, in the moment that he was proximate to them, he had been able to understand and characterize their situation—that they had been married that afternoon and were impatient and bristling with hormones.

Jurgen never achieved the top of the rope. As he neared it, the rope abruptly collapsed, lifeless, collecting sloppily upon itself on the floor of the stage. Jurgen landed on his ass with a very loud thump. Rhonda Byng appeared beside him and cocked her arms, throwing one hip out sideways. People began to applaud hesitantly. It took a moment or two to get going, but before long the audience members were clapping with brutish enthusiasm. Some even screamed and whistled like football hooligans. Jurgen stood up and rubbed his butt vigorously. Rudolfo ventured out onto the stage, acknowledging the roar only curtly. Jurgen reached out and took Rudolfo's hand into his own. Tugging hard, Jurgen drew his partner forward to accept the ovation.

Chapter Twenty-two

"So," announced Preston, although it was said in the middle of the night, and there was much about the word that was a sigh, "enough about me. What about you?"

Miranda rolled over in the bed. "I don't mind talking about me," she said, "but I'd just like to make a point of clarification. We don't talk about you."

"We don't?"

"We do not." She locked her fingers and made a cradle for the back of her head. "Mostly we talk about your father."

Preston grunted.

"You know, you hold the grunt in too high esteem as a conveyance of meaning and/or emotion."

"I just didn't realize I talked about the old man that much, that's all."

Although it occurred to him that the last story he had told Miranda—the tale that occupied the spell between their love-making and this new, rather awkward silence—had had to do with Preston the Magnificent, and the time his father had gone to Africa as part of a contingent of do-gooders and well-wishers from the United Nations. Preston couldn't imagine what had persuaded his father that this was a sound career move and suspected that one of the organizers was a comely young woman. Preston the Magnificent was always getting his head twisted by comely young women. He would become hopelessly and helplessly fuck-foundered and could be made to do most anything. So that is likely why he boarded a small airplane along with Martha Raye and Shecky Greene. The entertainers landed in Timbuktu; from there they were piloted up the Niger River, finally arriving at the junction with the Bani, and the city of Mopti. Then they went by jeep and donkey to the village of Sangha. The people there were the Dogons, which signified nothing to Preston the Magnificent, although he should have done a little research, because the Dogon people were magicratic, governed by wizards. They were not especially grand or powerful wizards, just men who shared a few secrets and knew a few basic moves. They could pull beetles from their ears, they could make stones fly, invisibly, from one hand to the other. So the people were not at all impressed with Preston the Magnificent when he performed the same illusions (producing a bouquet of flowers from a gleaming pan, translocating silver coins), thinking him simply some bureaucrat visiting from afar. They watched his act with heavy lids and stifled yawns. Even Shecky Greene, who, not surprisingly, spoke not a word of the Dogon dialect, did better, repeating his punchlines at greater and greater volume until the audience laughed in an effort to quiet him. Preston the Magnificent seethed inwardly and redoubled his efforts. He performed tricks he'd never attempted in public (including a multiple card production shown to him by his plump and splay-footed teenaged son, a knucklebuster that the boy did with infuriating ease) but the Dogon remained unimpressed. Preston the Magnificent likely knew more magic tricks than anyone in the world, but he soon ran out. The people stared at him. He stared back. He stared at the faces, at the frowns, the mouths slack and displaying varying degrees of toothlessness. He was on the verge of giving up, on the verge of bowing curtly and backing away, on the verge of finding a bottle to consume and a woman to shag mercilessly, when a thought occurred. He righted himself (he'd been slouching, despite his own admonition "bearing betrays breeding") and took a step forward. "Ladies and gentlemen," he intoned grandly, "I hereby present the greatest wonder of my confraternity." And with that, Preston the Magnificent reached up and removed his false teeth.

The Dogon gasped, their eyes popped wide. They erupted with applause, with loud whistles and cheers. Preston the Magnificent always held that as his finest moment, and immediately amended his resumé to indicate that he was an honorary leader, an elder, of the Dogon people.

"Okay then," said his son, Preston the Adequate, "enough about the old man. What about you?"

"What about me?"

"Well, you're in kind of an odd line of work. How'd you end up being a box-jumper?"

"Thaumaturgical assistant."

"Yeah."

Miranda bit her lip and considered her answer, weighing certain sorts of honesty. For example, she could easily answer, "Coincidence" or, more portentously, "Fate," and then list the chain of events that brought her from Maple Creek, Saskatchewan, to Las Vegas, Nevada. She'd awoken one morning, at the age of eighteen, looked out the window and seen, across her father's endless fields, the huge tents and metal wheels of the Hickey and Winchester Circus and Fair. She didn't throw her belongings into a gunnysack and leave that day. She waited until the late afternoon before venturing near, and even then she just hung on the periphery, her hands driven deep into the pockets of her Levis, her back humped bashfully. Young carnies grinned and whistled at her, handsome young men decorated with tattoos. Miranda appreciated this; at least, minded it a lot less than the sputtering, crimson-faced leering that the menfolk of Maple Creek seemed to feel was discreet. She ventured nearer. Arranged around the big top were several small tents—"blow-offs," in the argot of the trade—and these attracted her the most. It's hard to say why. An easy answer would be that each tent could only accommodate fifteen or twenty people, and Miranda felt she could cope with fifteen or twenty people. She also liked the signs that were erected outside, signs with garish illustrations and bold lettering. One showed a woman, dancing, turned away, her naked body draped with transparent veils. "SALOME" announced letters that curved and bulged in an attempt to look foreign. Another sign heralded the The Amazing Leonidas and showed him to be a gaunt man, his face made even longer by the spiked goatee that descended from his chin. Both these tents were to have special significance for Miranda. Her first job was to dance as Salome, to parade about a tiny stage dropping uneven squares of nylon. Even though the last veil revealed nothing close to nakedness (she kept on a beaded bra and diaphanous diaper arrangement that somebody thought appropriate), the Bod's portrayal of Salome brought with it arrests and show closures. This is how Miranda ended up assisting the Amazing Leonidas, who did indeed own a goatee. That was all he had in common with the likeness painted outside. The flesh and blood Leonidas was too much of the former (he weighed three hundred if he weighed a pound) and too little of the latter (he was pale and doughy).

But it was neither of these tents that made Miranda steal out of the farmhouse at three-thirty in the morning with a small collection of underwear and sweats. The tent that got her sat apart from even the blow-offs. The canvas was painted light blue and festooned with puffs of white, so that from certain low angles

it disappeared into the sky. A sign erected beside it read: THE
MUSEUM OF NATURAL WONDERS.

Miranda moved toward the tent. After all, she herself was by
way of being a natural wonder. She pulled the canvas apart at the
opening and slipped into the shadows.

There were a number of wooden tables arranged hap-
hazardly. The nearest supported a large glass bottle, a carboy
stopped with a thick cork. Inside the bottle, swimming in a
cloudy little sea, was a tiny dead calf with two heads. Miranda
shrugged and blew a little raspberry. After all, she'd seen that sort
of thing before. Monsters come each birthing season on a farm,
one or two anyway. There was a sheet of paper, covered with
uneven typewriting, Scotch-taped onto the table. Miranda took a
step closer: ANOMALIES OF EMBRYONIC CONSTRUCTION AND
IMPERFECTIONS IN THE GENETIC ENCODING CREATE THE
HIDEOUSITY THAT YOU SEE BEFORE YOU. She moved away.

The next table held a model of a cathedral, a tall magnificent
cathedral, rendered out of long, thin pieces of what she guessed
was alabaster. Again, there was a piece of paper taped to the table.
Miranda read: OLIVER HARWIN GREER, OF KNOXVILLE, TEN-
NESSEE, RENDERED THIS PERFECT COPY OF KING'S CHAPEL,
OXFORD, EMPLOYING ONLY THE BONES OF ABORTED FETUSES.

"Nice hobby," said Miranda and turned around, because it
was her intention to leave the tent which had definitely become
creepy. Then she saw the horn.

Miranda didn't know it was a horn, she knew only that
something very strange stood upon a table some feet away. It was
perhaps a foot high, and curled like soft ice cream settled into a
cone. The thing was covered with hair, short, hard bristles of
dark hues. The paper (a much whiter sheet than the others, covered with typewriting made with a newer, more tractable machine)
said, THIS HUMAN HORN WAS CUT FROM THE FOREHEAD
OF ANTOINETTE KINGSLEY of LAS VEGAS, NEVADA.

Miranda reached out a long forefinger and ran it down the horn's length. She was, she supposed, trying to determine its authenticity; at least, that was the best and only reason she could give for touching the thing. She ran her finger down and then ran it back up again, disturbing and exciting all the tiny bristles, which were much, much softer than they appeared.

It occurred to Miranda that beauty and monstrosity could live next door to each other. What set her into motion was the corollary: where beauty and monstrosity co-exist, all things must be possible.

So she ran away with the circus.

Not only had Preston had very few relationships in his lifetime, he'd had very few conversations. This one now ranked as the oddest. He took out a deck of blue-backed Bees and sought grounding in the familiar. He ran some cards, threw off, ran some cards, threw off, his mind silently chanting a mathematical equation that would set up the ducats for Dai Vernon's Poker Display, which, he hoped, he had never shown Miranda.

But she was having none of it. "I guess you figure I'm kind of weird, huh?"

"Well…" Preston drew a breath. "Being flawless, as you are, you were probably very attracted to the horn as a kind of symbol…"

"I travelled with the fair for about two years. I learned how to assist the magician. I learned how to cover the angles, how to block sightlines to the shifts and sleights. I learned how to turn in the sword box, how to suck in my stomach so that in the middle I took up a space three inches wide."

Miranda pulled hard on the conversational wheel, changing subjects like a hot-rodder changes lanes on a freeway. "What did Rudolfo want?"

"Oh," said Preston the Adequate, who could not stop a note

of sadness from singing in his throat. "You know what he wanted. He wanted to ask questions about the books. Same as you want to ask questions about the books."

The Hickey and Winchester Circus and Fair burned to the ground in Albany, New York. There was no loss of life, no loss of human life, anyway, although an ancient Indian elephant succumbed to smoke inhalation, charging through the flames without harm but then teetering and timbering dead on the grey grass outside.

After that, Miranda spent three years traversing the country, spending much of her time seeking out the little museums that dot the countryside like pimples on a puberty-twisted face. The state of Ohio alone took her four months to get through, because every mile or so there would be another little edifice dedicated to some trivial or bizarre aspect of human behaviour. There was the Hoover Museum of Vacuum Cleaners, for example. The Zane Grey Museum in Zanesville. The Museum of Power and Water, dedicated to the history and glorification of the Enema. Miranda went to them all, looking at the oddities, searching for possibilities.

Eventually she achieved the desert, and on the outskirts of Las Vegas she found The Oasis, and on the top floor she found Emile Zsosz. Her timing was impeccable. As she stepped off the elevator, Zsosz's assistant stepped on. The woman's fury was hugely apparent. Her black bodysuit was disarranged, the material covered with paw prints. Emile Zsosz himself wobbled nearby, still reeling from a blow to the face, but too drunk to actually fall over. The elevator doors closed on the assistant, Miranda took her place, and there is reason to believe that it never registered in Zsosz's soggy brain that a change had occurred. "It's showtime," he whispered, extending his hand toward Miranda.

Miranda rose from the bed and started dressing, even though dawn was still hours away.

"Where are you going?" asked Preston the Adequate.

"The damned Abraxas."

"How come?"

"I just don't like the direction this conversation is headed."

"Miranda, I look at you, I look at me, I gotta think there's some factor I'm not entering into the equation. It's got to be the books."

"Hey, dorkus. I was with the guy who's got the books. Remember? I left him to be with the guy who no longer *has* the books."

Preston found something in that statement that quieted him, although one couldn't tell from his expression whether it was sense and reason or a deeper, bluer mystery. After a very long moment's silence, Preston lit up a cigarette and said, "Hey, want to hear a joke?"

Miranda smiled, nodded, peeled off the clothes she'd thrown on and climbed back into bed. A large and clumsy man, Preston received her as gingerly as he could.

"Okay, here goes," he said. "There was this magician, this cheap, untalented magician who only knew a few old, tired tricks. And one day this genie appears, you know, poof, this big genie appears and the genie says, 'You get one wish.'"

"Only one?"

"Yeah, only one. And this magician says, 'For one night, just one night, I want your powers. I want to be capable of doing real, true magic.'"

"Yeah."

"So the genie says okay. And he waves his hand and the magician goes and does his show and he's a huge success. And the next day the genie reappears and says, 'How did it go?' And the magician says, 'Great. I pulled a rabbit out a hat, I made some coins disappear into thin air … '" Preston the Adequate allowed his voice to fall away into silence.

"It's a good joke," noted Miranda. "It's not very funny, but it's a good joke."

It had seemed to Samson as though he might escape his long life with-out having to confront danger. He has become comfortable in his cow-ardice. A case could be made that Samson was in fact addicted to his cowardice, because people become addicted to anything that limits their choices and makes life even a smidgen easier. The fact that Samson is a big albino cat doesn't really change the nickel-ante psychology. His life has been easier, because all he has had to do is turn away from danger and the unknown, tuck in his tail and start licking his ghost balls. True, there is always an awful moment when shame explodes within him, because he knows deep down that his birthright is courage, that he should roar wildly in the face of death.

But the situation is this. Das Haus *has been invaded. There are tiny creatures everywhere, little gnomes and poltergeists. And there is a larger being creeping about, black-clad and faceless, Samson's silent tormentor.*

Samson ducks behind a couch when two little people enter the room, tiny versions of Jurgen and Rudolfo. They are looting and pil-laging, their anger whetted by the fact that the kitchen yielded no food other than spoiled raw meat. They kick at the little animals in their path, starving creatures who no longer have the strength to scuttle out of the way. The little Jurgen and Rudolfo see the huge television set, which slows down their rampage momentarily. Ironically, there is a nature show being broadcast, a documentary on leopards. The little Jurgen and Rudolfo watch one of Samson's cousins, a brightly spotted male with huge testicles, run down a gazelle. They watch the cat bury its face in the gazelle's neck, they watch the geyser of blood, then the little Jurgen picks up a lamp and tosses it through the screen.

The light explodes.

Chapter Twenty-three

"Barry Reno," said Curtis Sweetchurch, "can go fuck himself."

He slipped a hand over the mouthpiece of his cell phone and looked over at Bren. The two men threw their shoulders up and down in silent mirth. Whoever Curtis was talking to remonstrated at quite a pitch, forcing him to peel the telephone away from the side of his head. "I know, I know, last time you were doing me a favour. I know that, snookums. But I have my clients' best interests at heart."

Rudolfo walked into the Gymnasium at this moment, stripped down to his workout briefs. He was startled, even horrified, to find the two men in there. Curtis was straddling the stationary bike, although he was not pedalling. Bren was doing wrist curls, his hands clutching enormous dumbbells.

Curtis turned around—the bike was faced away from the doorway so as to reduce distraction—and saw his client. "Rudy, baby," he said, folding up the telephone and hiding it deep within the pockets of the enormous shorts he was wearing. "Where's Jurgen?"

It was not lost on Rudolfo that all anybody seemed to ask him these days was, "Where's Jurgen?" As if he knew. He knew the options, he alone held the list of possibilities, but he rarely had any idea where Jurgen was. Every night, he knew, Jurgen showed up to do the Show. He didn't always drive in with Rudolfo. Sometimes he did; sometimes as Rudolfo was climbing glumly into the back of the limousine, Jurgen would appear suddenly, his eyes blazing, his robe tattered and dull. He would address *der Schwarze* in a strange language, his mouth opening with exaggerated volume and modulation, his tongue making clicking sounds against the roof of his mouth. The chauffeur would bow deeply, as though in the presence of royalty. But other nights, Rudolfo would close the door to the car and tap the glass separating the cab. He would sit alone and silent during the drive through the desert. Jurgen would be at the Abraxas, waiting.

Where could Jurgen be? Well, he could be in the Grotto, reading the books, although he seemed to be spending less and less time there. Rudolfo got the impression—formulated through rare sightings and an informal surveillance of the rock that blocked the Grotto—that Jurgen was no longer spending hours and hours locked away in that shadowy cave. Instead, he seemed to be dashing in and out. But where did he go when he left the Grotto? Rudolfo had no idea.

"Reno wants you guys back," said Curtis. Rudolfo's presence unnerved and unsettled him. For one thing, he failed to respond to questions—where *was* Jurgen?—and simply stood there brooding, his lips pursed, his brow moulded with thought. For another thing, what was with that underwear?

The other place that Jurgen could be, Rudolfo was thinking, was actually inside the Davenport Spirit Cabinet. Rudolfo hoped not, because this possibility terrified him the most. He hated it when he came upon the hideous wardrobe with its door closed; light struggled from its cracks and openings, light so weak that it only made it a foot or two before being swallowed by darkness. Animals crawled and flew from the cookie-cutout holes, not furry or feathered animals but scaly creatures that even Rudolfo, avid amateur naturalist, could not identify. Rudolfo hated it when Jurgen was shut in the Spirit Cabinet, but he hated it even more when the doors flew apart and Jurgen emerged, ghostly white and glowing.

Bren spoke up. "We told Reno to get stuffed." He possessed a very low voice. Rudolfo turned toward Bren and blinked several times, but he was still not moved to speech.

"You know what?" demanded Curtis, who hated silence in general, and weird silences in particular. "You guys are too big for Reno. You guys are too big for *television*. I'm not talking to anybody who is not from a major studio, because my vision now is one of motion pictures."

"I've written a treatment," announced Bren. "I haven't shown it to anybody, but already there's a lot of interest."

"There's very strong buzz," concurred Sweetchurch, staring at the sullen Rudolfo, "and no one even knows about the project."

"It's an adventure slash comedy slash drama slash motivational type thing," said Bren. When he said *slash* he smote the air brutally with the dumbbells.

"Is funny," said Rudolfo suddenly. Curtis almost fell off the bike. "Because Houdini, you know, he sell fucking books because he lose money in movies." Or, at least, that was the story. It was possible, it suddenly occurred to him, that the lost revenue had nothing to do with it. That may be just a cover-up story, *ja*, it was possible, likely even, that there was otherworldly contagion, a virus attached to the books, or contained within the mouldy apparatus—cultured within the smelly Davenport Spirit Cabinet itself—and Houdini sold the Collection so as to get rid of the disease.

And why did Eddie McGehee decide so suddenly to auction off the Collection?

Because, Rudolfo saw now, he had discovered the sickness.

"Curtis Sweetchurch," Rudolfo commanded, lofting a finger and stabbing it toward his manager. "You will find for me Eddie McGehee."

"Oh, sugar," whimpered Curtis, "I'm a busy beaver. I've got no time—"

"Do as I say."

"Now, now, Rudolfo—" Bren started, curling the weights significantly, popping veins the length of his forearm.

"Find me Eddie McGehee. Get me his address. I must go have speaks with him. Now get out. I am making exercise in the Gymnasium."

Cowed by Rudolfo's sudden reclamation of his previous hauteur, Curtis slipped off the stationary bike and slunk toward the door. Bren lingered, his knuckles tightening around the steel grips of the weights he was holding. Sweetchurch jerked his head at his assistant, and Bren allowed the dumbbells to drop to the ground with a resounding thud.

Then Rudolfo was alone.

Dizzy with energy, he yanked off his cap and wig, climbed aboard the stationary bike and pedalled furiously nowhere.

He sensed, but didn't see, Jurgen enter. There was a mirror on the wall some twenty feet in front of him, but it started half-way up to accommodate the racks of dumbbells and bars, the squat trees of clamps and plates. If Rudolfo had lifted his head he might have seen his partner, but he chose not to. He wanted to avoid the deathly pallor and the pale eyes, so he pretended to be in the final stages of the Tour de France. He hunkered down over the bars, leaning heavily on his forearms with his rear end elevated behind him. He considered saying something— demanding to know what was in the books, demanding to know

why it was so important, demanding to know what was wrong—
but instead he chose a heavy, panting silence and concentrated on
the pistonlike motion of his legs, the rhythmic displacement of
his two-cylinder butt.

He was startled to feel, suddenly, Jurgen's hand on the small
of his back, the fingertips slipping just underneath the elastic of
his tiny trunks. The hand dove in, cupping first one pumping
buttock, then the other, over and over again, as if maddened by
choice. Rudolfo's penis sprouted, pushing easily out the front.
Fingertips brushed the base of his scrotum, and Rudolfo shivered and the motion of his cycling was for an instant all confused,
then he found the rhythm, and settled into it, and matched his
breathing to it. He folded his arms across the handlebars and
laid his head upon them. The fingers slowly climbed his shaft,
and then they encircled the head, and as Rudolfo came he threw
himself bolt upright and saw flashes of light, so intense he was
nearly blinded. And that is why, many minutes later, he mis-
trusted, and discounted, his impression that he had been the only
man reflected in the mirror.

It was to Searchlight—a tiny town clinging to the edge of the
Mojave Desert—that Edgar Biggs McGehee (Eddie's grandfather) first repaired with the Collection, after making his bargain
with Harry Houdini. Edgar lived in a small hut, not much bigger and certainly no better constructed than the Spirit Cabinet.
Eddie, out of homage to his forefather, left this structure standing, although he himself lived in a huge mansion a hundred yards
away.

And it was to Searchlight—a tiny mote on the Nevada road
map—that Rudolfo came.

He was driven by Bob, that being the name of the mysterious dark chauffeur. At least "Bob" was what Rudolfo called him,
although the driver himself, stabbing a thumb into the middle of

his chest, produced a sound that was bracketed on each end by plosion and plosive, the middle a long, drawn-out sheep's yodel.

Bob had driven to Searchlight with unerring steadiness. Indeed, he was turning out to be quite the best chauffeur Rudolfo had ever employed. He was respectfully silent, communicating mostly with humble nods and half-bows. He understood his employer and his desires. So, for instance, when Rudolfo handed Bob a piece of paper with the word "Searchlight" scrawled upon it (in Curtis Sweetchurch's loopy and hasty handwriting), the driver merely stared at it for a long moment and then nodded. His one fault was an unnecessary musicality. He whistled much of the time, a fluttering sound that rode high in the air. Sometimes he added percussion, slapping at his own body with his ink-black, creamy-palmed hands. And occasionally he would alarm his passenger by pumping at the gas and brakes in funky rhythm.

Bob stopped the limo at the end of a long driveway. He leapt out, threw open the rear door and stepped back in order to allow Rudolfo grand and ceremonial egress from the car. Rudolfo stepped out and immediately wilted. "Fuck..." he moaned. "Is hot like hell."

"Hot," agreed Bob. Or at least, he echoed it, grinning widely, as if he found the very voicing of the word amusing.

Rudolfo began to perspire, the heat sucking moisture out of his body. Because he lacked hair, the sweat ran freely from underneath his wig and baseball cap and flooded his eyes, blinding him. He held out his hand and Bob lifted his elbow and offered to guide. Rudolfo held the black man's arm and they began a halting march toward the mansion.

"Is like one hundred and twenty fucking degrees," muttered Rudolfo. It was the middle of August, the dog days, so-called because some people feel that in August the planet is influenced, even governed, by the dog star, Sirius. Sirius is worshipped by the Dogon tribe of Mali. (Bob is of Dogon ancestry.)

The doorbell was answered by a dark woman in a crisp white uniform. She pulled the door open and waved them in. The woman and Bob exchanged whispered words and then they disappeared, leaving Rudolfo standing alone in the marbled foyer.

"Hello!" A man, presumably Eddie McGehee, rounded the corner into the foyer. He was a very tall man, slender to the point of emaciation. He wore a fluffy bathrobe; the sleeves were too short, and where the pale arms emerged was plywood flatness knobbed with wristbone and knuckle. Below the robe were long lengths of twiggy leg, the knees ballooning like boles.

"You are Rudolfo," he pointed out. McGehee wore a golden fez and oversized wraparound sunglasses, mirrored so as to reflect Rudolfo's image back into his own eyes. His face was decorated with daubs of sunscreen, but it was an obvious case of too little, too late. The tip of his nose, the rims of his ears, his brow and cheeks, were as burned and flaky as discarded snakeskin. Where it wasn't crisp and lobster-pink, the skin had the shade and texture of copy paper.

"I am Rudolfo. You are Eddie McGehee."

"Let's go out by the pool." McGehee turned and wheeled away. His toes, long, crooked and naked, gripped the tiles with lazy prehensility. "Preston said you'd be coming today."

"How would Preston know?" wondered Rudolfo—aloud or to himself, he couldn't say. He was no longer making much distinction between the two. But speaking of that, why hadn't Preston reminded Rudolfo that Eddie McGehee stood closest to the heart of the mystery?

"Preston is a very clever man. Guess what?"

"What?"

"He's fucking Miranda!" McGehee announced this with bubbling glee. Rudolfo shuddered; his skin would likely have become goosebumpy, except goosebumps blossom around hair follicles, so all that happened was that he became a little clammy and damp.

"Preston's rather a lovely man," McGehee put in. "He has beautiful eyes."

Rudolfo remembered his eyes as puffy and bloodshot, the centres dark as pitch.

The pool was a huge lopsided circle. The water it held was crystal clear; on the bottom and sides were odd designs rendered with bright red and yellow paints. There was a small patio table, shaded by a huge polka-dotted parasol. McGehee gestured to one of the wicker seats and claimed another. Rudolfo sat down and came right to the point.

"Why you auction Collection?"

"Hmm." It was a *hmm* to suggest that McGehee had never thought about it before. "Well, you know, I am the end of the McGehee line. I have left no offspring. There's no one for me to bequeath the Collection to. So there."

"Charity."

"Sorry?"

"You could leave it to charity. Or a library. Or a university."

"Yes, good point. Okay. Here's answer number two. I needed the money. It's not like I have a job or a profession. I don't generate income. And let's face it, I have an expensive lifestyle. So I needed the money."

There was something peculiar in McGehee's manner, some kind of teasing mockery. Rudolfo reached across the table and gathered together the lapels of the terry cloth robe, pulling McGehee halfway across the table. Rudolfo watched his own twisted face zoom and loom, reflected in McGehee's mirrored sunglasses.

"Listen, bubby-boy," he began—although Rudolfo was suddenly distracted, *very* distracted. Over Eddie McGehee's head he saw Bob in satyric pursuit of the housemaid. Both were naked, both had bodies that had been pricked with design; raised welts and scars formed moons, stars and lightning bolts upon the gleaming blue-black surface of their skin. Both Bob and the maid were laughing, the maid with a measure of breathlessness, Bob with rhythmic concentration.

They ran across the lawn and disappeared. Rudolfo shook his head and recommenced his bullying.

"I am desperate man," he said, keeping his voice low, barely audible. "I don't know what is going on but is going on terrible. Jurgen, every day he changes. Every day I wake up and I must think to myself, *oh no, today something else will be different*. Every day I think, *today there will be something new that I will not understand, Jurgen will be a little farther away from me, he will be more lost to me, and what can I do about it?*" Rudolfo took a few deep breaths. He stared at his reflection in McGehee's sunglasses. "Nothing." He tightened his grip on the terry cloth lapels. "So tell me what I need to know or I will make you hurt."

"Okay," said Eddie cheerily. "Here's the scoop. My grandfather, Edgar Biggs McGehee, he left quite a complicated will. It's full of riders and codicils. And one of those codicils has to do with the Collection. Basically, Rudolfo, I *had* to auction it off. That's what my grandfather wanted."

Rudolfo released McGehee and sat back in his chair. "It was in will...?"

"Oh yeah. Detailed instructions. Gramps was really quite specific. The Collection had to be put up for auction on April the sixth."

"Why? What is April six?"

McGehee rose and turned to face the swimming pool. "Do you mean, what is the significance of April the sixth?"

"*Ja*," snarled Rudolfo.

McGehee's long crooked fingers worked at the knot in the cord that kept the bathrobe together. He peeled the garment off and revealed a lactescent body, its nakedness hidden by a loin-cloth, at least, a soiled length of sacking that clung to the man's jagged hipbones like brush clings to a scarp. The openings for the legs were many times larger than they needed to be; wrinkled bits and pieces dangled below. McGehee reached up and removed his fez. A gossamer topknot was uncovered, curled up as though sleeping. Released, it tumbled down the length of the man's back, bouncing along the ridge of vertebrae.

"Among other things," McGehee answered, "April the sixth is Harry Houdini's birthday."

He then removed his sunglasses, tossing them nonchalantly onto a nearby chaise longue. He raised his hands above his head, bent his knees and prepared to execute a dive of antiquated fussiness. Just before he did, he turned and stabbed Rudolfo with his silver eyes.

Samson knows the true source of all this trouble—the Grotto. He knows better than anyone, because at night he stood outside that strange room and listened to what was going on inside. He has large ears and could hear what Rudolfo could not. He could hear the little whimpers that Jurgen had sometimes made in there, whimpers caused by quick, sharp pains. Samson has also heard low moans, caused by pain of more substance.

.   And the place smells, although human beings don't seem to notice. It reeks of decay. And the air itself is odd, it bristles like the air above the desert when a violent storm is approaching.

So the Grotto is where Samson must go if he is ever to confront his fear. He pauses to rethink. He could still avoid the confrontation. He could set his weary bones down right here on the cold, cold tiles; he could let his eyelids fall heavily and allow his last breath to pass over his pale, pale gums.

But...but damn it, thought Samson, I am a big cat. And as they like to say out there on the savannah, big cats are not big pussies.

Samson barks, a trick he learned back in the Münich days. It hurts his throat, clogging his windpipe with a fuzzy phlegmball. Samson shakes his head and hacks, not only to clear his throat, but to clear his mind of all such fakery and affectation.

Then he tilts his head back and roars.

Chapter Twenty-four

Rudolfo held a jar of cream, expensive cream, cream that was made in a small factory in Luxembourg, cream that was kept in an exquisite china jar adorned with etchings of linked flowers. Rudolfo held the jar in the palm of one hand and with the other he applied the cream to his partner's body. Jurgen sat, very still and patient. He glowed like a low-wattage light bulb much of the time now, and this is why, an hour before Showtime, Rudolfo had appeared with the jar, to cover the colourless radiance with cream.

Rudolfo also surreptitiously prodded him, under the pretense of cream application, gauging the progress of the sickness that had claimed his lover.

Jurgen didn't perceive himself as being sick, of course. Curtis Sweetchurch didn't think of Jurgen as sick either; indeed, he seemed to think that Jurgen was as healthy as could be. Curtis was talking about adding shows. The box office turned away hundreds of people daily who'd traversed continents and oceans in order to get there. But Curtis, thought Rudolfo bitterly, didn't know how bad things were. For instance, once, as Rudolfo rubbed cream onto his left shoulder, Jurgen's hams slid off the leather of the chair. But instead of plummeting to the ground, Jurgen just hovered there. Rudolfo placed a single finger upon his shoulder and pulled lightly, drawing him back to his perch.

"One time," said Jurgen, "Harry Houdini—"

"Why you talk about Harry Houdini? He's dead."

"Oh, certainly, he's dead," admitted Jurgen. "But that's no reason not to talk about him."

From the dressing room next door came low howls and moans, halting but adamant. These sorts of sounds came often from the little cubicle given over to Rhonda Byng, who hadn't been fired because Rudolfo was too enervated to do even that. He imagined that she had some greasy boyfriend who came to service her crudely before the Show, to bend her over the make-up table and stab at her dispassionately. This is what Rudolfo imagined, but it is not what he knew to be true. Because Rhonda arrived each night alone, solitary and pining for Jurgen. She made shy smiles and ducked into her little room long before she was due to appear on stage.

"One day Harry was riding in an automobile. Of course, this was in the early twenties, when automobiles were something of a novelty. At any rate—"

"*Hold still*..." Rudolfo's words sounded clunky and awkward in the dressing room. He realized he'd spoken in German; part of his mind had decided that, what with Jurgen speaking so eloquently, they must be conversing in their mother tongue. But the German sounded foreign and furtive, as suspect as a spy. Jurgen was speaking in English.

"He was being driven by a friend," continued Jurgen, "not that he had that many, you know, he was a private and humour-less man..."

"Shut up," muttered Rudolfo. "Just fuck the shut up." He

shattered the china jar across the floor. From next door came orgiastic bombinations.

"It's simply a little anecdote I'm relating," Jurgen protested.

Rudolfo placed a thumb in his mouth to bring about a pause in which he could think. But he'd long ago ingested most of the pale cartilage on his fingers, reduced his nails to jagged ridges so low they bisected the fingertips—there was no more nail to chew, "Okay," he whispered. "Tell me the story."

"Well..." Jurgen rose slowly. He picked up a long soiled piece of muslin and began to swaddle his netherparts. His penis was erect and twitched at the end, but Rudolfo had given up noticing. (Rhonda's throaty belling continued to leak through the walls.) "The anecdote is simply this. It has, you'll agree, a certain whimsical irony."

"Just tell me the antidote!"

"Well, Harry was being driven by his friend to his apartment, and when the man pulled up beside the curb, Houdini turned and looked at the passenger door for a long moment..." Jurgen giggled. "And then he said, *Hey, how do you get out of this thing?*"

He drifted over to the corner to where his filthy robe hung beside his old lamé garb, his sequined vestments, the flaming elastic bodysuits that he no longer wore. He shrugged himself into the robe—Rudolfo ignored the feeling that it was helping with the process—and when the garment had settled upon him, Jurgen clapped his hands together, producing an unearthly hollow sound that bounced off the walls of their tiny dressing room. (Rhonda cried out sharply, once, and then there came nothing but soft whimpers.)

"Okey-dokey," said Jurgen. "It's showtime."

Preston ducked out of the George Theater. The collar of his jacket was turned up and his neck was withdrawn, turtle-like. He wore a rumpled fedora that he tugged as far down as possible over his forehead, although that was not very far. He suspected that the hat had belonged to his father. Preston had not been able to separate himself from his father, despite all his best intentions. The Magnificent's belongings were always turning up in his closets, a kind of eerie bequest. His father's money had gone to Syndi, the last of his little pixilated girlfriends, but his old clothes were always turning up, or monogrammed cigarette cases, tarnished seltzer bottles, silk scarves, sheepskin condoms, all the leavings of the Magnificent's strange life.

Still, the hat, although a little small, hid his telltale greasy ringlets, and Preston was therefore a little less recognizable as he hurried along the street.

He was not sure who, exactly, he was hiding from. Miranda was lying atop the bed in the George, her flawless nose stuck inside a thick novel. She was going nowhere. Miranda tended to stick to any task with mulish perseverance, especially the reading of a book. Preston couldn't think of anyone else who would care what he was doing.

(Although, in a limo parked down the road, he was being pointed out to two very large and brainless men. "There he is now," crackled the voice, and the large men wrinkled their noses at the foul air that came wafting from the back seat.)

Preston, perhaps the finest stage magician that ever lived, was off to attempt his most awesome miracle, the improvement of his appearance. He was going to climb aboard an exercise bicycle and try to pedal away puckered fatty deposits. He was going to sit in a steam room until his pores popped out their blockages. He was going to stand at the shaving bar and work with great care on his beard and his hair. Preston knew he was behaving in many ways like a teenaged boy, and his only excuse was that he had never before behaved like a teenaged boy, certainly not when he was one. As a teenager he had done little but practise sleights and subterfuges. Seven hours a day, seven days a week, Presto would send coins flying invisibly from one hand to another, he would pluck cards from the air and then fire them back into nothingness. So now, all these years later, he was acting ungrown and enchanted. He was doing odd things, like ponying up a thousand bucks to join a health club. He shrugged and spoke aloud. "Fuck it," he said, in peevish self-defence. "I'm in l—"

Before the word was spoken, the two large and brainless men knocked Preston over like he was a bowling pin, then loaded him into the back of the sleek black limousine. Preston scrambled across the leather, and when he finally managed to right himself, he was staring into the pinched, pale face of the world-famous Kaz.

"No more Mister Nice Guy," said Kaz quietly.

"Hey, Kaz," said Preston, "there never was any Mister Nice Guy."

"Are you really fucking Miranda?" demanded Kaz. He looked terrible, far worse than he ordinarily did. He had a queer, mottled appearance, the paleness blotched by patches of flaky, irritated skin. What little muscle tone Kaz had acquired was gone. And his breath had worsened, although Preston would have thought there was little room for deterioration. Each of Kaz's words came accompanied by wild, roaring gusts of putrescence. "Are you?" Kaz repeated. "Are you really fucking Miranda?"

Preston considered various answers, some of which would respond to Kaz's acrid immaturity, some of which would defend the vague but vicious attack upon Miranda. What he finally said was, "Yes."

Kaz drew a deep breath. Sucking back his own air seemed to make him feel queachy and a pained look swept across his face. "That's okay. I fuck plenty of showgirls. Plenty."

The windows were tinted; even so, the streets of Las Vegas gleamed and glowed, lit by the afternoon sun. The limo was travelling down Paradise Road, bunched in with a lot of other limousines, a wild pack of luxury automobiles.

"You fucked me over at the auction," said Kaz. "And don't think I don't know why. Anti-Semitism."

"I beg your pardon?"

"You're an anti-Semite. It's obvious. That's why you made sure the Collection went to those two fascist faggots. By the way, I've got a private detective working on this thing. He's working on a few leads concerning Jurgen Schubert's conduct during the War."

"I'm sure it was atrocious. After all, he would have only been about three years old."

"They are Nazis and you are an anti-Semite."

"I am not an anti-Semite, Kaz, and even if I was, I didn't know you were Jewish."

Kaz looked momentarily crestfallen. "You didn't know I was Jewish? What did you think I was?"

"I had no goddamn idea, Kaz."

Kaz bounced his hands off his knees a few times—not in anger so much as a boyish inability to contain energy. He turned to stare out the window and spoke as though Preston the Adequate was a great distance away. "Just tell me. Tell me what's in the books."

"There's nothing in the books."

"Look, Preston, I don't mean you any harm. I am not a violent man. But I swear to god I will shoot you through the heart if you don't come clean. Because I *know*."

Preston the Adequate reached up and took his face into his huge, clammy palm. He rubbed his eyes, pushing his thumb and fingers into the sockets and pressing hard. "What is this you know, Kaz?"

"Listen. I travel around the world, going to these fairs and conventions. Sleeping with women that are *twice* as good-looking as Miranda. Anyway, at these conventions, at these fairs and conventions, you hear about these rooms. Not at first. I mean, for a long time, even when I was National Champion, I wouldn't hear about these rooms; I'd just go and maybe I'd get invited to dinner at the mayor's house or something, but it was a long time before I started hearing that there was a *room*, there was a special fucking room and a few guys were going there. Fucking *invitation* only. But finally, *finally*, I started hearing about these rooms. And a couple of times, I got invited into them."

"Well, then. Happy ending. I'll just get out at the next corner."

"In these rooms...these hotel rooms...there's usually only three or four guys sitting around. Magicians. Names we all know. I saw your old man in these rooms a couple of times."

"You never did."

"He was there. And there was always this weird little guy, dressed in robes, with a tuft of hair sticking up in the centre of his head. This weird little guy talked about the books."

"The books."

"I know that there is information, concrete information. About magic. Not about illusion, about the real deal. That is what I want. And that is what I will do anything to get."

"I don't know what's in the books. I never read the books."

"Liar."

"I never cracked one open," said Preston. "Don't think I didn't want to. Don't think I didn't sit there all night sometimes with one of those big honking books on my lap and my fingers trembling. But I'm a magician, Kaz. I'm not a wizard."

"You're afraid."

"Maybe."

"I'm not. Okay? I am not afraid. I have taken this as far as I can—as far as any human being can—and I am ready to take the next step. I am ready to become a wizard."

"Kaz, you got to figure that if there is information, it's about a few little, I don't know, cracks in the wall. It's about a few places in the universe where the corners don't come together. It's not about unlimited power."

"Okay, then please explain to me why Jurgen Schubert is all of a sudden doing this stuff, he's doing fucking legendary stuff, the Hindu Rope Trick, for fuck's sake, and guys have seen it and said they can't see any rigging or anything. So explain that to me."

"The Hindu Rope Trick is a venerable illusion. Lots of people know it. My old man used to do it."

"Yeah. Well, like I say, your old man was in those rooms."

"He never was."

"What is it with you and your father?" demanded Kaz.

"My old man was *never* in those rooms. Because my father was no fucking good! Why do you think I hate him so much?

"I thought it was because he turned your mother into a fat, drooling drunk."

Preston took a deep breath and calmed himself, but not before smacking Kaz in the face, cracking his nose and snapping the oversized spectacles in half. Kaz bent over with his face between his hands, but he couldn't stop the blood from spurting all over the leather seats.

"I'll just get out at Hacienda." Preston pointed helpfully through the tinted windows. "I've got to go to my health club."

Kaz nodded through his bloodied hands.

Chapter Twenty-five

Rudolfo pulled open the front door and allowed Dr. Merdam entry.

Dr. Merdam seemed to have gained a few pounds in the weeks since he'd last paid a *Haus* call. It was as though he'd finally crossed some critical line, tipped the scales so that gravity might become his complete and utter master. The extra fat on his cheeks, for example, tugged down over his starched white collar, dragging much of his face with it. The weight of his cheeks pulled at the skin under Merdam's beautiful almond eyes so they appeared sad, even forlorn. His eyebrows were yanked at the outer corners and cocked upwards interrogatively. His belly, a bulge of prodigious proportion, now plummeted toward the earth as though leaden, contained desperately by the buttons of his finely tailored vestments. Still, picturing himself an elfin man, Dr. Merdam danced into the hallway daintily and shook hands with Rudolfo.

"How is he?" he asked, removing a handkerchief and lightly dabbing at his lips.

"Not good."

"How so?"

"His skin…" Rudolfo reached forward and raked his fingers through the air, searching for words.

"Is he pale?"

Rudolfo found himself laughing and unable to contain it. He laughed until tears welled up in his eyes. Then he blinked as furiously as he could, but his eyes, lacking lashes, couldn't do much to staunch the flow. The tears spilled over.

The boulder was rolled back and the hole to the Grotto gaped. Jurgen was in the bedroom, busy with Dr. Merdam. It was the middle of the afternoon. Rudolfo ducked into the Grotto before he could talk himself out of it. He stopped just inside and caught his breath, which was roaring in and out of his mouth, making his chest shudder.

Jurgen usually lit the place with candles and lanterns, balanced on stacks of books and contrivances rendered from ancient wood. Now the Grotto was lit only by the wash from the corridor. Rudolfo stood motionless and allowed the shadows to take shape. Slowly he saw the columns of volumes, the books balanced off-kilter so that each stack had a distinct list, all inclining toward the centre. He was then very alarmed to see, at the circle's centre, the outline of a human take form. The figure had both hands raised, the fingers spread wide, the hopeless gesture of a hold-up victim. Rudolfo let out a small moan, a mouthful of fear. Then he noticed the tall domed shape of the creature's head, and he realized that he'd forgotten about the wooden automaton *Moon*.

Moon was rather crudely carved, his face a collection of ridged bulges, but he had been carefully painted, with fine arched eyebrows and rouged cheeks. It was impossible to tell whether the mechanical doll had been designed to represent an old or a young man. There was a simplicity to his features that suggested childhood, but the varnish had been cracked by time and temperature, giving him the aspect of great age. The figure was costumed in a bizarre fashion, wrapped in silvery pantaloons, a satin smoking jacket and slippers with toes that curled like snail shells. A turban, made out of sackcloth or at least, Rudolfo thought, something very scratchy, balanced on top of the automaton's head. He sat, cross-legged, upon his pedestal of thick, clouded glass.

As Rudolfo stared at Moon, the Grotto filled suddenly with the sound of fine gears turning and meshing. It was, Rudolfo thought, a lifeless version of the small noises the bushbabies made, in the middle of the night, when the tiny furry creatures paired up to copulate. Occupied as he was with this idle thought, Rudolfo did not notice, for a moment, that one of Moon's hands was jerking back and forth, the fingertips twitching. When he did notice, he leapt backwards. His left foot landed on a silver ball that one of the first magicians, Katterfelto, had used in one of the earliest cup and ball routines. Rudolfo's leg kicked out and he flew back. He wrenched his arms behind his back in order to break his fall and was sufficiently nimble and athletic that he was able to somersault as his butt hit the ground, ending up in a pose of twisted supplication.

The hums now amplified in volume, and the mechanical man began to bounce up and down, a studied and mathematical rendition of shaking with mirth. Moon's mouth popped open with a loud clacking sound and the jaw and bottom lip, a separate articulated piece of wood, began to jiggle and jounce. Rudolfo realized that the automaton was laughing at him, and he could not prevent volts of anger from colouring his hairless body.

He flipped over onto his hands and knees and in doing so brought his eyes within a foot of the Grotto wall. There was just light enough to illuminate the marks and scratches there. This time his shock was so great that he could not help speaking aloud.

"Fuck shit," he said—for inches away were the cyphers and runes that had troubled him so as a toddler, those made by Albert Einstein upon the walls of the walk-up at Kramgasse 49.

Rudolfo was up on his feet in a trice. He'd already persuaded himself that what he'd just seen was a trick of the imagination. He was so determined to rid his mind of the image (which floated eerily across his field of vision, like the afterimage left by a flashbulb) that he crossed over to the mechanical man, made a kind of bow and said, "Hi, baby."

The automaton's hand again began to jerk back and forth. It was, Rudolfo realized, waving. Rudolfo raised his own hand, spreading the fingers, and moved it back and forth like the baton of a broken metronome.

Moon's other hand suddenly appeared before Rudolfo. Clutched between the wooden fingers was a deck of cards. They were odd cards, longer and more slender than those that Rudolfo was used to. The design on the back was a simplistic representation of the night sky, a black background adorned with six-pointed stars and a large sliver of moon. As Rudolfo looked at the cards, the machine's hand snapped, and instantly the deck was spread and fanned into a perfect semicircle. Then the hand raised the deck and then lowered it slowly, and Rudolfo understood that he was to pick a card, any card.

He reached forward, placed his fingertips on a card and then cannily moved them to the right, digging out a card from within a denser grouping. He was smugly pleased with himself, until he flipped over the card and saw that he'd drawn the two of hearts.

Moon's jaw clacked open and the machine began its soundless laughing. Rudolfo yanked the cards out of the wooden hand and flipped them over, sure that every one would be a two of hearts, that this was some elaborate trick rigged by the increasingly odd Jurgen Schubert. But the cards were different and randomly ordered. Moon continued to laugh with silent clockwork glee.

"Shut up, facefuck," whispered Rudolfo, and then he spun about, alarmed at a rustling at his back.

A huge patch of shadow floated toward him. "We have to find his secret," whispered Dr. Merdam, the whiteness of his eyes gleaming brightly. He tore the top book from the first pile he came to. He threw back the leather cover and took the ends of some brittle pages between his fingers. There was a little poof and a small mushroom cloud and then his fingertips were covered with dust.

"What secret?" demanded Rudolfo.

"The secret of dissubstantiation. The secret of corporeal evaporation."

"What are you talking about?"

"He only weighs fifty-eight pounds," whispered Dr. Merdam.

"You don't want that secret, Doc."

"Yes, I do. It is what I dream about. Weightlessness."

"Doc, Doc. Don't say this."

"I'm a massive blob of protoplasm that's gone out of control. I'm huge and heavy and the Tony Anthony mental exercises are exhausting. I suffer headaches. I'm addicted to no end of prescription drugs. I long for nothingness."

"You're not fat, Doc. You just got big bones."

Dr. Merdam picked up the next book, held it at arm's length and focused on the gilt letters on the cover. "*La Magie assyrienne.*" Merdam lifted his sad eyes and translated quietly. "*Assyrian Magic.* Sounds hopeful."

"Besides," said Rudolfo, "is just trick."

There was a buzz and a click and Moon swivelled about, one of his wooden hands bumping into Rudolfo's shoulder. Rudolfo was not really surprised to see that the whittled fingers held a new deck of cards, blue-backed Bees. He obediently withdrew a card, flipped it over to note that it was, in fact, the two of hearts, and tossed it away.

"Trick?" echoed Dr. Merdam. "It's no trick, my friend. My scales are accurate to within a hundredth of a pound."

"Yeah, yeah. But magic is making assumes."

"Assumptions?"

"Sure. Your scales say fifty-eight, you *assume* that Jurgen losing weight."

"He must indeed be."

"No, no, Doc," said Rudolfo, waving a finger in the air. "He just not being *affected by gravity.*" As he spoke these words, it occurred to him—in a burst that left him flushed with adrenalin—that if Jurgen were no longer with Dr. Merdam, he was very likely on his way back to the Grotto. "Erps," gasped Rudolfo, and he took hold of Merdam's soft elbow and tried to spin him about. "We got to get out of here."

But it was too late. The light from the corridor—which spilt in through the huge irregular circle left by the remote-controlled boulder—was filled suddenly by a silhouette. Jurgen folded his hands upon his hips and turned his head slowly back and forth.

"So, Jurgen," said Rudolfo, surveying the Grotto with an air of idleness. "Have you ever thought about renovation?"

Jurgen remained silent, causing the other men to stir uneasily on their feet. He was dressed in his robe, filthy and soiled, indistinct in the gloom; all Rudolfo and Merdam could make out was his dark outline. They watched him raise his arms; the material from the robe rolled down to collect at his elbows. His forearms glowed like neon.

"Uh-oh," came a small voice. Rudolfo turned to look at Dr. Merdam—Merdam turned to look at Rudolfo. They realized that neither of them had uttered "uh-oh," and both glanced then at Moon. The automaton had raised both its wooden hands to cover glass eyes.

There came a long whine, like the sound of a crone keening at the funeral of a child. The papers strewn about the Grotto— pieces of parchment, broadsheets advertising Ehrich Weiss, the "world's greatest mystifier and self-liberator"—stirred and rustled on the floor. Then they lifted into the air, borne by the wind— for it was a wind that was howling—and began to whirl above the heads of Rudolfo and Dr. Merdam. The towers of books shook, trembled and toppled. The leather covers flew open and the pages flipped from front to back and made little drum rolls.

Jurgen remained in the doorway, blocking the one avenue of escape, moving his arms like a symphony conductor.

"Okay, Doc," Rudolfo said quietly, "we better be going now."

Dr. Merdam exploded toward the doorway, his four hundred pounds accelerating so quickly that he'd achieved maximum velocity by the time he hit Jurgen. Rudolfo never saw, quite, what happened, because Merdam's bulk plugged the opening as tightly as the remote-controlled boulder. Then, with a long sucking sound and a clownish pop, the doctor was through. He executed an elegant pirouette, trying to decide which way to go, then disappeared.

Rudolfo moved toward the doorway.

"Don't go."

Rudolfo turned around slowly. He was actually hoping that the words had come from the fucking wooden doll, even though that was a fairly horrifying prospect. But he'd recognized the voice.

Jurgen sat behind the small schoolboy's desk, his square brow propped on a luminous hand. His eyes pored over the pages of an ancient tome while his fingers deftly and rhythmically turned the pages. "Don't go," he repeated. "Stay a while. Read a book."

"I can't read," sighed Rudolfo. "You know I can't read. If I could read, I don't know if I would read. Maybe I would. Sometimes I want to. But the fact is, I can't read."

Jurgen looked up then, and smiled gently. For a moment his aspect changed. The glowing abated, briefly, and flesh tones, mottled by fever and spackled with illness, returned. His dark eyes suddenly filled with emotion, at least, Rudolfo was fairly confident he could see emotion back there, trapped and restless, like a big cat in an iron cage. "Rudy," said Jurgen quietly, and then his eyes deadened and his skin became incandescent and he looked down at the book once more.

The intruder in the Grotto—who wears a black bodysuit and a bala-clava, large spectacles balanced on the blunted nose and pinching the flattened ears—has made a few discoveries. The automaton, for exam-ple, when set into motion, surveys the circle of books and ends up facing a particular stack. The machine then produces an ancient playing card, always a spot, never a face; that number is counted off in the stack and reveals the book to be looked at and investigated. At least, that's the theory the intruder has come up with, although—he pauses momen-tarily and wonders at a loud, long sound that must be distant thunder, yet seems to come from within the bizarre mansion—the practice does-n't yield much in the way of results. One book tends to refer the quester to another book, that book to yet another, and while each might have some small kernel of information, the accumulation of knowledge is infuriatingly slow. The intruder had been hoping there was one book, one ancient volume, that held the key, something that could be stolen.

He hears someone clear his throat, a dainty "ahem" such as a librarian might come up with if a patron were absent-mindedly drum-ming a pencil on a tabletop. The intruder turns away from the books and there, in the hole that serves as the Grotto's doorway, stands that fucking ghostly tiger.

Samson roars, a very long roar, because it feels good—the mouth-expansion, the way his jaw muscles and tendons stretch to the point of pain.

The intruder jumps. The spectacles pop away from the mask and tumble to the floor.

Samson steps into the cave and begins to circle. He lifts and drops a paw, carving up the air into thick slices.

The intruder pulls off his balaclava, desperately relying on the fact that he is world-famous. "Look," says Kaz, "it's me."

Samson, of course, roars even more loudly now, because he hates Kaz, wouldn't even eat him with a side of fries. He snakes his head forward, trying to bounce candlelight off his fangs, trying to make them glisten.

"Aaagh," says Kaz, a sound that is almost hidden by the gaseous bubbling erupting from his backside.

Samson chuckles lowly, but immediately becomes fearsome once more. Roar, snap, swipe, roar snap-snap, swipe, man, you never really forget this stuff.

Kaz shrieks, so high-pitched that Samson winces, and then he lights out for the doorway. Samson wheels around and takes after him, but only for a few steps. Kaz disappears down the hallway. Samson tilts his head and listens—in a few seconds comes the sound of glass shattering. Kaz has driven himself through a plate-glass window. This sound, in turns, terrifies the small marauders inside das Haus, *and Samson can hear them scurrying, the footfalls fast and frantic. Then all these sounds disappear.*

He wanders over to sniff at Moon. Perhaps his nose brushes some button or switch—Samson has no sensation—but suddenly the Grotto is filled with the grainy, hushed sounds of clockwork. The mechanical man begins to laugh with silent mirth. Samson lifts a paw and bats the automaton off its perch. Moon tumbles to the ground and, being made of old wood and rusty metal, cracks into many pieces. Samson swivels his backside, then sprays a little stream of steaming piss all over the pile of lumber.

It seems as though, after all those years of timidity, Samson is now nothing but rage. He circles about the Grotto knocking over stacks of books. The stacks in turn knock over the candles, and the two lie together on the floor, old paper and flame. Samson knows what that means. But he does not leave the Grotto. Instead, he sniffs about and locates the remote control. He takes it into his mouth, bounces it about until his *left incisor comes to rest on the button marked ><. He bites down and sets the huge boulder in motion. As it rolls to block the entrance to the Grotto, Samson calmly begins to chew. There are a few sparks and electronic hisses.*

The rock falls into place, stopping the hole forever.

Chapter Twenty-six

Within a few days, Miranda had crowded the sleeping quarters at the George Theater with lumps of clay, blocks of wood, easels, canvases and acrylics. And, although it had taken her a few hours, she'd persuaded Preston to sit for a portrait. And, although it had taken her a few additional hours, she had gotten him to pose naked. He now sat on a wooden chair, his hands resting open on his lap, although they twitched restively quite often, eager to cover his crotch. "Why," he demanded, "am I butt naked?"

"On account of I have a theory," said Miranda. Her palate was crowded with pigment; to approximate Preston's skin tone she found it necessary to combine almost all of them, even Royal Purple and Flaming Magnesium. "You see, a real magician wouldn't wear all those fancy clothes. Fancy clothes—tails or whatever—are just saying, *look, I'm hiding stuff every-frigging-where.* Right? So a real magician—at least, this is my little artistic conceit—would be starkers. Now sit still."

"I am sitting still."

"Your eyes. They're, like, pulsating."

"Anyway, I'm not a real magician."

"I see." Miranda took a step backwards and appraised her painting. It wasn't too bad. She was determined to capture her lover faithfully, so it would be a long time before she'd rendered every wen and maculation. She dabbed her brush in burnt umber and started in on his belly.

"I'm just a carnival huckster."

"Okay. Sit still."

"That's all I am. A charlatan and a mountebank."

"You seem to be labouring under the impression that we are debating this point. You are a carnie, I am a carnie. Now, shut up and sit still. I am trying to immortalize you."

"I just, I just—" Preston took a deep breath, which caused the fat on his belly to roll.

"Shit," scowled Miranda. "Now look what you've done." The freckles and moles were suddenly realigned, the constellations had changed.

"I just want to make sure you understand that."

"Right."

"Because it quite often makes no sense to me."

"What's this now?"

"You and me."

"How so?"

"Because I'm fat and ugly. And you're flawless."

"Preston, we're sitting here in Las Vegas, where dice are getting rolled every second of every day. So I don't know why you haven't learned by now that almost *everything* is chance, happenstance, which includes the nature of our physical beings. So I've got the Bod and you've got, you know—" She gestured both at Preston and at her painted rendition of him. "Anyway, our bodies have been doing what bodies were designed to do. No problem there. At least, very few problems."

"Huh?"

"Baby, just let me paint. I don't like talking so much."

"You always change the subject."

"What fucking subject?"

"You know."

"I do not know. I don't change the subject. I respond. One sentence leads to another. The focus of our conversation shifts." Miranda's hand jerked and scraped a gash of clown-cheek red across Preston's painted belly. She threw down her brush. "Fuck." She raised the back of her hand and wiped at her face, leaving behind a wide smear of colour where there had been a tear.

Preston remembered a certain morning, long ago. The memory slept like a drunk in an old rooming house, buried beneath the threadbare blankets of memory, snoring and shaking the walls.

This conversation with Miranda jarred it awake—his eighth birthday party. He'd managed to assemble quite a collection of children for the party, a truly impressive number considering he had no friends. His mother fed them hot dogs, chocolate cake and huge goblets of cola. After the feast, before Preston was allowed to tear into the little pile of gaudily wrapped presents, there was entertainment.

Preston the Magnificent appeared suddenly, in full performance gear—a morning suit, puffed cravat, shoes so polished they gleamed and blinded. The children were transfixed by his hair, which was pomaded into an unlikely monolith of curls and locks. "Behold before you," he said, "a world-traveller, only newly returned to these shores. In my journeys, I have studied fakir miracles, both great and small, in the private chambers of Mohammedan rajahs! I have studied the art of levitation in Tibetan lamaseries! And I, alone in the Occident, am tutored in the secrets of the greatest wizards civilization has thus produced, the fabled Cingalese!!"

"Hi, Dad," muttered little Preston. This was not the scheduled entertainment. There was supposed to be someone named Sniffles the Clown. What little Preston didn't know (it would be years before his mother told him) was that his father had confronted Sniffles outside, sending him away with idiosyncratic gestures clearly designed to convey rudeness. Preston the Magnificent also hurled verbal abuse upon Sniffles and his ilk, decrying the craft of clowning as "sheer, mindless bumbletry." Then he attended to his hair, sharpened the points of his moustache and descended upon his son's birthday party.

Preston didn't know why he was dreading this performance—he'd spent months bargaining for it. What good was having a dad who was a magician if the guy wouldn't even do magic at his own son's birthday party? But his father had demurred, waving his beautiful, delicate hand in the air. "Nay, nay. I labour upon the proscenium or I labour not at all."

Preston had begged, but his father was obdurate, indeed, lived his entire life in an advanced state of obduracy. "I shan't, boy. Beg not. It lacks dignity."

So Preston settled for Sniffles, resigned himself to the buffoon, and was inexplicably panicky when his father showed up in the clown's stead.

For a while, things went very well. Preston the Magnificent pranced about the dining room herding balloons, which he then pricked with a long needle. The rubber would explode to reveal some little treat, an ice cream cone, for example, a chocolate bar or a bottle of soda. The children applauded tirelessly. Then, once everyone had received a treat ("Give them something to stick in their orifices," Preston the Magnificent advised his son years later), he moved on to stagier effects. He produced eight silver rings, banged and clanged them to illustrate their solidity, and then made the rings form links and chains. He blew upon the metal and the rings seemed to melt into and out of each other.

The children didn't enjoy this illusion so much, mostly because there was no payoff involved, but they did applaud and those who had mastered the art placed dirty fingers in their mouths and whistled.

But then something in Preston the Magnificent's manner changed. He stiffened, his vertebrae crackling audibly, and peered at his chubby son. "At this point I will require the assistance of an auxiliary," he said quietly. "And being as it is the natal anniversary of my only begotten offspring, who would be more appropriate?" He extended one of his hands, the nails milky and carved into perfect little shields. Preston eagerly pushed his chair away from the table, sending it toppling over. The edge of the tablecloth was caught in one of the folds of his corduroy trousers, and he hauled down a plate and two empty glasses. His friends laughed cruelly, but then again, they were not his friends, they were by way of being business acquaintances, Preston being far and away the most successful collector of marbles in the area.

"Yes," Preston the Magnificent intoned, "he is exceedingly graceless. Perhaps he is not the right boy or girl—"

"Please, Pop," said Preston. "Let me do it."

He had no idea what he was expected to do, but he desperately wanted to be part of his father's act.

"Very well." The Magnificent shook his hand and a small velvet bag appeared. He patted at it, kneading it with his fingers, showing it to be empty. "I hold the satchel of the ancient magi Therebes, who practiced his venerable arcana beside the banks of the mythical White Nile. In those days gone by, many times would the land be a'visited by pestilence and famine. Locusts would raze the crops, the sun would scorch the fields, rendering them barren and devoid of animation. Then would Therebes produce the magic satchel."

Preston the Magnificent shook the velvet bag and a few children snapped out of their monologue-induced reveries and applauded madly. The man's eyes began to smoulder like coals. "Reach into the satchel of Therebes," he commanded no one in particular, although his son was canny enough to intuit that this was his cue, "and withdraw sustenance!"

Preston shoved his hand into the velvet. His fingertips came to rest on something smooth, hard and vaguely round. He gingerly extracted an egg.

"See before you a continuation of vitality, but for an individual only! But witness again the magical satchel of Therebes! Thrust away, boy."

Preston bit on his lower lip and reached in again. Once more his fingers came to rest upon the coolness of eggshell. He pulled it out and exhibited the egg eagerly.

"Aw, it's a trick," muttered someone. (In his adulthood, Preston decided it was most likely Billy Hirschberg, whose father was a snarling and withered divorce lawyer. The larger question was why Preston as a grown man spent so much time wondering just who had heckled the old man.) "I betcha it's not even a real egg."

"Oh, miscreant!" snapped his father viciously. "I counsel only patience. We shall see what we shall see. Note once again that the sack is empty." Preston the Magnificent tilted the bag and pulled it open roughly, like he was checking the gums of a nag destined for the glue factory. Then he held the bag toward his son. "Go, boy."

Preston the Younger produced yet another egg.

"Yet again."

The boy transferred the third egg into his left hand, where it nestled comfortably with the previous two. He reached into the velvet bag and pulled out another egg. "Go, boy." There was no room for the fourth egg in his left hand, so he folded his forearm across his belly and positioned the eggs along this new ridge. "Go, boy." The fifth and sixth egg fit there nicely, too, but then

Preston again ran out of room. He spread his left hand and began to form a pile of eggs in the hollow of his palm.

Around about the tenth or eleventh egg, he began to get panicky. He had a sudden inspiration and began to stand them upright on their larger end, so they took up less room and were a little more stable. But this only eased the situation temporarily, and then the boy was completely stymied. The other children began to laugh and hoot, their voices sharpened by barbarity. "And again, boy," said Preston the Magnificent. "Reach into the miraculous satchel of Therebes."

"I don't have any more room for eggs, sir," whispered Preston. He turned to look at his father pleadingly; his attention was arrested by a rippling of his father's sleeve, the black material of the morning suit briefly wavy with reflected light. And then an egg popped out and fell into Preston the Magnificent's fingers, the three digits that were hidden behind the black pouch whilst it was held twixt thumb and forefinger. The three fingers seemed to comprise an independent entity, and they nimbly shifted the egg until it stood upright, hiked it and sent it quietly over the lip of the velvet bag. "Reach away," commanded Preston the Magnificent.

Preston did nothing.

"Reach in and grab the egg," whispered his dad, "or I'll take a brush to your fat backside."

Had he truly believed that his father was causing eggs to materialize inside the satchel of Therebes? (This was a question that had been posed by many analysts, in those years when Preston felt that analysts might be of some assistance.) Of course not. He had long understood that his father was not a magician in the sense that, say, Merlin was a magician. Preston the Magnificent was involved in Show Business, his son knew that. His son even knew that from time to time his father's magic didn't work, that audiences booed and men from newspapers wrote disparaging things.

But he had supposed that his father was up to a more un-
accountable order of trickery than merely hiding things up his
sleeve.

At any rate, what happened that day was that Preston
released the eggs he had stacked and cradled. They exploded
upon the floor, a riot of yolk and albumen. The other children
hooted and howled and banged ice cream spoons upon the tabletop. Preston the Magnificent pointed at the mess and declared,
"Behold! Fakery or deceit? I think not!"

The chubby little boy began to weep. He was embarrassed
about the eggs, true, but, really, the little act was designed so
that some schmuck kid would drop them all over the floor, that
was pretty much the point of the gag. Preston the Magnificent,
noting his son's tears, dealt him a look of stern admonition and
then abruptly turned and stormed away.

Preston continued to cry; he alone was aware that what had
been broken was not a dozen eggs but a sense of wonder.

It struck him with force that Miranda was packing away her
paints with some fury. He hadn't been speaking aloud, he hadn't
actually related this memory, although part of Preston was very
disappointed to realize this.

"Don't fix what ain't broke," Miranda was saying. "I don't
know why you worry about us all the time."

"I don't know why, either," muttered the Adequate.

"What, *exactly*, do you think I'm doing here, then?"

Preston sighed, and said words that he knew weren't true
so much as easy to speak and difficult to deny. "Because of the
Collection."

Over the course of the next couple of hours—when they weren't
arguing with varying degrees of ferocity—Preston related the
handful of facts he possessed about the Collection's history. Some

of the information was scholarly, reflecting his former position of curator. He knew, for example, how Ehrich Weiss had managed to get his hands on the Davenport Spirit Cabinet—he'd gotten it from Ira and William D. themselves. Houdini, thirty-five years of age and the most famous man on the planet, tracked the brothers down to an old folks' home in Sprucefield, New Jersey. There he found them, withered and pale, unrecognizable except for their trademark long moustaches, although the moustaches were white and wispy and contained only a few hairs. The Davenport brothers had never heard of Houdini. Their fellow inmates had—they pestered him for autographs and even pilfered a restraint jacket from supplies and persuaded Houdini to don it and then escape from it. He gave a thrilling exhibition of writhing and bone-bending, although the old folks hadn't really been able to fasten the straps with much conviction. But Ira and William still didn't know who Houdini was. They were friendly enough—they seemed to have been expecting *someone* to show up—and they answered all of his questions as best they could. Houdini gave them some money, a little money, and a few days later added the huge, hideous cabinet to his burgeoning amassment of magical books and curios.

Preston related all this in a voice flat and uninflected. He was aware that he was infuriating Miranda; he was aware that both her tone and her colour were raised. "Now, many people wonder why, if it were such a prize, Houdini would include the Spirit Cabinet with the stuff he sold to Edgar Biggs McGehee."

Miranda protested that she was not, in fact, one of those people.

Preston smiled slightly and continued nonetheless. "I think it was part of the deal with the Davenport brothers. Yeah. Part of the deal with the Spirit Cabinet is that you *have to get rid of it*. It has to be passed on."

Miranda gathered up more things, the small things she had

brought to make the ancient room seem more like a home. She had ceased to yell, but had taken up instead an incessant, boiling mutter. The word *asshole* cropped up often.

"You see," explained Preston, spreading his hands didactically, "the reason that Eddie McGehee put the Collection up for auction is ... *he had to*. It was in his grandfather's will. The Collection had ..." A part of Preston's mind registered the fact that Miranda was vanished. Here, then, was an illusion that Preston could pull off every bit as well as the old man. Preston the Magnificent had done it more often, true, making all of his ditzy lovers disappear, capping his career with the vanishing of his wife, making her materialize days later in a wooden box, her wrists stitched and the seams hidden by cosmetics. "It was in Edgar Biggs' will," he repeated quietly. "The terms were really quite specific. Within a certain time frame—and really, there was only latitude of a week or so—the Collection had to put up for auction. It is part of a plan ..." Preston began moving around the empty room. He enunciated clearly and drew large sweeping arcs in the air, as though trying to illustrate arcana to people sitting far away. "It is part of a plan put in place a long, long time ago. That is really about as much as I know. I myself ..."

The easel rose up in his path. Preston, drawing a deep breath, rounded it to take a look at the abandoned portrait.

"I myself," he finished, "did not look at any of the books."

In the painting, much of Preston was cloudlike and amorphous. His belly, for example, was simply a large suggestion rendered out of flesh tones, the edges vague and ill-defined. It was hard to tell where Preston began and shadows ended. Bits of him, though, were finished with photographic precision. His eyes, for example. They were darkened by the overhang of a large, furrowed brow, but Miranda had carefully added tiny slivers of light. Miranda had also finished the mouth, which was lifelike without being particularly realistic, because Miranda had fashioned a smile. More than a smile, really, a grin, a real shit-eater. Preston scowled, as if to show his portrait what it ought to be doing.

And Miranda had completed the hands, the hands that lay open in the naked, fuzzy lap. Sitting safely in the cup of the hands was an egg.

"Preston," says Miranda, "is damaged goods." She lies on the huge circular bed beside Rudolfo and stretches, because the Bod is bored and needs a tiny bit of activity.

Rudolfo never used to dream at all, and now everything is a dream. Miranda's story seems to him like a fairy tale, the sort of thing a mother might tell a child, so he searches for meaning and moral. "Everybody," he says, "is damaged goods."

"I don't consider myself damaged goods."

"Hoo boy," sings out Rudolfo. "You got it bad."

"Plus there was this thing," says Miranda with a touch of urgency, "this thing that looked like it was always going to be there, this thing about the Collection."

"Ja?"

"See, when we did the Sub Box in the Show, Jurgen and me, something would happen. I mean, I did what I was supposed to do, I jumped down, slipped in the false back, up into the sack, I did all that—hey, I'm the best box-jumper in the city—but something else was going on. Something I can't really talk about. And it made me think, you know, that maybe...maybe there was..."

"Magic."

"Sure. But Preston says it's no good if there is magic. Preston says that what's special about human beings is that they make magic."

"Good point."

"I wanted to know. Preston always hated me a little bit for that. And he wouldn't tell me. So I guess I always hated him a little bit. So we split."

Rudolfo notices a bird struggle out of one of the small holes in the *door of the Spirit Cabinet, a bird he does not recognize. He suspects it has not been seen before.*

"Yeah, but now you go do a nudie show."

"Topless."

"So is not like you make big step forward in life. Is like you go backwards because you feel like shit so you treat yourself like shit."

"When did you become insightful?"

Rudolfo laughs lightly. "Everybody is damaged goods. Everybody got bumps and dents, ja? But sometimes two people fit together, and the bumps go into the dents, and you have a whole thing like a potato."

"Okay, listen, maybe I didn't have the best motives when I first went to Preston, maybe I just wanted to get close to the magic...if it was really there, he would know...but, I mean, I got involved. Okay? I got connected. But Preston...like I say, damaged goods. Sometimes it's not just bumps and dents, right? Sometimes it's like the heart gets squeezed smaller and smaller. Maybe Preston just doesn't have any room in there for anybody else."

"Preston? Preston got heart like a fucking ham hock. He got room for everybody. He got plenty of room for you."

"What do you know about Preston?"

Rudolfo closes his eyes and tries to remember. "He tried to show me something once. I put my hand over the card, and he said that I had to believe, some little thing in me had to believe, that when I take my hand away..."

"What the hell is that?"

"Remove my hand, I mean."

"No, listen." Miranda sits up on the bed, wraps one of her hands behind an ear. "What's that?"

"Oh," says Rudolfo, because he hears it always, "is the doorbell. I made it to play La Bohème. *"*

"No, no, no. Listen."

Rudolfo does listen, then, and realizes that the chimes are silent. But then he hears a distant roar, full of hiss and cackle.

Miranda's nose twitches, and in an instant she is off the bed, racing for the door. "Fire," she whispers. "I'll go see where it is. You stay here. I'll be right back." Miranda disappears.

Rudolfo pulls himself off the bed languidly. He is not surprised at the pronouncement; indeed, he realizes vaguely that he has spent a year turning das Haus *into a tinderbox. He has not attended to the pumps and sumps; the moats, goldfish ponds and swimming pool have all dried up. The desert has claimed the land that the mansion sits upon; dry winds have wrapped around the brickwork like tendrils of ivy.*

Rudolfo pauses before the Spirit Cabinet. Light leaks from the cracks in the woodwork, a light so strong and pure that even these tiny slivers of it cause him to squint.

He cocks his head, because he can hear music. Not La Bohème, *something else, something he has not heard for a very long time. Perhaps it is simply an illusion, perhaps there are whistles and rhythms wrapped within the fiery roar, but Rudolfo thinks he can recognize a German folk song, "Du, du liegst mir am Herzen." Jurgen always loved that song. Rudolfo always hated it, of course, and hates it even more at this instant, because it forces tears from his eyes.*

Chapter Twenty-seven

The last public performance ever given by Jurgen and Rudolfo proceeded like this.

The crowd was ushered into the showroom at the Abraxas Hotel, and although ushers and usherettes tried to corral them toward the little seats and flip-top tables, almost everyone save the very elderly ignored these, preferring to press as close as possible to the stage. They crammed their bodies together without fear or embarrassment, haunches to buttocks, breasts to backs. It was therefore possible to get far more people into the showroom than was legal.

The showroom soon grew unbearably hot. People shed jackets and sweaters; they loosened buttons; one or two stripped down to fairly presentable undergarments.

The Show began abruptly, without fanfare. The house lights neither dimmed nor brightened, they simply remained on, casting an industrial glare over the goings-on. Music leaked quietly from the speakers. It was nothing by Sturm and Drang.

The night previous, Jurgen had appeared suddenly by the

huge, circular bed. Rudolfo had been sleeping, although none too soundly, and with Jurgen's arrival he rolled over and his eyes fluttered open. Jurgen was naked and glowed. Rudolfo could hear little hisses and spitting noises, beads of sweat exploding upon the surface of Jurgen's white skin. Jurgen, though motionless, was not still; his outline in the darkened room quivered. Rudolfo saw that his penis had all but disappeared. It was as small as a three-year-old's, and his testicles were nowhere to be seen.

"Hi," said Rudolfo, too tired to be surprised or terrified, tired enough to be enormously and endlessly sad.

"Hi," said Jurgen. "I want you to change the music for the Show."

"Oh." Rudolfo folded himself up until he was ready again for slumber. "All right." He closed his eyes.

The air around him suddenly grew chilled, and charged somehow, as though the heavens intended to open momentarily and drop huge rocks of ice upon them. Rudolfo opened his eyes and saw Jurgen floating down upon the mattress. "I'm very tired," Jurgen said. His eyes were open, empty and silver.

"*Ja*, you go to sleep now." Rudolfo reached out and placed a hand on Jurgen's chest, except it fell through and came to rest on the sheets. He withdrew the hand, snugged it up against his own breast. "Good night," he whispered.

"Sweet dreams," said Jurgen.

"Oh..." said Rudolfo as he tumbled again into troubled slumber. "I don't dream."

But he did that night. He dreamt many, many things, so many that in the morning he couldn't believe that he had slept for just one night. He'd dreamt his whole life, a strange version of it, anyway, with new endings and altered circumstances. He dreamt of the walk-in closet in Bern—his mother Arnold and her artist friends rampaging drunkenly just beyond the closed wooden door—but instead of his crib being surrounded by plush, stuffed animals, the closet was filled with a menagerie of breathing creatures. He dreamt that he woke and stumbled out of the closet, rubbing sleep from his eyes with tiny, clenched fists, and there in the apartment was a man with a moustache like a chimney-brush and an air of distraction. The man was by the walls on hands and knees, scratching away with a pencil. "You know," he said, catching sight of the little boy with the albino leopard clutched to his breast, "I think I fucked up here."

Rudolfo spent the next morning digging through his vast collection of CDs. He knew exactly what he was looking for, although he was unwilling to name it even to himself. It took almost two hours to find the right album, and when his fingers finally touched it, he began gasping, suddenly desperate for air yet unable to drink it in. His selection—*La Bohème*—acknowledged what Rudolfo was unable to: soon, Jurgen would be gone forever.

So that was what the audience was listening to now, Rodolfo's lament for the dying Mimi.

He walked onstage and received a smattering of applause. Rhonda Byng ran after him, flushed, already so sweaty that her costume clung to her and made her appear naked. The two wandered through the huge silver geometric objects.

Jurgen descended from on high, the grimy hem of his robe rising up, the garment puffing out like a parachute. The crowd sent up a howl that was awful and deafening. Jurgen merely raised his hands gently and they were silent.

"Okay," he said, as his toes lit upon the stage. "It's time for Up Close and Personal."

In the audience, Lois Sweet rose uncertainly. These words were her cue —*up close and personal*—and she was a professional. She slowly made her way to the stage.

"Hi, Lois," said Jurgen.

Rudolfo couldn't help himself. He rolled his eyes and tsked. Then, operating more out of habit than anything else, he asked, "Where you from, Lois?"

"Fort Dix, New Jersey," she answered.

"No, you're not, Lois," said Jurgen. "You're from Sandusky, Ohio."

Lois nodded slowly.

Jurgen opened a hand and revealed a deck of cards. "Name a card, Lois," he whispered. "Any card."

"The six—" began Lois.

"Any card," Jurgen corrected himself, "except the six of spades."

"But—"

"I like a challenge."

Lois Sweet had left Sandusky, Ohio, years and years ago, when she was young and pretty enough to think that she might become an actress. Now here she was, a stooge in a magic show, and things were still fucking up.

"The queen of hearts," she snapped.

"Yes," said Jurgen, and he tossed the deck of cards high into the air.

The cards hovered there, like hornets smoked out of the nest.

"Put out your hand like so," commanded Jurgen gently. He demonstrated for Lois, rolling out his fingers and baring his palm. Lois did as she was told. The cards continued to swarm in the air above.

"Very good. Now, you said the queen of hearts, correct?"

"Yes," she whispered.

"You spoke the name of the card with a certain amount of bitterness. The ironic tone was not lost upon me. *The Queen of Hearts*. But, Lois, you will now see that all things are possible."

One of the cards bumped its way free of the cloud. It sat in the air for a long moment before dropping gently into Lois' palm.

Lois returned to her seat clutching the playing card between her fingers.

"Now, everyone who's wearing glasses," said Jurgen. "I want you to take them off." He spoke quietly, his voice no louder than he might pitch it in a kitchen; still, all the people wearing glasses responded. They responded with alacrity, because they'd heard about this trick. "Take your glasses," instructed Jurgen, holding out an invisible pair by way of illustration, "and twist and mangle them. Stomp on them until the lenses are broken." The showroom filled with crunching sounds. "There." Jurgen was suddenly out of breath, and this last word was more gasped than pronounced. He reached up and rubbed at his own eyes, removing the makeup from around them, making the upper part of his face shine with milky radiance. "You don't need glasses," he whispered.

Rhonda Byng was inspired to step forward and spread her arms in an emphatic, though silent, ta-da.

The crowd murmured as they looked around the hall and at each other. There was a sigh of great happiness and a smattering of applause from the people who had never needed glasses in the first place.

Down in the laundry room, meanwhile, an industrial-sized washing machine, made cantankerous from years of stained bedsheets, shuddered to a stop as its wiring unravelled. Sparks shot out and bombarded the wall, made of cheap particle board. Fingers of flame took hold.

Jurgen brought up his hands and smacked them together. "Ladies and gentlemen." The robe fell away, revealing the ghostly body, the dingy loincloth. "Laddies and lassies," said he, "the next miracle is the globally celebrated and much ballyhooed Hindu Rope Trick. I, alone in the Occident, possess the arcanum of this wonder, having learnt it firsthand from the Cingalese. But, hear me, why should I perform this *chef-d'oeuvre* inside this theatre, opening the doors for accusations of subterfuge and chicanery, insinuations of thin wire attached to the lighting grids holding up the rope? Instead, I shall perform the deed upon the *boulevard without!*"

It took Rudolfo many long moments to figure out *was zum Teufel* Jurgen was on about.

"You should therefore stand and effect an egress in an orderly fashion." Jurgen stepped from the stage. He did not tumble into the audience, because, as Rudolfo had rightly pointed out to Dr. Merdam, he was no longer obeying the law of gravity. He raised his hands and pointed toward the recesses of the showroom. "The youngsters in the last row should go first," he said, "then the penultimate, etcetera. Follow me and you will see a miracle that shall go down into the vaults of historical annals!" Jurgen floated over everyone's head; his course was not true—he wavered and pitched like a party balloon, sometimes rising and bumping into the lighting grid, sometimes dropping fast and grazing the people's hair. "Follow me!" he commanded, while Rudolfo gathered up the small animals and loosed the big ones from their cages.

The hardened gamblers didn't pay Jurgen much attention as he floated past. Many were annoyed that their concentration had been momentarily destroyed, but they squinted and reapplied themselves to heavenly whim. Less ardent players, vacationers from out of town, found themselves caught up and marching along with the crowd.

Cocktail waitresses abandoned their trays to follow him. As the crowd neared the doors, the pantalooned pituitary giants gave up their posts and sentry boxes.

So it was that several hundred people spilled out of the Abraxas Hotel and filled the long circular driveway.

Rudolfo stood among them, craning to see over the heads. But Jurgen—isolated in the centre of a huge circle that the respectful, even fearful, crowd had made—found Rudolfo with his empty eyes and waved his hand. "Come on," he urged. "After all, this *is* the Jurgen and Rudolfo Show." Rudolfo pushed people aside and joined his partner. They linked hands and took deep bows and then—even though Rudolfo had absolutely no idea what was about to happen—they clapped with unearthly synchronicity.

Jurgen waved toward the ground where a rope lay coiled into an orderly column. Rudolfo had not noticed the rope, of course, but that meant nothing. This was the realization that had descended upon him over the past long months: there were many things he didn't notice, but that didn't mean they weren't there. Indeed, *everything* was there, *somewhere*. If one were careful and observant, all would make itself known.

Samson and Rhonda Byng stood inside the circle, too. Samson stared at the ground dolefully, occasionally lowering his huge head to lash a tongue through the gossamer tufts that blossomed out of his paws. He wasn't really disinterested, of course. But he was a shy cat, and wasn't given to public displays of emotion. Not like Rhonda, who bawled and bawled and didn't bother to wipe the tears from her face.

Jurgen pointed at the rope and an end worked itself free. It ascended a few inches and twitched rapidly, like a serpent's tongue searching the air for the taste of prey. Then the rope drove upwards, the coils disappearing. It stretched to a height of twenty or so feet and then stopped so abruptly it produced a throbbing low note that filled the world. Jurgen reached out and steadied the rope, wrapping his hand around it. He tested its strength and flexibility. The rope seemed as solid as a metal pole. Jurgen turned and faced the crowd. A grin spread across his face and he opened his eyes with delight, almost blinding the people in the front, because his eyes gleamed like quicksilver.

Jurgen wrapped his legs around the rope and then began to climb hand over hand. His ascent was rapid and effortless. He reached the top of the rope and disappeared into the heavens.

If all you knew of the strange case of Jurgen Schubert were the reports given in *Personality* magazine, then you would believe that this was the last that was seen of him, that he reached the top of the rope and dissolved into the welkin. The most fanciful eyewitness reports have it that Jurgen Schubert was picked up by a hovering interplanetary spacecraft, but these are discounted by almost everyone. Most people say they saw him explode into dots of white light, almost as though he had been a projected image and the projector was suddenly unplugged. But the more skeptical and sober-sided claim that he disappeared, not into nothingness, but into the first of the clouds of black smoke coming from the Abraxas Hotel.

This is possible, because the huge hotel was, indeed, on fire for many moments before anyone noticed.

The gamblers inside didn't notice until pieces of flaming chandelier fell upon the gaming tables.

The people outside didn't notice—they continued to stare into the sky, awaiting Jurgen Schubert's magical return—until an awful siren sounded, a mourning wail that could be heard for miles around.

It was heard in the desert, where Miranda sat in the moonlight, depressed and pissed off. She turned and saw a strange glow bloom above the dark shadow of the city.

The wail was certainly heard inside the George Theater. Preston lifted a finger and wiped a tear from his cheek.

Somehow Rudolfo managed to find the long white limousine that evening, to open the rear door and climb wearily into the cool leather interior. Bob was turned around in the front seat, his black face glistening with tears. He nervously removed his hatband and began to speak in his native Dogon. Rudolfo waved a hand at him rudely.

"*Ja*, never mind any of that. Drive me home."

Bob nodded and smiled, although tears continued to stream out of his eyes, and drove the limousine away from the tower of flame. Fire engines and police cars screamed by them, hordes of curious onlookers, tourists with their videocams screwed over their eyeballs. Soon, though, all that was left behind. Rudolfo stared into the streets. He saw tiny figures parading along the sidewalks—gremlins and poltergeists, witches and familiars. He realized that it was Hallowe'en, All Soul's Eve, that spirits were free on this most special of nights.

So he was not surprised, when he entered his bedroom later that evening, to see Jurgen floating in front of the Spirit Cabinet, clutching the back of a chair to prevent himself from ascending to the vaulted ceiling. He was vaporous, now, except for a few strands of hair (the colour of bone in the desert) and his eyes. His eyes were of a hue rarely seen, the colour of elements in the triple digits of the periodic table. They were at the same time endless and impenetrable.

"Hiya, Rudy!" he sang out.

Rudolfo sat down on the chair that Jurgen was using as a tethering place and reached up so that he could lay his hand upon Jurgen's. But his fingers met no flesh, only wood and upholstery and the smooth heads of tacks, so he removed his hand and folded it into his lap.

"Well," said Jurgen, "I think I have to be going now."

"No."

"Yes."

"Wait a bit. Let's talk for a while."

"Okey-dokey."

"Okey-dokey."

"I think," Jurgen said softly, "that Düsseldorf will win the FA Cup."

Rudolfo closed his eyes and a few teardrops were forced out.

"That was a joke," said Jurgen.

"Yes. I know."

"Because Düsseldorf is no good."

"Jurgen, I want to say something to you. But I don't know the words. I don't know them in English. I don't know them in German."

"Just speak, Rudy. Don't worry what language."

Rudolfo did speak. He did not know what language he was speaking in; the words simply arrived like guests at a party. "I think about my life, Jurgen, and how it was. How very strange it was."

"Everyone has a strange life, because life is so strange."

Rudolfo allowed a little video to play in his mind, filled with quick cuts, short clips. He saw himself briefly in the furry bosom of the only real family he ever knew, four bears in a stone pit in the capital of Switzerland; then the institutions, *die Berufsschulen*, where he had been sent, not for any real wrongdoing, but for becoming hairless and freakish; then the wrong-doing, of course, the taking of another man's life, which stung very badly because he'd been trying to *save* General Bosco, so not only was he a monster, he was an incompetent monster; then he'd been a beggar in München and he'd followed a couple of freaks to Miss Joe's mouldy establishment…

"I just think," Rudolfo said suddenly, as if he'd been gathering his thoughts instead of letting them run free, "that it's a miracle we ever met."

"Oh," said Jurgen, and he lifted one hand away from the chairback so that he could raise the index finger with scholarly precision, "it's not technically a *miracle*." Half-loosed, Jurgen started to rise, like steam from a pot when the lid's been removed. He pulled the free arm through the air and managed a descent, enough that he could grasp the chair once more.

"Well," said Rudolfo, "I don't know as much about miracles as you do."

"No."

"It may not be a miracle, technically," shrugged Rudolfo, "but it feels like a miracle. That's the important thing."

"Not precisely," noted Jurgen. He wouldn't free a hand this time, so he underscored his point by unwrapping both index fingers from the perch on the chairback.

"Oh, shut up," said Rudolfo. "I'm trying to talk to you. To tell you something."

"You'll have to tell me quickly, then." Jurgen jerked his head toward the Spirit Cabinet. His head glowed so brightly that it left behind ghostly traces, smears of luminance. Rudolfo saw that light leaked from the Spirit Cabinet, and strange sounds, too, harmonious zephyrs, winds that wailed and keened. "I've got to be going," Jurgen whispered.

Rudolfo sighed. "Go, then."

"Okey-dokey." Jurgen released his hands and floated away. He pulled through the air with both arms, then added a strong frog kick, because, don't forget, he'd been an amateur swimmer, a member of *die Haie*, the winner of three small, tarnished trophies. He reached the Spirit Cabinet and the righthand door swung open. Rudolfo tried to peer inside, but the glare was too much. He had to turn his head away and even so was forced to close his eyes.

"I love you," he said. He never knew whether Jurgen heard, never knew if his partner was then inside the Spirit Cabinet or merely entering. He never heard the sound of the door being closed—he could hear nothing except the wind raging in the room, sending up a howl that had driven all the animals in *das eindrucksvollste Haus im Universum* to seek shelter in the shadows.

Then there was light, pure and radiant, and then there was nothing.

The lefthand door swings open. Before he can stop himself, Rudolfo Thielmann steps inside the Spirit Cabinet.

Chapter Twenty-eight

A few days after the fire on the desert, the one that had destroyed *das eindrucksvollste Haus im Universum,* Theodore Collinger took himself down to the George Theater.

He was an elderly man. His hands, once long and graceful, were stained with age spots and shook uncontrollably. Collinger had been renowned as a magician, his speciality being the Chinese rings. It was quite some time ago that the rings had begun to clang and clatter whenever they neared each other, begun to meld when they should have stayed distinct, and separate when Collinger tried to display a chain. Since then he had applied himself to the art as a kind of scholar and amanuensis. He wrote a column for *Hocus Pocus* magazine in which he related news concerning the craft. "Collinger's Corner," it was entitled and he often reflected, bitterly, at how apt the title was, because in whichever sense a magazine can possess a corner, that was what was alloted to him, a tiny space in which it was impossible to get comfortable. And it paid nothing. His monthly stipend was pitiful, forcing him to live in a shithole motel with a clutch of aged showgirls who played Scrabble and discussed farfetched plans for restoring lustre to their sagging breasts. Collinger had taken to drink, of course.

He knocked on the glass doors of the George Theater and peered through into the foyer. The velvet within was blurry with dust and cobwebbing. He reflected that he may have come too early. He lifted his thin wrist and tried to catch a quick look at the watch there. Eight-thirty-seven. Hmmm. Perhaps a little ill-timed. He recalled that when he was young and played all the big hotels, he likely wouldn't have even made it to bed by eight in the morning. Unless it was with a comely young person, gender immaterial. Theodore Collinger scowled, feeling decrepit and sexless.

Preston descended hurriedly from upstairs, fastening his robe, evening the sides about his pale belly before drawing them together. He worked at the lock for a long moment and then pulled open the theatre door. "Hi, Mr. Collinger."

"I'm sorry. I've arrived a little prematurely."

"That's all right. I was just…" Preston waved vaguely in the direction of his sleeping quarters upstairs. "Come in, Mr. Collinger. Come on in."

Preston pulled open the door slightly and Collinger, ever a slim man and these days even more so, slipped through. As he passed by Preston he noticed an acrid, musky odour. It reminded him of something, although he couldn't quite place his trembling finger on it. "I've brought two things," said Collinger, getting down to business. "One is a cassette recording of what was actually heard on the evening in question. The other is a transcript of the same, translated into English."

Preston shook his head slightly. "Okay. Now, I didn't quite follow this on the telephone. This was a seance, last Thursday…"

"Hallowe'en."

"Sure." Preston nodded. Hallowe'en was, of course, the most popular night for seances, seeing as ghosts were out and about and looking to drop by for visits. Many people held seances, chanting low invitations to disembodied spirits. Mind you, some people were more particular in their incantations and awaited only the arrival of Ehrich Weiss.

Many know this story: in Montreal, in the year 1926, Ehrich Weiss was reclining on a sofa in his dressing room in the Princess Theatre. Two young men burst in, eager to meet the great Houdini. One of them, a McGill student named Whitehead, asked Weiss if it were true that punches to the stomach did not hurt him. Houdini pursed his lips and shrugged with what little modesty he could muster. Popular legend has it that Whitehead then struck him without warning; historians have it that Houdini did prepare himself, but rather ineffectually. He did not rise from the couch, for example, and Whitehead was able to shower blows from above, striking Weiss hard on his tiny stomach. Something inside Houdini burst. Some believe that something was already broken, that Whitehead's blows merely exacerbated the situation. At any rate, Houdini left Montreal, took a train to Detroit, even managed to give a show: a newspaper reported that he looked "more than a little tired." Afterwards, he was rushed to the hospital, where doctors attended to him frantically. Houdini slipped in and out of consciousness. Once, he looked at the young man caring for him and whispered, "I wanted to be a doctor. When I was young. I wish I had become a doctor."

"But, you're Houdini."

"But what you do is real. I am just a fake."

Houdini died on Hallowe'en.

Ehrich Weiss had stated on many occasions that if there were some way of getting back from the Other Side, he would find it. Since then, people have assembled every Hallowe'en and awaited his return.

Theodore Collinger took a deep breath and managed to get his shaking hand into his trouser pocket, pulling out a folded piece of paper and a small cassette tape. He waved these in front of Preston, who took a few moments to judge the speed and modulation, then pinched thumb and forefinger together, stabbed out and intercepted the stuff.

Collinger's attention was now drawn once more to the staircase where a young woman was descending. She was measuring out the sides of her robe, giving the terry cloth a little shimmy before drawing it closed across her nakedness. Collinger's innards were suddenly molten. He was so shaken that his hands were stilled. He lifted one, as though in greeting, although he was really holding it in front of his eyes to block the view, much as one would if forced to stare into the sun.

"Hiya," said this young woman, making a knot in the sash. The robe split high to allow her legs to take the last couple of stairs. "I guess you must be Theodore Collinger."

Collinger nodded; the name sounded familiar.

Preston, meanwhile, had lumbered behind the snack counter where there was a small tape recorder. Mrs. Antoinette Kingsley had long ago grown bored with Preston's Show and preferred to spend the time sitting behind the counter listening to Tony Anthony tapes. Preston plugged in the cassette, placed his thick forefinger on the "PLAY" button and pressed.

The tiny speakers issued forth a silence thick with static and human breath.

"There were four of us," said Collinger. "Myself, Kenny Bental, Louisa Hoyle and Freddy Myztyk."

"Oh, yeah." Preston scowled. Of the three people named, Bental was the most sane, and he was only allowed out on weekends. Louisa Hoyle was rich enough to avoid hospitalization; Freddy Myztyk was so loopy that his presence caused radio interference and local blackouts.

"Listen!" said Collinger suddenly, pointing at the tape recorder. "There's the first voice."

The "first voice" was laden with zizz and cackle, hard to distinguish beneath the ethereal roar. "*Hallo*," it said.

"And here—" said Collinger. The second voice came too close upon the heels of the first for him to announce it. "*Oh*," went the voice. "*Du bist es. Der Typ der mich im Bauch erwischt hat.*"

"German," noted Preston. He unfolded the piece of paper he held in his hand.

"*Das tut mir leid*," returned the first voice.

"*Es macht nichts. Heh. Gib mir einen Spot.*"

Miranda shivered suddenly and pulled the collar of her robe together, running her hand upwards like a western tie until the terry cloth was knotted around her neck.

"*Ich kann nicht. Ich muss gehen.*"

Preston ran his eyes over the page and found the appropriate words. "*I can't. I have to go.*"

"*Gehen? Keiner kann gehen.*"

"*Go?*" translated Preston in as soft a voice as he could manage. "*No one can go.*"

Then there was silence, which somehow seemed much louder than the eerie, tape-recorded words. Collinger said, "That's it," and Preston the Adequate switched off the machine. He pulled at his face, the pasty jowls seeming to stay stretched for many moments after he removed his hand. "Well," he said. "The German is a problem."

"Not really," argued Collinger. "The Weiss household spoke German. Houdini spoke German with his mother exclusively."

"Sure, but the first voice. I mean, for this to make any sense, that first voice would have to be Whitehead's. Wouldn't it?"

"Point of information," said Miranda. "What did they say?"

"Oh." Preston read from the sheet of paper, running a finger underneath the words as if to lend them a sort of forensic rightness. "Hello."

"I got that part," said Miranda.

"Oh. It's you. The guy who hit me in the stomach."

"No shit?"

"The translator," pointed out Collinger, "notes that the verb used is actually somewhat vague. 'Hit me in the stomach, got me in the stomach, something like that.' But the stomach part is clear enough."

"So what else?" Miranda prompted.

"Let me see. I'm sorry about that. Don't worry. Hey. Give me some scorn."

"What the what?" repeated Miranda.

"*Spott*," said Collinger, adopting a scholarly tone, "apparently means *scorn*. Ridicule, mockery, that sort of thing."

"No," said Miranda. "I bet he said *spot*. In English. You know. As in weightlifting."

"Aha!" declared Collinger, and only partly because the gap between the bathrobe lapels had dropped deep between Miranda's breasts. "More supporting evidence. Because Houdini, an adherent of the physical dynamism espoused by Eugene Sandow, spent many hours occupied with muscular training and improvement."

"Yeah, but," said Miranda. She fell abruptly silent.

"Yeah, but what?"

"This is wild," she declared, with considerable enthusiasm. "Houdini pulls off the Big One."

Preston spun around. "It doesn't make sense," he said slowly. "Why would Whitehead speak German?"

"Preston, you unimaginative schmuck," countered Miranda, "we are dealing with the Great Beyond. I'm guessing you can speak whatever language you want."

"But—"

"You got hold of something pretty special there, Mr. Collinger," said Miranda.

"Oh, I don't suppose anybody will believe it. A few, here and there. But there's a few here and there who will believe pretty much anything."

Preston popped the cassette out of the machine. He had to take hold of the old man's wrist, which seemed as thin and fragile as an icicle at noon, steady the hand and tenderly slip the tape between the vibrating fingers. "Hey, Mr. Collinger," he asked quietly. "What do you believe?"

"Me?" Collinger shrugged. "I suppose I believe that there is life after death. But I had pretty much come around to believing that, anyway. It's easy to believe that when one is about to die."

Miranda came close and kissed him on the cheek. "Thanks for coming and playing that for us, Mr. Collinger."

"My distinct pleasure." He turned and shuffled out the door of the George. The old man sailed slowly down the sidewalk, turned the corner onto Paradise Road and—having checked over his shoulder to make certain there were no eyes upon him—faltered briefly, hitching his shoulders and stumbling forward, an old man's version of kicking up one's heels.

"So what's the deal?" demanded Preston.

"Hmm?"

"Didn't you recognize the voice?"

"Sounded familiar."

"It wasn't Houdini."

"That so?"

"Shouldn't we have told Mr. Collinger?"

"The way I figure it, he'll take that tape to a television station or something, and he'll find someone who believes him and there'll be someone who doesn't—someone who says *why are they both speaking German?*—and in a couple of weeks everyone will have forgotten about it."

The two were ascending the circular stairs, leaving terry cloth bathrobes in their wake.

"And that would be good? That would be preferable to conclusive proof of life after death?"

Miranda tsked her tongue. "Man, you know that better than anyone."

"I do?"

"It's about wonder, right? Wonder. We need it."

"We?"

"Humanoids." She took the stairs two at a time now, drawing ahead of him. She mounted to the top and then dove for the fusty daybed. Preston swayed by the perimeter, breathing heavily—winded by the stairs, despite the fact he'd given up smoking—and staring hard. "Yeah," he agreed, "we need it."

"Come on, Preston," said Miranda, "we've got work to do."

"Work?" Preston waddled forward and fell, bouncing his bedmate into the air. "This isn't work."

"That's what you say now," said Miranda, landing on top of Preston's belly. "But let's hear from you in an hour or so."

"An hour? What are we going to be doing for an hour?"

"We," said Miranda, wedging her hand between their bodies, guiding Preston inside her, "are going to be creating little Preston. Preston the Wonderful."

"Right," grunted the Adequate. "Preston the Improbable."

"Preston," whispered Miranda, "the Splendiferous."

"Preston the, uh, Marvellous."

"Preston, uh, Preston, uh, the Stunning."

"Uh Preston uh the Uh."

"Uh the Uh."

"Uh."

And in that region of the blue world known today as Sri Lanka (but known once as *Cingal*, from the Indian word *sing*, for lion) two peasants, a young couple of the ancient Veddahs, crouch by the side of a snakelike, dusty road. In a small mesh basket before

them is their son, a few months old. The child is pale and labouring for breath. They have been to see the old woman who knows
about remedy and ritual, but she told them nothing. The old
woman merely touched the baby's forehead, pursed her wrinkled
lips until they vanished from sight, and then turned and hobbled
away on the sides of her twisted feet.

So the couple are returning to their village. All will has
abandoned them, leaving them hunkered, desolate and beyond
tears, in the middle of nowhere.

Over a rise in the road comes a man wearing only a soiled
loincloth, so loose and thinned by time that it does virtually
nothing to hide his nakedness. The man's body is odd; it is
improbably muscled, every group, subgroup and ligament clearly
visible just beneath the skin. And the skin itself is strange; it
seems as smooth as glass or porcelain. The sunlight explodes on
the man's body; the Veddah couple shade their sore eyes with
trembling palms.

The man's face is ageless, or at any rate, the age is impossible to determine. There is evidence of decrepitude—hairlessness,
chiefly, except for a thin topknot of gossamer hair—but there are
no wrinkles on the brow or at the corners of the mouth, even
though the mouth is pulled into the widest of grins. The man's
features are heroic somehow, his beauty all but perfect. The only
thing amiss is a peculiar colouration around and across the eyes,
where the skin tone changes from bronze to an ill-looking purple. The eyes themselves are shut, the lids sealed by a gum made
of rheum and tears. The man carries a staff, working it along the
road, displacing rocks that lie in the path of his naked feet. The
young couple dismiss the man as a blind beggar; they turn away
and look down to the ground, although they are both really looking into the deep pools of their own sadness.

The blind man stops before them. The young man and
woman catch their breath. They try to remain as still as possible,

praying that the beggar will soon shrug and continue on his way. But the baby betrays them. Its breath breaks through a windpipe squeezed tight by illness. The wheeze is whisper-quiet, far softer than the breeze, but the blind man cocks his head and turns.

"Our son—" the young man begins by way of explanation, but he is cut short. The beggar opens his eyes, slowly lifting the mulberry lids. The couple is startled, almost panicky. The beggar's eyes are not milky and lifeless, they are a radiant silver. At their centre are dots of denser metallic stuff like beads of mercury.

The beggar lowers his head, aiming these eyes at the baby. The woman starts forward, reaching toward the basket, but her husband places a hand on her arm. They exchange looks, and the wife slowly withdraws her hand. As she does so, the basket begins to rise.

The beggar's face is set in concentration. Although his brow does not yet wrinkle, the skin itself seems to crack, marbling with taut veins. The old bruises that surround the beggar's eyes become darker; the eyes themselves glow more intensely, giving out lambent pulsations.

The basket rises high into the air, above the hands of humankind, and begins to spin slowly. The silence is then broken by a sound, strange to the young couple because they haven't heard it in such a long time. It is the child laughing.